Ice Ghosts

Book Two
of the
Noctiluca
series

Prologue: The story so far

It has been three months since the adventures of Myron, Isobel and Ishyan that culminated in the defeat of the mercenary Ulrich Bessek and opportunist Michelle Glade along with the sinking of the *Jah Mahal* off the coast of Egypt.

In the immediate wake of the police investigation it was revealed that Isobel's father was incredibly still alive, and not assassinated in a freak luxury yachting tragedy as first thought. This discovery alone brought troubling untold questions. However, as both Isobel Fortuna and her rescuer Myron McGivney began to settle into normal everyday business, the Fortuna's soon did what they did best; become insatiably restless.

After the announcement by the newly created *Federation of Space Exploration* (*FoSE*) to commence orbital civilian flights as well as moon excursions, a new tourist boom literally exploded over night.

Isobel's father, Alessendro Fortuna, almost pushed to the point of cabin fever whilst in hiding, now returned with a bold venture indeed. He intended to take *FoSE* head-on and become the first company to succeed where others had previously failed. Due to the size of the project *FortunaCS* was soon partnered by the massive global conglomerate *TIC* (*Templar Innovative Community)*, run by the eccentric billionaire Harrison Templar.

Myron, a man who seldom enjoyed the limelight, began to recede further and further back into the shadows of the *FortunaCS* empire whilst his newfound love, Isobel, transcended toward the limelight like a moth to a flame.

Both knew the dangers of a company like *FortunaCS*, but nevertheless neither were in control of events untangling around them and, like other lovers around the world, soon found their private lives to be anything but.

Myron turned to Ishyan Stölles, the *FortunaCS* loyal bodyguard, for assistance in ensuring he could fulfil his newfound employment responsibilities, even though his personal life was falling apart.

However, other dangers were lurking in the shadows, in the aftermath of the sarcophagus affair. Sebastian Nolan had spent three months in hiding until Bessek's mentor finally handed him a project that could re-define military combat. Nolan soon discovers that he is about to transcend from underground terrorism right into the governmental playground. To aid him however, he now has a friend in a very high place.

For occasionally there comes a time when the dust settles just long enough to visualise what it's been hiding all along. For Myron this illuminates a horrendous truth.

Halfway around the globe Myron's friend Kirill Volkov suddenly falls ill and his condition is quickly linked to the red gem from Lake Kivu. It also awakes a memory thought buried forever.

A recollection of the past but born from the present;

The ice ghosts.

Betrayal

Reunion Island: Arabian Sea: Tuesday; 16:56

Lieutenant Gemma Andrews sat in civilian clothing within a small non-assuming restaurant at the foot of the mighty Piton de la Fournaise, a formidably active shield volcano that dominated the southern half of Réunion island. It was late afternoon, although there were still a few hours until dusk.

She caught snippets of the conversation her plain clothed soldier was having with the manageress; Andrews was convinced her rough translation had the last eruption dated to only a month ago. The Lieutenant knew the type of volcanic activity witnessed here was worlds apart from her native and infamous Mount St. Helens, but it still added another dimension to this mission that she could easily deal without.

For her soldiers this was merely a training exercise, she however knew differently. Their primary objective was a simple search and reconnaissance, but her secondary objective, based purely on the identification of one individual, was one she alone kept secret, for now.

The male soldier thanked the manageress for her time and turned back to sit with Andrews. He was loving this clandestine role play.

'Any chance I misheard the recent eruption bit?' Gemma asked as Arturo sat down opposite her.

'No,' he smiled. 'There is however a monitoring station halfway to the summit, which she recommended all climbers sign both in and out during their visits. Apparently, the summit isn't completely stable, so they like to keep a watchful eye on the holiday makers.'

'Sounds sensible,' Andrews replied. 'Any updates from the rest of the team?'

'Not yet,' Arturo said, switching his phone screen from sleep mode. 'I'll send a group message once we leave here anyway, then we can race to the top.'

'Yeah, great idea,' Andrews nodded sarcastically. 'I don't want you and Lake competing to the point where we have to call in a rescue helicopter.'

'That was a one off,' the young man smiled. 'Plus, I won.'

'It doesn't count if you set off a mini-avalanche,' she sighed impatiently. 'What did you order me anyway?'

'I stuck with carbs and protein, plus a high calorie drink for good measure.'

'Does it have a name?'

'Does it matter?'

'You still annoyed with me for not pretending to be your girlfriend?'

'Ah come on,' Arturo smiled. 'Don't hold that over me, it would have been a great cover story.'

'Maybe,' Gemma replied. 'You do have previous, remember.'

'Hence why it's such a great cover story,' he smiled ruefully.

Gemma looked up as the manageress brought over two drinks, napkins and cutlery.

'Merci,' Andrews smiled.

'Here,' Arturo said, taking out a battered looking map. 'This is the climb and rendezvous points.

Between us all we'll cover the zone you highlighted on the map.'

'Good,' the Lieutenant nodded. 'After that we're all staying in different towns tonight, so we can continue the training exercise there.'

'Ok,' he nodded.

'And purely reconnaissance ok, we can't have anyone identifying us or my reputation will end up in tatters.'

'Come on boss,' Arturo smiled seriously. 'Look. We're here because we're the best. I know we're a bit cocky, but what do you expect? Here, I've got a present for you...'

'What's that?' she asked looking down at the bright yellow cap her soldier had just produced from his rucksack. Gemma read the writing on the front. 'The big reunion?'

'Yeah,' he smiled. 'We're on Reunion Island and we can prete...'

'Chuck it in the bin,' Andrews stopped smiling instantly. 'We're not on safari. We're supposed to be incognito.'

'You're no fun,' Arturo sighed. 'No fun at all.'

Out around the countryside of the shield volcano Lieutenant Andrews' Special Operations team made their way slowly, but simultaneously, toward the summit. They had worked hard to remain incognito during their travels, so much that they now blended in with other holiday makers walking steadily up and down the dirt trails.

Salvadore took a sip of his water bottle as a puffing and wheezing Jackson slowly reached their next stop. Both knew their extra padding under their clothing and facial prosthetics was a mere test of disguises, but it did not stop them enjoying their roleplay.

'Could be worse,' Salvadore muttered above the warm wind that had started to chase them up the mountain. 'We could be running back down away from an eruption.'

'There is always that,' his colleague smiled, taking out his phone. 'Looks like they've finally left the café.'

'Good,' Salvadore replied before looking back to the summit. 'I'd hate to have to rub it in that we made it there first carrying all this garbage,' he indicated by prodding his stomach.

'It would be a tad embarrassing,' Jackson nodded. 'Look where you're standing you oaf,' the solder pointed, as he indicated the *"Beware"* sign next to them.

'What's that there for?' Salvadore muttered.

'It's to note the underground basalt tunnels,' Jackson said, pulling forth his guidebook from his back pocket.

'Oh no...' Salvadore reacted instantly. He knew only too well what was coming.

'Oh yes,' the soldier smiled broadly. 'Here we go. The basalt tunnels are indicative of shield volcano's around the globe where bursts of volcanic activity result in the outer parts of the lava flow solidifying where the inner core, still molten hot, then keep progressing.'

'Please stop.'

'Then,' Jackson held up his finger. 'In some circumstances the inner lava flow dissipates completely, leaving a hollow tube. This tube can be known to fail when pressure is reacted upon them, so often treated with respect and caution by scientists and volcanologists.'

'Finished?' Salvadore questioned impatiently.

'Yes,' his colleague nodded triumphantly. 'Bet you didn't know that.'

'I also didn't want to know that,' the soldier replied.

'Anyway,' Jackson noted. 'At the very least, don't walk on them, just in case one of them disintegrates, which with the weight of us now if a definite possibility.'

'Of that I agree,' Salvadore nodded. 'Gemma wouldn't be happy if we had to be airlifted for falling in a hole.'

'Not another rescue helicopter, come on,' his colleague whispered as he caught sight of movement off to his right. 'That looks like Lake and Williamson, let's aim to cut them off and ask them for "assistance" for the last bit of the climb.'

'I do actually need some help,' Salvadore exclaimed. Although late in the day the heat was still rising as they neared the crater's edge, and they still had another hour's climb at least. It would only get hotter the more they progressed toward the crater.

Lieutenant Gemma Andrews followed Arturo up the loose winding path past tourists that were now heading back down from the summit. The late afternoon was closing in on them, but that was fine for her, they had enough kit to assist them in poor light. Besides, the less people up on the summit of the volcano would only assist them. Then they could make their way into the towns and villages later tonight for further reconnaissance.

The mission was beginning to bother her. For something so straightforward Gemma was beginning to feel unbelievable tension in her stomach, as if something terrible was on the verge of occurring. The Lieutenant put it down to the fact that they were climbing an active volcano before pushing all thoughts out of her consciousness altogether.

'I can see some silhouettes on the horizon,' Arturo offered from in front of her. 'Should have brought my camera, that's a lovely shot from here,' he pointed at the red sky behind the summit, where the black shadowy figures stood.

'If nothing else this is a good workout,' she replied, her legs pounding into the stones and pebbles.

'Balls,' Arturo moaned. 'I forgot about that, I bet Lake is already up there, just waiting to gloat.'

'Knock it off,' Andrews whispered. 'This isn't a race and I won't have you two messing this mission up for a simple display of whose brain is smaller than the other's.'

'Funny,' Arturo shrugged. Looking around he suddenly felt quite alone on this desolate mountain, as the sun began its dip behind the crater's ridge. His tension was obvious.

'You ok?' Gemma asked as Arturo came to a halt.

'What are they doing up there?'

His question took the Lieutenant completely by surprise. She could just make the figures of Salvadore and Jackson, if only by their fake rotund figures, poking the side of the summit with their walking sticks. Andrews looked to her right. She saw the sign and the top of the basalt tunnel.

Lieutenant Gemma Andrews did not even have chance to speak before Arturo's body was flung backwards into her side. His weight pushed her onto the side of the loose slope, his lifeless figure obvious to her before they both hit the ground.

Then she saw the dust spurt out of the pebbles to the immediate right of her head and heard the instantly recognisable sound of a metallic ping; a bullet.

Sebastian Nolan lay down his binoculars on the warm volcanic rock where he lay. He was covered by a dull grey camo-sheet, essentially masking him from the surroundings. From his vantage point, with the sun setting behind him, Nolan held the initiative over the approaching Special Ops team.

His assignment was simple, yet risky, nevertheless. He had been tasked with eradicating this team, without trace of his involvement. Sebastian lifted his sniper rifle and gently brought it up to eye level.

There was little chance they would see him from his hideaway, but this didn't ease his quickening pulse. He was on the verge of something ground-breaking and, if Doctor Harding was correct, they were about to hold the world to ransom.

Nolan delicately rotated the sight around to the first of the soldiers. They wouldn't know what hit them. His eye withdrew from the sniper sight then gazed down to the phone by his side. All six faces were illuminated on the screen. Two women and four men. The sender only Harding knew, but that didn't worry Sebastian.

Ever since the Sarcophagus affair his world had been turned upside down. First his mentor Ulrich Bessek had been killed, then his entire network of mercenaries had either been run underground or had simply disappeared. Bessek's boss had also vanished, without trace. He had followed the original plan and contacted Anthony Draven, but had given the maniac too much leash, and now he was also off the radar at present. Nolan knew that Draven would surface eventually and was not sure if he would like what followed.

It was Doctor Harding who now had given him this golden opportunity to bring their enterprise back to fruition. Nolan could identify four of the team near the ridge now, the other two no doubt would enter his target sight soon enough.

He waited. His pulse slowed as he began to take control of his thoughts and emotions.

Williamson was the first to offer a sensible opinion.

'Probably just a bit of volcanic gas?' she mused as Salvadore prodded the basalt tunnel yet again. He was convinced it would crack at some point.

'And here we are standing around his royal clueless as he pokes it,' Lake joked. 'I'll get out my gas mask, shall I?'

'It won't be gas,' Salvadore muttered. 'Look, there are tunnels all over the place. How come only this one made a noise?'

'We have been through this,' Jackson noted, again raising his guidebook and wafting in the air for Salvadore to see. 'Some tunnels are left completely void of lava, others solidifying as they cool, so creating solid rock.'

'So, my theory is also a good one,' Salvadore noted. 'If I heard something from within, it can only be hollow.'

'Yes,' Williamson replied. 'In theory. Boys, here comes Andrews, think we'd better start acting a bit more professional.'

'No need,' Salvadore smiled. 'We're incognito, we can act however we want here.'

'Almost,' Lake replied. 'Maybe give the volcanology lesson a rest for five hey?'

'Ok,' Salvadore sighed and turned away from the rounded tunnel roof. He caught Lake's eye before inhaling quickly. 'Change of plan,' he yelled before jumping backward, twisting in the air then ploughing his walking stick into the tunnel roof. It finally cracked and, with Salvadore's additional weight, the walking stick continued to travel for another metre before hitting something solid. Salvadore lost his balance and hit the ground hard.

'You ok?' Lake laughed as he bent down and took Salvadore's hand. Williamson bent down and withdrew the stick.

'Oh f...,' she started as the walking stick pulled downward in her grasp. As she fell to the ground an arm punched its way through the tunnel roof, grabbed and pulled her head down into the darkness.

'No!' Lake shouted, dropping Salvadore and jumping to her aid. Another arm shot through near his body and grasped his leg. The pain was excruciating, it was like he'd been caught in a giant vice. Lake turned and hit the hand with anything he could find; rock, stone, but nothing seemed to release him from the agony.

Lake finally felt the hand try and gain a renewed grip and he managed to wriggle free. He pulled at the limp body of Williamson before trying to clamber to his feet. As he turned, he saw two more bloodied bodies being dragged toward another broken basalt tunnel. Lake could not believe what he saw. Then he heard loud breathing from behind him. He turned slowly.

Lake's last moments were spent looking despairingly straight into a pair of lifeless eyes.

Andrews scrambled wildly from the open and barren rock surface toward a pile of boulders nearby, if only to gain the momentum for an instant. As she dived head straight over the rock, she heard another bullet ricochet off the hard stone.

She quickly took off her rucksack before throwing it down the mountainside. Another bullet followed the diversionary tactic and Gemma knew she had milliseconds to make the most of the bluff.

The Lieutenant followed the rucksack, scoping it up in mid-run, before heading for another outcrop of raised volcanic rock. Five metres from her target an arm shot up from the floor beneath her sending her spiralling down the rockface.

As she stumbled to regain her balance Andrews changed direction and this time utilised the dust she had created only moments before, potentially hiding her movements from whoever the shooter was.

Andrews could only guess if she could continue riding her luck as she first found larger boulders before the beautiful green sight of sapling trees came into view.

The Lieutenant did not hesitate but hit the green line at full speed before beginning to zig-zag through the undergrowth as fast as she dared, always keeping her body as low as possible.

It was only when she reached the larger forestation, and a well-used pathway beyond, that she slowed and tried to regain her bearings. Andrews took out a pair of binoculars from her backpack and turned back to face the volcano.

As her pulse raced her heart pounded with the realisation that her team were gone. There were no signs of anything up there, apart from the now settling dust.

'Eboulement?' a voice sounded from behind her. Gemma turned so quickly she startled the elderly man. She was glad she was only holding binoculars, otherwise she might have raised a weapon instead. 'Pardon madame,' he held his arms aloft to indicate he had not wished to scare her. He stared at her for a second more before continuing, his own fear receding. 'Anglais?' he asked before pointing to her shoulder. It was bleeding, and he was indicating for her to follow him down toward the main road.

'Oui,' Gemma managed, suddenly feeling the sustained injury start to throb as the adrenaline began to dissipate from her fatigued body. Had she been shot? Was it just a graze of a bullet or had she hurt herself from the fall?

Suddenly her training kicked back in. As Andrews saw the roadway beckon her, she started to run, thanking the old man as she passed him. If the bullet had been laced in poison, then she didn't have long. She headed straight for their hire vehicle and clambered in quickly.

The Aéroport de Pierrefonds was about 20km away, as was their small plane. If she could just get a bit of distance under her belt, then she could use her medi-pack and the various boosters and injectors within.

Either Saint Joseph or Saint Pierre would do for a pitstop. After that she had no option but to take to the skies.

Sebastian Nolan did not waste time waiting for an opportunity to shoot once the fleeing woman had become hidden by the undergrowth. Réunion was an island after all, there were only a handful of locations she could go in order to escape quickly.

He folded up his sniper rifle before climbing down into the belly of the volcano. He replaced his facemask over his eyes, nose and mouth before heading to his temporary retreat.

Halfway into the inner crater there was a newly cut opening, just big enough for Nolan to clamber into. Inside he switched his night-goggles on and began to twist through the hard granite rock before reaching an old basalt tunnel beyond. There he was greeted by a pair of intense, if ultimately lifeless, eyes.

Nolan signalled to the trooper to follow him, as he turned and made his way back to the open air. There, in the darkening skies, Sebastian climbed back into the crater, followed by a group of strange looking soldiers dragging five bodies behind them.

Sebastian pointed down at the open lava pit beneath them. Each soldier then pulled their prey toward the fiery hole before throwing them in. Nolan took a moment to look at the fire and heat, before looking skyward as if in prayer, but ultimately for him toward only the darkness and the cold of space.

Nolan swore within his facemask, understanding only too well his mistake. He headed back up to the crater's edge, sniper case in hand and his group of soldiers in tow behind him. They had one more fish to catch.

As he once again looked out toward the Arabian Sea, he took off his protective facemask and withdrew his phone from his pocket.

'Hi,' Sebastian said coolly as his call was picked up. 'We have a small problem.'

Lieutenant Andrews did not stop the jeep as planned, but simply pulled open the medi-bag as the vehicle slowed at the first set of lights. She knew the procedure quite well and felt better to remain moving.

It also brought back chilling memories of the last time she had to use such injections. She had suffered an Indian Red scorpion sting whilst they were concluding a mission in Sri Lanka, and although Gemma was fit and healthy the effects of the venom would have affected her abilities and ultimately compromised her team.

Admiral Goldhawk had been in command that day and the lieutenant remembered his words over the headset as if they were yesterday. There was no option but to keep going, applying the antidote and adrenaline as they drove through the busy streets.

Andrews was with her team that day, she wasn't now. However, the procedure stuck with her. She thought back to Goldhawk's softly spoken words.

Buy yourself time. Apply the adrenaline compressor she thought.

Battle the poison. Eradicate the venom by supressing the effects and pushing the dirty blood to the extremities and away from the heart and brain.

Flush out the system. Attach a sifter to each arm to dilute the effected blood supply.

Each process was only designed to minimise the effects as much as possible, but it also pushed her onwards mentally. With each second she hesitated it would make her worse, every second she acted and pushed on the daylight would become brighter.

She felt one of the side-effects almost instantly take hold and grimaced as the cramps intensified throughout her chest and upper body. She knew nausea would also take hold soon, so grabbed a bottle of water and kept drinking until it made her retch on the seat next to her.

Wiping her chin with her arm Andrews took out another bottle of water and began drinking again. Sooner or later her stomach would accept it. Although she drove with a purpose, her reflexes were beginning to slow. Time was against her from all angles now. Andrews needed to obey the laws of the streets as she couldn't afford to be stopped by police, yet if she took too long then she could simply become unconscious at the wheel.

From up ahead the lieutenant saw the tower of the small airport and calculated how long it would take to get there. She then began the counting process in her head. Anything to keep focusing. Anything to ensure Andrews made it off this island alive.

Once she was in the air, she could take another boost of adrenaline, but not yet, not on the civilian highway. There were too many possibilities for anything to go horribly wrong. Out over the sea, then it would be only her and she could start taking risks. Gemma could live with that.

Steering the jeep into the small airport Andrews drove the vehicle right over to where her plane was parked. There was nobody near it, but the lights were on, so she rushed as fast as her body would allow her. She threw her bags and medication into the co-pilot seat before rounding the other side of the plane and hauling herself up into it. Gemma started the plane.
'Non, non!' she heard one of the engineers' shout as they exited the hanger with a maintenance toolbox. The lieutenant turned and gave him the thumbs up as she punched the plane forward toward the main runway.

It was complete lunacy to fly at night in such a machine, but Andrews had no choice. They would be hunting her down at present, and every second wasted would only let them catch up.

The injections were now kicking in, any poison or potentially lethal gases from the volcano should now be eradicated, or temporarily delayed at the very least.

The weather was also now beginning to wage a fight against her. Andrews felt the wind pickup as she took the plane toward the main runway. Some rain began to buffet the window to her right. She doubted if it would help her escape.

Gemma had stored her mobile in her rucksack and had now turned all the planes internal lights off. Once in the air Andrews would sabotage the flying lights on each wing by pulling out the fuses from the electrics panel beneath the cockpit, so into the darkness she would go, completely blind but also, hopefully, unseen.

Andrews just hoped the wind direction would change. If not, then she stood no chance of making Madagascar alive.

Only time would tell.

Nolan opened up his laptop in his apartment and watched the various images on his screen change before his eyes.

The radar was currently picking up the escaped soldier's plane, but that would disappear the moment she got out to sea, unless panic set in of course and she remained at high altitude. The weather was starting to deteriorate and only the most skilled or completely insane pilots would dare fly so low in such weather.

Sebastian picked up his phone as soon as it began to ring.

'Hi,' he started. 'She's heading out to Madagascar as presumed. The plane doesn't normally have such flight distance, but it may have been upgraded to fly her squad here in the first place.

No, some good news here sir,' Nolan noted to the question from the other end. 'According to the engineer at the airport it had yet to be fully fuelled. They weren't due to leave until tomorrow.'

Nolan listened intently to every word that the calm voice was instructing him.

'Yes sir,' Sebastian nodded. 'I won't fail you.'

Andrews flicked the fuel gauge several times before accepting the inevitable. In her rush to escape the island she had committed the most idiotic of aeronautical mistakes. She had taken an aircraft that couldn't get her to her destination. The plane was obviously lighter with just her, but even so, she needed more fuel, much more, to get her to Madagascar.

The lieutenant kept the plane at a low altitude to avoid radar, but therefore could not kick it into autopilot. She grabbed the stick with one hand as she pulled the map from her rucksack. With one eye on the darkening horizon she quickly estimated her flight distance.

Her heart plummeted. She was not going to make it by some distance. Andrews had no choice but to turn back.

As she looked up out of the windows to both her left and right, she saw the other two planes higher in the sky almost instantly, brightly lit through the ever-increasing rain. There was one on both sides, flanking her. At that height both would be on radar and no doubt being tracked by others back on land. Andrews looked out again to the horizon and instantly realised their plan.

They only wanted to push her out further into the open water.

Sebastian Nolan watched the two blips of his soldiers' planes on his radar continue out from the island in perfect synchronisation. Neither of his planes would contact him, that was not the way of these soldiers.

They were however not only explicably loyal to their cause but formidable in combat and followed every order to its absolute completion. They still gave Nolan the creeps though.

It didn't matter how many times Doctor Harding had tried to convince him; Nolan found it very difficult to completely trust these soldiers. As the images on the screen headed out over the ocean Sebastian's mind drifted back to his case file on his phone.

Nolan opened the file and flicked through to the combat trial pages. This current mission was only their third out in the open, but currently the soldiers just seemed to be growing exponentially more and more competent.

'The Menazee,' Nolan sighed as he read the notes he had already written before tonight. 'Second Order. Initial trials suggest these superhuman warriors lack some individual thought required for more complex missions, but when following a set of orders or maintaining a certain criterion then they excel more than fail.

Need to update this,' Sebastian muttered as he flicked to the third mission write-up. He switched the voice application on and tapped where in the document he wanted the text to start.

'Mission Three – Stealth,' Nolan began. 'The Menazee illustrated both highest endurance levels and patience infiltrating the island allowing identification of their true nature. Once in the rim of the volcano they dug a hideout with basic if diamond tipped tools, before venturing into the lava tunnels and waiting for the enemy to approach.

There was some engagement that had detracted from a complete mission accomplishment, but whether this was due to a Menazee failure or external factors no doubt we'll have to establish this after returning to base.

With one of the Special Ops team surviving the Menazee were then ordered to utilise two planes and follow a simple order to ensure the escaping plane be left with no possible route of escape.

They were instructed that there would be no reason for a confrontation and,' Nolan hesitated as he checked his laptop, 'currently they are following this command without question.

The lack of vocal communication from the Menazee is unnerving nevertheless, but currently I have no reason to see this as negative feedback. The Menazee have evolved far more efficiently than I ever gave them credit for.

They are strong, incredibly resourceful but almost alien to me,' Nolan reasoned. 'Yet they are without doubt the answer to all our problems. They crushed a Special Ops team as if they weren't even there, and one escaped only due to bad luck, which will soon be rectified,' Sebastian smiled as all of a sudden the two blips that were on his radar turned and headed back to land.

Game over.

Gemma let go of the joystick as her crudely made autopilot contraption held as the winds continued to buffet the small plane. She could not leave the cockpit for long, but the plane was still too heavy for the precious fuel left.

The winds had changed direction and from the clutches of despair Andrews now contemplated the incomprehensible; that she might yet make it.

After turning the light back on within the tiny plane, she worked fast pulling out as many of the loose fittings and boxes as possible before heading to the tiny door near the rear of the plane. This was not a good idea, but it was the only option she had left.

Gemma heard the motors whine and realised that the weight at the rear of the plane was beginning to make it climb. Andrews however let fate dictate the next and possible final hour of her life. She might appear back on the radar, but it was too late to worry about that now.

Lieutenant Gemma Andrews opened the rear of the plane and spent her last remnants of energy pushing out as much cargo as she dared or had time to loosen.

Once she managed to close the rear door she picked up the last remaining lifejacket and returned to the cockpit, took back control of the plane and then decelerated as much as possible to save fuel. She needed to buy some time. This was a major shipping lane after all. Anything was now possible.

Gemma pulled free her binoculars again, turned off the lights, and whilst the weather outside worsened she tried to keep her spirit positive. She quickly calculated just how far the plane would take her and changed her direction slightly to ensure the winds were pushing her along, instead of slowing her down.

Maybe the engineer had contacted the aviation authorities and a rescue operation was already underway? Even if not then the local ships in the area would have been notified and would now look out for a stray six-person plane.

With a crack of thunder rocking the aircraft, Andrews took the plane yet lower, hoping that sooner rather than later the two planes high above her would lose sight of her darkened aircraft against the white horse backdrop of the stormy sea. From her vantage point she could no longer see them, but that did not mean they weren't still trying to track her.

As for being rescued, something would come along. Something would save her. It had too.

Angel of the Seas

Madagascar: Arabian Sea: 13:48

Myron McGivney sat patiently on the quayside as the transfer boat moored itself. Next to him a couple were busy flicking through their documents whilst other tourists were gathering their luggage and belongings.

He had caught sight of the huge luxury liner *Angel of the Seas* around thirty minutes ago, his own emotions suddenly in turmoil again. Isobel Fortuna and her father were already on the ship, having already completed half of their Australasia tour – part media extravaganza and part business catchup.

Myron had realised quite early on that he was interested in neither. In the end it had been an obvious, if difficult, choice to give Isobel the space she needed to return the Fortuna business back to its reign of power. So why was Myron here then, unless he still felt there was something to fight for?

He sighed and thought back over the last few months. Both Isobel and he had been drawn so close to each other in the wake of the near disaster her brother had help orchestrate. It was almost both of them versus the world at that time.

Then the inevitable bursting of the bubble, which Alessandro Fortuna had managed to do almost instantly with his hold over his daughter. Myron did not blame the man, as a father he obviously wanted what was best for his daughter. Myron knew deep inside however that at some point the old Isobel would return, one which would again have the weight of the world back firmly on her shoulders. Myron could not protect her from that, not with the Fortuna's in the limelight in every city, with every news feed having some mentioning of their name each night.

Alessandro knew just how to play the media as well, his puppet strings hanging over all the continents, and in every business he either owned or had the opportunity of acquiring. Myron was just a simple man, or so he had first assumed.

Like anything else he had ever done Myron did so with one simple premise; to be truthful to himself, and others. Like before, this had now left him in a position that he did not relish, that he would be the last one holding onto something that obviously did not exist, whether that was an ideal or a belief in someone that now seemed so distant.

Myron did not blame Isobel of course, how could he? His feelings for her were so complex that he realised he would never actually be able to tell her exactly how he felt, but of course that no longer seemed to matter. For within his pocket was something that might do all the talking for him, he just had to find the right time.

Isobel Fortuna leant onto the rail overlooking the eastern coast of Madagascar and breathed in the fresh sea air. *He was out there*, she knew. This both pleased and unsettled her. Although Isobel was now firmly rooted back within her role as deputy of *FortunaCS* it could not ever replace what had happened between them only months ago.

And no matter what either Myron or her father would say, she knew the truth. Myron had risked everything to find her, absolutely everything. Isobel sensed something had broken within Myron in that sacrifice as well, for he was never truly the same afterwards. Isobel sighed heavily. Was it her that had caused the rift, her position, her father or simply Myron?

On days like these she could easily think back to the initial aftermath of the sarcophagus affair, where Myron was there for her whenever she wanted, but that had all changed now.

Of course, her father had wanted "more" for her than to fall for Myron, even though the emotional advice from Alessandro was also contradictory. Isobel knew that her father was being overprotective but wondered just how much was due to his own personal anguish after losing his wife and her mother. She could understand how he would want to save her from such pain, but it was not his place to oversee her whole life.

Isobel remembered her father's words only too well; "You can't control your emotions, but you can control your actions."

This was true, she inevitably was responsible for how her life would turn out, and although Isobel loved being the deputy head of probably the largest courier firm in the world, it no longer seemed enough.

This was mostly due to the people she met – they were rich, powerful and talented individuals but ultimately bland compared to Myron. She smiled at this thought, so would he, Isobel imagined. It was odd just how much one man could change her life forever, and in a way she could never have contemplated before three months ago.

Turning to view the deck she caught sight of her father approaching – it was not easy, but she had to choose a new life at some point. Here he was again, not even allowing her time on her own, just in case Isobel started to develop dangerous thoughts. Maybe he was scared, not just for Isobel becoming hurt by a lover but also of being left alone. It was truly a ridiculous premise, but would he be content if Isobel stepped down and they eventually would have to sell the company he had built with his bare hands. Probably not, Isobel considered.

And that, she thought, was the whole problem with her life. She was torn between being dutiful and being truly happy, if risking everything she knew for that happiness. Isobel smiled, let go of the handrail and wandered over to her father.

Myron held firmly onto his holdall resting on his lap as the transfer boat bumped across the waves toward the *Angel of the Seas*. Myron had to revel in its absolute majestic beauty as the ship grew with every metre, they drew closer. It was simply ginormous.

There were a few tourists on his boat that were obviously very rich, but ultimately the wealthiest would not be seen on such a crowded boat or share such a primitive mode of transport. A helicopter cruised overhead, which instantly answered Myron's question.

Maybe he should have accepted Isobel's invitation to go premier class, but that was not his style. Myron wanted to go under the radar, wanted to live his life how he had planned it, not as some pretentious guests expected him to behave.

Myron knew he'd embarrass Isobel again at the meal tonight. He just did not fit in, and although he always tried, it seemed too false. Should he have come? He doubted it. Did he want to see her again? That, he had no doubt. Would it be the last time? Now, that was a question he didn't want to dwell on, not for even a millisecond.

Ishyan Stölles was as ever eager to blend into the background, but even he felt it difficult on a cruise ship. Eventually he had taken to speaking to the Captain and gaining access to a maintenance cabin on the lower deck, a uniform and toolkit. It seemed like an instant success as he had become almost invisible straight away. Maybe on another day Ishyan would have taken exception to this obvious depravity in human behaviour, but not today. The whole remaining members of his adopted family were on board the *Angel of the Seas*, and he, as ever, would be their watchful guardian.

Considering even the invite for this cruise required the highest security clearance, Ishyan knew his job regarding the guests was largely unrequired for both him as well as the visible security on board. However, so much could go wrong on a ship this far off the coast from South Africa, as they were venturing into very dangerous waters.

Ishyan caught sight of the transfer boat, and with his interest at usual high peak, looked down from the gantry toward the new holiday makers. Ishyan kept out of sight as they boarded but felt a small smile trickle onto his lips as he noticed the usual out of place Myron McGivney almost stumble onto the deck of the huge ship.

Stölles leant back into the shadows, happy to have his newfound friend on board. Myron was almost a lucky charm for Ishyan, and since the sinking of the *Jah Mahal* the bodyguard had always reserved a special place in his heart for him.

They had both parted as equals, something that Ishyan knew Myron had difficulty in accepting, but

Stölles realised just how much the man had sacrificed to rescue Isobel. There had been a lot of luck going with him of course, but that was fine. Myron deserved it.

Ishyan kept out of view, but moments later checked his phone and the passenger list. It didn't take too long to find where Myron's cabin was situated and Stölles had to laugh. It was one of the cheaper cabins, miles away from the main areas of entertainment. Typical.

Myron, Ishyan thought in amusement. Always looking to watch from the outside, always ending up slam bang right in the middle of a situation. Stölles picked up his toolkit and began the slow meandering walk down to where Myron's cabin was situated.

The captain of the *Angel of the Seas* opened her arms in a grand gesture as both Alessandro Fortuna and his daughter, and only heir, entered the bridge.

'Signor Fortuna,' she smiled warmly, ushering the visitors toward the centre of the room, and right in front of the huge bank of ship's consoles and screens.

'Captain Adriane Yusuf,' Alessandro shook her hand before turning to his sibling. 'My daughter, Isobel,' he said. 'I promised her a quick tour.'

Isobel smiled as they talked amongst themselves, the view of the bridge reminding her of the last few hours onboard the *Jah Mahal*. The *Angel* however was significantly larger, and even though the weather was threatening to hinder the cruise later today, Isobel knew its sheer bulk would force through most of the seas without even unsettling the crystal chandeliers.

Myron lay his suitcase down on the bed, opened it, looked inside for inspiration before giving up completely and lying down instead. He stared at the ceiling for what seemed like an eternity before a knock at the door interrupted his empty thoughts.

Myron got up, crossed the small cabin and opened the door. There on the other side was a man wearing a maintenance uniform.

'Afternoon sir,' Ishyan smiled. 'I have a broken tap reported for this cabin?'

'Um, yes,' Myron replied. He ushered in his friend, closed the door and waited for an explanation.

'Undercover,' Ishyan beamed maniacally.

'Yes, I got that,' McGivney replied sarcastically before smiling honestly and warmly embraced the older man. 'Good to see you Ishyan, very good to see you.'

'Same here my friend,' Ishyan returned. 'It's been a while.'

'It certainly has, why the disguise?' Myron quizzed with some concern in his voice. He hoped there was not something on the horizon that might suddenly spring up and surprise him.

'Nothing like that,' Stölles replied, noting his worry. 'Alessandro has so much security on board I felt like I was sticking out, thought I'd go undercover, just in case.'

'Yes,' Myron mused. 'Just in case, I know how you think Ishyan. Just in case usually means you're hiding something from me.'

'Not this time,' Stölles offered. 'However, what with all the media attention over the Fortuna's at present, I'd prefer to keep a low profile.'

'I don't blame you,' Myron smiled before turning his back on Ishyan. 'Drink?' he asked, opening the sideboard bar.

'Tonic and ice if you have it,' Ishyan smiled. They both pulled up a seat and sat sipping their cooled drinks, both wondering what the other was thinking. Myron spoke first.

'I'm going to step down from my position,' he almost whispered. Ishyan nodded and fully understood his friend's decision.

'You both deserved more,' Ishyan said slowly. 'Alessandro rescued me; Sergio used to play with me, but it was Isobel whom I grew fondest of. Her smile was so...'

'Infectious,' Myron offered.

'Yes,' Ishyan laughed softly. 'Infectious, but in a good way Myron.'

'In a good way,' his friend agreed. 'Yes, I can't disagree on that one.'

'She will never forget you my friend,' Stölles swirled the ice around in the rapidly emptying glass. The lack of alcohol was refreshing, Ishyan disliked having his reflexes tinged by any substances.

'I know,' Myron replied. 'I guess I never really had a chance, and it was fun whilst it lasted.'

'Fun?'

'The bits after the explosions,' Myron winked. 'The gunfire and sinking ships I won't miss.'

'Maybe,' Ishyan sighed.

'No,' Myron said more sternly. 'I won't miss it. I'm no thrill seeker.'

'I didn't say you were,' Ishyan shrugged. 'Just remember how it would have turned out if you hadn't gone after her.'

'She'd have been fine,' Myron told himself more than Ishyan. 'It would have worked out ok.'

'Don't kid yourself,' Ishyan replied. 'You needed me, and I needed you. Neither could have done it alone, at least agree with me on that one.'

'You win then,' Myron nodded. 'Plus, don't forget Sofia, Darius, Kirill and Tucker.'

Ishyan laughed heartily. Myron smiled and finished his drink before offering another.

'No thanks,' Ishyan replied. 'I have to get back out there, keep my eyes open for anything out of the ordinary.'

'Ok,' Myron smiled. 'Just one last thing,' he said before Ishyan had chance to leave.

'What is it my friend?' Ishyan asked.

'Here,' Myron replied as he put his hand into his pocket and withdrew a cylinder full of dark red liquid. Ishyan's look asked a thousand questions. 'It's mine,' McGivney continued, pointing at the phial of blood. 'Keep it. Hide it. When the time comes, get it checked out.'

'Why?'

'Isobel doesn't know everything about the rescue,' Myron told his friend. 'I have to admit, nor do I. Initial indications suggest a small presence of hallucinogenic and behavioural performance heightening toxins most likely from the blood red gem I took from Bessek and wore between London and Venice. It didn't take long to enter my bloodstream, and the concentration was miniscule, but believe me, the effects have been monumental.'

'What do you mean?' Ishyan asked seriously.

'This is what I've been trying to tell you,' Myron sighed. 'I'm no hero, never was. This is potentially the reason why I risked everything for Isobel. I might be miles off, but such an influx of chemicals could explain why I ran after her, showed no hesitation and simply waded into the battle on the *Jah Mahal*.'

'Or,' Ishyan continued as he pocketed the phial. 'You're looking for excuses. Trust me Myron, you weren't high on drugs.'

'Maybe.'

'Maybe nothing,' Ishyan rested his hand on Myron's shoulder. 'If that gem did alter your perception in some way, then so be it, you still had to get up off your softly padded behind and go after her in the first place. Forget this, my friend. It'll lead to no good if you let these thoughts linger.'

'You might be right,' Myron replied, suddenly feeling very tired. He also felt as if a huge weight had been taken off him. Ishyan now had the phial, and he trusted him implicitly in doing the right thing if required.

'I am right,' Ishyan nodded. 'Now my friend, whatever happens we will meet again one day, and when we do, we celebrate in style.'

'That's a deal,' Myron replied before hugging his friend one last time. 'Take care Ishyan, and I hope you manage to stay out of trouble.'

'Doubt it,' Ishyan smiled. He picked up his toolkit, propped open the door and turned one last time back to Myron.

'Just be yourself kid,' Ishyan winked at him before stepping out into the corridor.

Myron remained standing for some time after the door closed, wondering if he would see Ishyan ever again. Maybe not, but even he would not put it past

Ishyan to have eyes on him, wherever he was. This made Myron smile.

Isobel made her excuses before exiting the bridge and heading for the main deck, partly for fresh air but mostly to clear her head of her father's constant application of business protocol. As heir to his empire now, more than ever, the responsibility of following his onerous procedures and duties was becoming abhorrent, but nevertheless it seemed to be her destiny.

As the sun's rays threatened to make her day better, she caught sight of something that brought conflicting emotions. Only a few months ago Isobel would have run to his arms, but now, strangely, she almost contemplated stepping back from the rail and walking the other way. She also still had the choice as Myron had yet to see her. He too seemed to be lost in thought looking far out to sea. Isobel sighed, hoped they could at least talk civilly and began the agonizing walk along the deck and down the steps to the next level.

'Myron?' Isobel almost whispered as she approached.

'Hi,' he smiled warmly, which caught her slightly off guard.

'Sorry,' she said. 'Didn't mean to startle you.'

'No, it's fine,' Myron replied, catching her eye as if they had only just met. 'I was miles away. How are you?'

'I'm fine,' Isobel replied, unsure what else to say. She had half-expected this to be awkward, instead Myron seemed quite relaxed to be in her company.

'I have to apologise,' Myron offered quietly. 'I'm not good at all this Iz, so I snook onboard via the transfer boat. I hope you don't mind?'

'Of course not,' she waved away the apology, even though the reason was all too similar. Myron just didn't feel comfortable being amongst the Fortuna's, but something else warned her of her potential misjudgement. 'It's not me, is it?' Isobel asked, before she could hold the words back.

'No,' Myron almost laughed. 'It's never been you. Of that I promise,' he said before turning to face her head on. 'Look, Iz,' he began before a shout from along the deck made them both reel to face the loud voice.

'Templar,' Isobel breathed. 'He's an investor in the space project.'

'I had gathered that, it's hard not to have heard of him,' Myron smiled. 'You're going to have your hands full for a while.'

Isobel did not have time to react to her friend's comment before Harrison Templar was walking toward them, his arms gesticulating in every direction at his excitement to be onboard.

'Miss Fortuna,' Harrison began. 'This ship is amazing; I've got lost twice and found a bar on both occasions!'

'Well, that's not quite the usual writeup the ship receives but glad you like it,' Isobel replied, before turning to Myron next to her. 'And this is my good friend Myron.'

'Good to meet you,' Harrison offered his hand before shaking Myron's vigorously. 'And you, Miss Fortuna, saviour of the space race,' he held his arms out wide before hugging her.

Myron smiled at Isobel's obvious discomfort at such open affection. *That'll teach you*, he thought slyly.

'Saviour?' Myron questioned the last statement. 'I was under the impression this was a collaboration, with both companies due to make equal advantage?'

'On paper yes,' Templar replied before Isobel had a chance to interject. 'However, if truth be told Isobel has...' he looked over at Miss Fortuna as if to check he could continue, '...potentially become a game-changer, and allowed us to have a great advantage over all our competitors.'

'Maybe we should continue this talk later, over dinner?' Isobel offered, before realising instantly she had just burnt Myron's fingers. She chanced a look across to him, but he seemingly had let her get away with it.

'That probably sounds a better idea,' Myron noted. 'I'll leave you two for now and hopefully will catch up with you later Harrison,' he smiled. 'Your ideas on civilian spacecraft as well as atmospheric re-entry are truly ground-breaking, I just hope I'll get the opportunity to see one of your manned shuttles in person one day.'

'Well,' Templar started before looking again at Isobel. 'Tell you what, why don't we pop on upstairs to where we're meeting for dinner and we can chat about it? I'm sure Miss Fortuna will get you up to speed with our test facilities. It's no secret after all, is it Isobel?'

'No, Harrison,' Isobel replied. 'It isn't.'

And as she followed the two men, Isobel reasoned that the space test facility was no longer a secret simply down to Harrison Templar. Why was everything so complicated?

As Isobel contemplated what to do next, she caught sight of Myron turning as he reached the upper deck, looking back her way, smiling and sending her a friendly wink.

Isobel returned the smile and wondered where the last few horrible weeks had gone. She had expected confrontation and bitterness from him but had been met with a smile, a loving gaze and even playfulness.

What had changed? Isobel thought. This scared her as much as it warmed her soul.

Harrison Templar stepped over to the bar and ordered what he thought to be the perfect beverage for a late afternoon on a clear blue day. The billionaire was therefore somewhat taken aback when both Myron and Isobel merely sipped their alcoholic drinks before settling them back on the marble counter.

'Is that it?' Harrison asked. 'We're on holiday guys. Enjoy the glorious seas whilst you can.'

'I'm on medication,' Myron told him, a half truth after all. Plus, Templar's reputation proceeded him by about thirty-six hours, which was usually the time it would take to recover after one of his parties. 'But,' the younger man added, noticing Isobel's subtle behaviour at his side, 'happy to take you on at a game of shuffleboard out on the deck. I have absolutely no experience though, but always wanted to try it.'

'You're on,' Harrison smiled, a little surprised. 'As long as you have fun, I'm in.'

Myron almost rolled his eyes in response to his colleagues well-rehearsed one liner. Harrison turned and passed back his empty glass to the bar staff.

Isobel caught Myron's gaze and mouthed a silent "thank you" as he grinned at her knowingly. There was obviously only so much of Templar that even Miss Fortuna could take.

'I'll leave you two to battle it out,' Isobel offered as Harrison re-joined the couple. 'I need to freshen up.'

Allowing Isobel to leave without causing a fuss, Myron followed Templar as they strolled out onto the main deck. As they passed a few onlookers to another deck game, Myron was not surprised in the slightest as Harrison Templar ventured toward not only the most populated game area, but also one that had been raised above those all around. The young British man smiled. Always a showman.

Isobel wandered back to her luxurious cabin half-hoping that Harrison Templar, the billionaire innovator, would not get Myron into too much trouble. The other half of hope she reserved for Myron continuing in his current form. She so much wanted her father to approve of him, but that was never going to happen.

Now, Templar she knew that Alessandro would approve of, which only annoyed her bitterly. Harrison was amazingly intelligent and charming, but she also saw right through him to the infantile approach the American had to everything in life. Once he had achieved it, he always moved on. This was exactly her worry now with the space project. Her father had passed it on to her to work alongside Templar, but Isobel knew how long this project would take. Or at least, how long the "whole" project would take.

Miss Fortuna had left this final part of the equation from both Harrison as well as her father.

Ishyan knew, but she had made him promise never to let her father know. Considering she had asked in the aftermath of her father's impossible return, she thought Ishyan may have agreed simply due to the turmoil of his emotions. Not that Ishyan ever showed any emotions mind you. Well, that was not completely true.

Myron had managed to break that rock-hard stone truly open. Isobel had never found out what had occurred on the *Jah Mahal*, but she already knew Myron's actions to be heroic. Whatever had happened on that fateful day had made a massive impact on Ishyan, almost to the point where she would never be able to get her sometimes bodyguard to side with her against Myron.

Not that Ishyan had ever needed to say anything, he always managed to juggle both her father's and her wellbeing, whatever the current situation might be. Isobel noticed the subtle ways Ishyan either included or made sure Myron was kept in the loop about Fortuna matters, which slightly irritated her sometimes. Mostly as it should be her letting Myron know. Maybe this was exactly the problem.

She had strayed far too near the fiery emotions of love and was now paying the price dearly for it. Myron too. Isobel should never have let herself be consumed by the relief and overwhelming ecstasy of her rescue, where the very next day she had discharged herself from the medical bay and had personally sailed to see Myron. They had then whisked away into the ocean and spent the next few weeks almost in paradise.

It had been Elysium, Isobel told herself. They had loved each other, even if it was only the overly emotional high of recovering from the enormity that they had both been through. Reality had soon sunk in and they had returned to Earth with a hefty bump.

Earth. Now that was a problem. Isobel laughed as she conceded for the first time that this whole space project was merely on the rebound of her and Myron taking a break in the first place. *Get hurt, get a project*, was her motto. Now she wanted to venture into space. Isobel knew she had some deep-rooted psychological issue but trying to find the answers amongst the stars was surely the biggest nonsensical idea of all time.

Well, she mused, that was almost the answer. Myron had managed to fuel her more than she first realised. Isobel knew he had suffered due to his ordeal at the hands of Bessek. She had heard him many times, mostly after their arguing, calling out in his sleep from the next room. Isobel had of course simply blamed it on their ever-fracturing relationship. But when she let it, she did wonder if Myron had suffered from any post-traumatic stress from the whole episode.

Isobel flicked open her file of notes, trying to push him from her mind. It still hurt her immensely, which was partly a relief to her, partly only made her want to push on with this next project even more.

As she turned the page two words struck her immediately, almost as much as they had all those weeks ago: dark matter.

Isobel sighed heavily then sat back onto the bed. Ishyan knew what both Myron and her true plan was, but nobody else. She had wanted to tell her father but had ultimately decided upon that in the end.

Dark matter: it seemed intrinsically linked to both her and Myron's troubles in every way. Isobel had researched post-traumatic stress disorder as it seemed to make sense, but nothing then added up. She should have been happy, and secretly hated herself when she was not content with every dead end that she encountered from her research.

So here she was, assisting a billionaire in a media frenzied space race, but her true goal was something far more scientific. Isobel had every intention of launching their ship with a satellite that would view through the heavens with a different sort of lens, and then maybe some answers in her life would be answered, even if she knew they weren't what she originally set out to discover.

Isobel replaced the file on her desk and decided to run a bath. She sighed again. For her whole life Isobel had managed to operate the simple operation of turning a tap without an issue. She had given Myron a few months of him treating her like a princess that now Isobel found herself gazing in deep thought at the running water.

Yes, there had been pain. Yes, there had been anger. But Isobel knew deep down that she should have fought more for what they had; they both should have. Maybe they still had time. Isobel thought about the space project. If their feelings for each other were true, then she had to let him know.

'Bloody Ishyan,' she whispered as the bath suddenly felt a lot more inviting. 'He planted those seeds in my mind.'

Harrison Templar walked with the utmost vigour onto the large central deck of the *Angel of the Seas*, and right toward the raised shuffleboard arena that he had requested the Fortuna's arrange solely for him. Spread around this raised bit of decking were other more traditional shuffleboard courts, with their markings set in white and players busy shooting and scoring in the late afternoon sun.

The American of course liked to be different, and here was no exception. Harrison loved his indoor shuffleboard tables where instead of a marked endzone there instead was a pit, a final dropping point where sometimes a mere millimetre was the difference between failure and glory.

Templar now strode purposely up the few steps to the gantry point of the raised shuffleboard arena, waving over another drink from the deck bar as he did.

'You still up for a game?' he spoke back to Myron, who followed like a man who was keen to watch, but no more.

'I'll give it a go,' McGivney replied. 'The other courts had too much oxygen for you, did they? Nice vantage point from up here by the way.'

'Ha ha,' Harrison smiled. 'Yes, I might get noticed a bit more up here, but look Myron. This is true shuffleboard...'

A few faces from below looked scornfully at him. *Typical Templar*, thought Myron. Doesn't care who he annoys.

'This game is the definitive version,' he continued. 'Notice the pit at the end, sheer theatre if we're lucky.'

Myron took an opportunity as the barman approached with Templar's second drink to walk along the moat surrounding the shuffleboard arena, noting the no-play zone, the initial high 1st scoring line then the 2nd and 3rd scoring lines before the drop – where a hanging puck would score an additional point. Like curling, only the puck or pucks nearest the far drop pit would score. Potentially with luck on your side, and if your opponent was completely incompetent, you could end up with 16 points in one session from four pucks.

'First to seven to start us off?' Harrison asked from down the polished board. Myron pushed the potential 16-point single end victory from his mind and back to his opponent.

'You're not going to take a no so let's just get on with this,' Myron winked as he strode back up the moat toward Harrison. There was quite a crowd gathering already, and Templar had not even started his theatrics yet.

'Ladies...'

'Oh my word,' Myron sighed.

'...and gentlemen,' Harrison started, quite to the annoyance of a few traditional shuffleboard enthusiasts who were playing their games in the usual quiet manner. 'I, Harrison Templar, innovator of the high seas...'

'Good grief,' McGivney whispered.

'...have been challenged...'

'Has he?' Myron said out loud this time, but it still did not deter the grand speech.

'...by my good friend Myron McGivney here, who you might remember being the hero of the *Jah Mahal* only a few months ago.'

Myron's expression said more than a thousand words; had this man no shame? During his trip from Cairo to Madagascar, at all times over the last twelve weeks, Myron had managed to keep his identity unknown.

Two minutes with this billionaire and the whole boat now knew. His eyes rose to the sky in disbelief, coming back to face Templar who had a smile beaming from ear to ear.

'That makes it a bit more interesting,' Harrison smiled as he offered his hand ready for the competition. Myron shook it firmly. As Templar began to loosen his muscles up, Myron turned back to the upper deck, which overlooked the main deck. He was convinced that he had seen Ishyan lurking about up there just now. If that was the case, then this was no ordinary game. But why, it was up to Myron to find out.

Alessendro Fortuna heard the commotion from the upper deck and wandered over to see what was occurring. He smiled as he saw Harrison Templar literally in the middle of the hubbub.

What Alessandro did not expect though, was Myron to be there alongside him. His emotions toward the man were torn. He owed Myron so much for assisting in the rescue of his daughter Isobel, even if the how's and why's he had still to extract from Ishyan. There was also more chance of extracting an apology from a politician than to get a straight answer from Myron. He seemed almost the opposite of Templar.

Where Harrison was ruthless, Myron had heart. When Templar used cunning, McGivney was resourceful. And as for Isobel, the billionaire would set her up for life, but what could Myron possibly offer her?

So, two men, both with clear intentions for his daughter. Harrison's built on economies of scale and Myron's on a rather old-fashioned premise, and one

Alessandro swore he wouldn't contemplate ever again. You could rebuild an empire; you couldn't replace the irreplaceable.

He knew that Harrison enjoyed his indoor shuffleboard, the billionaire had two at his ranch retreat where Alessendro had stayed upon his last visit to California. What he didn't know was why Myron had apparently challenged him, although knowing Templar that too might have been concocted right out of thin air.

Alessandro almost felt sorry for Myron, the guy had no chance. A figure sat down, out of view of the upper deck, on a row of plastic chairs behind Alessendro.

'What is it?' the Italian owner of *FortunaCS* asked subtly.

'I think this game wasn't fair to begin with, let alone trialling out a bit of your space kit along the way.'

'Better to test it here rather than anywhere life threatening,' Alessendro replied. Ishyan sighed.

'Sir, you know I respect you more than any other person on this planet,' Ishyan began. 'And I love you as a father.'

Alessendro turned to face the other man, his expression betraying his concern.

'What is it Ishyan?'

'You are not aware of everything,' Ishyan simply spoke quietly, feeling the vial of Myron's blood in his pocket. 'Don't push Myron away, you will need him in the end.'

Alessendro stared at the other man as he kept his patience at bay, a trick he managed to achieve only due to Ishyan's life-long service and loyalty to his family. Stölles was also rarely wrong about anything.

'Okay,' Alessendro nodded finally. 'You're temporarily relieved. Go where the cruel wind takes you, and when the time comes, then you simply give me the sign.'

'Yes sir,' Ishyan replied without a smile. 'Thank you.'

'It's ok,' the old man managed before his bodyguard turned away. 'I trust you; I just don't like the thought of the end. Not again.'

'Nor do I sir,' Ishyan replied. 'Nor do I.'

Alessendro gave the younger man one last nod before turning and letting his whole concentration be taken up by the sight on the main deck below him.

Let's see what these two gladiators can conjure up for me, Alessendro smiled. He desperately needed a distraction.

'After you,' Harrison offered the pushing stick to Myron as they both stood at the players' end of the raised shuffleboard arena.

'Considering this is my first game,' McGivney replied, not accepting the stick, 'I'd have thought it was only the height of good manners for you to show me how to play with you commencing the game and pushing the first puck.'

'Why, of course,' Templar half-smiled through gritted teeth. 'What did I say? First to eleven?'

'Seven I believe,' Myron muttered matter-of-factly as he stood to the side and looked down the polished wood to the far end. There was quite a crowd gathering now.

'Ok,' Harrison agreed. 'First to seven, let's see if one of us can get a few scores this round,' he smiled, repositioning his sunglasses back over his eyes. He then gripped each of his forearms with the opposite hand once or twice to get the blood circulation going.

Alessendro knew better than that of course. Both the glasses and ultrathin body glove underneath Templar's clothes should combine state of the art technologies, allowing each puck to be pushed at the perfect trajectory toward the scoring lines. However, the kit was still in testing phase and Fortuna was always one for testing equipment to its limits.

He had already tried the kit first-hand in an indoor climbing arena *FortunaCS* had hired, cleared and utilised for a whole weekend just to trial the body gloves. They were not unique at all, exoskeletons had been in circulation for years now, but Alessendro wanted his technology to become almost part of everyday clothing. Maybe military weapons were not quite his style, but he knew only too well what kept projects bankrolling in this world, and almost losing his daughter to Bessek had given him a bit of a sway in this direction.

Plus, his daughter's and Templar's fascination with the commercial space race had bred another use for such clothing. Imagine slim fit astro-suits which could keep the body's temperature regulated as well as making the human body stronger and more agile.

It was all a pipe dream a few years back, but some innovations were literally popping up all over the world at present, and Fortuna wasn't one to stand around and marvel at each one. He wanted part of the circus, even if his intentions were borderline in some cases.

Alessendro watched as Harrison's first puck slid in just before the third scoring line. It was not the best opening shot as it left the scoring zone empty, but the old man had to allow a small smile to creep over his features. There were not many players who could walk onto a foreign court and play such a shot of perfect length right away. Next Myron took the pushing stick.

'Your go,' Templar mused as he stepped aside and took another sip of his drink.

Myron stepped forward, pulled the pushing stick back, then forward a couple of times, just like a golfer taking a practice swing before he approached the puck.

It was easier for Alessendro to notice from the higher vantage point, but something struck the old man about the way Myron was now prepping for his first shot. Alessendro watched in disbelief as Myron's shot glided along the polished wood, parking itself perfectly in front of Templar's first shot. It had not even nudged it, yet from this position Harrison couldn't knock it out of the way either, not unless he risked removing his own puck from the field of play. Considering the length of the shuffleboard arena, the shot was a near miracle.

Harrison seemed to have the wind taking out of his sails momentarily before the clapping and cheering from the crowd egged him into replying quickly. Templar looked at the far end of the shuffleboard, let his glasses focus on the exact spot he wanted the puck to end up, then let his second puck fly. Again, it slowed just as it reached the third scoring line, almost identical in length to his first puck. This was not lost on Myron.

'So, you're a one-shot magician, are you?' McGivney smiled innocently as he took the stick from Harrison. 'In that case, maybe I should try the same?'

Templar looked on as Myron's second puck again came to rest their side of Harrison's first two pucks but pressing flush up against it.

'You know,' Harrison began, unsure of what Myron was trying to achieve. 'All you're doing is protecting my pucks, so with half the first game gone, I'm currently four up. Going at this rate it's going to be over after this frame?'

'If you say so,' Myron replied, his voice strangely resilient compared to the man Templar had been introduced to earlier.

Harrison took his gaze away from the other man, prepped his puck and then pushed off again, this time with less gusto. He was not sure what Myron had planned, but there was no point in playing anything risky at this point, not with Myron having the final puck, the hammer, at his disposal. His puck fell short, but he was still four points up.

McGivney tilted his head to one side as he considered the various shots and angles from the shooting end. One stuck in his head, the fact that it was almost unachievable did not seem to register with Myron's brain at all.

He pulled back the pushing stick and let loose a tremendous shot, the puck flying off at high speed down the polished wood. There were many gasps as first Myron's puck hit Templar's third almost head on, sending it ricocheting into Harrison's second, before they both fell off the side and into the far pit and moat respectively.

Next to him Harrison groaned. In just one shot he had lost two points, and now had only one puck left. Templar walked across to the barman again, picked up his drink and played for time. He took off his sunglasses, laid them on the tray momentarily and began to walk down the moat alongside the shuffleboard arena to get a better view of the pucks.

Myron was almost convinced that this was against the rules, but let Harrison think he was getting away with it. The billionaire's sunglasses had been left on the tray after all. McGivney let Templar reach halfway down the board before making his calculated move.

The crowd were all congregating around Harrison's feet now, all talking about what their own preferred shot would be. Up above, Alessendro was enjoying the spectacle but with it this brought other dangers. Templar was not a man to mess around with, but Fortuna and his daughter would bring him around, whatever the result here. There was no doubt Myron had flustered him, and Alessendro had never seen that with Templar before. He had also never seen Myron act like this either. What a strange but enlightening day it was turning out to be.

By the time Harrison had returned to the shooting end of the raised arena, the crowd had all silenced again and normal play seemed to be about to resume.

Templar picked up his glasses from the tray, placed them onto his head before seemingly hesitating in playing his fourth and final short of this frame. Myron looked on knowingly.

Harrison took a few seconds to recover, then pushed his final puck forward. The shot had less finesse than those before it and didn't even creep past any of Myron's pucks.

The crowd all moaned in disbelief, before hushing each other as Myron stood up to the shooting line. Templar was still two points ahead at present, but Myron had the opportunity of sending his final puck into his own first puck, and if enough force was applied it would send Harrison's clear off the board.

That would have been a great shot and would have allotted Myron six points, but this now became all about winning the game in a single frame. He moved himself to the left of the board and lined up his final puck with his third, the one that had cruelly dispatched two of Templar's pucks only a few minutes ago.

Myron let his body sink controllably to his left knee as he pushed the puck away from his body. It glided down and slightly across the court as it headed for Myron's third puck. He heard the crowd grow in volume as first his final puck gently nudged his third puck, which then headed across the board at an angle and right into the side of Templar's scoring puck. Within moments Harrison's first puck had dropped out of contention at the side of the board, but the crowd were witnessing something more, something very special.

McGivney's final third puck neatly ricocheted further into the scoring zone, moving slower and slower, further and further toward the drop point. He heard a few ecstatic shouts but already knew what he had achieved. The cheer a second later, as well as Harrison's whole body dropping in defeat, told him everything he needed to know.

Myron had managed to score a hanging shot on his final roll of the dice, along with three other scoring pucks. He heard the score erupt from the far end and turned to shake Templar's hand. Myron half expected some anger to be sent his way from the other man, but instead received a firm handshake.

'Mr McGivney,' Templar pulled him in close. 'I have underestimated you to my own detriment. I might have a use for you,' he smiled thinly, before letting the theatrics seep out of his bones once more. 'Ladies and gentlemen,' Templar boomed as he held Myron's hand up aloft. 'I give you the saviour of the *Jah Mahal*, now champion of Shuffleboard!'

There were cheers of laughter as well as congratulations, but Myron suddenly felt he wanted to be anywhere but here. It had begun again.

He turned to Templar, thanked him, told him he would see him at dinner later before making his way through the cheering crowds back to his apartment. Myron found himself almost running at one point as his brain began to become disorientated, his focus started to wane in and out, and his body temperature soared.

Fighting nausea, Myron managed to enter one of the deck doors he recognised before heading to the stairs. Knowing instantly he could not climb up nor down, he turned to the lift instead and pressed one of the buttons.

As the lift door opened Myron felt a strong grip on his arm push him inside and then heard the doors close again. He heard the word "*breathe*", knew the voice, but could not force any of his thoughts together to make any sense. Myron felt the sickness drive up in him again, a mixture of feeling paralytic and vertigo, mixed in with an unbearable heat all over his body.

Within what seemed like minutes another door opened, and he fell onto something white and soft, before a blackness sank over his whole body.

As Myron McGivney's body lay on the bed, face down on the covers, Ishyan Stölles pulled out a syringe and injected the man with a clear but powerful sedative.

'Sweet dreams my friend,' Ishyan said solemnly as he took out some medical monitoring equipment from his toolkit. 'Let's hope that helps.'

Isobel finished her leisurely bath, took her time getting ready for dinner and finally even wondered why not one of her family nor close friends or even a work colleague had come to her cabin.

Eventually, as the ship began its long trek to Cape Town, Isobel called the cabin boy who quickly set her straight. She thanked him for her time before heading up to the lounge area, where Harrison was already in full swing with the guests.

'So,' Isobel asked subtly as she stepped toward her father. 'What did I miss?'

'Quite a bit my angel,' Alessendro muttered. 'Your boyfriend gave Harrison here a thrashing at shuffleboard this afternoon, and ever since Myron has been in hiding and Templar, well, exactly the opposite.'

'Oh, good grief,' Isobel sighed. 'The day you finally call Myron my boyfriend and Templar's acting up like this?'

'Yes,' Alessendro replied calmly. 'Bit of karma I expect on my behalf. Don't worry, I've already requested the bar staff keep his refills as alcohol free as humanly possible, and once we get some food in him, he'll calm down I'm sure.'

'Maybe,' she replied. 'Although the guests seem to be entertained for now.'

'Ah,' Alessendro smiled. 'He's noticed you. Good luck.'

'Thank you, father,' she replied sarcastically before a slightly drunk Harrison Templar made his way over to her. 'Isobel!' he called unnecessarily. 'We need to chat, I have a proposition for you, and Myron for that matter.'

'Really?' Isobel asked, unsure where he was going.

'Yes,' Templar said as he grabbed her arm and led her away to a large window overlooking the ocean. 'You see, I challenged Myron to a game of shuffleboard today, I know, stupid me trying to be king of sports. Anyway, your boyfriend absolutely took me to the cleaners.'

'Were you drunk by any chance?' Isobel asked, even more unsure of where this was going now.

'No,' Harrison replied, even feigning hurt at this last comment. 'Let's put this in context. The astro-suit, we've tested it yes?'

'We're always testing it,' Isobel remarked, before the penny dropped. 'What did you do Harrison?'

'Nothing...much,' Templar reasoned. 'Nothing dangerous anyway. But you do owe me another pair of sunglasses...'

'Not one of the prototypes? Templar, I thought I could trust you with this tech?'

'It was Myron's fault!' Harrison whispered back. 'But I'm getting side-tracked. You missed something incredible today Iz, your father's already seen it, he must have told you.'

'He mentioned something about Myron handing your ass on a plate back to you.'

'Cute,' Harrison smirked before continuing. 'I wore both the ultrathin suit and glasses, as a test only, to see if the zoom vision could guide my body to push four pucks down to a specific area of the shuffleboard scoring zone.'

'And?' Isobel asked intrigued.

'Well, it would have worked fine...' Templar began.

'What happened Harrison?' Isobel asked impatiently. 'How did Myron beat you?'

'What happened with him on the *Jah Mahal*, Iz?' he asked back, staring deep into her eyes. 'Something was different about him as soon as he stepped onto the shuffleboard raised arena.'

'Nothing,' Isobel replied, knowing full well there had to be something, and she had missed it completely.

'I need something from you,' Harrison began.

'Careful what you're going to ask,' she warned him.

Templar simply smiled.

Myron opened one eye, then the other. His body was dripping with cold sweat, but the nausea had now passed. As he sat up, the smiling face of Ishyan greeted him.

'You had me a little worried there my friend,' Stölles began. 'And I can see why Isobel threw you out with all your sleep talking,' he winked to break the ice.

'So much for not seeing you for a while. How bad was it?' Myron asked. He'd recorded his own sleep time and again to make sense of the ramblings, but it didn't mean much to him.

'Bad enough,' Ishyan said. 'Come, we need to catch the dinner reservations otherwise we're both in trouble. I've got your Black Tie ready.'

'Thank you Ishyan,' Myron offered. 'Again.'

'It's no problem, Myron,' Stölles smiled. 'I know you have a journey to make at some point, I just hope it isn't quite yet. But when it is time, make sure Isobel knows why.'

'She will,' Myron nodded gratefully.

Ishyan stood, smiled once more, then headed out of the cabin.

Myron entered the main lounge of the *Angel of the Seas*, with his invitation in hand, and was quickly ushered over to where the Captain was greeting new arrivals.

'Mr McGivney,' Captain Yusuf smiled before shaking his hand. 'Thank you for coming onboard my ship and attending this event tonight, I hear you're quite the celebrity after the Shuffleboard shenanigans of this afternoon.'

'Thank you,' Myron replied. 'And my sincere apologies to any other deck players for the cacophony both Mr Templar and I seemed to create. It wasn't intentional.'

'Maybe not on your part,' the Captain smiled. 'Fortunately for Harrison any nuisance he creates he usually manages to sedate by merely opening his wallet and buying a few rounds.

I read all about your exploits regarding the *Jah Mahal*,' Adriane continued. 'Dreadful business. You'll be safe in our hands, don't worry.'

'To be honest, I've never felt so relaxed since I boarded,' Myron lied. 'The ship is absolutely beautiful. I just hope the weather holds.'

'We've a bit of rough conditions coming in later,' the captain admitted. 'But nothing she can't take in her stride.'

'Glad to hear it,' a familiar voice from behind Myron spoke. Isobel quickly slipped her hand into his, almost as if fearing rejection. Myron closed his hand warmly around hers and returned a smile. 'Captain, do you mind if I tear Myron away from you?'

'Of course, Miss Fortuna,' Adriane replied. 'I'll catch up with you both later.'

As the captain turned to welcome the next guests Myron let Isobel guide him over to a less crowded part of the lounge area.

'You ok?' he asked.

'Sort of,' Isobel replied. 'I think we need a heart to heart.'

'Now?' Myron whispered. 'Here?'

'No, of course not,' Isobel rolled her eyes at him playfully. 'My cabin is near; we just need some privacy.'

'Ha,' Myron laughed as he saw Harrison's head duck between guests as he caught sight of them. 'Not sure we're going to get that tonight, but we can try.'

Isobel turned to see Templar heading their way and gripped Myron's hand instinctively. Myron frowned unintentionally. *What was it?* he tried to read her thoughts.

'My favourite two partners in crime,' Harrison boomed over the crowded lounge area. 'I wonder if I might have a private word in the boardroom?'

'Of course,' Myron nodded. Even he understood when there was no chance of escape.

'Come, please,' Templar urged. Harrison led them to the private area, ornate but small, airy but with no windows. There were a few monitors on the walls, but apart from that this room had the ability to change to whatever function was required. For now, it was required for confidentiality.

'What's the matter Harrison?' Isobel asked with all seriousness. Myron turned as Templar closed the door and waited for the man to speak.

'Look,' he said slowly. 'I'm going to be completely honest with you both, which is not always my way,' he smiled slyly. 'But time is against us. I've just learnt that *FoSE*, as they like to call themselves, has set a date for first launch.'

'Already?' Isobel asked, thinking to the original *Federation of Space Exploration* group that had been made up of multiple countries across the world. Next to her Myron took a seat and poured three glasses of chilled water. This might take a while. So much for any alone time with Isobel.

'Yes,' he nodded to Isobel before seating himself opposite Myron. 'Thank you,' he indicated regarding the water.

'What was the original timeline for their launch?' Myron inquired, half-knowing the answer.

'We were talking years, but they've pushed it forward to only six months,' Templar admitted, and he was more than just concerned.

'Spill the beans Harrison,' Isobel said sternly. 'Who do you have on the inside?'

'His name is Doctor Harding,' Templar admitted. 'He has his fingers in many pies, as you can imagine from a leading scientist, but he has had his morality tested by what he's found out over recent months. It seems not all is above board as it should be at *FoSE*.'

Myron, in is brief time with *FortunaCS,* had soon begun to learn about the politics and mind games that are played around boardroom tables, and this was no different. He did not trust Templar, no more than he trusted Alessendro. To be honest the only two people he trusted on this ship were Isobel and Ishyan, and even then, knew how well a poker hand both his close friends could play.

Ishyan never revealed his hand until the right moment, where Isobel managed to materialise winning hands right out of thin air. Myron didn't even need to catch Isobel's eyes to know what she felt, they had almost a telepathic understanding when in this situation. It however was when they relaxed that they seemed to suffer and sour their relationship.

'Go on,' Isobel said coolly.

'There's a program there,' Harrison continued. 'They called it SOMWar, the Second Order Menazee Warrior project.' He turned his attention to Myron and pulled up his long shirt sleeve. Myron saw the thin body armour underneath. 'This should have beaten you today,' Harrison half-smiled. 'That linked to my glasses should have put in four scoring pucks, but somehow you beat me.'

'Luck,' Myron replied a bit too quickly for his own liking.

'Maybe,' Harrison answered. 'But this project has gone one further than mere exoskeletons. They've developed enhanced fighting machines based on the human and chimpanzee DNA, a unique coding to create the most lethal, and loyal combat fighter. This is something I hadn't anticipated.'

'So, what's your recommendation regarding our own timeline?' Isobel asked solemnly. 'We were tight before; we have a test flight in three days. We'll be showing the world where we are, and *FoSE* will eat that up.'

'Yes, about that,' Harrison began hesitantly. 'This is where I haven't been entirely honest with you Miss Fortuna.'

'What?' she asked stunned, although next to her Myron was less than surprised.

'I had a secondary option for the project,' he offered quietly. 'It is far riskier, hence why I never put the proposal on the table.'

'Really?' Myron asked.

'Yes,' Harrison shot him a look. 'You believe what you want about me Mr McGivney, but I do have a soul. I left it off the table as I did not want to endanger Isobel or her father, but that has all changed now. You've also stepped into the light.'

'What?' Isobel asked.

'Come on Iz,' Harrison began. 'Surely your father has already spoken to you?'

'No,' Isobel began. What is going on here?' she asked both men.

'I didn't win by luck today Iz,' Myron spoke without looking at her. 'I took Harrison on at his own game, just like that maniac Bessek.'

'What do you mean?' Isobel turned toward him, confused.

'You know Iz,' he finally turned to face her. 'Have you ever asked yourself how I could have come after you, and actually managed to find you, let alone rescue you, and survive?' he spoke softly. 'I was infected from the beginning. As to why, I have no idea. But the gem I picked up from the warehouse in London altered my personality, my physiology and metabolic state.'

'Exactly,' Templar agreed. 'And today, when I challenged you out of the blue, you reacted with something I wasn't ready for. It was not just a warrior stepping up for battle, it was a gladiator who knew that loss would mean certain death, something that I have not seen for a very long time. Your intensity blew me away.'

'And thank you for cheating,' Myron smiled sarcastically. 'I wondered why Alessendro was so interested in the match.'

'Templar?' Isobel reacted angrily.

'Oh, come in Iz,' Harrison waved away her comment. 'You know your father far better than me. He's always looking for the next opportunity. He knew what this ultra suit could do, both for the military and the space mission.'

'Don't lecture me about my father,' Isobel began before she felt the swift touch of Myron's hand beneath the table. What was he trying to say? She dared not look at him but waited for the next grip of his hand around hers.

'I'm just saying that Myron might be our golden ticket,' Templar began. Isobel felt his hand quickly tighten around hers to note the warning. She knew he was not warning her of his own safety but of something else, something the Fortuna's could not possibly comprehend at present.

'I'm not with you,' she stated clearly.

'*FoSE* are light years ahead if you forgive the pun,' Harrison smiled. Myron felt a twinge of rehearsed dialogue in his voice. 'Myron is an enigma, something that has fallen into our lap. What if that bloody gem was part of this *FoSE* project as well? Doctor Harding is ready to spill the beans, I can at least find out what he knows?'

'Ok,' Isobel replied, knowing not to trust Harrison, but also eager not to push him away too far. *Keep your enemies close*, she thought. 'Where does Myron come in?'

'Take him to the training camp,' Harrison replied. Templar could see Isobel twitch as soon as he mentioned it, but Myron's expression did not betray his own feelings. 'Let us see what he can do? Maybe we have the answer to all our problems here?'

Myron squeezed Isobel's hand one last time before raising both his hands to the table and taking another sip of his water. Next to him finally came a response.

'Harrison,' Isobel began hesitantly. 'What happened to Myron on the *Jah Mahal*, only a select few know about.'

'I understand.'

'Not even my father knows,' she warned him through teary eyes.

'Miss Fortuna,' Harrison interrupted her. 'Please believe me, I have no intention of causing discomfort to either of you. Please.'

'It's ok Iz,' Myron said softly. 'Let's run some tests. If the ultra suit performs above what you expect, or hope, with me at the helm then great,' he said. 'If not, then we'll have to find another way to beat *FoSE* in getting a commercial spacecraft around the globe. But just remember, both of you,' Myron spoke slowly. 'This is not a race, first across the line doesn't mean anything if a few months later the rest of the world finds out you cheated to get there first. The truth has a strange way of always floating to the surface, no matter how hard you try and hide it.'

'I agree,' Harrison nodded. 'Miss Fortuna?'

'You have my agreement also,' she said. 'A pact then?'

'Yes,' Templar nodded and held out his hand. Isobel lifted hers from her lap. Myron took one more swig of his chilled water before adding his.

'To whatever's out there,' McGivney smiled.

'Done,' Templar nodded.

'Yes,' Isobel added.

'And now,' Harrison sighed as he stood, adjusted his tuxedo, and made his way to the doorway. 'It's time for dinner. Please enjoy yourselves and don't worry about a thing. We're going to do this.'

As Templar exited the room Myron and Isobel waited a few seconds before following, hand in hand. Both could tell from the subtle twitching of their fingers that they were not happy, but that they had no other choice. Harrison was going to win the commercial space race, by means fair or foul, more probably the latter. Isobel had never felt more threatened by anything in her life, and that said something after the sarcophagus incident. She also never felt more afraid for the person who now held her hand. The man she desperately had tried to stop loving, and now had completely failed to do so. She hoped Myron felt the same way.

'Dinner,' he whispered closely into her ear as the other guests began taking their seats. 'Can't we just get takeout and retire to one of our rooms?'

For the first time since Isobel could remember at a VIP function, she found herself wanting nothing more than to turn and take Myron far from here. She knew they were in danger, and her father at that.
Templar scared her.

The Captain was on her third or fourth speech, one between each course, when Myron made his excuses and left the table for the toilet. He had kissed Isobel lightly on her hand as he left, a sign that he was going "for a walk" as he knew it would be hard for her to leave both her father and Harrison plotting their world domination.

Myron chose the outside as his friend for the night, the chill and freshness of the air bringing quiet relief back to his tired body. It did not matter where in the world he had ended up, he always felt as if his home was the distance away from Isobel's current location.

He knew it had always been his decision in London all those months back to go chasing after her. He could come to terms with that. It was his personality that had made friends and contacts across Europe with first Kirill on the Orient Express, then Sofia in Venice and even Ishyan and Tucker on the island of Assos. However, the other part of him; the part the gem had influenced, that was the part he could not truly understand.

Without the gem Bessek would have stopped, and probably killed, him in London. The jump from Sofia's boat plane would have injured most people far fitter than him, and of course he had somehow managed to climb the castle walls to infiltrate the prison. Then of course was the collision with the helicopter on the *Jah Mahal*.

None of it was him. He had been infected. It was also nigh traceable. He had given Ishyan a vial of his blood for tests, but that was only recently. He had left Kirill the gem itself, and here lay the next issue. He had left his good friend with the reason he now had nightmares, nausea and unexplained superhuman reflexes and insight, even if only for short periods of time.

Myron could not ignore this anymore. It might not be his fault he was originally infected, but before he could cure himself, he had another human to warn; his good friend Kirill Volkov.

He just hoped he was not too late.

Myron wandered along the deck, almost oblivious to the rising winds around him before something caught his attention at the edge of his peripheral vision. At first, he thought he had imagined something, but knew better than that by now. He looked around him and saw one of the staff quarters nearby.

'Excuse me,' he said as he knocked on the door then entered quickly. 'Do you have some binoculars?'

As they were passed to him, Myron did not wait to give an explanation but headed back out on deck. His heart raced as he caught sight of a light aircraft through the binoculars to the east of the ship. One of the crew had followed him out into the brisk air and noticed Myron's concern.

Before Myron could even ask, they gave him the thumbs up and headed up the metal gantry quickly, toward the bridge. Myron turned his attention back to the ocean waves and felt his stomach twist violently.

The craft was dropping rapidly.

Neither Isobel nor Harrison missed the fact that the captain seemed to leave the dinner before dessert was finished, nor that Myron had still not returned.

'You thinking what I'm thinking?' Harrison asked.

'I hope not,' Isobel replied as she stood and made her excuses.

By the time the captain had reached the bridge the whole room was a hive of activity. The first officer quickly updated her, as the rest of the crew already began emergency procedures.

Out from the control tower, Myron had already made his way down to the launch deck, where two rescue crew members had prepped the lifeboat. Between them they had also pulled together enough medical supplies for anything but the direst of situations.

'You saw it go down?' one of the crew asked.

'Yes,' Myron replied. 'Almost due east of us, although I'm going to need a pair of eyes back on the ship to get us there.'

'The weather's coming in,' another mentioned as she lugged a medi-bag onto the boat. 'We need to go now Lyle. We can't wait any longer.'

'Okay, Lucy,' her companion replied. 'We're going to need your help,' he simply told Myron.

'Whatever you need,' McGivney replied.

As the boat set off from the *Angel of the Seas* Myron glanced a look back and caught sight of Isobel and Harrison come to the railings, just as the seas began threatening to close off his view back to them at all.

Myron raised a hand in goodbye. He then turned to concentrate his full attention to what lay before him. The waves rose and fell, but his eyes continued to look straight ahead. Whoever it was just had to hold on a little bit longer.

They were coming. They would save them. They had too.

Ice

St. Petersburg; Russia; 19:49

Kirill felt the truck judder to a halt and hands were laid on him immediately. He was almost picked clear up off the floor as he was dragged out into the deadly cold air. Underneath the visor his throat almost seized up due to the dire drop in temperature, but his soul remained as strong as ever. He would choose his moment, but Kirill would fight until the bitter end.

It wasn't until several minutes later that his headwear was removed, but by then he was already underground. The walls were cleanly cut from ice and shone as the soldiers' headtorches glistened off every surface. Kirill remained silent, saving his breath for later. His body was already sapped of energy anyway, it wouldn't take much to defeat him at present.

The Russian heard a metal door unlock up ahead and sensed he was nearly at his journey's end. The hands pushed him forward but was then aware that the footsteps turned and left him. For the soldiers who had ushered him here had played their part and Kirill would now carry on the rest of this surreal journey on his own.

Kirill stood and waited, allowing the metal door to swing shut behind him. It wasn't much warmer this side of the security boundary, but it was infinitely more silent, and almost completely void of light.

'Kirill Volkov,' a voice spoke through the darkness. 'You seem to have taken a wrong turn...again.'

'Major Fyodor Chugunkin,' Kirill replied instantly, recognising only too well the voice from his past. 'Why am I not surprised to find you amidst the depths of hell?'

'Kirill,' the major began. 'Please, we are but comrades here. Why do you always see the bad in me?'

'You know full well,' came the reply.

'Maybe,' Fyodor replied, flicking on a lantern as he approached Kirill. 'Our country needs us to bury our bitter past my old friend. What do you say?'

'If this is about the Americans in Norway then they are more resilient than you give them credit for,' Kirill warned.

'Yes,' Chugunkin sighed. 'They are testing my patience. Luckily for us I have a remedy for that problem.'

'Really?' Kirill replied. 'The last I heard that debt had been paid.'

'Mere propaganda,' the major offered. 'You must have more faith in your fellow countrymen comrade.'

'I do,' Kirill said bluntly. 'But the ones I trust seem to be murdered in their sleep or made traitors of the state.'

'Some mistakes have been made,' Fyodor noted solemnly. 'However, we are now trying to rectify them by whatever means necessary. Come and look for yourself...'

Kirill woke in a cold sweat in the armchair, his breathing heavy in the relative silence of the crackling embers of the open fire. Larissa entered the drawing room from the kitchen.

'What is it dear?' she asked. 'I heard you call out.'

'Nothing,' he lied. 'Just dozed off. I need a drink of water,' Kirill added as he stood up, wrapped his dressing gown around him and headed out to the kitchen. 'You go up to bed, I'll be up shortly.'

The house seemed so peaceful even at the early onslaught of night, a chilling mirror image against the silence of the icy hallways of his dreams. *No*, Kirill thought. *Those hallways were not silent.*

Another flashback entered his mind, but this time no visuals accompanied it. Just the sounds of the screams of men.

Kirill shook his head as if to dislodge the resurfaced memory. What had happened to him over the last few weeks? His whole life seemed to be turning upside down, memories Kirill swore he never had were beginning to surface in his subconsciousness, causing him to question his sanity.

He had told Larissa nothing, but that would have to change soon. Either he was experiencing a complete memory recall or had started to hallucinate. He wasn't particularly pleased with either option.

Opening the fridge and grabbing some ice for his water, Kirill froze again as another memory hit him. This time he knew the resurfacing memory was real. Everything slotted together. He knew the place.

'Pyramidian,' he whispered. 'But why now?' he sighed sitting heavily on a kitchen chair. He ran over the last few weeks to identify where this episode could have originated but found no solace in his activities. Nothing made sense.

Then it clicked, as if by magic.

'Myron,' he whispered.

Myron's head bobbed up and down as the rescue boat almost flew between the peaks and troughs of the brooding ocean. Time was short, he knew that. The approaching darkness, the wind and now rain all conspired against them but only made Myron's concentration grow infinitely more focused.

Without looking back Myron raised his right hand slightly to indicate for the boat to turn toward starboard. He then gave the thumbs up as he continued to look up over the turbulent seas.

Behind him both Lyle and Lucy were hanging on with dear life to the rib as it bounced across the waves at high speed. Neither felt safe out here, but were strangely compelled to follow Myron's navigation, even though they could not see anything through the blackened stormy seas.

Without warning, Myron rose himself to full height right onto the front of the rescue rib, holding strongly onto the bow mooring line. The pilot had to ignore his instinct to stop the boat, in fear that Myron could go overboard.

As a flash of lightning crisscrossed the sky, Myron rose his arm once again, but this time with complete decisiveness. As Lyle kept an eye on Myron's navigation, Lucy picked up a bright orange doughnut shaped lifebuoy and prayed they were not too late.

Myron kept his arm outstretched until they could all see the remnants of the plane. There was no obvious sign of life, and it was sinking fast, so Lyle grabbed at a flare gun and fired it into the sky. As the flare gradually descended through the sky Myron caught sight of a figure slumped over some wreckage about thirty metres away. They had a buoyancy aid on, but with no movement being shown he feared the worst.

As Lyle piloted the rescue boat closer, Myron checked his own buoyancy aid's fasteners and prepared himself to jump overboard. Neither of the two crew members tried to stop him.

The depth of the water hit Myron far more than the temperature. Before resurfacing the human could feel the unfathomable depth beneath him, and he dared not open his eyes to look down. Myron had never sensed this before in his life but swore that he'd never forget it.

Mere milli-seconds later he was back above the water and swimming towards the wreckage. Reaching the body Myron tried to manoeuvre the figure onto their back so that they would not drown. It was hard work, but he finally managed it.

Then he noticed it. Something glistening under the flare light; dog tags.

Myron did not hesitate but pulled them free from the figure's neck before pushing them down his own top for safety. It was a reckless and impulsive act. Myron just hoped it would not have any dire implications.

Behind him he heard the rescue boat above the winds and pulled the figure tight to his chest, their back to his front, their head nestled up against his neck. He then shoved them both free from the wreckage and simply waited for the boat to pick them up.

Myron felt the hands on him and assisted to lift the figure into the boat. He then followed. After a few seconds of catching his own breath, Myron then assisted with the figure's recovery.

'She's alive,' Lucy said and smiled. 'Good job.'

Myron smiled as the pilot span the boat around and plotted a course to where they had just come.

Military, Myron thought. This could get tricky.

Isobel stayed on the deck as the rain began. One of the cabin crew quickly wrapped her in a heavy-duty cagoule, whilst Harrison and her father went straight up to the bridge.

'Come on Myron,' she whispered out into the night. Up above her multiple searchlights bounced off the rising waves, each trying to illuminate the potential whereabouts of the rescue boat.

Behind her Isobel heard the static of a radio punch through her thoughts, with one of the searchers quickly answering. Pandemonium followed and for a few seconds Isobel felt her breath taken away from her, before the searchlights finally converged on one location in the near distance.

Isobel breathed a huge sigh of relief as she saw the rescue boat head back. The ship's medical crew were already waiting on one of the lower decks, but of course they were now hindered by the turbulent ocean around them. The ship's special side hold cargo door could not be opened due to the waves, so they were left with the tricky option of sending down a rescue ladder and safety harnesses.

As the rescue boat came close, she noticed another problem, the waves were now smashing into the side of the ship. Above her she heard the unmistakable sound of a winch being activated.

Isobel didn't have much faith in winching up the rescue boat as it was, nor trying to remove the injured person off the boat onboard either. They were in a bit of a predicament.

As she watched the winch drop toward the sea beneath her Isobel saw Myron prepare to catch it. Surely, he was not going to...

Before Isobel had time to shout a warning to him, Myron had managed to pluck the winch out of thin air and pulled down as much slack of the rope as possible into the boat.

She watched on as the rescue boat crew secured the injured pilot to the winch, then lifted them to their waist height. As the boat continued to bob up and down Myron then got underneath the person and pushed them up, the winch taking the strain just as another trough appeared out of nowhere and seemed to devour the rescue boat.

As the injured pilot swirled in the wind Isobel saw the winchman raise the rope as quickly as possible, hands from the deck below keeping the body from hitting the side of the ship, then quickly pulling the person onboard.

Isobel looked back at the rescue boat and saw Myron lying prone on the floor, another crew member trying to help him up. The boat withdrew a bit further from the ship for a few minutes to regather their thoughts for the next phase.

Harrison came to her side.

'Iz,' he began. 'I've got no idea what they're going to do next. They had so much luck with getting the injured pilot onboard. Not sure how they can ever get the rescue boat back on.'

'They can't,' Isobel replied before pushing past him and down the metal ladder toward the deck below.

She was damned is she was going to be a spectator in all of this. Besides, she had "previous" with a winch.

As she drew close to where the injured woman had been taken onboard, Isobel grabbed the winch head and lifted it over the side, leaning over herself as she did. Isobel ignored the various shouts coming her way, looking down at the rescue boat as it prepared to pull alongside once more. As a hand grabbed her to make sure she did not go over the side, Isobel turned and told the crew member to tie her onto the winch head.

At first the man seemed dumbfounded, but then twigged with her request. He shouted across at his crewmates and within minutes they had devised a rescue winch similar to that from a coastguard helicopter. Alessandro rushed to her side but knew better than to try and talk her out of it. She was lighter than most of them anyway, strong and with more than an ounce of stubbornness to follow.

'Be careful,' Isobel's father instructed as she climbed onto the ledge. Alessandro looked up at the winch control and signalled to take in the slack. Isobel almost laughed, half in nervousness and half at her father instructing the crew to give him a walkie-talkie to inform winch control just how to do their job.

Isobel felt the rope grow taught, tightening the lifejacket around her as she was lifted a few inches off the ground. She held the circular and padded pickup-rope out in front of her, ready for the rescue boat crew to cling onto her, one by one as they were winched back onto the *Angel of the Seas*.

She knew that the boat would inevitably be left behind in the seas, but that was an insignificant price to pay for saving the injured pilot. Isobel felt the winch swing, and before she had time to prepare herself, she was dangling feet first over the blustery seas.

As she looked down, Isobel saw Myron wave her down and could only imagine what her father was saying to the winch control. She tried to smile, egging on her humour and imagination as she was lowered further down toward the boat.

After what seemed like hours her foot was guided toward the centre of the boat, Myron eager not to hold her tight just in case the waves blew the boat off course.

Isobel felt her feet hit something hard, then almost instantly saw the face of a rescue boat member pushed heavily into her circular pickup-rope. Myron shouted something incoherently over the wind and once again she was in the air, this time with another person in tow. Isobel looked down at the frightened face and tried to smile, the roar of the waves still deafening her.

Going up seemed to be easier for her mind to accept and held out her arm for the deck support to grab. Isobel saw her father's huge grin as she was pulled onboard, the legs of the rescued crew member almost dragged onto the deck. She was unfastened from Isobel's clutches before being taken off by the medical team. Her father came close and looked her deep in the eyes before patting her on the shoulder. He smiled warmly, his eyes welling up with pride.

Then Alessandro led her back to the edge for the next run. Slapping her on the back she then leant over the edge, and again waited for the winch to take her weight. Isobel knew Myron would wait until last, which helped her a little to pace herself. She had two more drops. Just two.

Isobel was lowered once again, this time the descent was notably shorter, or at least in her mind anyway. She knew what to expect this time and it was no surprise that when the hand grabbed her leg before the rescue boat pilot almost pulled her down right onto him. He instantly pushed himself up through the circle of rope and they were going up again, just as Myron veered the boat at an angle to combat a nasty set of perpendicular waves heading toward the ship.

The ocean was becoming worse. The *Angel of the Seas* was currently almost at walking pace, but if the storm worsened it would have to pump some more power into the turbines to counter the ferocity of the waves. That would not bode well for Myron at all. Isobel felt the urgency in the crew members as they pulled the pilot out from her grasp, before she was sent on her way once again, this time without a rest.

As she began the final descent Isobel felt the winds change direction again, this time sending her toward the ship's metal bodywork. She quickly pushed out her legs to brace for impact, bending her knees just in time to avoid any injury. Isobel looked up and saw some more activity, before the winch mechanism seemed to push her further out from the boat, but without going further downwards.

Great, she thought. *They're extending the arm to its maximum*. That would keep no doubt her from danger whilst hopefully still being able to support both her and Myron on the way back up. However, in this weather all they needed was to get tagged by the boat or the sea and the combined weight and force could potentially break the arm right in two.

Isobel dared to look down and saw Myron bring the boat around one last time. He was fiddling with the steering wheel console, and she wondered if he had tied the key to his jacket and therefore setting the boat to stall once she rescued him. It would make sense that the boat would then simply float away into the night without the risk of it accelerating and veering right into the ship. She heard a boom and noticed a huge wave splash out from the boat below. Myron was indeed struggling as the boat was now being tossed between waves.

Looking up at her father's silhouette one last time she gave him the thumbs up to descend, and instantly Isobel felt the cold spray of the stormy waves hit her already tired body. This time instead of waiting for a hand to grab her she kept checking for the boat. Myron could not steer it, prepare to disengage and guide her in. Isobel kept manoeuvring her arms and legs to counterbalance against the wind and the threat of the winch coil constantly turning her one way or the other.

As the winds seemed to settle for a few seconds Isobel realised that this was it, she had to go now. She gave two thumbs up to the crew above her and prepared to descend to the boat below. It was almost in reach, then with one final swing grabbed at the stern of the boat.

As a huge wave hit the rescue boat side on, she felt the almighty tug of the force throw her sideways, her body instantly becoming tangled with the mooring line of the boat. She heard Myron shout before his hands were on her a few seconds later, manoeuvring her battered body from the entanglement. A huge shriek roared above them as the winch arm tore sideways through the thundery night sky.

Seconds later the coil slammed through ninety degrees and toward the other side of the winch as another wave buffeted the boat across the ocean surface. The ice-cold waters showered over them as they both continued to fight against the ropes that now bound them.

Isobel saw the silvery flash of a blade as Myron pulled a rescue knife from his jacket and sliced through the boat's moor lines and her own binding. As soon as the winch rope broke loose from her restraints, they both dived for cover on the floor of the boat, before clambering to the relative safety near the wheel. Myron reinserted the key and powered up the engines once more. Isobel turned to view the winch through the searchlights as it first hovered above, then began to lower once more. Her cut jacket and part of the rescue rope still dangled from it, she held up her arm for her father to see.

Isobel felt the boat surge back toward the winch, the black shadow on the horizon a mere subconscious blur at the corner of her eye before one of the searchlights hit it. Isobel turned to see Myron disengage from the wheel and rush toward her. She turned and rose her arm one last time as the almighty wave crashed a mere twenty metres from them and bored its way through the black sea toward them.

As Myron reached her side, they both clambered to the side of the boat, and as the winch rope came close, they jumped in unison, desperately hanging onto Isobel's jacket that was still attached to the winch rope. Isobel felt herself swing round and clatter into Myron as they both wrestled to get a better grip. The sound of the wave reached a crescendo as it crashed toward them.

As the winch coil crept back upward, they both held tight as the white-water hit them midriff and pulled them through the sea parallel to the ships hull. Isobel felt her shoulder writhe in pain as she lost her grip only for her arm to become trapped in between the rope, the rescue apparatus and Myron. As she screamed out in agony Myron tried to wrap his arms and legs around her, whilst they both battled with keeping their bodies above the water.

'Stay with me!' Myron shouted above the roar of the water, his gaze not upon her, however. Isobel recognised his expression only too well. Something was not right. 'Hold on,' he whispered in her ear.

Just then the winch creaked and almost bent in two as the combined weight of the force of the sea pulling the two figures along became too much. They were both sent plummeting into the cold dark sea, the waves instantly crashing over their heads and forcing the air from their lungs. Myron could feel Isobel struggle against her binds and instinctively reached again for his knife, but it was no longer there. He pushed his free hand around her and tried to force her free, but instantly could sense the pain he was causing her so gave up. One of the searchlights hit their location and, as Myron looked through the bleak water towards her, saw the life begin to drain away, but yet she still smiled as she looked at him, if only in sadness.

Myron unbuckled his legs from her and, pushing her upwards using his arms, kicked with all his might toward the surface, willing them both upwards. His lungs burnt and his eyes stung but still he kicked, and somehow Isobel managed to force her body out from the binds of the winch. Finally, they broke through the thin veil between death and life and sucked in the sweet elixir of oxygen once again.

The sound above the surface was deafening, and Myron could instantly see why. The whole winch arm was wrapped against the side of the ship, the coil slowly rising but digging into the paintwork as it rose. Myron grabbed the end of the receding rope and tried to keep both his and Isobel's head above water. He was not sure if the rescue apparatus would even hold their weight anymore but tried to bind his right arm into the nearest part of material which was tied to the winch rope. Myron knew she was injured, her expression constantly told the story each time either he, the waves or the coil jostled her. She did not give up however, she wouldn't let herself.

Myron then heard another monstrous sound from above, before the coil shot up the side of the ship by around five metres. Their bodies were hauled unceremoniously out of the water and they hit the side of the ship as they rose, and heavily, before coming to rest. Myron's right arm felt as if it had been ripped from its shoulder blade. Metres above the waves they dangled, but finally out of reach of the ocean's deadly white claws.

Then, slowly, inexorably slowly, they were pulled up the side of the ship. Myron rested his head next to Isobel's cheek and kissed it warmly, his left arm around her waist, his legs simply clinging onto her any way possible.

'Some rescue,' he whispered in her ear. 'I love you so much.'

As Myron held her close, he knew she had already slipped into unconsciousness, but that was not why he had chosen that moment to say what he had.

He would have said it anyway. After tonight, the fight for her father's approval would be nothing.

How little Myron knew about his future.

'I'll take over,' Alessandro smiled at Myron as he laid his large hand on his shoulder as thanks. 'For now. You go and get showered and changed and you can take the graveyard shift for me in an hour or two.'

'Thank you,' Myron replied before heading for the cabin door. The crew had evacuated four smaller cabins so that the injured pilot, Isobel, the rescue boat pilot and the other rescue medical person could all rest and recover in peace, but all within a small radius of the ship's medical team. He stepped into the corridor and waited patiently. He felt the dog tags in his pocket and wanted to return them before the soldier awoke, even if he managed to slip them into her pocket for later.

A few medical staff exited one of the rooms and Myron greeted them. One of the doctors patted Myron on the arm as thanks for his part in the rescue, before heading to the other cabin.

Myron turned and left; the returning of the dog tags could wait. He needed a shower, a change of clothes and maybe even a whisky on the rocks. This made him smile. He could not stand whisky, even when something was worth celebrating.

As Myron headed down the corridor and away from the commotion, he felt someone watching him. The sixth sense that eluded most people haunted Myron constantly, ever since he had picked up that damn gem. He knew there was something that he needed more explanations for but did not know who to ask. He had given Ishyan his vial and knew his friend would assist wherever he could, but his mind kept focusing back to Kirill. What could Myron do to help?

The young man turned another corner and saw his cabin. Time for a shower, he mused. If he was being followed, he no longer cared. It could only be Harrison or Ishyan, and to be honest he could scare them both off with a quick disrobing of his clothes.

Myron entered his cabin and took off the thick jacket that he had worn throughout the ordeal. He let the cabin door swing close on its own, leaving the invitation for whoever was out there. At least Myron was not disappointed.

'Gemma Andrews isn't it?' he asked as the lieutenant crept into his cabin after him.

'Sorry,' the soldier replied. 'I played "dead" once you found me, thought it was the best way.'

'It might well have been,' Myron smiled, before reaching into his pocket and pulling forth her dog tags. He handed them to her. 'I wasn't sure how it would have gone down, so removed them. Nobody knows.'

'Thank you…'

'Myron.'

'Myron,' she nodded. 'There's probably a thousand questions you want to ask right now?'

'There'll be a thousand questions the captain will want to know once you wake up in the morning,' Myron warned. 'If it's going to get tricky, we need to get you off the ship as soon as possible.'

Lieutenant Andrews stared at Myron for a few seconds before comprehending a reply.

'What do you want to know?' she asked, somewhat simply.

'Absolutely nothing,' he smiled. 'I'd only have to lie if I knew the truth and I'm a terrible actor. Plus…'

he added as something else clicked in place. 'A contact in the US Military might have it's advantages. Nothing that would put you in harm's way of course.'

'Of course,' Andrews nodded. 'Now it's my turn. I have only one question.'

'Go ahead.'

'How did you know?' she asked. 'I was miles from the ship. How did you know I was out there? I had already disabled all the lights.'

'What were you running from?' Myron countered.

'Confidential,' she replied, smiling as she did so. She already knew what Myron's answer would be.

'Confidential,' he added, almost laughing. 'For now,' he raised his finger. 'The position you hold though might be paramount in finding me answers. You're more than welcome to any secrets you uncover. For now though, you have to return to your medical cabin. We can catch up tomorrow.'

'Can you get me onto dry land?' she asked.

'You might have to be a tad theatrical when you wake,' Myron considered. 'But I can't see why not. I need to find a way off this ship as well, suddenly I feel as if several planets have aligned.'

'Bit like how you knew I was in trouble?' Andrews offered.

'Something like that,' Myron noted. 'Now go. Whatever your little secret is, protect it, and pray you also got away with it. The fact that your plane didn't disintegrate on impact has saved you, but any floating wreckage might also keep you hunted,' Myron analysed, wondering where these dark thoughts were coming from. He was no soldier, yet kept being pulled back into thinking like one, or was it simply a survival mechanism?

'Okay,' Andrews nodded. 'I'll create a scene in the morning, will you be close by?'

'Yes,' Myron nodded sadly. 'I have someone who got injured tonight. She's based in a cabin very close to yours.'

'I'm sorry,' Gemma began.

'It's not your fault,' Myron admitted. 'She's my heroine. Sometimes I forget that we can get hurt.'

'Yes, we can all get hurt,' the Lieutenant replied, almost as sadly. 'Until the morning.'

'Until the morning,' Myron agreed. 'Goodnight.'

Larissa looked at her husband's body on the stretcher as the ambulance tore through the St. Petersburg streets. The words he had spoken tonight bore into her soul, her thoughts easily drifting to Myron, her emotions mixed with an unhealthy amount of hatred from what she had heard.

It was obviously easy to blame someone for Kirill's condition, but when that person also had subjected her beloved to what could only be an unprecedented level of toxic chemicals in his body and potentially his brain then she found her anger entirely justified.

The sounds of the siren evaporated as the congested crossroad was left behind her, but the blue and red flashing lights outside the window were a very pale reminder of what had happened.

She squeezed her husband's hands within hers and kissed him.

'Don't leave me Kirill.'

Myron sat almost fully clothed in the foetal position in the warm shower for around forty-five minutes until his subconscious fully returned. He awoke himself from his meditated state and plucked the disappearing thoughts from his memory before they vanished forever.

US Military. Gem. Kirill. Isobel. Templar.

The same thoughts kept repeating in his head.

Myron forced his breathing more slowly.

US military. Lieutenant Gemma Andrews. Crashed in a what looked like an eight-man civilian plane, although it could have been modified with additional fuel reserves to undertake more mileage. The only other islands within a 500-mile radius were Mauritius and Madagascar.

Myron ignored the latter for a second, as although this was a huge distance to travel, there was something about the French connection that reminded him of Bessek. No, Myron considered. Must be coincidental. Although...

The gem. How far did it's reach extend? The gem itself was not something that Myron would lose too much sleep about. Even if it had somehow populated his bloodstream with toxins and made him more observant, stronger and more focused then he only owed the gem a debt of gratitude for managing to defeat Bessek, Glade and their soldiers onboard the *Jah Mahal* all those months ago.

Kirill. Myron had left the gem with his Russian friend. This did unsettle him. What if the toxins which had stated to inflict Myron also had influence over Kirill and Larissa? He couldn't risk it. Not at all. Even just one phone call would relieve that fear, but not here, not on the ship. He needed somewhere private.

Isobel. His love for her knew no bounds. Myron already knew he would walk away from her if that meant she was happy, although over the last twenty-four hours he doubted very much as if that would be the answer.

Templar. No doubt he had much influence over many countries and political systems, but Myron continued to wonder just what his motives truly were. Money? Power? Or simply to win at all cost?

Myron exited his cabin with only one thought on his mind; Isobel. He made his way back up to the floor that had designated a wing to the medical staff and injured crew members, which housed of course Lieutenant Gemma Andrews.

As he approached, he saw Alessandro at the doorway. The older man signalled to Myron at a distance that everything was fine, and as they drew close outstretched his arm to shake the younger man's hand, before embracing him fully.

'You and my Iz,' Alessendro began. 'I'll never understand it, but then again, maybe I don't need to.' He smiled at Myron, before opening the door and ushering him through. 'She's asleep, but in good health,' he smiled. 'Goodnight my son.'

Myron smiled and thanked him before entering the room, closing it behind him. He suddenly felt so buoyant. Alessendro had used the words "my son". He picked up the blanket and pulled the chair close to the bed. Myron wasn't going to wake her now, even though she looked so angelic. He knew when she was peacefully sleeping and left it at that.

Morning would come, and when it did, he'd take it just as he took every other day in the Fortuna world. Myron would follow his instinct, his belief in the people around him and the justification of doing the right thing.

The only issue with that, thought Myron as reclined back in the seat, took Isobel's hand in his, closed his eyes and let sleep take him, was that it always led him out of his comfort zone and inevitably into trouble.

The last thoughts Myron had before he slept were of Gemma, and the darkness that would now invariably follow her.

Wednesday; 06:49

Isobel woke slowly, the pain in her shoulder now a dull ache, no doubt suppressed by countless drugs pumped into her over the last eight hours. She felt Myron's touch on her hand and looked across at him. However, he had started the night was not how he'd awake, that was for sure.

His head was almost buried in the side of the pillow next to her, his body hunched over the bed, her right hand engulfed by both of his as well as his forehead. At least he'd had the common sense to wrap himself in a blanket, although on second thoughts even this could have been done by a passing member of the medical staff.

Isobel smiled and kept her pain silent as she twisted to turn to face him. Myron stirred instantly; his eyes exhausted but fixated on her.

'You okay?' he asked simply. 'Your dad was in as well; we took it in turns.'

'I know,' she smiled. Isobel sighed with happiness. Her father was nothing if not protective, and to leave her alone with Myron after such an ordeal spoke volumes. 'How is he?'

'Worried,' Myron smiled. 'You're the talk of the whole ship Iz,' he played with her. 'Even this far out at sea you can't help but make the headlines.' Myron kissed her the back of her hand softly. 'I was worried as well.'

'So was I for a second,' Isobel whispered. 'Still, we had a job to do. How is the pilot?'

'Recovering well,' Myron nodded. He knew he could not keep any secrets from her, but this was also not the time. If she had guessed then she did not show it, but then again nothing surprised Myron anymore. If she woke up one day and told him she was telepathic then he would not have been surprised him either.

A knock came at the door, just at the right time for Myron's sake.

'Hi princess,' a familiar voice said as Alessandro's head crept into view.

'Hi daddy,' Isobel reverted to when she was a girl. Myron took this as his chance to exit.

'Drinks anyone?' he asked them both, quite smoothly he thought.

'Just water please babe,' Isobel told him. Her father waved away the offer with a smile. Myron stood and left his love with her father, only to almost bump into one of the stewards out in the corridor.

'Ah Mr McGivney,' the young man noted. 'We have a telegram come in for you. It's up in the comms room. Would you like me to bring it to you here? We knocked on your cabin, but understandably you weren't there.'

Myron looked at the man for a second. He seemed overly apologetic. This could not be good news, Myron guessed.

'If it's okay I'll come with you to get it,' Myron said. 'I just need to...hold on,' he said, grabbing a nearby pitcher of water and glass from a serving trolley, checked it was fresh before taking it to Isobel. Seconds later he returned to the steward. 'Let's go,' he nodded politely.

Myron's thoughts raced on the way to the comms room, and his heart thundered as the envelope with telegram was handed to him. He could easily read the two words *CONFIDENTIAL* and *URGENT* on the front, so thanked the man, turned and found his way outside onto one of the side deck areas.

Myron made sure he was alone before opening the envelope. The early morning sun glistened over the wet metalwork of the rail in front of him, but this all faded around him as his eyes fell on the black print against the morbidly white paper.

Time stood still as he read, then reread, the script. Then Myron simply pocketed the telegram and headed back to his cabin.

His thoughts were with someone halfway across the globe, and in deadly trouble.

Lieutenant Gemma Andrews fortunately awoke before the medical staff arrived. She therefore could pretend to wake, instead of how she would have normally, with quickened reflexes and potentially deadly force.

Last night had quickly come back to her; the plane ditching in the sea, the cold dark ocean and of course the rescue.

A savour had come, had taken her back to this ship, and had even protected her identity. Why? Only time would tell, but she instinctively knew that she had a friend onboard, just how much they could help however she'd soon find out. She had to get back to the Annlin military base on the outskirts of Johannesburg, where her squad had been stationed, and quickly. There was one member of her squad that had remained at the base. Her commander, back on home soil, would also need to be notified. Something had gone terribly wrong.

Gemma heard someone approach and began to play at being injured, just as her and Myron had agreed the night before. With any luck this might aid in getting her off the ship as well.

As for her dog tags, she kept them in her pocket for now, but did wonder just how she could get off this steel behemoth and back to base without letting loose her secret.

They would not simply fly a civilian back to shore just because they were injured, would they? Maybe it did depend on how bad they thought she was. Maybe Myron had another plan.

Gemma let her mind slip back to the crash and allowed the pain and anguish of feeling so alone in the ocean to ride over her. For once in her life, showing others that she was in pain would help her situation.

The medical staff heard the cry and rushed to help the rescued pilot, just as Myron entered his own cabin several floors below. There was not much he needed to pack, but there was a final plan that needed to be agreed, and quickly.

He sent the text from his smartphone, before pushing both the phone and other important items into a small holdall. Hesitating only to change his clothes from the night before Myron then headed back out of his cabin for the final time.

Without wasting any time Myron then headed back up to where Isobel lay, and hoped that she had recovered enough to understand his request. His heart and loyalties were now torn between three people; Isobel, his love; the Lieutenant, his responsibility; and Kirill, his fault.

Myron felt the twinge of adrenaline hit his veins as he headed up the stairs. For this to work he needed quite a bit of luck, and assistance.

He took neither for granted.

Isobel reacted to the cry in the same manner as her father, although she struggled to get herself out from her rest bed quickly. By the time she stumbled to the cabin doorway medical staff, crew members and her father had already entered the next cabin. It was the rescued pilot's room.

Isobel caught sight of Ishyan further down the corridor, his expression telling her more than a thousand words could. Stölles had also reacted to the cry, but it was not overly worrying the family bodyguard. So, if it was not a major concern to him, then the pilot's reaction had to be a ploy. Isobel listened as the medical staff assisted the pilot, before her father was ushered back out of the adjourning cabin. There was little he could have done, Isobel knew, but that would not stop him trying.

By the time Alessendro had returned to his daughter, Ishyan Stölles had made his way along the corridor to them as well.

'Sounds like she's awoken in shock,' the bodyguard mused, just loud enough for the crew around the cabin to hear. Isobel decided to play along with his game.

'She was in the sea for a long time, even if her body signs are normal, she might be suffering mentally.'

'Even looking fine, she might have swallowed a lot of water, not to mention other issues. Sir,' Ishyan spoke softly to Alessendro. 'Would it be too much to request hospitalisation back on land? It would be in the best interests of the pilot and all the crew.'

'I agree,' the older man nodded instantly. 'Poor soul. Ishyan, make the arrangements. Isobel?'

'I'm okay papa,' she smiled. 'Just bumps and bruises.'

'Okay,' he replied, his eyes switching between both Ishyan and Isobel. If he had guessed any ruse Alessendro decided not to show it. 'However, once Ishyan has sorted this out both he and Myron are going to be keeping a watchful eye over you until we reach Port Elizabeth. Agreed?'

'Agreed daddy,' she smiled, before noticing Myron approach from down the end of the corridor. This time Isobel knew instantly something was wrong, and by the way he looked at her it wasn't going to be anything nice.

Isobel sat back in her rest bed, in disbelief at what Myron was telling her.

'This is insanity,' she muttered. 'You're telling me that all of this time you knew but didn't tell me?'

'There was no proof,' Myron apologised. 'I still don't understand it all but Larissa contacting me cannot be sheer coincidence. Ishyan has a vial of...'

'Ishyan?' she shot him a glare.

'Ah,' Myron began. 'Look, I only passed it onto him today. Sit back down Iz,' he warned.

'Or what?' she shot back.

'Or I'll tell your dad you're out of bed,' he smiled before sitting on the duvet next to her. Isobel calmed as she heard his words, knowing he had thought about this a lot already.

'What are you going to do?' Isobel asked, reaching for his hand as she spoke.

'I have to go to Kirill,' Myron simply stated. 'I need to ensure he's ok. I owe him that, at the very least. What is it?'

'Ishyan,' Isobel replied. 'My father has instructed him to organise a helicopter to take the pilot to land. Guess you might as well go with her?'

'Guess so,' Myron smiled softly.

'I'll send him a quick text. Prewarn him. Have you told me everything My?' she asked quietly, knowing only too well that her father could come back into the cabin at any moment.

'Most of it,' Myron smiled. 'The pilot is an American soldier. I took her dog tags when we rescued her. Don't ask me why.'

'Because she was in danger,' Isobel offered simply, understanding his actions instantly. 'Soldier on her own in a ditched plane. It is suspicious.'

'Very,' Myron squeezed her hand. 'I have duties, for once,' he winked at her. 'But if I could have it any other way, I'd stay here with you.'

'I know,' Isobel replied. 'I don't want you to go either. You be careful.'

'With Templar around you do the same,' Myron raised her hand and kissed it warmly. 'I don't trust him.'

'Neither do I,' she whispered. 'But at least I have my father and Ishyan here. You'll be on your own babe; I don't like that.'

'I'm never alone Iz,' he smiled. 'Thanks to that damn gem my imagination goes wild at times, most of the time you're always right there by my side, talking to be, guiding me.

'Really?' she squeezed his hand. 'And there was me thinking we took separate routes from Cairo for another reason.'

'Yes,' Myron remarked. 'That bloody gem. It was starting to make me feel I was losing it. At least now I can have the blood sampled. That should offer some answers at least.'

'Maybe,' Isobel looked into his eyes. 'Just don't hold anything back from me, will you? Thought we were a partnership?'

Myron smiled and felt the weight inside his jacket of the ring he wanted to give Isobel. Now was not the time. However, he could offer her other sentiments.

'Once both Gemma and Kirill are ok, I'll return,' he smiled. 'I won't wait for the blood analysis; we can discover that together. It just made me feel as if I wasn't in control of my actions and emotions when I came after you.'

'Is that it?' Isobel almost laughed. 'Oh My. You came after me, nobody else. What is really worrying you?'

'It is just that,' Myron replied honestly. 'You know I always want to conduct myself in the right manner. I'm nervous around your father and his business contacts as I hardly understand anything they say, but it doesn't play on my mind. Not any more anyway.'

'Don't worry,' Isobel pulled him closer. 'What happened yesterday, all of it, was wonderful. You're my hero. I don't want you to go.'

'And you're my heroine,' Myron smiled before learning forward to kiss her gently. 'Here,' he said quietly as they embraced. He put his hand into his jacket and realised that he might as well give Isobel the ring. 'I bought you a present from Morocco. It reminded me of you as soon as I saw it.'

'What is it?' Isobel smiled as Myron pulled the elongated white box from his pocket. 'A necklace?'

'Can you stop guessing for a second?' Myron calmed her, knowing Isobel only too well. 'I bought it after our argument in Cairo. Not as a sorry present, but to show you how I felt. Don't panic,' he smiled at her. 'I'm not going to do anything rash.'

'That's a first,' Isobel grinned back, thinking of the night before. 'Anyway, we've only known each other for three months. If you did propose...'

'Yes?' Myron responded; his interest piqued.

'My,' Isobel blushed.

'Sorry,' he kissed her hand again. 'That was merely an opportunistic question.'

'I know,' she continued to look deep into his eyes. This time it was Isobel who leaned forward to kiss Myron.

'That doesn't seem like a no to me,' he smiled playfully.

'It's definitely not a "no",' she told him seriously. 'Think we've both got our demons. You have your gem; I have my responsibilities.'

'And I don't fit it,' Myron smiled sadly. 'It's ok Iz, I get it. Doesn't mean I have to like it though.'

'Demons are there to be vanquished,' Isobel whispered. 'My father seems to be warming to you more.'

'It only took a rescue,' Myron almost rolled his eyes.

'No, I don't think it was that,' Isobel smiled sadly. 'You never met my mother; she was the greatest. She also held the family together. I think my father saw something in us last night, the way we work together in a crisis, when it really matters.'

'We do seem unbeatable when we forget about everything else,' Myron smiled. 'But then there's the gem again, it only seems to kick in when I'm in those situations.'

'Maybe,' Isobel told him. 'But then again, does it kick in after you've already decided upon your actions? It's worth thinking about babe. Maybe it's not such a burden after all. Well, some of it.'

'The dreams I could do without,' Myron noted. He heard commotion near the door. Alessendro must be back. It was time.

'The necklace?' Isobel queried, also noting the noise from outside the cabin.

'Sorry,' Myron replied, understanding he still had hold of the present. 'Here. For you. From me. With all my love,' Myron almost choked on the words as for the first time he understood that he'd soon be leaving Isobel. When would he see her again?

'Thank you,' Isobel whispered as she opened the box. Inside was not a conventional necklace, but a ring on a necklace chain. 'Wow,' Isobel smiled. 'It's so beautiful, I think, yes, I recognise the engraving.'

'It's a guardian ring,' Myron smiled. 'Basically...'

'Whoever gives it will guard over the receiver for eternity,' Isobel understood. 'Thank you, Myron,' she smiled, before kissing it then handing it back to him. Myron looked at Isobel in disbelief.

'You keep it for now,' she said quietly as a tear rolled down her features. 'You have my love, and I want you to remember me whenever you look at it. Promise me. It might give you god speed to return to me.'

'I promise,' Myron replied before putting the necklace around his neck. 'Should have picked up another chain mind you...'

'Ha,' Isobel laughed through her tears. 'It's not very manly is it. Prefer some surfer's string, do you?'

'Sshh Iz,' Myron replied as a knock came at the door. Alessendro's voice requested entry from the other side. He made sure the necklace was hidden beneath his shirt.

'Come in dad,' she called. Alessendro's face instantly crept around the door.

'Not interrupting, am I?' he asked.

'Not at all,' Isobel smiled as her father entered the room. 'Unfortunately, Myron's had a bit of bad news, so I was wondering if you could assist him?'

'Certainly,' Alessendro nodded instantly. 'Anything.'

'Myron needs to make landfall to contact an old friend who's just been taken ill,' Isobel offered smoothly. 'I heard the pilot was being airlifted to shore, could Myron hitch a lift?'

'Of course,' Alessendro confirmed. 'I'll just let Ishyan know, and Myron' the older man smiled warmly, 'if there's anything else you need just let me know. Anything at all?'

'I will sir,' Myron thanked him. This made Alessendro laugh.

'No more sirs,' he replied, looking at his daughter happily. 'Just call me Alessendro. I insist.'

'Thank you,' Myron replied, before taking his cue to leave. He quickly turned to Isobel, took her hand one more time and kissed her goodbye. 'I'll contact you when everything's sorted,' he looked at her, his expression hidden from Alessendro.

'Be careful,' Isobel whispered, knowing only too well that Myron thought he was heading into unknown territory. His cryptic statement to only contact her when it was safe was an old agreement between them, but it still chilled her bones. Why now? Why at all?

Myron smiled one more time before turning to leave and smiled to her father as he exited. Isobel stared at the door before it closed, her father remaining quiet until the silence began to make him feel nervous.

'And you only need ask as well,' Alessendro finally spoke. 'It's not as simple as you made out is it?'

'I thought I was a good actress?' she half-smiled apologetically.

'You can't bluff me, my princess,' her father said as he walked to her bedside and sat with her. 'And as for Myron. He can't act his way into a television commercial. How bad is it?'

'It's linked to Bessek,' Isobel found herself saying before her eyes began to well up. Her father pulled her close and soothed her.

'It'll be ok,' Alessendro offered. 'Let me get Ishyan on the case.' As Isobel let her father embrace him, she looked over his shoulder and toward her bedside bag. Something had caught her eye.

Myron had left his phone and wallet with her. His intention was obviously to go completely off the radar.

Isobel hugged her father harder.

Myron wandered out along the corridor before a familiar face greeted him.

'Ticket to ride?' Ishyan asked politely.

'Oh no,' Myron smiled, remembering the words from London. 'I forgot I told you that.'

'Here,' Ishyan said as he passed him a metal suitcase and a few other items.

'Thank you, my friend,' Myron offered. 'I don't care what either of them ask you to do, don't come looking for me.'

'Really?' Ishyan looked at him quizzically. 'How would you even know?'

'Good point,' Myron conceded. 'Just don't put yourself in harm's way for me.'

'Yes, you know me so well,' Ishyan almost laughed, before regaining a serious tone. 'This is all interconnected. Trust me. It's inevitable that our tracks will cross again in the very near future. Until then, just be careful and be you.'

'I will,' Myron said. 'Thank you, which way to the chopper?'

'I'll take you,' Ishyan smiled. 'Last thing we need is for you to get lost on the way.'

Lieutenant Gemma Andrews felt her stretcher lift and meander through the ship's corridors before they exited into the fresh morning air. The sound of the helicopter hit her as instantly as the sun's rays, but she fought the instinct to let her emotions lift. She had no choice but to keep "playing ill" a bit longer, at least until she was back at her base.

Andrews kept her eyelids closed and instead made ultimate use of her hearing, even if it was difficult above the aircraft rotors. One voice however did stand out. Why was he here?

Gemma felt her stretcher click into position before her restraints were tightened. As the door was shut, she felt the presence of another in the rear of the helicopter.

'Unfortunately,' Myron began over the sound of the whirling rotor blades. 'The ship couldn't spare any medical staff, so you're stuck with me for the journey. In which case if you're going to have another episode then you might want to reconsider, unless it involves simple bandaging.'

'That's ok,' Gemma spoke quietly. 'I'll be fine. Where are we heading?'

'To your temporary base in Annlin, near Johannesburg,' Myron offered. 'You said you had another team member based there?'

'Yes,' Andrews noted. 'She's been undergoing assessments. I felt bad for her at the time as it was my call to leave her behind...'

'Well,' Myron stated. 'At least you have a friend there. That's a start. The trip won't take long, you ready?'

'Don't worry about me Myron,' she whispered. 'I've got everything under control.'

'Right,' he considered. 'You do realise that you're currently lying on a stretcher don't you, and spent I don't know how long last night clinging to a floating bit of debris in the Indian Ocean?'

'Had worse,' was all Andrews replied. She winked at Myron as the helicopter flew from the ship.

'Of course,' Myron replied smiling. 'Should have guessed.'

Harrison Templar looked over at the helicopter as it left the *Angel of the Seas* and contemplated the inevitable.

That's interesting, he thought.

On face value the transfer of the pilot back to the mainland was a simple enough precaution, but with Myron also travelling off the ship it did swell Harrison's interest. What was the man's intention back on shore? Templar had first presumed the relationship between him and Miss Fortuna to be a mere fad, but after spending a few days with them both now knew they both cared immensely for each other.

That was not necessarily an issue, in fact it might even prove most useful in the long run. Emotions and affections are wondrous bargaining tools in his trade, if applied at the correct time. Templar of course did not have time for either, but that did not mean he couldn't make use of everyone else's.

Harrison simply looked on and wondered how Myron would fit into the rest of his plans. There was obviously now no room for him in his immediate space program, but that was not necessarily an issue. For the long run though he wanted both Myron and Isobel in the front seats of the business, as although Harrison was a highly respected businessman around the world, there would come a time when the world would want to connect with two lovers as they took the next step into the cosmos. It was sound commercial sense.

For now, Harrison had agreed with Ishyan to pass on the suitcase with his thin exo-suit within, although Templar had parted with it with more than an ounce of regret. It still required further testing, but as he always knew, sometimes for a bird to fly you had to simply step back and let nature take its course.

Of course, he could have tracked the suit, and Myron for that matter, but it was not worth the possibility of getting caught. Whatever now happened to Miss Fortuna's lover, any news would eventually come back to him. Templar just preferred to keep all his chess pieces in sight. He wondered…but quickly dismissed the idea. Too tricky, or was it? Dangerous thoughts. Harrison almost had to shake his head to get rid of them.

Templar instead turned his attention to the pilot, as this seemed like a complete unknown. Time to do a little digging.

Who exactly was the injured pilot?

Draven

Wednesday; 08:54

As the helicopter touched down at the Annlin military airbase on the outskirts of Johannesburg, both Myron and Gemma were first taken to the medical wing, before the Britain then left the Lieutenant and was shown a side room in which to wait.

Myron knew that he was an outsider here, and no matter what Andrews thought of him, she was now in a hospital ward where she would stay until she recovered completely. No doubt someone would turn up eventually, but Myron was already concerned about the telegram message and wanted to find out what it meant as soon as possible.

There was a clock on the wall in the room, almost the only furniture apart from a small desk and two chairs – both plastic and potentially very uncomfortable. Myron therefore did the only thing he felt in control of, to give the administration here a clear ten minutes to come and get him, or he'd start to cause some trouble, although completely innocently of course.

Myron had left almost everything that linked him to *FortunaCS* with Isobel back onboard the *Angel of the Seas*. He only had three things still in his possession. The first was the small aluminium suitcase Ishyan had given him. Myron knew what was inside but did not see the need for such technology here. He also had a fake passport in the name of Leon Chamel (who else?). And finally, on his wrist, was his beloved watch; the one Isobel and he had built by hand whilst visiting Venice as part of their newly love tour. One of the hidden components inside the watch was a simple but secure chip linked to an offshore bank account, which Myron had purposely decided not remembering the location when Isobel had told him the details.

The watch had been Isobel's idea, in fact the whole trip to Venice had. Myron had winced on several occasions when she had finally opened up and told him her account of the *Jah Mahal* story. The kidnapping, the feeling of isolation, the betrayal of her brother and then his subsequent death, all this before the final realisation that her father was alive after all.

Myron's story had been an adventure, but not one full of darkness, so as soon as he admitted that he'd already been on the Orient Express then Isobel decided for them both to retrace their steps, but at their leisure and without any danger on the way.

Starting their journey from London to Paris via private jet, they then spent the night at the Shrangri-La hotel, breakfast on a private veranda overlooking the Jardins du Trocadéro, the river Seine as well as views of the slightly iconic Eiffel Tower. Next, they boarded the famous Orient Express the very next morning. Myron was greeted by an inform Walter, who singlehandedly managed to embarrass him for a full twenty minutes as he regaled in retelling Isobel all about Myron's first visit upon the Orient Express.

Fortunately, Brigitte soon greeted them in Bar 3674 and made them a special cocktail to celebrate both their recent adventure and on finding "love". Myron had to admit that there was nothing like travelling with friends, and in this case with the woman he absolutely adored.

The trip, unlike his last outing, was over almost before it started. He was not left with only his own thoughts for even a second, and before he knew it, they were approaching Venice.

Although Isobel had threatened to borrow Sofia's seaplane, they instead simply spent most of the weekend wandering the streets before finally revisiting Darius' watchmaker's shop, where Isobel had a little surprise awaiting him.

There, the elderly gentleman had started to make a one-off watch just for Myron, as a special present from them all for his part in Isobel's rescue. Myron was simply lost for words as he was sat at the watchmaker table with Isobel, and they finished off the job by adding the main cog and spring, before Sofia noted there was just room for a few minor upgrades that should suit Myron's troublesome nature.

Isobel had smiled her wonderful smile as they had finally screwed the watch shut, and Myron had tried it on.

'Now Myron,' Darius had begun. 'The extra items we added are all in sleep mode, so won't get picked up on any security sensors, so when you need them simply break the front and pull them free.'

Myron remembered asking if it was better if he unscrewed the back instead, only for Darius to rant about how he would manage to get out a precision screwdriver when being chased by a shark, outrunning an avalanche or complaining about heights. Myron had nodded sheepishly and at that point remained completely silent, as Sofia laughed and Isobel, seated next to him, had simply hugged him.

Myron smiled at the memories. Yes, he still wore the watch, and yes, it could aid him in escaping from this room if required.

He looked up at the clock and then at the door. Ten minutes had passed, and Myron knew that was long enough to be stood waiting around. However, as he approached the door, Myron noticed someone walking along the corridor in his direction. Surely, they weren't letting him go leave already?

'Sir?' a young cadet offered as she entered the room. The door had not even been locked. Brilliant, thought Myron sarcastically.

'Yes?' Myron replied, trying not to look vexed by his own incompetence.

''You're free to go sir,' she added. 'And as thanks for your assistance in the Lieutenant's rescue I'm to take you to your place of choosing.'

'Really?' Myron started. 'Thank you...'

'DT sir,' she replied. Myron nodded. He had no idea what that meant but didn't push it. 'If you'd like to follow me?'

'Lead the way,' Myron smiled. A free ride? That should make his journey to the city centre a whole lot simpler.

The traffic in Johannesburg was congested, but they still made their way quickly through to Myron's drop-off point. His thoughts were elsewhere, but DT's driving was exceptional through such tight quarters.

Myron sat in the passenger seat and began to think about Andrews and wondered just how much this soldier knew about her. It might have been a long shot, but he had nothing to lose.

'I guess you've been informed not to speak to me at all about Lieutenant Andrews?' Myron began, the question opening his mind instantly to another thousand questions he had yet to have time to consider fully.

'Yes,' DT replied. 'Fortunately, we both know something has occurred that can't simply be brushed under the carpet. It just depends how we're going to approach this. I don't know you; you don't know me. Yet we both know the Lieutenant.'

'Well,' Myron began. 'You obviously know her better, but I'd like to know why she was forced into downing a light aircraft into the ocean, so near to Madagascar and other islands. Also, why she was alone.'

'The Lieutenant had a squad under her command,' DT began. 'They were all on a training mission, but that's all I know. I'm still taking some exams, so Andrews dropped me from the team just to concentrate on testing my skills at the base instead.'

'Which are?' Myron asked inquisitively.

'I'm a sniper,' DT smiled from behind the steering wheel.

'Really?' he replied. 'Got a lot of respect for that profession. Bailed me out on more than one occasion.'

DT's eyes looked across at Myron as he looked outside the car. She hesitated to continue, her thoughts drifting to why this character had ended up in the helicopter with Andrews.

'What happened?' DT asked simply as she let her instinct throw caution to the wind.

'I saw her crash,' Myron answered matter-of-factly. 'We rescued her, brought her back on board the *Angel of the Seas*, gave her one night's medical attention then brought here this morning. I don't think anyone knew on the ship who she was.'

'Really?' DT asked.

'Sort of hid her dog tags,' Myron replied sheepishly. 'Felt like the right thing to do at the time.'

'Weird how that works out isn't it?' the driver replied.

'Yeah,' Myron laughed. 'Right now, I have a suitcase in the rear seat with me that obviously I might have difficultly taking on an airplane. I was thinking of simply leaving it in the back…'

'You know how to potentially get someone into trouble don't you?'

'Actually,' Myron sighed. 'I was hoping that it might help Andrews out in finding who had done this to her?'

'So, you're not going to help?' DT asked seriously.

'I am,' Myron replied. 'But I need to go offline for a bit. I have a friend in need. However, I'm hoping that he might be able to assist me get some context on all this. It could be a training accident, but I'm not sure.'

'I knew those guys Myron,' DT replied. 'This was no accident.'

'Okay,' Myron replied, understanding her pain only too well. 'Sorry. I'm not sure what I can do, but there's nothing new there,' he admitted. 'I can promise you though that I will try my utmost to discover what happened, and where possible, will try and ensure it doesn't happen again.'

'Thanks,' DT replied. Strangely she believed Myron. There was something about him. He was not a soldier, far from it. But he did have an underlying strength, almost a stubbornness to continue when the rest of the world was against him. 'Here you go. There are a number of governmental buildings in Parktown.

I'm sure you'll find the right one. The information centre is just over there.'

'Thank you,' Myron said as he opened the car door. 'Be careful, and hope the little present helps a little.'

The soldier watched him wander across the pavement and up the steps into the government building. True to his word Myron had left the aluminium suitcase. DT wondered what was inside, and how could it possibly help Andrews?

However, above all else DT knew that South Africa was no longer safe, for any of them. She would go back to the base, reason with Andrews and get back to their homeland as quick as possible. DT had a feeling that this chapter of her life was only just beginning.

Myron entered the almost brand-new building, quickly finding his way to the reception area. He smiled at the assistant before stating the transmission number he'd written on a small scrap of paper.

'Here you go sir,' the assistant said as they passed the envelope labelled for him. Myron thanked them and took it to one of the confidential isolation pods that littered the side of the reception area.

Closing the glass door behind him and switching on the secrecy button the outside word turned dark, with the inner light illuminating only the desk before him. Myron opened up the envelope and read the words within. It was from Larissa. Myron's heart missed a beat. It was about Kirill.

Myron read the confidential letter, the words cutting at his soul as he instantly knew what had happened. It was the gem. He had entrusted Kirill with it and it had done an incredible amount of damage.

Kirill was now in a coma and showed no signs of recovery. Myron knew he had to do something but did not even know where to begin. He felt lost, and very afraid. Within the near darkness of the pod Myron put his head into his hands and could not stop the tears.

It was his fault. It was all his fault.

Anthony Draven sat in the rear of the Sedan, his attention currently on the images before him on his smartphone.

A lot had happened in the last twenty-four hours, but here he was, thousands of miles from home at the beckon call of a scientist that potentially held the key to his future.

The first message was from Nolan. A partial success from the Reunion Island. The military's Menazee project was not at the centre front of Draven's curiosity, as it seemed to be with everyone else he ran into. No, the Menazee were no doubt ferocious warriors and key to their overall success, but Doctor Harding had already hinted at something far more sinister. And fortunately for Draven, the scientist had not even suspected its true potential. How fatal that error could be.

Draven rubbed his chin. So, someone had escaped the trial on Reunion. Interesting, he thought. That itself was no mean feat. By the lack of information that Lieutenant Andrews had managed to let seep out into common knowledge before she had returned safely to Johannesburg was a massive illustration of aptitude. She was a formidable opponent indeed. Draven wondered how he should play this. This game of chess was not as simple as black versus white, where the last king standing wins.

No, here he would have to guide each piece from both sides, just to get him into striking distance for the ultimate kill. His prize currently sat in a secure facility almost half the world away, but if he ever lay his hands on it the whole world would suddenly understand his dream.

His next move was about to happen. Draven looked up from his smartphone to the building and noticed the figure materialise right in front of his eyes.

'That's him,' Draven mused. The driver muttered something into his ear-comm-link and almost instantly two suited figures appeared on both sides and flanked the figure, manoeuvring them toward the awaiting vehicle. Anthony waited patiently for the car to move away from the curb before even contemplating speaking to this individual.

DT watched through her rear-view mirror as she noticed the black sedan pull up next to the curb, with two well-dressed bodyguards approach Myron from behind and ushering him into the vehicle swiftly. She was glad she had not simply driven away as something was obviously amiss here.

She still had plenty of time to get back to her Lieutenant lying in the hospital ward, and potentially this might throw some light on the whole incident saga anyway. DT took note of the registration number, just in case she would have to track it later on. The sedan drove away from the curb, which left DT little time to plan any strategy. She quickly slipped open the street map of Johannesburg and mentally jotted potential routes that the vehicle might now take, whether it be to the airport, outskirts or to another location within the city boundaries. Obviously, she would tail it, but sometimes in following you had to outsmart your target rather than simply follow in their footsteps.

As she headed out into the traffic, DT was confident in her ability to tail a vehicle if required, although it was not her forte. Looking back at the map there were plenty of possibilities that Myron might be in mortal danger, so if that was the case she'd need to act quickly. She had neither the weapons on her nor was she an expert in hand-to-hand combat so the thought of using her own vehicle as a weapon came quickly to her mind. Then something caught her eye on the back seat; the aluminium suitcase Myron had left.

'Leon Chamel?' Draven amused himself.

'What do you want?' Myron replied to the voice. He had been ushered into the rear seat of the Sedan but cutting the rear of the vehicle in half was a large glass panel, which was blackened. It was like he had exited one pod and entered another. 'Bit secretive isn't it?'

'Maybe,' the distorted voice spoke through the intercom. 'For both our sakes I'd prefer to keep my identity secret.'

'Okay,' Myron replied. 'So, what do you want with me?'

'A simple favour, and a promise,' came the voice. Myron grimaced; he had a flavour of what was coming.

'Firstly,' Draven began from the other side of the screen. 'I have a request that will assist both of us. You seek answers to a dilemma, yes?'

'Yes,' Myron confirmed.

'Well,' Draven continued. 'I have a contact that could possibly help. The only fee for that assistance is a sharing of any information found. You have a contact in Russia I believe that took control of the Lake Kivu gem, am I right? And now he is sick?'

'Yes, correct on both parts,' Myron replied.

'Well then Mr Chamel,' Draven began. 'This is your lucky day. For on this very coastline lie the Agulhas current kelp forests, an incredible beauty I'm sure you'd agree, but also home to some deadly fish. Although sometimes hallucinogenic, I believe that creature will allow you to create an antidote for your friend's illness.

Now, I am not one to waste such valuable resources, so I would like the results of how the antidote works, and a sample in return as a favour. Your every move will be tracked by my associates so don't worry about carrying around my phone number, once you succeed in your mission, they will come for you.'

'Understood,' Myron answered, feeling a deep chill run down his spine.

'And as for the promise Myron,' he heard the distorted voice say his real name for the first time. 'I know Isobel's every move. You betray me, I kill her. Understood?'

'Yes,' Myron heard himself say, the fear in his voice noticeable before he had time to compose himself. 'There's no need to implicate her, I'll do as you say.'

'More than that Myron,' the voice replied. 'You stay away from her, forever. You go anywhere near her and I won't hesitate. I won't hesitate at all.'

Myron looked at the darkened screen to his left but could only see his pale reflection. Then he heard a sound and a slot between the two sides of the vehicle opened and a small sheet of paper passed through.

'This is your contact,' the voice offered. 'Simply save your friend and you'll live. Disappear and so will Isobel. Anything else I kill you both.'

With that the car pulled over to a kerb and Myron's door was opened by one of the smartly dressed bodyguards. He got out and watched helplessly as the car drove away.

In Myron's hands lay the opportunity to save Kirill, he just hoped he was up to the task.

Noting the Sedan steadily moving through the traffic, DT quickly leant back and pulled the suitcase onto the front passenger seat. The suitcase was not locked so in an instant she had it open with her free hand and briefly surveyed the contents.

DT laughed out loud over the steering wheel, for it was both comical and potentially a lifesaver. The suitcase simply held a body-hugging exo-suit. It was similar to ones the military used for certain warfare requirements but of such lightweight and molecular design that it would fit under clothing if required. Well, if nothing else, she had leant had the edge over Myron's kidnappers in a fist fight now.

She closed the suitcase and returned to concentrating solely on tailing the Sedan, her eyes fixated on the traffic all around. Without notice, the Sedan pulled over and the side door opened. DT followed suit and pulled over behind other parked cars, hopefully still hidden from sight.

To DT's amazement, Myron left the vehicle and the Sedan instantly shot off into the traffic. She quickly juggled the prospects of which to tail and decided upon the Sedan. If Myron had somehow pulled the wool over her eye's and was now working with the enemy then the fashion that he was escorted into the Sedan, plus the suitcase he had already given to DT, didn't quite add up.

She started the car and turned into the traffic a healthy distance from the Sedan and left Myron behind. DT just hoped she had made the right call.

Draven gave the nod to the driver who pulled away and made their way to the nearest airport. Anthony thrust his hand into his inner jacket pocket and pulled out a sheet of paper, now severely creased due to how many times it had been read.
He perused it one more time, the case files already digitally stored on his phone with hard copies in his flight bag. The letter intrigued him, constantly, pulling at his every facet of curiosity.

Dearest Anthony

Firstly, I must apologise for not contacting you sooner, or in person. I'm sure you understand the precautions, but since the dreaded Fortuna affair I've been hastily relocated far from all potential links with this terrible event.

I write to you now with a proposition, one which I hope you'll accept with most haste. I also have one request, just to ensure that the rumours I hear of you are in fact true.

And so, to the proposition: I have recently been relocated to a scientific installation far from watchful eyes. There are secrets here that only I and my superiors are aware of, yet they are in deep ignorance of their potential. To you therefore this glorious responsibility now awaits.

The request? I merely ask for some evidence of your work. If indeed the tales are true then I will send you my location, and the power I hold within my grasp I promise will change your life forever.

Yours sincerely
Doctor Arnold Harding

DT had the luxury of driving a car with a registration recognisable by airport security to allow her to park very close to the proximity of the main entrance. She was also fortunate of being completely oblivious of the owner of the black Sedan, so there was almost every chance that he also did not know she existed. DT would take precautions though; she had been the one to drop off Myron in Johannesburg and had probably been tailed at some point. Either that or they knew where he would be at a given time, which was less likely.

The soldier pulled a jacket from the rear of the car before entering the airport, trying to look like a civilian as much as humanly possible. It was odd as DT knew she stuck out like a sore thumb in the academy, so at least should have been comfortable in these surroundings. She was not. Typical.

DT followed the mystery man as he meandered his way through the airport and towards the baggage boarding stations. She was not going to follow him much longer, she just needed to know which flight or at least which part of the terminal he was going to be in. The rest she could do from behind the scenes.

Noting the man glide towards one of the ticket booths up ahead DT quickly made a mental note of the flight number before heading off toward the security sector of the airport. She had her military ID on her so gaining access to at least the entry level CCTV area should be no major feat. DT only wanted some still shot images anyway, so she could take them back to her Lieutenant. Then, if they were lucky, maybe Andrews' old commander might be able to assist. Maybe.

DT approached the security desk and as casually as possible laid her ID on the counter and spoke softly her requirements. The man behind the screen looked at her with trepidation until she noted it was for tracking purposes only. Obviously the very real possibility of a terror attack had entered his mind immediately.

The soldier was waved through the door and taken with earnest toward a bank of wall monitors that illustrated the busy airport. DT noted to one of the operators of the flight number and terminal and he filtered one of the wall sections with those images only. Once DT had noted the mystery man in one image the operator then began scrolling through each CCTV footage until there were 12 images of the man, all at different times and locations but all of high quality. DT smiled.

The head of the security then entered, DT quickly explaining the reason for the tracking. Although the security could do more to find out the identity of this man, the head soon understood that it might be counter-intuitive so left DT with digital images from the screens. She thanked them all then left, eager to offer them to Andrews. There was something eating at DT's mind and knew her Lieutenant might still be in trouble.

The soldier left the airport and headed back to her car, knowing full well that she was probably being followed and that at any moment they could strike. Only the mystery man had boarded the flight after all, so his bodyguards, whoever they were, were still out there, waiting.

Time to get Andrews up to speed.

Rogue research

Richard's Bay: South African east coast: Wednesday; 12:37

After the tension of running through the Johannesburg station and catching the correct train for the journey, Myron's first impression of his contact Ashton Mehrtens was one of, surprisingly, utter nonchalance. After the taxi dropped him off at the harbour entrance, with its magnificent stone archway and cobblestone walkway beyond, Myron began the unenviable task of trying to locate him along the high stone walls.

The tide was out, and although there were many dinghies littering the jetty below, there was not anyone who seemed to resemble a research scientist amongst the people bustling around the harbour.

Myron continued to walk along the quayside, keeping clear of the workers who were moving fish, fuel and other deliveries either to or about to leave the mainland. It was almost as if he was in completely the wrong location. He soldiered on anyway, trying not to get run over by any heavy machinery in the meantime.

As he negotiated the various slipways and storage facilities eventually the buildings ran out and he was left with the older, and narrower, harbour wall that jutted out into the Indian ocean. It was inevitably more peaceful at this end of the harbour, and Myron thought, if nothing else, that he'd manage to at least get a few minutes rest and recovery before trying to locate Mr Mehrtens.

Up ahead of Myron there were located a few benches, so he strode purposefully toward the first. As he approached, he noticed that the bench wasn't in fact free, but that a body was already lying prone across it. Probably catching forty winks, Myron humoured himself. The figure wore a huge black weathered leather cowboy hat over his features, probably to mask the sun, but no doubt (due to the colour) almost cooking the face underneath. Next to the bench was a large rubber crate, the type surfers use to store their wetsuits in.

As Myron began to walk past the bench his eyes caught sight of movement in the crate. He could not help but stop and take a secondary glance. His eyes deceived him obviously, for in the crate, along with a floating tennis ball and half-eaten sandwich, was a ginormous coconut crab. Myron was not sure, but it looked the size of a baby Kangaroo.

'What the...,' Myron began as the words came out of his mouth before he could stop them.

'Whoa,' came a voice from underneath the black hat. 'Gringo, you sound far from home. Need a lift buddy?' the stranger said in a broad Australasian accent. Myron sighed in realisation.

'Mr Mehrtens?' he asked, half knowing the answer.

'Ah right,' Ashton smiled. 'You the limie from the email? Sorry mate, didn't expect you so soon.'

'That's no problem,' Myron replied as his attention returned to the rubber crate and its inhabitant. 'Is he yours?'

'She,' Ashton corrected him. 'I call her Meredith, after my ex,' he smiled sadly.

'Of course,' Myron found himself saying. Why wouldn't you name a two-foot crab after your last girlfriend?

'So,' Ashton began as he scooped himself off the bench and into an upright position. 'You need some specimens from the kelp forest? That's some pass you've managed to get us, that baby is highly protected.'

'So I heard,' Myron replied. 'Hopefully we won't need to risk any wildlife on our search of the kelp.'

'Ha,' Ashton chuckled. 'It ain't the kelp I'm worried about mate, since they protected the area the bloody sharks have been coming back in droves. If we need to get some samples then it might get a bit nerve-wracking.'

'Don't we have fishing tackle for catching samples?'

'You haven't fished for kelp bream before have you?' Mehrtens replied soberly. 'Merry here has more chance of picking up a plucky fish than we do with a line. Nah My, we either get in the drink or we come up dry.'

Myron took a few seconds to translate Ashton's comments before realising the enormity of the task ahead. No wonder Draven had let him go so easily; Myron might end up dead just trying to secure an antidote.

'Why the frown?' Ashton continued. 'You're in safe hands, I've tackled that kelp forest at least half a dozen times, nothing major has gone wrong yet.'

'Nothing major?' Myron replied.

'Exactly,' Ashton smiled. 'Anyway, can't chinwag all day, the tide might be out but that damn sun likes to take a kip each night, so we'd better get onto the rolling blue as soon as poss.'

'Less of the rolling,' Myron muttered.

'You've got two hopes,' Ashton smirked. 'Give me a hand with Merry would you. And no bloody *Lord of the Rings* gags wither, she doesn't appreciate them at all.'

'Didn't know they had a coconut crab in the book?' Myron replied, bitterly confused.

The dinghy was small, tiny in fact, but this didn't stop Ashton remarking on how safe it was. Myron had other ideas. It seemed to be one harbour crossing from sinking altogether.

'Where's your boat?' Myron asked.

'You're in it?' Ashton replied with a blank face. 'I call her the "Merry rose again", after...'

'Your crab, I get it,' Myron sighed. 'I meant the one we're supposed to find the kelp forest with.'

'Ah,' Ashton realised. 'The science ship. Yeah, it's on loan from the local University so we gotta be careful. No ketchup on the couch if you know what I mean.'

'I have no idea,' Myron began before almost jumping out of his skin as one of Meredith's claws snapped out of the side of the crate.

'She's getting hungry,' Ashton evaluated as he twisted the throttle a bit more. 'We'll drop her off on the way, where we're going is no place for a crab.'

'You mean the sea?' Myron replied. His head was beginning to hurt.

Myron lifted his head and looked back at Mehrtens. The further they got from dryland, and nearer the boat, and the actual job they were trying to do, the more Ashton seemed to focus. McGivney smiled inwardly. Maybe this guy could help him after all.

'Do me a favour and pat Merry on the back of the head would ya?' Ashton asked. 'It'll calm her down a bit. She hates dingy rides.'

And on the other hand, Myron thought. Maybe not.

After dropping Meredith, the coconut crab, off on Pelican island, which was a secluded part of the quay, Myron held the dinghy still by the ladder of the science ship whilst Mehrtens climbed up over the side of the rail and onto the deck.

McGivney followed up the ladder, after first securing the dinghy to the buoy at the rear of the boat. Whoever had financed the vessel had surely a sound and wealthy investor. Myron half guessed that it might lead back to Draven, and potentially Bessek as well. Money, money, money, Myron shrugged. Even when it was doing good things it was probably being washing machined by something bad.

'And welcome onboard the *Flying Shark,*' Ashton smiled. 'Our home for at least twenty-four hours, maybe less if we get lucky.'

'I'm all for luck,' Myron smiled. 'What do you need me to do?'

'Just unhook us,' Ashton replied. 'Once we hit the sea you can take over at the helm if you like, it's pretty straightforward, although I have to check on the weather as the engine efficiency is a little complicated.'

'That's fine by me,' Myron replied as he looked around the ship. He had learnt a bit from his sailing with Isobel. 'Have you got a mixture of solar electric, HFO and traditional wind assisted sailing?'

'Yeah,' Ashton grinned from ear to ear. 'She's a real beaut.'

'I'd say,' McGivney agreed before tying the spare rope in a knot to the side of the decking.

After spending about ten minutes on deck admiring the sheer beauty of the open water, Myron clambered down into the heart of the boat as Ashton had his head bent over multiple maps and charts.

'Bloody weather,' Mehrtens vented. 'We were due a good spell until the weekend, but nature's thrown another spanner in the works.'

'I know what you mean,' Myron commented, thinking back to the rescue onboard the *Angel of the Seas*. Then the weather seemed to change at the blink of an eye as well, although in the end maybe that had assisted the Lieutenant's survival.

'It's gonna be close,' Ashton continued. 'We could eat our way into the fuel reserves just to get us to the kelp as soon as possible, and hope we have enough sun to recharge the batteries to aid us getting back, just in case this little storm gets worse.'

'I'd rather play it safe,' Myron countered. 'I was under the impression that apart from the risk of not finding this dream fish, the rest of the trip would be quite event free?'

'Who on earth told you that mate?' Mehrtens turned and almost laughed at Myron's innocence. 'We're about to head out on to the Agulhas current, one of the most volatile seas in the world.'

'Great,' Myron sighed under his breath.

'Don't worry yourself too much though,' Ashton replied. 'This baby was designed to take on storms headfirst. Maybe on this occasion we take it easy getting to the kelp? Unless it is important, which I thought it was?' he half-asked, already knowing the answer.

'Fine,' Myron conceded. 'We'll do it your way; I just want to make it back to land.'

'Ah mate,' Ashton grinned again, but this time infinitely more maniacally. 'I ain't making promises like that. Last time I did my girlfriend...'

'Ex?'

'Yeah,' Ashton hesitated slightly. 'Thank you. Anyway, last time I had to promise her I'd return to dry land, you know what happened? A bleeding sub had to rescue me. Who knows what we're going to find out there?'

'Just go,' Myron whispered, hoping that any incoming storm would relent just long enough for them to gather some kelp fish and return home safely.

DT arrived back at the military hospital an hour later, her route elongated partially trying to ensure that she wasn't being tailed. However, if anybody did have the ability to track her registration number then they'd know it was from the airbase in Annlin anyway.

She headed as quickly as possible toward the hospital ward and her superior. There wasn't much else DT could do right now and she trusted Andrews' more than any other soldier she had served with. The fact that they were still on foreign soil did nothing to alleviate the constant concern from her mind, however.

Lieutenant Gemma Andrews was sitting up, looking slightly bored and fidgeting with her bandaging against the nurse's advice when DT approached.

'Thank goodness,' Andrews smiled in relief. 'Someone sane at last to talk to. DT, can you let nurse

Roberts here know that I'm quite capable of looking after my own medicinal intake. The scorpion story should do.'

DT looked over at the nurse, shrugged then decided to play the honesty card instead.

'We've got a complication,' she noted, the words indicating to the nurse instantly that her ears should be listening elsewhere. They were both quickly left alone.

'What is it?' Gemma asked with obvious concern.

'If I'm right' DT noted, 'then we need to get out of here before sundown.'

'You're always right,' Andrews groaned. She picked up her tablets and contemplated how many could be taken to offer her the most haste without any side effects.

'I had a good teacher,' DT smiled. 'Your friend Myron has an enemy, one which might be linked to your squad.'

'Really?' Gemma asked as all the humour drained from her features. 'Is he okay?'

'I think so,' DT acknowledged. 'Somebody picked him up, but he seemed to be left unscathed. I then tracked the car to the airport. I have some images,' DT explained. 'But not here. Can you get in touch with Goldhawk?'

'I can try,' Andrews admitted. 'But not here. Can you get me out of here when the rota switches?'

'I'd rather do it after nightfall' DT acknowledged, 'but it could be too late by then.'

'Yes,' Gemma mused. 'Don't play into their hands. Be a bit unpredictable. Don't do what I'd do.'

'What?' the soldier asked.

'We were compromised at the volcano,' Andrews noted. 'They knew our every move. I can't be involved in the decision making. You'll have to shoulder this one on your own.'

'That's ok,' DT nodded. 'I noticed an ice-cream van doing the rounds earlier. That won't raise suspicion. Joking,' she smiled as Gemma's mouth opened involuntarily in dismay.

'Although...' Andrews considered.

'Just leave it to me,' DT winked, and turned to leave. The ward was not particularly secure. One side was almost completely full of windows. However, being on a military base there should not have even been an issue.

Consider every eventuality, she thought back to her training, and her mentor only a few feet away. As DT took in the surroundings, she was well aware that Andrews was focusing on her, but that didn't deter her train of thought. If the base could be breached, then her Lieutenant was in very definite trouble. They would locate her easily.

'You mentioned sciatica?' DT questioned innocently as the nurse approached them. 'I suffered from that after Portugal,' the soldier continued, fully aware that this was a simple code for meaning absolutely nothing at all. 'They put me on the cycle machine to wind out the muscle knots.'

'Guess that will have to wait,' Gemma responded. 'No bikes down here.'

'Um,' the nurse pretended to overhear by accident. 'If you're suffering from lying down, we do have some sporting facilities for rehabilitation, but it's on the other side of the camp.'

'I'm happy to push her?' DT offered, looking around for a wheelchair. She hoped her superior would play along.

'Hey,' Andrews muttered. 'I don't want to be any trouble to you both. It just feels as if my body is seizing up here, where it should be fighting these cramps and bruises.'

'I'm never going to stop anyone who has the fight in them to recover,' nurse Roberts nodded. 'I'll get you a wheelchair, I just need some documents signed.'

'Sure,' DT happily agreed. 'Pass them here and I'll fill them in whilst we wait. I'll give you a hand.

Andrews watched on as DT followed the nurse over to the counter. What was she up to? Gemma thought. Then the penny dropped. DT had taken two of the forms. Clever. She would fill in both then complete the ruse whilst the nurse wasn't watching.

One form for the nurse, and the other which they would switch just before leaving. It would not only keep them safe, but if they played their cards right, they might even have a glimpse as to who was on their tail, if anyone.

DT returned to Lieutenant's side and smiled.

'The rehab centre is near the recovery barracks,' the solder smiled. 'Nurse Roberts says they're currently decorating the barracks so it's currently empty of personnel. Nice place for a trap…'

'I don't want to know,' Gemma sighed, but with a positive esteem for DT. 'Thank you.'

'Oh, I forgot,' DT realised, remembering something from earlier that day that would deflect this bout of emotion. She was not good at such compliments or genuine gratitude. 'It might help us later if your battered body is really going to cause you some difficulties, but your friend Myron left you a little present.'

'Really?' Andrews asked suspiciously. 'What is it?'

'A suitcase,' DT offered innocently.

'Aluminium?' Gemma asked inquisitively. She had seen him with it on the helicopter journey.

'That's the one boss,' DT returned. 'Got a little number inside that'll make you look great on the dancefloor.'

'Oh,' Andrews replied with interest. 'Well, better have it at the ready, just in case.'

'Yes maam,' DT smiled. 'Here comes nurse Roberts, you ready to do the switcharoo?'

'Just tell me what you need me to do?' Andrews asked. 'Then just weave your magic.'

'Ok,' DT nodded. 'It's showtime.'

Forest

Anthony Draven sat in the VIP lounge of Johannesburg's O.R. Tambo International airport, sipping at a rather unsavoury latte macchiato, whilst preparing a quick message on his phone for encryption using military software.

Draven had never met Doctor Harding but had, via Bessek and Nolan, acquired the assistance of the man currently in command of a very profitable little enterprise. Anthony wondered just how much power the doctor had, and if there was yet another puppeteer who resided above them all, like a marionette.

He looked down at his phone before submitting the message. It would become encrypted within minutes before finally sending, but that wasn't an issue. There was no rush here, he was due to head back to the United States first anyway. Hopefully later he would rendezvous either with Sebastian Nolan or Doctor Harding himself.

Draven read the encoded message one last time.

Transmission #63452

To: Doctor Harding

Please excuse the encrypted message but I too now seem to have prying eyes lingering over both my work and movements.

I have sent three digital files that will arrive separately in your secure drop-box within the next twenty-four hours.

I hope these will not disappoint.

Regards AD

Draven had already read the documents on Ulrich Bessek, Sergio Fortuna and Michelle Glade, as well as the pivotal roles the *Chameleon* had played in rescuing Miss Fortuna from their clutches.

It had not taken long for Nolan to expose the *Chameleon* once Alessendro Fortuna had resurfaced. The enigma was a simple ruse used to allow multiple people passages across the world under one simple name.

They were no secret agents however, although Draven did still wonder about the true identities of those that had assumed the *Leon Chamel* persona over the years. He had now met one, but how many others were there?

Bessek's death on the *Jah Mahal* was inevitably unfortunate for them all, as was the delay in trialling the Menazee now under Nolan's command. Just half a year could have been the difference between success and the failure that had occurred. Was it an overconfidence in Bessek's abilities, or had the red gem really allowed someone to infiltrate the castle of Assos as well as the *Jah Mahal* and almost singlehandedly take out the whole of Bessek's army?

Or simply the plan itself? Thought up by a disillusioned son of a billionaire, eager to conjure folk lore out of thin air. Had it all been a bit too extravagant?

Draven's thoughts raced. He thrived on how people's minds worked, and especially their limitations, or lack of them. The heroes of the *Jah Mahal* intrigued him as to outwit someone like Bessek would take a military mind, not one of a civilian persuasion. However, although the official report seemed to heavily rely on military intelligence before the counter strike of the supercavitating missile utterly destroying the *Jah Mahal*, Anthony now knew different. He had delved deep over the last months to try and find out what had actually occurred.

There was a simple truth, Draven had not been involved. Myron McGivney should never have been allowed in touching distance of the red gem yet be allowed to take it and along with it their fate.

Amateurs, though Draven. As he had his flight announced the contempt began to sweep away from his thoughts. He had three flights to endure until Anthony would be where he wanted to be. Draven needed to start again, and he knew just where to begin.

Under thirty minutes later Anthony Draven sat next to the window within the Air Express International plane, with only one way to kill the sixteen-hour flight. He had his files. He would re-read each and every one, where possible trying to thrust himself into the minds of the unfortunate victims.

Anthony picked up the first of the files and stared at the title for a few seconds. *Asylum*. It brought shivers up his spine just thinking about various stories from mental institutions he had visited over the last ten years.

Yet in one such facility he had found someone who had potential. Maybe not what Doctor Harding had time for, but Draven knew a lost soul when he saw one.

Reclining back into his first-class cabin's seat Draven opened the file and began to read the report, his mind twisting the printed words so that he could imagine his own place within those cold white walls.

It was not difficult to pretend he was in another man's shoes. He had visited so many institutions alongside Suzannah Fray in the last few years. He could quite easily picture the inmate Patrick Symion's imagination running wild in a world that he was completely oblivious to, one which held so much horror in his own shadow.

Anthony Draven hesitated as he read the transcript "I need some guidance". He knew just how Patrick had felt. Anthony too needed a new direction, but at least was happy to be on a flight heading back to America.

It was a positive move and hopefully soon to be a profitable one. Draven returned his thoughts to the file in his hands...

Patrick Symions had murdered his whole family only five years before, and soon after had undergone a complete mental breakdown. Although he was institutionalized against the will of the whole town in which he had lived, in a strange way justice was being undertaken.

Anthony Draven had seen first-hand how the cyclicity of the murderer's personality had created its own hell, the pattern of a clear and joyful mind only too soon comprehending the madness of his own actions. Suzannah had far more dealings with the individual but she had noted in her own reports of how Patrick had almost blamed another for the murder, a man named Adam.

Anthony Draven stopped reading the report just as his eyes began to feel heavy. He decided to recline his seat and catch up on a few hours' sleep. There had been no Adam of course, never was. It was simply a guilty man realising too late what he had done. It was

amazing what the human mind could invent just to protect their own mortal soul.
Thanks to the excellent detective work Suzannah Fray had undertaken, the story of Patrick Symions had whetted his appetite for further answers. He had two more reports in his bag but kept them where they were for now.

Instead he sought and found sleep easy. His dreams however were mottled with bizarre images of the last few months, ranging from the sinking of the *Jah Mahal* right up to the revelation of Patrick Symions' suffering. Something seemed to connect them all, but it was not anything that Draven already had knowledge of. It seemed to be something yet to be discovered, by him at any rate.

It called to him from the shadows.

Wednesday afternoon

It was late in the afternoon when a constantly irritable Myron McGivney gazed first at the scuba gear then back at Ashton, then out of the boat and down towards the deep blue depths beyond.

'What?' he simply replied in disbelief.

'We need to get a quick specimen,' Ashton replied matter-of-factly. 'If you need some raw material it needs to be fresh.'

'Can't we just fish for it?' Myron reasoned, quite sensibly he thought.

'Well, we've already discussed this,' Mehrtens mused. 'However, if you're not going to listen to me then just get the rods out and try it your way?'

'Ok,' Myron smiled. Anything was better than going down there, he thought.

Ashton sat on the side of the boat and sniffed the air. All he smelt was the stench of his own lies.

'There's no fishing rods here!' Myron screamed from the internal cabin.

'Ha,' Ashton mock laughed. 'Exactly. You ever fished in kelp melon head?'

'No,' Myron replied patiently. 'Do enlighten me.'

'Have you ever fished in seaweed then?'

'Um,' Myron began to think back to his childhood. Often during school holidays, he would sit with his father for hours on end, only losing tackle after tackle to seaweed.

'There you have it,' Ashton remarked as the realisation dawned on the other man. 'It simply won't work. You'll just snag every effort on kelp. Come on, we're wasting time. And don't forget your harpoon.'

'Didn't realise we were catching fish that way?'

'That's for protection my friend,' Mehrtens said as he slipped on his own face mask and neatly fell backwards into the ocean. He didn't resurface. Myron however did hear a muffled voice over his headset that sat in his lap. He shrugged before lifting his own gear over his head and followed Ashton into the depths, his harpoon being held very tightly in his hand.

The view underneath the boat was one that instantly took Myron's breath away. The afternoon sunlight only aided to heighten the beauty of the vision before him. The floating kelp forest almost moved magically beneath him, flashes of the brilliant sunshine reflecting off various fish as well as the fauna which clung for dear life on to the kelp.

Myron could already make out Ashton in the depths below, his wake dissecting the kelp as he concentrated instead on his net and catching a bream fish. The Britain would have loved to ignore the darker side of the kelp forest but knew that where there was an abundance of food, and him, then there was also danger. Myron kicked with his feet but kept his harpoon steadily pointed out in front of him.

As he crept into the forest of green Myron suddenly found his heart racing and almost jumping out of his chest. He was convinced that there were other things down here, moving far too fast for anything but his peripheral vision to catch. McGivney tried to calm his breathing, but it was a far simpler task to think about than resolve. Everything down here was like a shroud, and Myron did not fully understand whether the kelp was protecting the weak or merely hiding something far more sinister.

Mehrtens for once did not seem interested in winding up Myron with any tomfoolery but instead underwent the search with the utmost professionalism. The way Ashton moved underwater was also a revelation, he seemed to almost glide without effort between kelp stems, his interaction with the other life down here completely natural.

Myron hesitated slightly as the depth continued. Finally, when he could take it no more, he lifted his hand to the side of the facemask and opened the communication channel.

'Ashes,' he began. 'What do you need me to do to make this quicker?'

'How about being bloody quiet,' came the reply. *Typical*. He let go of the comms button.

Just then Myron saw a sight that should have petrified him. A fully-grown whale shark brushed right through the kelp forest, a seemingly army of smaller fish either in close proximity or following in its wake.

'Right,' Mehrtens whispered almost immediately. 'Stay still, get your net out and try and bag us some of those bream fish. The small ones following the that Rhinco. This might be our best chance.'

Myron did not respond but simply expanded his net to maximum width before allowing his concentration to be drawn away from the dangers of the darkening seas and towards the shoal of various fish that now darted past him.

Myron already knew he was in the better position, through luck more than anything else, and it was now up to him. Unless Mehrtens had guided the behemoth his way of course, which Myron took into consideration as more than a remote possibility.

However, now that was all irrelevant. What mattered was only the catch. McGivney extended the net out as far, and as quickly, as he dared. Then he waited for the right moment. Out here, hundreds of miles from dry land, Myron would usually have been focusing on the immediate threats around him. Once again, the toxins that had once plagued him now returned to his aide as his concentration intensified whilst watching the shoal swim past.

Myron's body became almost lifeless as he completely relaxed. His breathing slowed to almost a standstill, his whole entity and the extended net becoming one with the ocean current.

In an instant Myron felt the change of the kelp environment switch from idyllic pastures to one of hunting grounds, as something barged past his body and into the shoal of fish. Multiple bombardments came from all around, but Myron resisted the urge to flee, instead simply keeping his net at full length and allowing multiple fish to become netted as they escaped their hunters.

Within seconds the realisation of the attack dawned on Myron and he withdrew his catch within the net, before heading to the depths where he knew Ashton was awaiting. He saw Mehrtens beckoning him towards the kelp before daring to look back upwards.

There, in stark silhouettes, were the shapes of something half-imagined circling their pray.

'Good going net boy,' Ashton remarked over the headset, along with a thumbs up. 'Looks like you found a few good specimens for me there.'

Myron did not reply but allowed a small smile to settle on his face. There was a question he wanted to ask his colleague but felt that this was a good situation for ignorance to play a part in proceedings. His question could wait until they reached the ship.

Myron pulled himself up onto the main deck of the *Flying Shark*, puffing and wheezing after the swim upwards. He had tried not to look as if he was swimming as if his life depended on it, but that was clearly a lie. The enormity of the claustrophobia had finally gotten the better of him, and like may episodes before, his short-term act of heroism soon descending back to normal panic in no time at all. Ashton followed him a few minutes later, in no rush and with the utmost calm.

'Chuck us the bucket My,' Mehrtens asked as he pulled free his facemask. 'Let's keep these fish as fresh as possible. With any luck we can send them back if we don't need them.'

'Sounds ominous,' Myron commented. 'What parts of them do we need? Blood? Small tissue sample?'

'The brain,' Mehrtens stated. 'But we don't need much. Any other day I'd simply use yours ha ha.'

'Yeah, funny,' Myron remarked.

'Come on bud,' Ashton continued as he pulled the net onboard. 'You did great down there matey, thought that dolphin pod was going to give you the scare of your life.'

'It did,' Myron replied honestly. 'You see a fin and you automatically think the worst.'

'Ha ha,' Ashton laughed loudly, a huge belly snort that almost brought tears to his eyes. 'Myron mate,' he chuckled in between gasps of air. 'Take off your oxygen tank and take a look at the rear cylinders.'

McGivney did as he was told and looked at the rear tank. Several cylindrical devices were crudely attached. 'Your own design I take it?' Myron asked, already knowing the answer.

'Hey, how did you guess?' Ashton remarked, hurt by Myron's tone. 'These are homemade, yes, but still state of the bloody art!'

'How do they work?' McGivney asked inquisitively. He was eager to have any advantage over the dangers of the sea.

'Well,' Mehrtens smiled. 'There's already plenty of tech on the market, but you really want sharks to be deterred way before they even know you're there. The one on the right sends out a nice little radio message I custom made for *Shark FM*, nice little number called "*I like to sing in my shower*", which I then distorted to a frequency range suited for our little fin friends.

Now, that should repel most Carcharodon, but just in case they simply wanted more of the Ashes, then we move on to repellent number two, which defines smell. Or, in this case, neutralises mine, as much as humanly possible of course. Sharks also react to pressure as well as vision, but by that point they're probably very annoyed at me for causing them a headache, which then leads us to the last few cylinders.

Now, this tech isn't new, simple electro pulses sent out over a twenty metre radius to instantly deter the most unwanted of guests, but I have one setup to always send out a signal, the other two as my backups, because, and I have to warn you here My, once I set those babies off the water almost turns white, it sends them off the Richter, if you know what I mean.'

'I'm half following,' Myron nodded. 'Does it hurt them?'

'I must be honest, I haven't stopped and asked,' Ashton shrugged. 'Thought you wanted to be safe?'

'Sorry.'

'But,' Mehrtens sighed he put the tank back down. 'I must be honest with you kid, I've only once had to activate those babies in anger and I'm glad I did otherwise I wouldn't be here right now. The fact of the matter is clear really, if I can create something better, then I will. I have a few more trials to do.

Hey?' he suddenly jumped up. 'Don't suppose we have time in our schedule to do a little trial-busting do we?'

'No,' Myron said sternly. 'We need to get to shore.'

'Ok,' Ashton sighed. 'Maybe next time.'

'We are good to go, aren't we? Can we make landfall tonight?'

'We could risk it My,' Ashton remarked. 'The sea can start to get a bit choppy around teatime usually, but if you're in a rush?'

'Bit choppy?' Myron considered. 'Yep, let's give it a go. Does she have enough fuel?'

'Plenty me old mucka,' Mehrtens patted him on the back. 'We had a bumper day down in the kelp today, the solar panels almost filled up the battery. Come on, let's sail for the next hour whilst we prep afternoon scones and tea, and then we can bring down the masts and put on the boosters.

You did bring scones, didn't you?'

'Why would I bring scones?'

'Ah man,' Ashton moaned. 'You are bloody English, aren't you? I was looking forward to them.'

The sun was just beginning to dip beyond the mountainous horizon as DT crept back into the rehabilitation centre from the recovery barracks. All had gone to plan, although the soldier had to improvise slightly in order to ensure that her trap didn't compromise the safety of the personnel within the military base.

'Should I even ask?' Gemma questioned as she shut the aluminium case and looked over at DT. The soldier grinned maniacally and switched off the light in the room.

'Everything's going to plan,' DT muttered. 'We're alone up here, with a good vantage point over the barracks. If anybody gains access to the hospital ward and reads your papers then that's where they'll head.'

'That was the only part of the duplicate ward sheet that you changed. Just my location?' Gemma asked.

'I could have added additional medical frailties, but the nurse seemed on the ball, we're risking everything just modifying the location slightly.'

'OK,' Andrews sighed in the near dark. The blinds were down and blocking out the dusk sunlight, with DT already setting up a zoom lens through the curtains of the window that overlooked the barracks. 'I'm not going to even ask what you've set up down there, just don't make it too over-elaborate. If they send the same hunters as before we can't risk getting too close. Plus, there was a sniper.'

'Yeah,' DT scoffed. 'If they had any worth you wouldn't be here now,' the soldier commented, allowing her own professional pride to rise to the surface just long enough to make Andrews frown. 'Sorry.'

'It's ok,' Andrews smiled sadly as she remembered Arturo's body clatter against hers as he fell from the single bullet. 'I wish you had been there. You might have saved the day. I just walked them all into a trap.'

'Crap,' DT swore, misjudging her intention to stoke her superior's fire and forgetting just how close Andrews always let herself become to her unit. Was it a strength of command or weakness? DT twisted the problem on its head and instead thought back to the dangers of the night. 'Look boss, we might as well be honest with each other, I was mightily pissed off with you for leaving me at the base but listening to your recollection there wasn't anything I could have done.

Yes, I wanted to be there but ultimately, what could any of us have achieved?' DT shrugged. 'Whatever you were up against though, I want to expose it. Whatever it takes.'

'Yes,' Andrews nodded. 'Exposure. That might be the key. Ahhh,'

DT smiled back at her as the realisation kicked in of the soldier's plan.

'The trap in the barracks,' Andrews understood finally. 'You want to light up the world on whoever is after us, don't you?'

'Why not?' DT nodded. 'Might be the only way of stopping them.'

'Can you rig that camera up to send images continually?'

'Of course,' DT smiled, already ahead of her superior. 'Just say the destination and I'll disable the firewall of the compound and we can send the images anywhere on the planet.'

'Ok,' Andrews smiled. 'We have a plan. Get the camera and trap primed and once the party starts, we simply get out of here using the chaos as cover, leaving the camera behind to record everything.'

'Who's going to be the lucky viewer?'

'Commander Goldhawk,' Andrews spoke softly. 'You were right, we contact him. He'd be the only one who would be able to put this all together.'

Ashton tied up the flattened masts and packed up the sail just as the seas began to become more turbulent. On deck Myron was already making his opinion heard to the sea life around him.

'Hey My,' Mehrtens began. 'You're better off in the water mate, at least your stomach won't gang up on you in there.'

'I'm fine,' Myron whispered. 'Can we just get going please?'

'Any second now,' Ashton nodded. 'We'll need to pick up a bit of speed to make land by nightfall, so unless you want to be on deck in the dark holding onto the kit then we'd better get this done now.'

'Okay,' Myron replied hesitantly. He liked the sounds of returning to dry land, but the speed bit did concern him a little. Although he had only known Ashton for under a few hours he already assumed anything Mehrtens thought was a tad reckless was no doubt an utter disaster in Myron's vocabulary.

'Just buckle those in tight My,' Ashton pointed as a few of the waves started to hit the side of the *Flying Shark* and send spray over them.

'Not again,' Myron sighed. He had started to hate the sea. Or at least being on it. When stormy. That was the mitigating factor he thought. Turbulence was the key word he wanted eradicated from any description of the ocean when he was on it. What he enjoyed was calm. Just calm.

Myron looked up and saw anything but calm. In fact, even to his limited seafaring knowledge, something was not right here. Ashton seemed to be rushing with as much haste in the last five minutes than he had done over the last half day. Something wasn't right.

'Ashton?' Myron questioned loudly; his expression obvious to the other man.

'Let's get below Myron,' the other man suggested as another wave buffeted the boat. 'I don't want the engines to stall or risk flooding in this.'

Myron nodded and followed the man into the bridge. Although Myron had already seen the console before, now that the sky was darkening the hundreds of lights and screens seemed to brightly light up the helm. It did not make him feel any safer.

'What's going on?' McGivney asked again, but this time made sure Ashton would answer.

'It's showtime,' Mehrtens replied. 'We're deep within the Aguhlas current, everything was fine until thirty minutes ago when we received a wave warning from a super tanker around twenty miles away. Seems the currents are converging there.'

'You mean the way we're heading?' Myron almost stuttered, noticing the location of the super tanker plotted on the radar screen in front of them.

'Yeah,' Ashton replied, almost sheepishly. 'I did tell you I was a research scientist, didn't I?'

'Yes,' Myron answered, not entirely sure of where this was going or how much he was going to like the answer. 'Hence why I was sent to meet with you in the first place.

'Well,' Ashton began. 'I am quite good at marine biology, but it's a secondary income revenue for my main research. Myron, I'm sorry mate but we can't miss this opportunity. Catching one is a once in a lifetime event man.'

'What the hell can you catch in a storm?' Myron asked sincerely. 'Surely not a shark?'

'I say catch,' Ashton continued as the boat powered up, and Myron felt the instant need to buckle himself in. Overhead a loudspeaker buzzed to life.

'Flying Shark,' the voice began. 'This is Rogue Research. We have a sighting marked at thirty-two klicks north - north east of your current position. Please confirm status and approximation of time of arrival.'

'Hi HQ,' Ashton began professionally. 'This is Flying Shark. We are on an intercept course with the rogue with an ETA of ten minutes. You will have our GPS and full status incoming ASAP. All systems here are booting up and sending out data via the satellite and buoys.'

'Thank you, Flying Shark,' the overhead speaker replied. 'Confirming status and signal coming through. Radio silence will commence whilst you carry out the mission. Good luck.'

'Mission?' Myron asked coldly.

'I got him to put that in,' Ashton replied. 'Makes it sound a lot more grandeur.'

'Ashton?' McGivney asked one final time, his belt becoming more and more tight with every wave the boat flew over.

'We're going hunting,' Mehrtens replied simply. 'For a rogue wave.'

Entwined

The turbulence awoke Anthony Draven, although he didn't mind. His scotch sat untouched in the holder of his chair, and although he could have simply closed his eyes and returned to slumber bliss, decided to instead read another file.

He sat himself up slightly, turned on the reading light and picked up the second file. It was a tad different to the Symions file, and he had only managed to piece together each part of the tale from key eyewitnesses, but it had proved profitable, even if from a slightly different angle than normal.

The story surrounded a set of identical male twins, both in their thirties. Draven knew there were established scientific links between twins, but never to the scale that was illustrated within this report.

There was also a terrible crime committed and a thirst for revenge, so Anthony was not surprised either of the bloodshed that followed. Draven could only take the key witness accounts at face value but following on from the Symions case it did illustrate that not everything was known about the human mind and its limitations.

There was a paranormal conclusion that Suzannah had noted upon, although Anthony had been keen not to disclose this with either the psychiatrist or serving police colleagues of either twin.

For one of the twins to have been touched by a soul of the dead was perhaps a step to far for most people to comprehend, and Draven had to agree that unless he himself had witnessed such a similar feat that he would also have simply dismissed it just as

quickly. But it did exist, it was true. Now Draven just had to prove it.
Anthony smiled as he finished reading the report. Suzannah Fray had again assisted him in the witness statements. He wondered at what point he would bring his protégée into the equation, but for now was happy to leave her where she was. There were plenty more patients to be catalogued anyway.
No doubt Doctor Harding also would ask him about the stash of stolen bank money the criminals had left behind, thinking it forever hidden. However, it was no longer there.

Anthony never left an opportunity go to miss...

Myron could not help but be impressed with Ashton's handling of the *Flying Shark*. It shot across the waves, the bumps down his spine with every impact lessened by the super carbon impact absorbing cockpit chair. It was like riding in tandem with a Formula One driver. On water. With waves. Or the way Ashton piloted the boat, like a rally driver on snow and ice.

Ashton's concentrated so heavily on the route before him that everything else was now secondary to him. He completely ignored Myron, which didn't bother the Britain in the slightest as McGivney preferred it that way whilst travelling at such speeds.

Even for oceanic waves Myron thought they were relatively mundane. Nothing, as yet, seemed out of the ordinary. He looked across at Ashton's radar and recognised a boundary ring coming up soon. Ashton seemed to read his thoughts.
'Ok bud,' he warned. 'We're about to enter into unknown territory. Once we pass the line there on the radar, we're in no-man's land. Basically, anything

goes. The currents could suddenly change direction, the crests, troughs or the cycle of the waves might alter at a heartbeat. Trust me, the worst place to be right now is on the surface.'

Great, Myron thought. He was sure Ashton was trying to get him to retract his statement earlier that day about hating it underwater. *You'll get no such satisfaction from me*, Myron thought.

'Jeez maloo,' Ashton almost screamed as a thundering wave rose just to the left of the cockpit. The boat turned to intercept and then rode over, spray engulfing the vessel. 'Did you see that My? That one came out of nowhere, hope we caught that on the recording.'

'So, we done then?' Myron asked in hope. He had heard about rogue waves and riding one face to face wasn't actually half bad, he considered.

'You kidding me?' Ashton almost laughed. 'That was a nailed-on sidewinder, a mere tiddler, but a good one to get the senses ticking.'

'Right,' Myron replied sarcastically. 'A sidewinder is a mere tiddler. Of course.'

'Yeah mate,' Ashton offered. 'You get them near the edges, where currents converge. What we want is a rare phenomenon near the centre. When the laws of physics all jump out the window in unison and mother nature decides to show us how small and insignificant we really are.'

'I already know that,' Myron replied honestly. 'I don't need proof.'

'I'll name it after you kid,' Ashton replied as he steered the boat back on its original course. 'Rogus Complainus.'

'Hilarious,' Myron answered as he viewed the cockpit to his left. The sun had now left them almost completely in the dark, wandering off behind stormy clouds. Then the world seemed to go black before his eyes. For there, to his right now, was a mountain of water, and it was growing every second.

Then it turned white as it crashed towards them.

'Brace!!!!!!!!' Ashton shouted before the white water thundered into them and sent the boat spinning side over side, Myron's consciousness was almost torn from him as he felt the GeForce batter his senses.

The ear shattering crashing continued as the boat was buffeted around, Myron's body hanging strapped and inverted in his chair as the deafening roar of the waves carried on relentlessly. He heard a moan from beside him and then Ashton was quiet, which he presumed correctly was the Australasian falling into unconsciousness. It was a miracle that Myron was still able to focus his mind.

Although the vessel was showing no signs of remaining still, it was now evident that they would remain capsized. Of all the times Myron wished that his mysterious alter ego would return, then this was it. But no, no inert focus and no out-of-body experience that would assist him in is plight.

Instead he simply hung there, the blood slowly running to his head. Within minutes his world would turn dark, Myron would become unconscious and probably death would be upon him within another few hours, whether from the sheer amount of blood pouring into his brain or the weight of his organs crushing his lungs. Myron could already feel both occurring.

Hesitating only to stretch his left arm out above his head, and toward the ceiling, which was now the floor, Myron wrestled to find the clipping mechanism of the seatbelt. When he fell, and if he hit the ceiling hard, then it could fracture or break bones. Being right-handed, the last thing he needed was his stronger arm out of commission.

Myron counted to three, then pressed the unclipping device. He had half expected to fall straight away, but somehow both his arms had become entangled with the straps. Using this to his advantage Myron let his body swing around until he was upright again, then dropped the remaining distance to the floor.

Instantly he vomited, as the blood began leaving his head and the reality of the situation kicked in. It was like being in a steel drum cascading down the Niagara Falls.

Myron tried to stand and felt for the body of Ashton still hanging upside down near him. He fought with the seatbelt fastener, prepared himself for the weight, then unclipped the other man. Both hit the ceiling floor hard. Myron quickly checked Ashton's pulse.

The man was alive, that was a start. Given time he'd wake up, and at that point maybe they could plan a way off this ship. The people Ashton had spoken to already knew their location, that was something, now they just needed a minor miracle.

For starters, the storm easing would be something.

It was almost three hours later that DT noticed movement on the monitor, and even though the images through the darkness were blurred at best it was obvious they were not South African military.

'That's them,' Andrews muttered quietly. 'Their size is a dead giveaway.'

'Okay then,' DT whispered. 'Guess it's showtime.'

She unhooked her phone from the camera and left it rolling, the network cable into the wall socket sending the images halfway around the globe. Next to her Andrews sent a simple text message with the camera http link attached.

'Come on,' Andrews told her. 'We can't risk sitting around once your surprise goes off.'

DT looked back at her superior and Andrews could easily see the vengeance in her features. Gemma simply waited for the soldier to make up her own mind.

'One day,' DT whispered. 'One day we'll have revenge.'

'Yes,' Andrews replied. 'But we need to have the upper hand first. For that to happen we need more intel. We're going home.'

That at least brought a smile to DT's features.

Within the heart of the R.O.G.U.E headquarters panic was the order of the day.

'What's the situation?' one voice asked over the silence of the control room.

'The *Flying Shark* has remained capsized, so any counter measures have failed. We have yet to receive any updates from the crew.'

'Status of the boat?'

'Offline, sir,' the voice offered dejectedly.

'Okay,' the most senior voice replied. 'Worse case scenario. The crew are incapacitated, vessel capsized, and the power or engines need rebooting. What can we do? Will the turtledrone work?'

'Potentially sir,' another answered quickly. 'We do need satellite link-up in order to enable TD into life, but it could be done. Potentially even using sonar if we have another vessel within a five-mile radius?'

'What about the dolphin pod?' another mused. 'Could we get Sheila's pod to transmit turtledrone's SOS call? Ashton has been testing with the pod extensively over the last few months.'

'Or,' came a thought. 'We'll get Sheila to send out all the SOS codes, even if TD doesn't work then the boat might recognise the sonar call and reboot the system automatically.'

'Worth a go sir,' a female voice began. 'In theory once the boat boots up it'll release TD anyway, and also the rescue buoy. We'd know if it works almost instantly.'

'Okay,' the senior voice began. 'Get Meredith on the phone. She needs to get a fix on Sheila's pod and get them to head for the *Flying Shark's* location.'

'Do you think it'll work sir? It is another one of Ashton's ingenious schemes.'

'It'll work,' he smiled. 'More often than not his genius works out in the end. Just hope they're ok onboard the *Flying Shark*. For all of its ingenuity, that boat can only last a certain time capsized in the ocean, less if the seas are still submerging it every five minutes.'

Sebastian Nolan had gained access to the military base quite easily. As with anything under Harding's enterprise there was not anybody who couldn't be bribed or extorted against. And it only took one weak link to break the chain. Nolan left the sorry soldier at the gate behind as he drove the truck into the compound. He had brought all the Menazee troops with him, he was taking no chances of letting his catch go so easily this time.

Twice Lieutenant Andrews had evaded him, for her it would be third time unlucky. The first was on the volcano. It had been bad luck that his bullet, intended for the Lieutenant, had hit another soldier. However, for her then to escape had annoyed him considerably. Then for her to survive the ocean night, that was simply bad luck.

Once the call had come in that an injured soldier had been airlifted from a cruise ship and to a Johannesburg military base then Nolan had quickly re-organised his plans to apprehend her. Tonight was not about killing her, he simply wanted to be in and out of this base before anybody knew they were here.

Purely stealth. A mission that once again could test the limits of the Menazee, although Sebastian considered this should be the easiest of the tasks he had recently given them. He had five troopers with him, all of which had been given certain roles for this exercise.

Firstly, they had gained entry through Harding's dubious military contacts. Nolan would operate the truck throughout the mission. He originally had to sneak into the hospital ward to find out Andrews' current location, but even that had been taken care of. It was just as well, the less sneaking around Sebastian had to do the better. He wanted to be in and out under sixty seconds.

The lieutenant had been moved to another part of the installation, which was out near the open ground of the basketball courts. This was particularly handy considering he wanted as little opportunities for his troop to be identified. They were all wearing full body cover, but still.
He then had one Menazee primed to cut the internal electrics so that any lighting around the compound couldn't be lit. Two were then in charge of disabling the doors to the barracks, as well as anybody who got in the way, using non-lethal means if possible. This was also a first. Nolan wasn't sure if they fully comprehended what non-lethal meant. The final two were then being used to apprehend Andrews.

As the truck stopped near the basketball court Nolan turned off the vehicle lights but kept the engine running. Sebastian knew he didn't have to say anything but still felt uneasy simply offering a silent commend, so instead just said one hushed word.

'Go.'

DT looked down at her phone as they crept down the staircase and toward the rear entrance of the rehabilitation centre. She could see the shadows moving across the grounds towards the barracks and knew they didn't have much time. Next to her Andrews waited for the light show to begin. They were on the other side of the centre to the barracks, but Gemma still didn't believe that was enough, unless the exposure of these soldiers to the military personnel and potential the media drove them back underground.

Andrews waited patiently, her hand hovering near the catch release of the door. Her body still ached from the ordeal over the last twenty-four hours, but Gemma's mind was still as focused as usual. They had to survive this, anything else was a bonus.

Next to her DT raised a single finger in the air. Showtime.

Ashton groaned groggily as his consciousness finally came back to him. It was pitch black. His head throbbed incessantly, and he released his pain gently.

'For the love of all that's holy and glowy,' Ashton began. 'What I could do for a bucketful of macroplankton right now. You alive My?'

'I'm here,' Myron said through the darkness. 'Just waiting for you to wake up after your fainting episode.'

'Ha,' Mehrtens laughed as he tried to get to his hands and knees. 'Typical, you've outlasted me. You're something. You stopped feeling seasick now?'

'I'm not sure if my body has become accustomed to this hellhole or simply my senses have given up completely,' Myron replied through the darkness. 'I could do with a bit of good news though. I heard some weird sonar signals over the last ten minutes. Any chance this boat has an SOS call?'

'Blowout man!' Ashton shouted in disbelief, instantly coming back to life. 'That's not the boat matey, that's Sheila.'

'Sheila?'

'Yeah, a dolphin pod based just off the coast,' Ashton explained with excitement. 'Ah man, if they managed to navigate their way to us do you know what this means?'

'That we're about to get rescued?'

'Well, yeah, there is that,' Ashton replied. 'Nobel prize territory dude. Dolphin and human interaction on a level never seen before. I need to see the data first though, but they could have been sent to find us.'

'And?'

'Ah,' Ashton replied. 'In theory the boat's PCU will reboot, the engines will power up, we right ourselves and hey voila, we'll be heading back to port by...what time is it?'

'It's just passed ten thirty, in the evening before you think you've been unconscious for around fifteen hours.'

'If we were still capsized tomorrow morning then we'd be in definite trouble,' Ashton remarked. 'We'd have sunk.'

'Ah,' Myron sighed. 'Haven't noticed any seepage yet. Who built this vessel anyway?'

'You know,' Ashton began. 'Not really sure. It was a bit of a secretive thing; some scientist guy was our benefactor. We've been collecting all sorts of specimens for him over the years. Never met him though. He doesn't really have the social skills I have either.'

'I can imagine,' Myron replied. Just then a few lights flicked on next to his leg. 'Better get off this console, just in case I press the ejector seat button.'

'I did ask for that,' Ashton replied. 'Silly idea apparently.'

'Yeah, I was being a little ridiculous.'

'*Flying Shark*,' came a familiar voice over the intercom. Instantly more lights and screens came to life before their eyes. Ashton clambered to one side of the console and flicked another switch.

'Ashton here,' he began. 'Glad to hear your voice again boss. Do you know if we're clear to right ourselves yet? The dashboards still coming to life this end.'

'Hi Ashton,' the voice continued. 'Give it five minutes and the boat might even self-right itself. We've got normal conditions in your location now. I know you've got more pressing concerns currently but some of the data you've captured is simply exquisite.'

'Really?' Mehrtens replied astonished. 'Guess it was all worth it after all.' He glanced over at Myron. The other man smiled back through the half-light of the bridge, if only due to sheer relief.

Ten minutes passed until the vessel began to self-right on its own. Ashton began to explain the process, but Myron bypassed all the necessary information, merely excited for the boat to be righting itself.

'How long until we can make shoreline?' he asked curiously. 'Just thinking of those samples.'

'Yeah,' Ashton replied absentmindedly. 'Maybe a few hours? There's no point rushing now.'

'I beg to differ,' Myron exclaimed. 'I have a good friend that needs my help.'

'Right you are,' Ashton almost seemed to break out of his hypnotized gaze. 'Of course, we'll get on it. I won't let you down My.'

McGivney thanked him and wondered what was spooking Mehrtens about returning to shore. It reminded Myron of his own concerns about the sea. Surely Ashton wasn't petrified about being on dry land?

Nolan waited in the darkened truck as with military precision first the lights of the compound shut down, then he caught sight of the remaining Menazee warriors storm the barracks.

Almost immediately the barracks erupted into a series of coloured light and explosions. Nolan swore and drove the truck forward as almost as instantly the troop exited the building, the fireworks lighting up the night sky. Sebastian ushered the soldiers back inside the truck, then accelerated across the compound and toward the entrance.

From nearly every doorway South African military poured out into the illuminations of the display, some instantly aware that the truck was not part of their vehicle store. A few shots were fired, but mostly in warning rather than with any accuracy. By the time the compound's soldiers had organised themselves the truck had already disappeared into the night. Behind the disappearing Nolan and the Menazee troop both Andrews and DT had also managed to pull off the same feat.

The camera however kept recording and sending images across the world. Minutes later Commander Goldhawk had organised a search and rescue operation for his two soldiers and pushed the images further up the chain of command.

It was time to burn a few fingers.

Antidote

Thursday 00:46

Myron sat in the front seat of the silver Mercedes minibus as both the research team, Ashton and himself were whisked off from Richard's Bay harbour and toward their headquarters which was nestled quite neatly just before the surrounding mountain range.

McGivney let Ashton tell the tale of their ordeal without interruption, mostly because he was too tired to intervene but partly because it would only remind him once again of his alter ego. Myron knew just how Bruce Banner now felt, albeit without having to order another set of clothing each time he had an episode.

Myron had absolutely no control over it, and now it was affecting the people he cared for. If the antidote worked then he would not hesitate to use it on himself either. He wanted an end to all this. Only when he was free could he ever be the man he thought Isobel wanted.

Even if ultimately it killed him? That was probably the billion-pound question. Without the toxin he wouldn't have survived the *Jah Mahal*, or thinking about it, maybe not even the roof attack in London. *Damn gem*, he thought. Even the origin of it eluded him, and having a total stranger tell him that a fish was a potential antidote only frustrated him more.

Myron had no doubt that the mysterious man's voice in the vehicle would make true his promise, so he had little choice but to run this through to its completion, with the creation of a working antidote. If he failed in his usefulness, then Myron only assumed the worst.

Here lay the key; save Kirill and maybe they could solve the riddles of whom this mysterious stranger was, whether Templar was trustworthy and his chance to get Isobel out of harm's way.

Myron left his thoughts and once again listened to Ashton's telling of their adventure. The man was an obvious genius, of that there was no doubt. His grip on reality however was slightly disengaged.

The van soon left the motorway and headed off into the relative darkness of the side roads, where Myron found himself gently drifting off into a dreamworld once again. Sometimes life felt so simple, other times...

He was awoken from his thoughts as the driver pointed to Myron the headquarters. The facility was part of an industrial estate, and just seemed to be a few warehouses strung together. As the van parked, Ashton gathered up the box with the specimens before illustrating to Myron that they would be going in a different direction that the rest of the team.

'Give me a few moments bud,' Ashton said coolly. 'Need to prep myself for the next part.'

'What do you mean?' Myron asked innocently, until he realised. 'Oh my word, does your ex work here?'

'Shush, will you?' Ashton replied. 'And definitely lose the "ex" bit.'

'Okay,' Myron answered, more confused than ever. 'What's going on?'

'Ah man,' Ashton began. 'I hate land stuff. Wish I could simply live at sea.'

'What is it?'

'It's Meredith man,' Ashton offered. 'She's not my ex, I just never seem to be able to commit to her, that's all.'

'Oh,' Myron replied. 'I wouldn't worry about that, you're hardly alone in the universe for being a complete putz with your girlfriend.'

'Maybe,' Ashton noted.

'Come on,' Myron replied. 'I'm getting cold out here and I need an antidote. You can create one, can't you?'

'Um, not me My,' Ashton grimaced.

'Can Meredith?' Myron asked patiently.

'Once we ask her, yes,' Ashton frowned. 'Knew I'd forgotten something.'

'Brilliant,' Myron sighed. 'Well, let's find out quickly. If it's a no then I'm telling Meredith all about what you've put me through.'

'That's harsh,' Ashton replied. 'It was a good adventure I thought?'

'Come on.'

By the time Draven was halfway back to the USA and Nolan and his troops were back in hiding within the South African mountain range, DT and Andrews were picked up by American military personnel in plain clothing within Johannesburg. They were quickly given a quick written debrief from Commander Goldhawk before heading to the air via a Chinook helicopter.

Soon they would be boarding a military cruiser and heading back to their home country, to where Goldhawk was waiting for them. DT, as ever, allowed the travelling to wade over her as she immersed herself back into her subconscious and attempted to consolidate all these new discoveries toward potentially finding a solution to their problems.

At least the superhuman troopers had a name now; Menazee. Goldhawk himself had managed to find that out, whether it was common knowledge before tonight was another question entirely. Her superior could deal with that one, DT just needed to know what their weaknesses were.

Andrews also found some solitude as soon as DT closed her eyes, only minutes after reading Goldhawk's official report. So, the military knew, or at least her commander knew something. Andrews considered this and decided they should keep a lid on it for now. The lieutenant needed to speak to Goldhawk, and to find out what they were dealing with. As far as Andrews was concerned, if anybody asked, she had no idea what these creatures were. Apart from the fact that they were obviously trouble.

Gemma felt the aluminium suitcase knock against her knee. She had no idea if this would help her in the next forty-eight hours, but at least wished she could test it before facing these troopers again. Not yet, though, she thought. Andrews had no idea who was watching her.

Meredith stared down the eyepiece lens of the microscope as she switched through the sample slides. The laboratory was quiet, as was the case at any time after six in the evening, but she worked better when left alone, so she was happy.

There was another reason of course. She was expecting company. The rescue had gone like clockwork although this did not calm her. Ashton seemed to have a death wish regarding his research, and she was not one for watching on as another human being killed themselves for a bit of fame and fortune. She heard the men approach from the corridor, only looking up when an unfamiliar voice spoke.

'Hi, Miss Meredith,' Myron asked, after knocking on the door and entering slowly. 'I'm Myron, a friend of the Fortuna's. I was sent to assist Ashton Mehrtens in attaining a rare sample of bream fish, in the hope we could create an antidote for a rare type of illness that has affected one of my colleagues.'

'Nice to meet you Myron,' Meredith looked up from the microscope. 'I take it Ashton got lost from the car park to the lab again?'

'You could say that,' Myron smiled warmly as he stepped across the lab toward her. 'Here,' he offered, putting the box of specimens on a clear part of the bench, away from the other experiments. 'I wouldn't ask if it wasn't important.'

'That's okay,' she smiled. 'You were the one onboard when the rogue hit weren't you? I half-wish that on Ashton at times, but not a stranger. You feeling okay?'

'Let's just say it's not an experience I ever want to repeat,' Myron chuckled. 'But considering what happened today, I do feel as if I'm enjoying a extra slice of luck cake today.'

'I'm going to be honest Myron,' Meredith began. 'An antidote is not something that can be created very simply.'

'That's ok,' Myron sighed. 'No need to apologise. I have the same issue in my bloodstream, so if you can detect any anomalies then at least we have something to start with. I've been guided here by a mysterious hand, so I'm starting from scratch I'm afraid.'

'Oh,' Meredith began, looking at Myron with concern, before she once again smiled. 'Give me your arm,' she continued. 'A quick blood sample should give me all I require for now. I'll need you to hang around though, no doubt I'll have hundreds of questions for you later as we proceed through the tests.'

'No problem,' Myron smiled, feeling a huge weight of pressure dissipate from his shoulders. 'Can I get you a coffee?'

'You can find Ashton and get his arse in here,' she smiled. 'A coffee would be nice as well, thank you.'

'He's really something,' Myron found himself stating before he turned to leave.

'He's definitely that,' Meredith shrugged.

'I mean it,' Myron continued. 'It's almost as if he's complete out there amongst the waves, he seems to struggle when being back on land.'

'Are you asking me to go easy on him?'

'No,' Myron smiled. 'I wouldn't want to interfere, but don't take his complete incompetence around you for not caring, that's all. I've been there, done that. Guess we're all a little guilty at times.'

'Maybe,' Meredith replied. 'I want to know what happened onboard the *Flying Shark*. His heartbeat went into bradycardia just after the capsizing. Was he still strapped in?'

'Um,' Myron began, but that was all that was needed.

'Does he know?' Meredith asked.

'We haven't discussed it,' Myron replied truthfully. 'I honestly thought he would have slipped out of his restraints anyway, when he didn't…'

'That's okay Myron,' Meredith bit back her tears. 'Why don't you bring him in, then run off to get a few coffees whilst I have a quick word with him?'

'Okay,' Myron replied and left the room. Halfway along the corridor Ashton was taking a sip of cold liquid from a water fountain.

'Everything alright?' Ashton asked as Myron approached him.

'Meredith's going to try everything she can to make an antidote,' Myron nodded. 'Think you have a bit of apologising to do though.'

'Ah man,' Ashton sighed. 'I'm no good at this My. What do I say?'

'How can you surf a rogue wave, battle with sharks yet find it difficult to say sorry to your girlfriend?' Myron quizzed him.

'She's scarier than both, that's how,' Ashton replied honestly.

'You're a melon head,' Myron offered. 'What's the worst thing you've ever done?'

'Well,' Ashton noted. 'There was a month last year where we almost had a wedding party each weekend, and I forgot my shoes on each occasion.'

'Each time?' stuttered Myron. 'How? What did you leave the house in?'

'My flippies,' Ashton shrugged. 'Second time I put them in a bag, then forgot the bag. Third time I put them in the car boot...'

'Then you took another car?'

'Right on My!' Ashton laughed, before seeing the error of his ways. 'You're right. What am I to do?'

'Just tell her you love her,' Myron offered and walked off. 'But make sure you mean it...'

Myron returned after around five minutes with some fresh coffee one of the other researchers in the area had made for him, and some refreshments from the vending machine. He had not had any money on him, but Darius' homemade watch had come up trumps again. Myron was not sure if the account could be tracked to this location but was relieved that he had only tried this on a simple vending machine, not anything that might alert the authorities.

As he returned to the laboratory Myron saw Ashton and Meredith finish an embrace. He half-began to turn around, before they noticed him and beckoned Myron back inside the room.

'Buddy,' Ashton began before running over to Myron and hugging him tightly. 'Meredith told me that I had passed out in my seat, you basically saved my life.'

'Well,' Myron noted. 'Not sure about that.'

'He's so modest,' Ashton smiled over at Meredith. 'And thanks to my baby here the dolphin pod came out to rescue us.'

'Really?' Myron replied. 'Thank you, I'm forever in your debt.'

'No, you're not My,' Ashton began. 'Meredith saved your life, you saved mine, and I make her life an absolute misery.'

'You could say that,' she commented. 'Tell Myron the other news.'

'Oh yeah,' Ashton continued. 'Your blood sample My, seen this bloody thing before. Gave me the creeps, some guy called Nolan visited me a while ago under the guidance of a Doctor something, from somewhere.'

'Harding,' Meredith offered, staring at Ashton in dismay. 'A huge benefactor.'

'Yeah, that's the one,' Ashton nodded in excitement. 'His wasn't a blood sample though, this Nolan guy had it stored within some kind of animal tissue. He said he had found it on a dead snow leopard, one which had gone mad and attacked a local tribe. His story was plausible, but I couldn't ever get his sample to match anything I've ever catalogued.'

'What is it?' Myron asked slowly. He was not sure if he wanted to know the answer if something similar had sent an animal crazy.

'Mild hallucinogen basically,' Ashton nodded. 'Nothing to worry too much about. When did you get infected?'

'About six months ago,' Myron replied.

Silence.

'What is it?' the Britain asked as the other two simply stopped looking at Myron and then at each other.

'That's impossible,' Meredith stated.

'It's bloody insane,' Ashton remarked. 'That should have diluted and left your bloodstream after a week, maybe a bit longer if you'd cut back on water. Six months? That makes no sense.'

'There isn't a hallucinogen on the planet that lasts this long Myron,' Meredith stated. 'I'm not saying it's impossible, but this simply doesn't happen in nature.'

'Okay,' Myron replied. 'You say hallucinogen. What else might it do?'

'Sorry Myron,' Meredith sighed. 'I can break this apart and get you more answers, but we're basically reacting to Ashton's initial findings. There could be other reasons, the story regarding the crazed cat was never validated either. It could have been a mistake, a coincidence, even a test someone had done on this beast before the incident occurred.'

'So basically, it could be far more than a simple hallucinogen that makes me have bad dreams?' Myron asked.

'If that's in you buddy' Ashton noted, 'then my baby will cure it. Given you've been carrying it around for six months, you look pretty healthy, so it's not all bad?'

'That's what I believed' Myron replied, 'until one of my friends lapsed into a coma. I believe he also had these toxins in his bloodstream.'

'Oh My,' Ashton groaned. 'I'm sorry dude.'

'It's okay,' he told them both. 'But I need to go to him. And I either go with an antidote or a way to heal him. Currently I'm out of many options.'

'I did keep a contact number of the Nolan character,' Ashton began. 'Although by no means should you follow this up if it's gonna go south.'

'I won't get into trouble,' Myron smiled innocently. 'Right,' he thought quickly. 'Here's the plan.

You two keep working on an antidote, serum, or whatever you think might assist me in keeping whatever's in my blood at bay. That includes notifying me of anything that might cause it to flare up or make me react to it. There has to be something, even adrenaline, anything.

I have to go. I need to be on the move. Keep me updated and I'll come back to you when I think it's safe. I have no contact details, so we'll have to play this by ear.'

'Just use our *Flying Shark* website,' Ashton smiled. 'We have fourteen readers at present, another one will be awesome. Meredith loves it. Don't you babe? Ah babe, don't give me that look. It's an awesome website.'

'Deal,' Myron replied. 'Good luck and thank you. Any sniff of trouble and delete anything you have. Don't risk anything for me.'

'Right,' Ashton rolled his eyes at him. 'I can be discrete you know.'

'I'll do the contact stuff babe,' Meredith whispered to him.

'Ok,' he replied disheartened. Myron laughed.

'Come here buddy,' Ashton said as he recovered and bearhugged the other man. 'You take care.'

'You too,' Myron thanked them both, then departed, alone, out into the cold night. Looking at his watch he instantly knew he hadn't thought this through properly.

The door opened behind him and Ashton stood there with a huge grin on his face.

'Gringo, you look far from home. Need a lift buddy?'

Anthony Draven woke for breakfast in a surreal state. He had already finished reading two of the three files in his bag, but ultimately had then dreamt about them as well. Although unsettling, as his subconscious mind mixed reality with fiction, Anthony did manage to recollect snippets of his dreams and store them for future use.

The inflight meal was bland, but Draven did not mind. His nourishment would come from another source. He had saved his most enlightening and promising file until last. Sipping at his orange juice he opened the final file.

It was only the beginning, Draven considered. Of all his case studies, Jake Connelly's had been the most opportunistic, and again for this he had Suzannah Fray to thank.

The woman was like an ancient dowser, able to use divination to locate the most suitable patients. Although almost a pseudoscience, Draven could not argue with her high percentage of effective results.

If it was a few hundred years ago no doubt he'd have thought of her as a witch, but in these enlightened times Anthony preferred simply to think of her as supremely gifted.

The key to Jake's case was simple timing...he had been a very troubled and emotional human being that had somehow lost his way. Whatever the reason behind the boy's suicide, once Jake Connelly had entered Draven's life there was an opportunity to take another step towards his dream.

As soon as the boy had been taken to hospital following his jump off Ephraim's bridge, his life signs were basically zero. By the time the ambulance had arrived the blue lights had stopped.

It hadn't taken much for Draven to get his hands on the body, and before anybody knew any better, he had managed to link up Jake Connelly's body to a life-support machine and start his work immediately.

Anthony thought again of Doctor Harding's letter and hoped this case study, if not the others, would illustrate Draven's potential.

Draven closed the last file and thought back to Maxine's police statement, and how she felt on that fateful day. Fortunately for Draven, Maxine had also been duped by both Suzannah and him. It had been almost fool proof if a spur of the moment decision to steal the body.

Anthony Draven leant back in his seat and contemplated how Suzannah and he had managed to reach the dying brain of Jake through the various latest technology at his disposal.

Their twenty-four-hour vigil of the boy had also been inspired. Yet, above all, unless Anthony and Suzannah had such a keen insight into the monitoring of brain signals and had fully utilised the prototype virtual reality skull-set then they would have failed.

What they had attempted was as ground-breaking as much as it was unethical and illegal. Yet they had somehow communicated with the boy and made him believe that he was still alive and had the opportunity to turn his life around. That much was evident from the eerie images they viewed on the screens in front of them.

Draven stopped reading momentarily. There was something about the town of Muhoi and Jake's family and friends that had given the boy strength, even when his brain was dying, and all his body's life signs were flatlined. He mentally stored this for later. Maybe there was a use for family and friends after all, he considered.

Technology had almost offered Draven the unthinkable, but in the end Jake had died. It was true that the one thing that can truly die was the unrepentant soul of a suicide.

However, before Jake's death it had illustrated to Anthony and Suzannah that there was something out there, something they bitterly wanted to find.

Anthony looked out of the window and then considered the next chapter of his life ...

Boardwalk

Port Elizabeth: Southern tip of South Africa; Thursday: 11:18

The sight of Port Elizabeth would never grow old for Isobel, but on this occasion the city which had always seemed so alive to her held a grave reminder.
Firstly, she had promised Myron that they would take in either a Southern Kings rugby game or cricket at the famous St. George's Park, but could now do neither. She already missed him dearly, which in a strange way soothed her.

His love for sport had been rather surprising, as was most of the things she had found out about him. For a man so secretive Isobel expected to uncover a few surprises, but not to the extent she had encountered.

She let a small smile cross her lips as the *Angel of the Seas* began its slow docking in the harbour. Myron was like a small child, uninterested in much she took for granted until he had had a little taste. Then, it was like opening the flood gates of a dam. Out would wash the fascination, the relentless thirst for knowledge and afterwards a lifetime of enthusiasm for something originally, he would have simply walked on by and ignored completely.

Isobel had obviously found this utterly bewildering but the truth had been simple. For much of Myron's life he had put his head down and worked hard, relentlessly pursuing a single goal that was laid out for him. Now however, he had been shown a brand-new path, but one completely alien to him.

Myron had even noted once to her that if he went the night without embarrassing her then he would be happy, but until now Isobel had mistaken that comment entirely.

It had not been his personality that had bothered him but his knowledge of the wider world, the world that he had paid very little attention to but now he had been thrust into so violently. It had taken Ishyan to remind her that he too had been pulled from his own homeland and expected to make a new life for himself. And Isobel knew that Ishyan had been given everything Alessendro had assumed would help as well.

They had given Myron nothing, yet what had he given them? For Isobel she owed him her life, whether he allowed her to think that there was any truth in this or not. Ishyan certainly gave the man his vote for what had happened only months ago.

Isobel took a deep, sad breath, and thought of Myron one last time before the madness would start again. For this *was* the Templar Harrison and Alessendro Fortuna show, and as much as she loved her father and respected his business partner, she could have done without their shenanigans for a few days until her emotions had settled.

Even when she had spent yesterday recovering in her cabin both had visited her on more than a few occasions. There was simply no downtime.

Secondly, although she had not visited Port Elizabeth for a few years now, that wasn't true for everyone she knew at *FortunaCS*, and this now concerned her. There were no absolutes regarding either Templar's business legality nor ethics, but now Isobel worried about her own mortal soul.

As soon as she had heard about her father's commitment to Templar's space venture, Isobel had found out as much as humanly possible about Harrison's company. It was whilst browsing through the conference dates that one had stood out, and Isobel had wasted no time coercing Ishyan Stölles into booking the presidential suite in the only five-star hotel in Port Elizabeth, in the eventuality of playing a rather dangerous game.

Of course, the hope was that Harrison Templar's business etiquette was all completely legit, but at the time Isobel could not have been 100% sure. And so Ishyan had stayed for five days under the *Leon Chamel* pseudonym, and prepared the suite for a potential Templar visit.

Now they were here, and no doubt Harrison would have booked the presidential suite for himself. As to whether Isobel wanted to go through the next stage of this plan was another question. Spying was not her game. However, if she wanted to find the truth behind Templar then she had no choice but go ahead with the plan. Either that or wait and see what Harrison had up his sleeve. Isobel did not want to take that chance.

So, even with a heavy heart she had a job to do. Isobel turned her back on the harbour and ventured back down below, to check on her cabin one last time before they left for dry land. The planned stop would be a few days, enough sightseeing time for most of the crew, an opportunity for her father and Harrison to talk more shop to the invitees to the hotel convention and of course for her, a rather more secretive mission.

Isobel ran into her father as she approached the cabin. He'd already passed his luggage to the stewards and was now preparing for the next step of their journey.

'Hurry up Iz,' he sighed. 'You know Harrison doesn't like to be kept waiting, and he's arranged an entourage on the harbour, just for us.'

'Guests of honour hey?' she smiled. 'What with booking out the whole of the hotel and conference suites who would have thought he'd also have time to conjure up a welcoming committee.'

'Iz,' her father warned her. 'You know the rules, this is a joint project and Templar has massive resources at his disposal.'

'All of them legal papa?' she almost whispered, brushing past him and into her cabin. Her father followed and shut the door.

'What's got into you?' he asked patiently. 'You told me the rescue hadn't affected you? Do you want me to call a doctor?'

'I'm fine,' she replied. 'I'll be back to normal once we're back on dry land, I promise.'

'Good,' his father smiled. 'We need you at your best for the conference. I take it that Harrison has filled you in for your parts?'

'Yes,' she replied, trying to step into business gear. 'He's taken the lead, no surprise there, but has left a fair amount of technical stuff to dig my teeth into.'

'Good,' Alessendro replied. 'I'm stepping back from all of this Iz, so I'll leave it to you and Templar. However, if you need me just let me know.'

'That's not like you?' she quizzed as innocently as possible.

'No,' her father replied as he bent forward and kissed her on her forehead. 'It's not is it.'

With that he left, leaving Isobel to try and translate her father's last words.

The motorcade was, by presidential standards, of a similar size. The main difference was the razzmatazz that seemed to follow Harrison's every step. Isobel almost grimaced as she heard her name being read out aloud over the tannoy system. She stood at the top of the gantry and now had to suffer the indignity of having people cheer for about thirty seconds as she slowly made her way to the harbourside. There was no point rushing, she thought. She'd only trip and fall.

At the bottom stood her father, waiting patiently. There seemed to be security everywhere, although Isobel had already noted that the whole harbour was now shut off anyway. Knowing Harrison also the local roads that led to the hotel. She knew it was not far, but Templar did like to make a fuss.

'Thought you'd never come,' her father whispered as she drew close. 'Come on, we've got this car to ourselves, so let's get off to the hotel.'

'What's he doing now?' Isobel asked as up ahead on another commotion was occurring.

'Ah yes,' Alessendro muttered. 'Getting into the spirit of things again. Harrison managed to get his Dodge Tomahawk motorbike aboard and wants to show it off at every possible opportunity. I was just glad he couldn't get it out on deck over the last few days, although I'm sure he tried.'

'Bloody show off,' Isobel replied before stepping into the awaiting car. 'I wouldn't have minded, but that thing's got four wheels, hardly a bike.'

'Um,' Alessendro muttered before catching his daughter's eye.

'What?'

'The design is patented, and currently we own the copyright,' he smiled. 'Just in case.'

'In case?' Isobel gazed back at her father, trying to work out his reasoning. He simply looked ahead as the car pulled away. 'Not for this project, surely?' Isobel continued. 'That machine is a death-trap.'

'The current version is,' her father stated. 'Think laterally.'

'Okay,' Isobel replied and relaxed back into her seat.

She instinctively closed her eyes...

...and placed herself on the tarmac next to the machine, but with one minor additional detail.

'Missing me?' Myron asked from beside her. She grabbed his hand quickly before her imagination whisked him away again.

'You're just what I need,' she replied. 'Look.'

'Yes,' Myron replied, taking in the sight of the motorbike before him. 'The Dodge Tomahawk, this looks like the latest version, but of course we both now know that not to be true.'

'What?'

'Your father's hints Iz,' Myron continued as he stepped forward and ran his hands over the shiny chrome frame.

'Well,' Isobel began. She knew he'd acquired the patent, but that didn't necessarily mean...

'Look,' Myron offered as he clambered onboard the bike.

'Get off,' Isobel warned him. 'You have no experience on these things.'

'No, I don't, do I?' he smiled back. Myron pressed the ignition button and revved the V10 engine loudly. The sound was deafening. Isobel shut her eyes and when she opened them...

...she was back in the car alongside her father.

'You're not planning on building this for the enthusiast, are you?' she smiled.

'No,' Alessendro beamed. 'However, keep it under wraps for now. I don't want Templar sniffing around this project, not yet anyway.'

'Okay,' she replied. What would her father want with the patent to this machine? It had four wheels, so potentially more rideable to the uninitiated. It was also ridiculously powerful with a V10 engine. Any normal person would simply walk away from this. So why the interest?

Could it be linked to their other project? Surely such a vehicle in space was nonsensical, but that would not stop him. No, there had to be a military connection here.

Isobel shook away the thoughts and concentrated instead on the present. Their vehicle was now part of a procession that was meandering its way along the harbour and out into the streets. Isobel could already see the hotel outside the window and was not even remotely surprised to see two flags whirling in the breeze from the main flag posts. One was the *FortunaCS* logo and the other the Templar family crest.

He never misses a trick, Isobel thought.

Harrison Templar climbed off his motorbike at the front of the motorcade, met the hotel manager on the steps before entering the huge five-star hotel. From within the lobby Harrison then met with some of the staff before waiting to officially welcome the guests.

Isobel and her father were about the fifth car to arrive, and they approached the hotel with awe. Either Templar had gone overboard, or the hotel manager had really outdone himself. The gardens were immaculate, the paintwork seemingly fresh and all the staff were welcoming them on arrival.

Once they had past the Dodge Tomahawk, conscientiously but obviously with delight parked right outside the entrance, they walked inside with Alessendro wandering over to Templar first, Isobel quietly in his wake.

'Once again Harrison, you've excelled yourself,' Alessendro admitted at the sheer voluptuousness of the luxury hotel. Isobel skirted around the central fountain before meeting up with them.

'It is truly beautiful,' Isobel agreed. 'What's out back?'

'Ah, you noticed the conference centre,' Harrison smiled. 'But guess what else? They've also got a go-kart track and archery field.'

'You and your competitions,' Isobel sighed.

'Come on Iz,' Templar replied playfully. 'I'm one-nil down thanks to your boyfriend, at least be sporting and let me have the opportunity to draw the series?'

'Okay,' Isobel retorted, acting bored. 'Archery it is though. You can keep your go-karting for another day.'

'Deal,' Harrison beamed. 'Three o'clock out on the rear lawn garden. That'll give us a few hours to unwind and catch up on business.'

'And to round up any companies who've arrived early for tomorrow's festivities,' Alessendro noted. 'Be a good time to carve up some more opportunities whilst you two provide the entertainment.'

'You don't miss a trick either,' Isobel smiled.

'Well, we've got a lot to live up to after the shuffleboard yesterday,' Harrison admitted. 'I take it you can't split one arrow with another?'

'No,' Isobel rolled her eyes. 'They're carbon weave Harrison, they'd literally disintegrate. Isobel Fortuna,' she spoke softly to the receptionist as her room key was signed for and passed over to her.

'Oh,' Templar mused, slightly crestfallen that this was the case.

'However,' Isobel reacted quickly. 'There's no reason why I can't shoot one of your arrows out of mid-air.'

'Ha ha,' Templar laughed as Isobel took the luxury suite keys, waved goodbye to both of them and disappeared off toward the staircase.

'She's not joking Templar,' Alessendro smiled.

'No,' Harrison agreed. 'She wasn't was she.'

Sebastian Nolan entered the open pit mine based just outside Bethelsdorp, a good five miles west of Port Elizabeth, with only one thing on his mind. For once he was to be the bearer of good news, but it came uneasily to him. He was no actor, and the part he had to play today did seem uncharacteristic of his normal behaviour. Anyway, it did not matter if his performance was dire, the site manager already seemed partially cautious as to the twelve-hour shutdown of the mine and wanted to meet Nolan as soon as possible. This he could deal with; it came instinctively to him.

As the truck came to rest, Sebastian jumped from the passenger seat and onto the dusty track. Behind him he left his troop of Menazee, all dressed in mine security uniforms, facial prosthetics in place and all sitting stationary either behind the wheel of the truck or in the cargo area behind. As usual they would wait his command. As usual they would be tested again tonight.

Nolan followed one of the security guards as he was led to an office situated just off from the main road. No doubt it wasn't used that much but seemed to be perfect for his requirement this afternoon.

The office was empty, and when the guard left him Sebastian quickly checked his watch. There was no rush, but he was expected to report in at some point. This mission had to raise no suspicion and had to be completed on time and without any failures.

Thinking back to the shield volcano on Reunion, Nolan remembered how he had taught the Menazee to quickly dig strategic holes across the volcano crater. Here he wanted to do a similar ploy, but this time the locations had to be carried out perfectly. Sebastian had fitted each Menazee with a GPS locator, diamond tip drills and a large rucksack each, all filled to the brim with remotely rigged dynamite.

In the volcano they had used diamond tipped hand tools, limiting the noise produced. This was a necessity due to the civilians around the shield volcano.

Here however, once the site had been cleared, his soldiers could make as much noise as they wanted. However, they had to be perfect with their hole cuttings, and quick with their placing and hiding of the dynamite.

Nolan awoke from his thoughts as he caught sight of movement from the security gate. Another van had driven up, and two men now approached. One Nolan recognised as the guard only minutes before, the other therefore must be the site manager. He was also looking very grumpy. Perfect, Nolan thought. He could play along with this.

'Afternoon,' the gruff voice began as the site manager entered the hut. 'Mr Hodges wasn't it?'

'That's right,' Nolan smiled as the false name. 'Thank you for seeing me so quickly, and for what's it's worth I understand your concern here.'

'Yes,' the bearded man replied as he opened up his file. 'I've done a little bit of research here, so apologies for my comments earlier by phone.'

'Not at all,' Nolan smiled again. 'As I'm sure you're aware, we have done this previously at other mines.'

'Yes,' he replied. 'I can see that now. You must understand that this mine has been my responsibility now for eight years, so I'm very proud of what we've achieved here.'

'So, what better way than to reward your staff with the casino night down in Port Elizabeth?' Sebastian offered.

'And free drink?' the site manager quizzed as he checked the report in front of him.

'Yes.'

'And accommodation?'

'Everything that is written on that sheet has already been authorised Mr Koarni,' Nolan promised. 'I'm here just to oversee any other requirements.'

'Like?' the site manager asked.

'Security is my forte,' Sebastian noted. 'However, this is a working mine after all, and even if operations shut down for twelve hours, you're still going to require certain machinery kept running and monitored as well as deliveries being able to drop off. That kind of thing.'

'Understood,' Koarni nodded. 'Here's the full itinerary for tonight, there's only a handful of machinery for you to oversee. You have to understand that until I found out about the other mines that I was somewhat...sceptical.'

'Harrison Templar knows how to throw a good party,' Nolan began. 'He also likes to reward staff who are excelling. This mine is no different from others he's done something similar to. If it's a success, then you get the gold star.'

'That's also a slight concern,' Koarni admitted. 'This mine isn't hugely profitable. I can't really understand why it's been chosen. My staff work damn hard, but previous owners have never even given them a festive day off, let alone a shift off duty to party.'

'Well,' Nolan smiled. 'That's Templar. Plus, he's not even an associate yet, let alone an owner. Your mine has clear potential, that's half the real reason for this generosity. The fact that your staff work hard and manage to create a profit when others are in decline should always be celebrated.'

'Noted,' Koarni mused as he thought over the other man's words. Takeover was always a possibility, but it was never something the staff took well.

'And the mine is what it is,' Nolan reassured him. 'If staff are worried about takeovers etcetera then just be honest, tell them that Templar has noticed them and wanted to include them in the festivities, just in case in the future they became his staff but he didn't then have the opportunity? Slight blurring of the truth, but it's in everyone's favour.'

'You have done this before, haven't you,' Koarni smiled wryly. 'Okay Hodges, you have a deal. I'll wait as last man and hand over the keys myself. I have a three-year-old suffering with night terrors at present, so I won't be drinking anyway. I'll still want some sleep though, so we say nine o'clock tomorrow re-opening for business?'

'Sounds like a plan,' Sebastian shook his hand. 'I'll await by the gate until you're ready and we'll go from there. There's a few larger bits of kit on here, but I'm familiar with those.'

'Thank you.'

Isobel entered her luxury suite and quickly took out a floorplan of the entire site. Harrison had taken over half the galaxy as usual and the hotel, conference suites, gardens and side rooms were now under his jurisdiction, as it were. However, she had one trick up sleeve. Ishyan had been here before.

From her bedroom window she faced the sea, as did all luxury suites. However, the presidential suite was different. It was on the top floor and entrance was via a passkey encoded lift. There was a fire escape, but this too was also key coded. Therefore, the suite had a full view of the whole of Port Elizabeth from its various windows.

From a security aspect all the windows were bullet proof, although Harrison seemed completely oblivious to his own safety most of the time whilst in public. She did wonder if it was all an act.

Isobel needed information, and within the presidential suite was the most likely source. It would be a secondary smart device, able to send texts rather than set up for social media. Without it she could not prove anything. With it?

Well, knowing whose side Templar was on was a start. Isobel was hesitant to think about much more than that at present. The authorities had yet to establish who had ordered Bessek to steal the *Jah Mahal* and try to fire an intercontinental rocket from its belly into Central Africa.

Could Templar really be involved, at any level? It was a wild jump, but if he was innocent then at least she could continue with their business partnership with only the usual level of mistrust. Her delving into her father's past had also come up with zero evidence so far, although she knew Ishyan had firmly put up a wall of silence to her regarding that matter.

Isobel knew that if she ever became endangered from not knowing then Ishyan would tell her, which only frustrated her more. She wished Myron were here, he would usually have something to say that would put her problems into context. Right now he'd probably suggest focusing on the next problem in hand, which at present was the archery contest. Isobel left the suite and headed back down to the reception area.

As she entered the lift Isobel contemplated that at least she did not say yes to go-karting. She wanted some secrets between Templar and herself, and her competitive nature would only unleash what she had been undertaking over the past six months. Myron knew, and had fully supported her. Harrison on the hand might see it as a threat.

'You're really missing me, aren't you?' Myron asked her as Isobel strode out onto the middle of the archery arena.

'This is your fault,' she muttered in her mind. 'You had to go and beat him. Now here I am in the middle of a hotel garden fantasizing that you're standing with me and getting ready for another pointless Templar competition.'

'You should have seen the shuffleboard game,' Myron noted. 'Templar likes being in control, but most of it he sets up in advance. Disrupt his train of thought, or his sneaky ways of contesting the game, and you'll win.'

Isobel shook away the daydream and thought intently about this. Was this already buried in her subconsciousness? When had she spoken to Myron about this? Or maybe someone else? Maybe she overheard it? She did not have time to worry about this now, so instead tried to view the world from Templar's viewpoint.

Magnet in the target? No, that would not assist just Templar, unless they were using a different target. So, to combat that she would simply recommend they use the same target. That was easy, if a bit of a remote possibility.

Special sunglasses? She knew Templar had already tried that with the shuffleboard game, so any issues there she would simple render them broken. Isobel would not do it subtly either. She wanted Templar to know if he was cheating, none of this gentleman bravado Myron had conjured up.

Wind assistance? Now she was pushing the boundaries of reality. However, there was one thing that Harrison liked more than anything else, and that was winning. This was where she was glad it was only archery. Isobel had no love for the sport, unlike the karts. Thanks to both Myron and Ishyan she was now competitive as any racing driver. Damn them both. But it was for a very good reason.

Isobel was also relieved for another reason altogether. Isobel had confided in Ishyan that she had wanted to be "in the running" for any space project, but knew of the commitment, intelligence and fitness levels required. It had been a million to one shot, but she thought it worth the chance.

Of course, Myron had found out literally five minutes later and had fully supported her regarding the training and exams. Together they had organised a strict regime over the following six weeks, to the point where Isobel had successfully passed most of the stringent exams and tests required for space flight.

Then the two men had dropped another bombshell onto her, just in case she had not been feeling the pressure already: dark matter.

They had "acquired" a small satellite that they wanted to build and test in space, out from the Earth's atmosphere. Neither men shared any of the reasoning behind this, and to be fair Isobel partially blamed herself for their secrecy. She was beginning to feel the strain of such training, and again knew that if they felt it would help, they would share the details.

Isobel had given up dropping hints to either of them but knew their fascination to be for the greater good. They both had no interest in keeping information to themselves, and maybe this was their mantra; to discover and share. Free information.

Would that set a new precedence within the world that she had been brought up? Definitely so. For all of the countries of the world to wake up one morning and have this information land in their laps at no cost would level the playing field as regards certain superpowers having control of energy, knowledge and therefore power and wealth. It was a dangerous game they were playing, hence why the satellite made sense.

It would be out of reach from most potential threats but there were still a few orbital satellites that could still destroy such a tiny vessel if required. Isobel switched her thoughts back to the present and the archery.

'Thank you, Myron,' she whispered. That had put this competition into context. It did not matter, but it could still prove useful for Isobel. How could she get Harrison to eat out of her hand? She still needed to gain entry to his suite later at some point, but how? Her mind raced as behind her she heard the commotion of guests starting to arrive.

Ishyan Stölles overlooked the rear of the hotel from his vantage point from around five hundred metres away. His hideout was simple enough, and as part of a series of rentable flats it was also guaranteed to give him the freedom of movement he so desperately required.

As for gaining entry to the hotel's network infrastructure, it looked as if the design had left him a few weaknesses in which to infiltrate. Ishyan linked up his laptop and tested the Wi-Fi strength. Isobel had already left the interconnecting device within a locker in the changing corridor outside the gym, and it seemed to work perfectly. Was there no place where humans couldn't exist without their smartphones being attached to them?

Ishyan chuckled as he looked at his. He was an exception surely? However, it did make a thought pop into his head. Disabling the network could have its advantages, but not here. Not now.

No, he needed to gain entry to the system as Ishyan had no doubt that Harrison Templar had set his suite up with a trip to counter anybody entering without permission. It would also send an alert to his phone, so the network needed to be compromised, but without anyone knowing.

Ishyan also needed Isobel to be clear and have an alibi; potentially with other guests involved. He looked down at the list, one in particular caught his eye. Luke Van Loggerenberg was a viable contender, for more than one reason. He was young, very good looking and the CEO for an artificial intelligence vehicular innovation company.

Isobel had encountered him a few times, and they seem to have got on quite well. Ishyan also could tell that Van Loggerenberg was clearly infatuated with the older Fortuna woman, and this obviously assisted their cause. Ishyan needed someone to stay exactly where needed for this to work.

Stölles picked up his high range binoculars and glanced over the hotel rear once again. There were the gardens, entrance to the casino as well as the raised terrace that led off from the restaurant, and above that all was the rear of Templars presidential suite.

The ivy that littered the fresh stonework had obviously been planted simply for effect, but this had obvious advantages. It had been bolted into place strategically around the guttering, so an easy place to climb. If required.

From this angle anybody at the party tonight would see a person climbing the ivy upward to the presidential suite, but there was another angle, one over by the casino leading off from the gardens. Due to adding a dry cover recently after the new build, which Ishyan could only guess would have been cursed by the architect, it then covered partial elements to both buildings. If Isobel could encroach around to this area, then nobody below could then see her.

Ishyan looked back at the floorplans and made some simple assumptions. Nothing had changed much since he was last here, although the thought of doing this for real, and with Isobel at the helm, left him somewhat torn.

It should be him that attempted this, but Isobel had instructed Ishyan to work from afar this time. Of course, he must arrive at the party just in time not to raise suspicion, but that was ok. If his tech in the apartment worked fine, then this would not be an issue.

Stölles put down the binoculars and made his way over to the apartment desk in order to start re-testing the mechanical arm that he would require to hold his binoculars later tonight. Without them he would be flying blind. He looked down at the sunglasses next to him. Well, if they were good enough for Templar, then they would be good enough for him.

The archery arena was simply a cordoned off part of the gardens, but with high hay bales at the far end, an obvious shooting stage as well as plentiful seating for the guests to view the spectacle.

Isobel wandered out and into the shooting arena and awaited further instruction from Harrison. The crowd was beginning to build now, and she knew that Templar would make a grand entrance at some point. She checked skyward just in case he should make a similar entrance here to another recent conference and arrive via parachute.

Hearing his voice from the foyer Isobel began the trek back toward him. Looked like today he was going for a land-based entrance, and hopefully not on that bike of his. Isobel swore at her jealousy. He didn't even have the guts to ride the thing at full speed, although at 400mph even Isobel had to concede that this was playing Russian roulette with a piece of metal sitting between your legs.

'Isobel!' Harrison greeted her in his usual overfriendly manner as he exited the grand rear steps of the hotel. He might as well have owned the company for the sheer amount of staff that seemed to follow him everywhere. 'Champagne?' he asked sweetly, with a grin that would embarrass a Cheshire cat.

'Don't mind if I do,' Isobel answered. 'That way if I lose, I can blame you,' she smiled.

'Oh, come on,' Harrison tested her. 'As if I'd stoop that low just to win an archery contest?'

'I do know something about the shuffleboard contest you had with Myron,' Isobel whispered.

'Touché,' Harrison admitted. 'That hurts Isobel. Just make sure the only blows are with your words rather than a stray arrow.'

'That would go down well in the papers wouldn't it,' she smiled. 'Fortuna rogue arrow spears billionaire business partner.'

'It would create a few talking points I admit,' Templar nodded as he drew her aside and toward the bow area. 'However, considering I'd be taking one for the team, and in such a painful manner, then maybe we'll skip on it this time.

I was thinking though,' he continued thoughtfully. 'We could play for something other than mere money or personal glory this afternoon?'

'What do you mean?' Isobel asked, suddenly concerned the way Harrison was speaking. Did he know? Did he even suspect Isobel was spying on him?

'Nothing too fretful, I assure you,' Templar spoke softly as he picked up one bow and passed it to her. 'More of an exchange of information.'

'What kind of information?' Isobel answered ruefully.

'Oh, just the kind that drops into our lap each day whilst, I don't know' Harrison muttered whilst waving his hands around in the air innocently, 'we rescue someone who it appears might have a military background, yet nobody informed the captain?'

'What do you mean?' Isobel faked her surprise, remarkably well as Templar was not ready for this response.

'Oh,' Harrison began, trying to shift his question to another angle. *Divide and conquer*, he thought.

Fake and thrust, Isobel considered. 'What do you know?' Isobel asked almost instantly. 'Myron went on the helicopter with her, is he ok?'

'I'm sure he is,' Harrison conceded quickly, his plan faltering at the first hurdle. *Damn it*, he swore internally. He could see Isobel physically reeling at his words.

'What do you know?' Isobel asked again, but this time with a clear sound of venom in her voice. Only she knew that she was acting, but somehow her emotions had become real at just the right time. Maybe it was hearing these words from another human, maybe it was that Harrison knew of something she thought was a sacred secret. Either way, she now had this man just where Isobel wanted him.

'Not much,' Templar replied finally, conceding defeat. 'I'm sorry Isobel, I misread the situation.'

'Yes,' she retorted with anger in her voice. 'You did. Now, unless you want to take an apple and stick it on your head and walk towards the bales of hay, then I suggest you allow me to return to my quarters and try to find out what the hell is going on with my boyfriend.'

'Of course, Miss Fortuna,' he heard himself say. As Harrison watched her leave, he knew he had fatally succumbed to a massive oversight on his part, and in the process had almost destroyed everything he had built up regarding their business relationship.

Templar picked up a bow and arrow and quickly set himself up with a target at the far end of the garden. He only had one thought as he fired the arrow and it connected firmly with the bullseye.

It is time, he thought.

Isobel closed the door behind her as she entered her luxury suite, the back of her watch passing on a Morse code message as the light tapping began moments after she had left the botanical gardens.

Ishyan had obviously seen everything and adding emotion to the proceedings might benefit them tonight. Yes, Isobel had now placed herself in

Templar's sights as a more than equal adversary, which in Harrison's world was almost a clear indication of a need to be eradicated.

However, emotion also breeds impatience and unpredictability. Both now lay as an advantage over Templar. He would either ignore or try too hard with Isobel at the gala that night. Either way she could use it to her advantage.

As Isobel entered the lounge area off from the bedroom there he was, sitting and tapping away at his laptop, a busy beaver with so much to do yet so little time left to do it.

'We on schedule?' Isobel asked Ishyan seriously.

'It'll work,' he replied honestly. 'There might be a last-minute switch of plan depending on where Templar is at the given opportunity, but we have some emergency measures just in case.'

'How much does my father know?' she asked sincerely.

'Nothing,' Ishyan replied, the partial betrayal obvious in his voice. 'But that's the way we play this.'

'And Myron?'

'Nothing, sorry,' Ishyan apologised. 'He's left everything which we could contact him with. I thought he boarded with the helicopter with his tracking watch, but it's not signalling a location yet.'

'He's wearing the watch,' Isobel smiled. 'A few days ago I wouldn't be able to promise you that, but after last night and this morning I can. He's wearing it. Just be ready when the tracker is initiated again, as he obviously doesn't need us...yet.'

'Understood,' Ishyan nodded. 'Right, I need to get out of here. Everything is ready. Just remember, once you enter his suite, I can delay the alarm, but we still need it looking slightly amateurish.'

'Is that a compliment?' Isobel asked.

'Yes,' Ishyan smiled. 'But leave our clue traceable, but not obvious. Just like we planned. And be quick.'

The Island

Ragged Island; Off the Coast of Maine, USA; Thursday afternoon

Anthony Draven picked up his luggage as the pilot called him over to the tiny four-seater plane. After stowing his suitcase away in the hold, Anthony followed the pilot around to the front and into the passenger seat.

'I don't usually let passengers ride up front, but any friend of Roc is a friend of mine,' Dusty, the pilot smiled. 'Haven't seen you before. From around these parts?'

'No,' Draven replied as pleasantly as possible. 'My work takes me everywhere.'

'Understood boss,' the pilot nodded and flicked a few switches to enable the propellers. 'Might be a bit bumpy today but it won't take long. Fifteen minutes max take off to landing.'

'Thank you,' Anthony added civilly. 'How well do you know this area?' he asked as the pilot trundled the plane to the end of the small runway.

'Lived here my whole life, man and boy,' Dusty admitted. 'Nothing much has changed this far up from the city, but that's just fine by me.'

'Are we then in a state of perpetual misinterpretation?' Anthony almost half-joked.

'No,' the pilot responded almost immediately. 'That bloody King bloke has been laying it on thick so much about Maine being the embodiment of evil that we've now had to stand up and fight against it.'

'Alright,' Draven replied. 'So, what do you think about the sanitarium on Ragged Island then?'

'I see where you're going with this,' the pilot smiled. 'Look, I know Roc quite well and there's no evil in Cove House. A few poor souls that have taken a wrong turn or two maybe, but that's it. I can see where Mr King got the inspiration from, but they're not on the island to segregate them from society because they're dangerous. Only to make them better.'

'Sorry,' Draven replied quickly. 'I didn't mean to offend, and I can see the instant link between a mental institution and making the jump to examining the state of the human mind, and what else is out there.'

'Ah, I don't take it personally,' the pilot continued. 'It's a lovely area and you just hear too many horror stories. If anything, the truth is very boring, nothing happens around here at all. But that's ok, if we need adventure we just head south to the big smoke.

Believe me, after a weekend in New York you'll be itching to get back to nature.'

'Ha ha,' Draven faked his laugh. 'Yes, I've been to a few big cities in my time. Not one have I wanted to stay in more than a few days. I guess humans are attracted to the lure of the thrill of the big city, but you're right, it becomes very tiring all too quickly.'

'Exactly,' the pilot nodded as the plane stopped turning at the far end of the runway. 'Just to warn you, the flight is short but the landing at the other end is a bit bumpy as Ragged Island only has a grass landing strip. Don't worry though, never had an issue there.'

'Glad to hear it,' Draven replied as the pilot began to increase the throttle and set the plane shooting down the runway. Anthony let the pilot concentrate on the job in hand, and once they were in the air took out the scanned letter that he had received after landing back on his home soil.

Dearest Anthony

My initial perception was true, you are indeed a man of huge potential yet to be realised by those who watch over us.

I have a few surprises for you. Firstly, I have noted your interest in Mr Patrick Symions and can confirm he'll be relocated shortly to Ragged Island, just off the Maine coastland. There is an 'institution' there that should assist with everything you require.

If I may be so bold, your current subjects seem to only offer small repayment for your efforts. I've found that an object falling from a greater height always makes more of an impact. To this end I have sent some recommendations from another colleague in your 'trade' that potentially offer more substantially handsome rewards. You will see that they have pulled themselves far from unfathomable depths. With just the right guidance they could 'fall' from an unbelievable height, and thus gaining you the biggest opportunity in your research.

Secondly, if you hadn't already managed to decipher my location, I am residing at the GSV – the global seed vault- in Svalbard, near Norway. Although it's pleasantly demilitarised there are certain zones here which are off-limits to all but the highest levels of security.

It is here that I am keeping my greatest treasure, and one which you will crave once you understand its power. It is called a 'Gatu Dojan' but please, don't use this name unless with trusted sources. It will draw deadly attention to yourself.

I have only touched the surface of what this device can achieve, the world will have to keeping waiting until it finally knows its secrets.

My work here is continually ongoing so look forward with anticipation to your visit. Until then, I have informed the doctor at Ragged Island to assist you in your quest, using any means necessary.

I hope this exceeds your expectations.

Yours sincerely

Doctor Arnold Harding

By the time Anthony had read the letter they were already gliding over the North Atlantic Ocean and toward Ragged Island. Draven noticed how there were multiple islands in the area, and also how wind and storm swept some of them looked. It was obviously an interesting life out here in the wilds.

Isobel finished getting ready for the gala and mentally went over the plan one more time. She needed an alibi; and she would have one in Luke Van Loggerenberg. There needed to be a quick, obscured route to Templar's apartment, and that had now been identified. Isobel required eyes on her at all times tonight, Ishyan had sorted that out by means of an automated system set up in an apartment overlooking the back of the hotel. She then needed herself, Ishyan and her father all to be visible at the "time" of the break in.

That was the tricky part. If Ishyan's delay to the Wi-Fi did not work, then she'd be caught red handed. If he managed to compromise the API that hung to ceiling inside the presidential suite, then all would be ok. It was only a delay she wanted. It would benefit it her more, rather to shut down the Wi-Fi altogether. She wanted the break in to seem quick, mysterious and ultimately poorly executed with no sign of theft.

That way Harrison would eventually realise it was a simple attempt at a burglary that didn't work, and therefore could be forgotten about. By then Isobel should have all she required.

Looking at her watch, she noticed that Ishyan should now have left his own apartment and be on his way to the gala. Isobel attempted some mental arithmetic and wondered where on the planet Myron now was. If he had decided to visit Kirill, then there alone was a strong enough reason why he had not contacted her yet. The other reason was also a possibility, but one that unnerved her.

They had always agreed on radio silence as a sign that something was not right. It might just be cautionary, but that would have been enough for either of them to remain silent. It could be as simple as Kirill's request to keep quiet until Myron returned to Isobel, but it might also be far worse.

Isobel picked up both her heeled shoes and put them on the bed next to her. She then put her feet into two inner liners that she'd use to climb the ivy infested wall outside of the hotel. They were extremely rugged and had been used before, in the indoor rock-climbing centre that they had also tested the space exoskeleton. They were also almost wafer thin, so remained hidden in her shoes.

She slipped on her heels then walked toward the suite's full-length mirror to ensure the inserts were not visible. They fitted perfectly, and for the price of the pair of inserts Isobel had to concede that she felt like she was walking on a million dollars.

Time to get the party started, Isobel thought.

The plane landed with a bump then an inertia shift as the pilot put on the brakes hard. The runway Anthony could easily see was as long as it was maintained. The far end, and the sea, approached them all too fast.

With a final rapid deceleration, the plane ground to a halt right opposite an old hut, which looked distinctively to Draven like an abandoned store.

'Last stop,' the pilot smiled to himself. 'Joking aside, you see the cove just ahead? That's Seal Cove, you want the next one along; Camp Cove. You can't miss the house, one track in, one track out. Give my regards to Roc.'

'Will do,' Draven responded as he took off his seatbelt and pulled free his luggage from the rear of the plane.

As he exited the plane a small jeep drove up the track towards them. A middle-aged woman was at the wheel, her features full of tension.

'Good luck.' The pilot whispered. 'Looks like Roc's sent you the battle horse to bring you in.'

Draven smiled as genuinely as he could muster as he approached the jeep. 'Anthony,' he remarked as the door opened and the woman stepped out of the vehicle.

'Angela,' the woman replied, shaking his hand strongly. 'Dusty get you here ok?'

'All very straightforward,' Draven remarked, thanking her. 'I take it we've got a rare few hours of calm between storms?'

'You could say that,' the woman replied, her tension slowly dissipating now. Anthony knew something had happened back at the institution but felt happy at this juncture only to skirt around the edges of the reason for his visit. 'Throw your luggage in the back,' she offered, opening the boot and taking out a holdall. She then wandered over to the pilot, leaving Anthony momentarily. Draven pushed his luggage inside, closed the rear of the vehicle then climbed inside.

There was one hell of a black cloud gathering on the horizon east of them. He was convinced he saw some lightening as well. Seconds later Angela was back in the driving seat and they headed the short distance back to Cove House.

Isobel Fortuna made her way to the conference suite for the gala opening, and it did not take long for her to catch sight of either her father or Ishyan. As for Harrison however, he no doubt was waiting to make the usual grand entrance once enough guests had turned up.

Taking a glass of pink champagne from the nearest waiter Isobel searched the room for her alibi. There was no immediate rush to re-establish her rapport with Luke, and the more coincidental their initial contact the better. Without engaging eye contact with him Isobel began a long wandering roam around the room, planning just when they would accidently bump into each other. If possible, just after Templar's grand speech, the less time she spent with Van Loggerenberg the better. She was not that good an actress after all.

As Isobel glided elegantly across the carpeted conference hall, she felt the rear of her tiny wristwatch inform her that the plan was ready to go. She'd never be ready, but something in her mind linked what they were doing to something far bigger, something that she had no intention of failing. Isobel decided to twist the problem on its head and instead attack it from another angle.

She was almost halfway across the gala floor toward Luke Van Loggerenberg before Harrison Templar made his dramatic entrance. The loudspeakers kicked into action, the main lights dropped, and the atmospheric effects kicked in around the hall. Isobel was glad the lights had dimmed, her response to Templar's entrances were now becoming tiresome but she dared let anyone onto her distaste for him. *Let him enjoy it*, she thought. At least Harrison's mind would be elsewhere.

'Ladies and gentlemen,' the tannoy system boomed as the two main doors swung open. It was Templar's voice; he would not even let anyone else do the introductions. Such vanity. 'Tonight, we witness the pinnacle of our dreams, the voyage into the heavens and the expedition of other worlds,' he began. Isobel viewed the 3D images that now littered the hall, impressed but unwilling to show it.

'We are now in a race,' Harrison continued. 'There is no dispute in the competition to light up the skies of innovation, and I am delighted to be in the cockpit alongside the Fortuna's in our conquest to be the first to colonise outer space.'

That was a bit of a statement, Isobel conceded. It was one thing offering space trips to the general public, but colonisation was another thing altogether. Both she and her father had also not seen anything concrete that would allow them to win this race either. The first look of the space transport was due to be revealed tomorrow morning, in Durban. Apart from that, if Templar had anything else up his sleeve then she wished he'd let them know as soon as possible. Then again, she could twist this in her favour...

'Tomorrow,' Harrison continued. 'You have all been invited to the grand unveiling of our Space Travel and Reconnaissance vessel, the *STaRship,* held at Durban airport, our home for this phase of the venture.'

That bit Isobel did know, hence why she had contacted various companies around Port Elizabeth, enquiring of restricted and completely confidential spaces where she could set up her space training camp.

There were three possible sites at present, with the open cast mine at Bethelsdorp on the outskirts of Port Elizabeth being the closest and with the most potential. The mine had multiple additional tunnels bored into the massive pit, and the site manager was also interested in her request. He had been looking to switch sites anyway, so with her investment could close one and move the short distance to another, all without any knowledge of to the general public, Templar or their joint competition of *FoSE*.

'And,' Templar let the word hang in the air for a few seconds. 'The potential of creating the ultimate space launching sites within the cradle of South Africa is no pipedream, but I need your support, we all need your support.'

The clapping erupted from all around Isobel, and she joined in, catching Harrison's eye as the main ceiling lights grew back to full intensity.

Anthony Draven's first impression of Cove House was not that of a modern asylum, but of the more traditional 19th Century style institutions. It reminded him of a typical English country house, not quite a mansion, but one that exuded history and family values.

Out across the ocean a storm was definitely brewing, the dark clouds ominous and the winds themselves beginning to grow in ferocity. Draven climbed from the jeep and did not wait for Angela, instead heading for the main entrance quickly. He noted the lone figure at the top of the white wooden steps, surveying not only the visitor but also the encroaching storm.

'Mr Draven, I presume,' Roc smiled, his enthusiasm for his guest obvious despite the conditions outside. 'Come, we have much to talk about.'

Anthony climbed the steps and accepted the offer, Roc helping him with his luggage as they entered the old house. Draven correctly assumed that Angela and Roc rarely saw eye to eye, they seemed like two ill-fated newlyweds in a badly arranged marriage.

Draven noticed how Roc seemed to be completely comfortable with his role, whatever it was, at this institution. Angela he could only guess either hated working here, knew too much or simply didn't have the say in trying to control matters for herself. Anthony had seen this time and time before. The solution for him was simple. Gain control and act; by whatever means.

Roc intrigued Draven. So did Doctor Harding. Neither were conventional doctors, but both promised so much more than anything Anthony had managed to gain from other quests.

The fact that Patrick Symions was in this facility should have been the crowning glory for him, but Harding's promises eluded to something much more potent. What was this Gatu Dojan that he spoke of? How did the Global Seed Vault fall into Harding's plans?

Draven knew of some of the dark secrets that had almost destroyed the Fortuna family only months before, but none of this drew in comparison to what

Harding had promised. Anthony would bide his time, get to know Roc, to understand all he knew, and just how Draven fitted into their plans. Anthony knew he had potential, but it was raw and without the proper funding and resources up until now. Even Harding had noticed that. That was why he was here now on Ragged Island, and later tonight, hopefully the next stage of his journey would begin.

'I'll show you to your room,' Roc broke Draven from his concentration. 'It's upstairs. We like to keep the ground floor for general use – lounge, dining room, study. You might have noticed an extension on your arrival, we've actually managed to house the kitchen and utilities there, out of the way of the clients.'

'Do they have free roam of the facilities?' Anthony asked carefully.

'Yes,' Roc confirmed. 'But there are set hours. They're currently all in the lounge at present, it's a weekly promise of a film if everyone is well-behaved.'

'And if they're not so well-behaved?'

Roc gave him a look which instantly told Draven all he needed to know. So, this was why there was a gulf between Angela and Roc. Anthony quickly understood Roc's attitude. However, he still wanted to know more, so decided to play the waiting game until he picked a side. Angela could still have a use after all.

Anthony followed Roc upstairs and to one of the rooms at the far end of one of the corridors.

'Your room is probably the safest of them all,' Roc noted. 'Furthest away from the rabble, multi-locks on doors and windows, and if all else fails I'm sleeping next door. We haven't had trouble here for months so I'm not expecting anything now. The only case we're keeping an eye on is Patrick, your man, but even he's currently in remission. According to your colleague Suzannah's calculations, we're not expecting another episode until this time next week.'

'Really?' Draven replied with remorse. 'I was hoping to spend some time with him, with the "real" him.'

'Don't let that bother you,' Roc told him as he urged Draven to leave his luggage and follow him. 'We have much to discuss, and with your current timetable not much time to do it in.'

'I agree,' Draven muttered. 'How much of Harding's work are you familiar with?'

'That can wait,' Roc simply smiled as Angela approached from along the corridor. Draven took the hint.

'Do you want to observe the bedtime routine?' she asked solemnly. Anthony nodded graciously.

Isobel flittered through the hustle of the gala hall and waved at Luke as he turned her way. His smile told her all she needed to know, and as soon as they greeted Isobel relayed his last comment to her as if it had only been yesterday.

'I thought you might have forgotten?' Luke offered as she ushered him to the bar.

'Never,' Isobel smiled pleasantly as she ordered two drinks, Luke's preferred beverage from memory. She had learnt early in her business days that ensuring a customer felt wanted and remembered was almost as important as talking about the actual business in hand.

'Ah,' Luke smiled as she passed him his drink. 'No, you don't forget a thing, do you? Thank you,

Isobel. I'm sorry, I forget just how busy you are and just how many plates you spin at once.'

'I do have assistance in catching them,' she joked, noting her father and Ishyan who stood at different parts of the room.

'Guess you do,' Luke nodded. 'I can't see Myron here, is he around?' the young man parried with a line that he intended to throw Isobel slightly off balance.

'No,' Isobel's smile waned a little, intentionally. 'Like your own private life Luke, not everything works out so smoothly all of the time.'

The words cut right through Luke's smile and he took a few seconds to recapture his vigour.

'Yes,' he nodded, understanding just how foolish he'd been to mention Myron at all. That was an amateur mistake and Isobel had rightly put him in his place, although the fact that Isobel knew about his relationship at all did make him feel partially better. At least he wasn't invisible.

'But let's forget about our troubles for tonight, will we?' Isobel began, taking a sip of her pink champagne. 'I didn't want to seem rude about speaking to you about the new style Ekranoplan you proposed, but as you know there is a time and place for everything. Would you be happy discussing it tonight? With all the talk about space I think a lot of clients are dreaming up the impossible before we even fully commercialise the likely.'

'Of course,' Luke noted. 'I actually like to call them GEV's rather than the traditional Russian word, but it's the same notion. Basically, we utilise a level surface to keep a winged transport in the air by maximising the ground effect produced the aerodynamic interaction between the wings and the surface. The Russian's originally used the Caspian Sea, but you could use ice or plains to utilise this method of transport.'

'And where in the world would you commercialise this?' Isobel asked, her curiosity tingled.

'Well,' Luke stammered. 'We've done some research, some of it in collaboration with NASA, and there are studies to show that passenger travel could lead to cheaper, increased accessibility and less polluted options.'

'Yes Luke,' Isobel winked. 'I'm not that rude I haven't done my research. I meant where in the world would you commence such a project first to maximise its potential?'

'Oh,' Luke replied, his eagerness to please obvious even if his details to hand were not.

'Come on,' Isobel told him. 'Let's grab some air. You look like you're getting flustered and that's not my intention at all.'

She led the younger man over to the opened glazed windows that led to the balcony area. *Well*, Isobel thought. *That's part one completed, now the really tricky part.*

Once the patients had all been put into their rooms, Roc illustrated to Draven just how they monitored the rooms at night.

'Individual sensors are placed at the entrance of each room, and then along the hallways and door wells,' he explained. 'Through the day we deactivate the system, but once night falls, we cannot risk any of the patients finding their way outdoors.'

'Especially on a night like this,' Draven nodded as a huge crack of thunder ripped through the night.

The sound didn't reverberate as much as Anthony had initially thought, and as he looked at the windowsill realised just how protected the building was to the extremities.

'We soundproofed Cove House as much as humanly possible,' Roc muttered. 'It helps the patients feel safe in more ways than one. We're under strict guidelines regarding how we look after our patients, but there are some loopholes we can implement if a particular case presents itself.'

'You mean Symions?' Draven asked.

'Yes,' the other man smiled. 'Harding sent me the files. I must admit that all the cases piqued my interest in different ways. However, I can see why the Symion's file was your favourite.'

'I'm not Doctor Harding has the same view,' Draven sighed intentionally. Anthony was unsure of the relationship between the two doctors, but he'd find out by the end of tonight.

'Maybe not,' Roc noted. 'However, the good Doctor Harding has a number of projects under his wing and I get the impression sometimes the rare gems that are presented to him are missed. Symion's might not be the ultimate case file for you Anthony, but that doesn't mean we can't learn a lot from him.'

'I agree.'

'Consider the sheer cyclic pattern of his demise into insanity, then almost recovers at a drop of a hat,' Roc noted. 'As for the twins file, I take it that you managed to locate the bank robbery cash?'

'Maybe,' Draven remarked, looking the other man deep into the eyes. 'As with anything I come across, if there's potential I'll rinse it for all it's worth.'

'That sounds like a good motto to have,' Roc noted. 'Come, we can't stand around all night. The fire will be ablaze downstairs and I need a drink.'

The two men wandered down the grand staircase and into the drawing room, which now had a roaring fire. During the day it was kept merely as an ornamental mantlepiece for obvious reasons. Fire was not always the most pleasant of friends for the inmates.

'Here,' Roc offered as he poured two measures of bourbon and sat down opposite Draven, handing him the glass as they sat. 'Now, tell me about yourself, the unofficial version of course.'

'Right,' Anthony replied. He had been preparing for such a time of course, but now it had come he'd been taken slightly aback at the requestor of this information. He had expected a military contact to be the originator of the question, not a doctor on a remote island in the North Atlantic Ocean.

'I'm not as you envisaged, am I?' Roc smiled. 'Don't let the pretence here fool you, although there is no basement of patients...here.'

Draven's eyes lifted hearing the manner of this statement.

'I'm searching,' Anthony offered.

'Aren't we all my friend?' Roc answered almost immediately. 'The question is for what? Money, glory, power? Knowledge?'

'The ultimate question,' Draven almost stammered. He had never told anybody his greatest desire, yet alone a stranger on a strange island.

'Ah,' Roc grinned. 'I once thought Harding would be able to solve that one for me.'

'You mean Doct...' Draven started, wanting to seem polite.

'I call him the "good doctor" when I require it,' Roc replied, his grin fading. 'Anthony, some men are given the opportunity to change the course of history, even to rewrite it, if there is such a thing.

However, once you're given that moment you do not let it pass. You do not hide behind political gains or military worship.'

'I'm sorry,' Anthony apologised. 'I meant no disrespect.'

'No,' Roc replied venomously. 'And neither have you insulted me. But there are men who falter when fate gives them the golden chance of victory. That is the reason for my frustration Anthony.

Harding has mentioned a bioweapon to you, I believe,' Roc quietened himself.

'The Gatu Dojan,' Anthony nodded, remembering the letter.

'Yes,' Roc nodded. 'In it's simplest form it could be described as a bioweapon, but testing was never fully exercised to reveal it's true potential.'

'Which is?' Draven asked, leaning forward in his chair. The conversation was leading to a place that neither men feared, but obviously others did not dare to tread.

'Pyramidian,' Roc noted. 'The answers were there all along.'

The slight warm wind blew Isobel's hair across her face as they walked onto the balcony. There were plenty of guests already outside, no doubt getting some air before Harrison's next bout of festivities.

'Oh,' Isobel sighed as she neared the veranda. 'Look Luke, I need the little girl's room, do you mind holding my purse until I return? I do trust you,' she winked.

'Um, of course,' Luke nodded as he was almost struck into silence by the request. Isobel almost hated herself for tricking him, but this was business. She headed off toward the toilets knowing full well she could cut back to the hotel wall on her travels and keep out of sight.

As she reached the sanctuary of the canopy, she pulled off her shoes and tucked her dress into her thigh length shorts she wore underneath. Twisting the heel clear of one shoe she retracted an earpiece and from the other a tiny camera. There was also a small piece of paper in one of the heels which she pocketed for now.

It was now or never.

Ishyan Stölles knew wearing dark sunglasses within the gala would raise attention to himself, so decided to counter this by also wearing the full security attire usually reserved for night club bouncers. The black suit, white shirt and black-tie combination, along with an intentionally noticeable earpiece, all helped to take away the attention from his sunglasses.

From where he was standing, he could see all the guests in the gala hall, the darkness on the outside of his glasses almost translucent from within. What there was however, was a thin film of digital overlay on the inside which allowed him to also view Isobel's real-time location on the outside of the building climbing towards Harrison templar's suite.

Back in Stölles' rented apartment, both the mechanical arm and attached camera were now filming her progress, inch by inch, as she climbed up the ivy walls. Ishyan also had a simple device in his pocket to send any Morse code to Miss Fortuna at a moment's notice. In theory he could also speak, but that might draw attention to himself, and to Isobel.

Ishyan pressed a switch on his phone and the camera on the mechanical arm switched views from Isobel back to Luke Van Loggerenberg's position on the veranda. So far, so good. However, as with anything, it would only take a momentary slip or for an unknown element to occur and all hell would break loose.

He hoped that Isobel was having things her own way whilst climbing the walls.

Isobel Fortuna discovered quite early in her climb that the ivy was no match for her weight, even though she was the trimmest she had been for years. However, as Ishyan had promised, beneath the ivy were metal rings designed to thread either plastic or wire coils for holding the vegetation. This did work.

The evening was now dark enough to hide her movements, although from her vantage point she could hear both the music and din of chatter from below. Somewhere behind her Ishyan's camera was keeping an eye on both her and Templar, just in case he wizened onto her plan. For now though, she was safe.

Halfway up the climb Isobel checked both the route up as well as the surroundings around her. She was almost to the Presidential suite veranda, where it would become infinitely trickier. However, on she climbed.

At the top Isobel vaulted the stone railing and walked briskly over to the rear patio doors. They would be locked, but she had the technology to override the digital access point. That was not an issue. What was inside however was. If Templar had even located any additional kit in the room, then she would not know until it was too late.

Ishyan had been scanning the room now since arrival and was happy that apart from the usual hotel security, nothing else had been added. Stölles had also reasoned that to calibrate such kit would take ages, and that was one thing Templar did not seem to spend time doing. He was visible most of the time he had been in the hotel.

Which made Isobel think that maybe Harrison had simply relied on the suite's safe instead, which meant Templar had fallen into her trap. Raising her watch up to the access point, she deactivated the patio door and quickly slipped inside.

There was someone waiting for her.

Harrison Templar strode across the gala floor, champagne in hand, playing the role of host as only he knew how to. With an overabundance of charm, wit and flair. The evening was going very well, the only chink in his armour was the unsavoury incident he had suffered with Miss Fortuna earlier that day.

We all make mistakes, he thought. He'd be a fool though not to try and rectify them. Harrison caught sight of Alessendro with a couple of old business acquaintances but could not see his daughter. Where was she?

Templar made his way toward the bar area and then decided to take a quick walk onto the veranda.

'What are you doing here?' Isobel asked within her mind.

'I could ask you the same question,' Myron replied. 'This isn't your suite?'

'Yes, thanks Sherlock,' Fortuna responded, somewhat venomously.

'Don't have a go at me,' Myron offered. 'I'm not the one breaking and entering.'

'Leave me be,' she said hastily before heading over to the safe, situated within the wardrobe.

'That was a quick survey of the suite,' Myron noted. 'Happy you haven't tripped any wires or there aren't any cameras in here?'

'Leave it.'

'What are you trying to achieve here Iz?' she heard the voice again. Finally, she succumbed to reason.

'Damn you Myron. Damn you and your morality.'

'Actually,' Myron responded from behind her. 'I'm here to stop you getting caught.'

'What?'

'Come on Iz,' Myron told her. 'You know Templar's untrustworthy, yet you still want to break into his safe. Why? What do you think you'll find?'

'I'm not sure.'

'Whatever he keeps in that safe will still be nigh impossible to break into,' Myron reasoned. 'Harrison won't trust any safe unless it's his own. He doesn't trust anyone.'

'But at least I'll know,' Isobel told him, before opening the wardrobe doors and commencing unlocking the safe.

'This isn't right babe,' Myron continued. 'And you know it.'

Isobel ignored him and continued to hold her watch up to the safe's digital mechanism. The device worked almost instantly.

'Last chance,' Myron spoke softly.

Isobel opened the safe's door and looked inside. There was only one item within, a smartphone.

'You lose,' Myron noted. 'You have no password, it'll also be linked to a physical security-key, probably his other phone…'

'Yes, I got that,' Isobel sighed.

'Just don't touch it. You might trigger a sensor.'

'I won't,' she continued. 'Do you think it's rigged for movement?'

'Let's hope that's all it's rigged for,' Myron told her, his voice obviously annoyed. 'Now you need to get out of here fast and don't get caught. He mustn't ever know you're on to him.'

'Guess you're disappointed in me,' Isobel refused to even turn. She knew there was nothing to see, but Isobel still felt like she had been told off. Who was she kidding? It had been a ridiculous idea in the first place. Why had Ishyan allowed her to do it?

Because she had told him, that's why. He had told her not to, but Isobel had been too pig-headed again. Isobel locked the safe back up and turned. What she saw almost made her laugh. Myron sat on the edge of Templar's bed, tuning his guitar.

'Am I suffering from hallucinations from that gem as well?' Isobel asked. 'You seem to be getting ready to serenade me?'

'Remember Paris?' Myron offered. 'We wrote that song...'

'Not now Myron,' she replied with emotion in her voice.

'You seem to have forgotten yourself, Iz,' he noted, gently picking at the strings to check his fine tuning.

'Not now,' Isobel said again, her emotions swirling. 'Please.'

Myron ignored her and began playing the song they had jointly written that night in Paris, using a guitar that was just a simple accessory in the suite. It was a simple enough tune, but both had opened their hearts that night, seemingly for both of them like never before.

Myron ran his fingers up and down the strings, simply switching from a G-major chord to an open set of strings, before switching to D-major then to C-major. However, the picking seemed to work. It seemed to exude life from every note.

The tune was slow and melodical, and pulled on every one of Isobel's heartstrings, not simply because of the pace and tune, but because she knew how much the words meant to her. They were simply part of her life, and everything she wanted to be. Damn him.

Isobel watched on, not needing Myron to sing a single word, the song was already in her head, along with the orchestra that they both had noted would add depth and emotion to the piece. Maybe one day they would record it, but for now Isobel preferred it to be their little secret, as it gave her strength in even her darkest moments, as it did now.

Isobel sat next to him and listened to the chorus, bridge and Myron's attempt at an acoustic solo, which in her mind worked for once. The song was the more beautiful than she ever remembered, and as the final chorus rang out, she felt the words rise to her lips.

Although Myron kept playing his eyes drifted to hers as she sang, the weight of the world disappearing instantly. His Isobel had returned. All too soon the song ended, and Isobel only wanted to embrace him. But she had precious time to waste and had to return to the reality…

Isobel blinked in astonishment, realising instantly she had not even ventured into the apartment. It had all been within her own mind. She had not even touched the patio door or even tried to unlock it. As for leaving any clue, Isobel decided that Myron had been right. Leave this place and the darkness surrounding it. She had to trust in herself and everything she wished to be.

Isobel sighed heavily as the truth hit her square on. So, she had not escaped whatever had infected Myron after all. Their time together had been intimate, and she did not regret that. Part of her was glad of this truth, as she now knew the struggles that he faced each day, and why he had become so distant. The other part of her however was angry, as this virus was clearly manmade, and she would not stop until she helped uncover the truth.

She smiled, thinking of Myron's face again. There it was, three months of knowing him and she had finally set her own moral boundaries, even if her subconscious had helped her define them. She had known deep down that this was not the right call after all but needed her guardian angel to point it out to her.

Miss Fortuna quickly headed back to the ivy climbing wall when she felt her watch relay a message from Ishyan. Just as a huge weight lifted from her shoulders, another thunderbolt come into play. Time was no longer on her side.

She had to get back down below.

Harrison Templar approached Luke Van Loggerenberg, whom looked slightly out of place holding a lady's purse.

'Mr Loggerenberg,' Templar commenced in his usual over-the-top manner. 'I see you've managed to lose your date?'

'It's Miss Fortuna's,' Luke replied, embarrassed.

'Oh right,' Harrison's interest increased.

'She's just popped to the toilet,' Loggerenberg continued. 'Really enjoyed your presentation.'

'You wait until tomorrow my lad,' Harrison noted. 'The unveiling is going to be spectacular.'

'Oh, I wouldn't miss it for the world,' Luke smiled. 'Mr Stölles?' the young man offered as Ishyan now entered onto the balcony. 'Bit dark isn't it for sunglasses?'

'Military grade,' Ishyan replied deadpan, not caring if he fooled anybody. Right now, he was key to giving Isobel enough time to re-enter the fray without suspicion. If he had to look like an idiot, then so be it.

'Give them here,' Harrison grabbed the glasses off the bodyguard's face. Templar then placed them over his own eyes. 'So, Mr Stölles, your dirty little secret is out.'

'Sorry sir,' Ishyan sighed, faking his apology. 'I love the Kings. I should have guessed I couldn't pull the wool over your eyes with trying to keep one eye on a rugby game.'

'You're a card,' Harrison laughed, impressed with the gadget. He looked at the inner screen from multiple angles. 'I'd already created such glasses to assist my Shuffleboard game but you only go and customise them for every bored man around the world. Genius. You're in the wrong game.'

'Yes sir,' Ishyan smiled. *No, I'm not*, he thought.

'So, where is...ah, here she is,' Templar almost rejoiced as he gave the sunglasses back to Ishyan. 'My dear Isobel. I come bringing gifts of a thousand apologies after today's misunderstanding.'

'That's okay Harrison,' Isobel smiled. 'As long as we understand each other.'

'Oh, most definitely,' Templar nodded. 'May I ask why the interest in Loggerenberg?'

The comment made poor Luke almost glow in the evening moonlight, but Isobel countered just as quickly. She of all people realised potential when she saw it, even if the young man was barking way up the wrong tree. His environmental objectives however were inspirational, and Isobel understood only too well that his younger generation of followers would assist the space program in areas they had yet to comprehend.

'Luke's done quite a job of commercialising his GEV project,' she smiled. 'But he now has a prototype for a potential moon project. Very ambitious but ultimately a ground breaker. Imagine the far side of the moon, crater filled and facing out into the void. What more could any hotel chain want but to have the potential to move around the Earth side, either following the sunlight or simply obtaining the best views, all by anti-gravity.'

'No,' Harrison tried to argue. 'You cannot have mastered such a feat surely? I would have heard about it.'

'Oh, dear Harrison,' Isobel sighed. 'Lost your touch? Maybe you shouldn't have embarrassed him about holding my bag? A woman scorned is one thing, a potential business partner humiliated...'

'Ah, you heard that?' It was Templar's turn to be ashamed.

'The toilets are just around the corner,' Fortuna noted. 'The queue is quite long, way out into the night. You get the gist...'

'I do,' Harrison nodded, completely obvious to the fact that Isobel had heard the conversation through the microphone concealed in her purse.

'Apologies Mr Loggerenberg,' Harrison shook the other man's hand. 'I can see that we'll be doing quite a bit of business soon, if you forgive my obvious impudence?'

'Of course, sir,' Luke nodded. He was bright enough to know when Isobel had planted a gift right into his lap.

'Catch up with you all soon,' Templar nodded, then left to talk to other guests.

'Thank you, Miss Fortuna,' Luke offered as soon as the billionaire was out of view.

'It's nothing,' she smiled back, as Ishyan folded his sunglasses and placed them in his inner jacket pocket. 'I know anti-gravity is a pipe dream but keep working on the GEV project for now and you never know, maybe we'll be able to get something working up on that big ball of stone up there.'

Ishyan looked upwards and new that the "big ball of stone" was the least of their problems right now. Stölles had his feet firmly on the ground, even if all around him were more interested in delusions of grandeur.

St Petersburg: Russia

Myron landed at Pulkovo airport and into a flurry of heavy snow. To make it worse the plane had to halt at the edge of the runway, so all the passengers had to trundle off the boarding steps and into a waiting shuttle bus to get back to the terminal. It was absolutely freezing.

The British civilian made his way through the terminal to the security zone and offered his fake passport and boarding tickets one more time. By now Myron was used to the security procedures, looks and chats between staff whenever he roamed anywhere in the world. At least Myron had the safety net of Larissa expecting him, which in this instance he knew would be enough. She wouldn't have asked for him otherwise.

Myron tried not to think too much about Kirill as the last thing he wanted to do was to seem emotional at border control. So instead he thought back to the environment outside, and the cold. It half worked.

As he was waved through Myron strolled with his hand luggage through the remainder of the airport toward the main entrance. He wondered if there would be a waiting party for him but decided to head straight for the taxi zone anyway. He had the address in his pocket, so it would be easy enough to simply get into the nearest awaiting cab and drive off into the snow flurry. Myron knew though it ultimately would not be that simple.

Inspector Reed had a more than a mild annoyance regarding Leon Chamel, so Myron did hesitate and wonder just what the *Chameleon* had done in Russia in the past that might cause him a few issues this visit. The reality however was simple enough; Myron had to risk all to gain all, and at present Kirill's life was at stake.

If his friends back in South Africa had been successful, the antidote would have already been delivered to Larissa which inevitably meant there would have been no reason for Myron to travel also. However, that was not his style, and there was no guarantee that the antidote would work. Therefore, Myron had agreed with Ashton that his visit was a necessary evil, but hopefully one that would breed the best result for Kirill. He knew that Mehrtens was also awaiting his call once Myron arrived at the hospital, just in case.

The British man noticed the man and woman who were potentially tailing him almost immediately, but there was something about their stance that confused him momentarily. Then it dawned on him; they were here to ensure he made it to Kirill.

That brought another more serious to the front of his mind; if that was the case, then who else might be here who might try and stop Myron?

Without trying to rush through the rest of the terminal, he looked at his watch and glided almost impatiently through the other airport visitors. *Pretend you're on business, pretend you're late and all will be fine*. There was not a day anywhere in any transport environment where someone wasn't late for a meeting and being incredibly impatient about it.

As the travellers in front of him approached the main entrances huge automatic doors opened and a chilly blast of air blew into the terminal. Myron was glad Ashton had lent him his spray jacket, but the cold still hurt his eyeballs and mouth. How did anybody manage to live here?

The taxi rank was already becoming congested, but Myron had no other choice. The two followers had also remained inside the terminal, for now at least. Myron began checking the queue and the remaining taxis as he understood just how easy it would be to pay off a driver, or even replace one, and kidnap him as they left the airport.

For what purpose though Myron could not fathom and knew here he had failed once again in his precautionary plans. He had yet to learn from Isobel's business mind and was now feeling like an amateur.

As the queue shortened, the group of four in front of him all took the same taxi, leaving the next for him alone. Myron took it and sat himself in the back of the vehicle along with his luggage. The driver turned around and smiled, waiting for Myron to offer a destination.

Play it safe, he heard Isobel's words, as if she was sitting next to him.

'Primorsky please,' Myron smiled. He sighed internally as the words rattled out of his mouth. The district was about ten miles from the airport but it was linked by a decent transport network. There, she'd saved him again.

If the driver had been sent to expect him, the answer of a different location than the one Kirill was located didn't show.

'English?' the driver asked. 'You pick good time for visit. Much snow expected over next few days.'

'Yes, I've noticed,' Myron nodded. 'It's absolutely freezing. How do you cope?'

'Cope?' the driver replied, confused.

Myron thought of a more suitable word. 'I mean, does the cold ever bother you?'

'This is not cold,' the driver stated emphatically. 'Look, car it runs! We can see road and your plane stopped on runway. Not cold,' he shrugged and drove the car away from the curb.

'Right,' Myron apologised.

'Now,' the driver stated. 'My brother is a deep-sea fisherman off coast of Murmansk, now that cold. Cold seas. Cold wind. Cold crab. Cold.'

'When you say it like that, this does seem a paradise in comparison.'

'Exactly,' the driver laughed before switching up the volume of his radio. 'Ah, Zenit, come on!' he shouted at the contraption before returning his concentration to the road. 'Champion's League tonight against the PSG, we need win or we out.'

Myron only half caught the general progress of the game but hoped for the sake of the driving that Zenit kept the game as mundane as humanly possible.

The trip to Primorsky was uneventful as could be expected, considering the Zenit goalkeeper had been sent off after the sixty-fifth minute and replaced with a defender. By what Myron could fathom the replacement goalkeeper had injured himself in the warmup, although he wondered just what kind of preparation for a football game would render your next available player completely side-lined. He thought best not to comment, and the driver seemed quite good at delivering both sides of the conversation anyway, so Myron just sat back and enjoyed the trip as much as humanly possible given the circumstances.

Once they arrived in the north-western district of St Petersburg, which itself was a heavy dockland area, Myron decided it was time to get in touch with Larissa. The call did not take long, although he still had another fifteen miles to travel.

Myron looked out across the dockland bay and out at the Gulf of Finland. He could just about see the faint outline of Kotlin Island, where Kirill was being looked after at Morskoy hospital. He sighed at the thought of how long it had taken him to get to this location, and just how upset Larissa had been.

The snow started to settle on his shoulders and Myron knew he did not have a choice but to continue his journey, even if it meant the heartache of finding his friend in a terrible condition. He owed it to Kirill and wanted to help Larissa. Myron just did not know if he was ultimately able to do either.

About five minutes had passed since the taxi and left him, so he flagged the next passing cab. He noted the new destination and sat back and rolled over every potential outcome in his mind, including the worst possible scenario of them all.

In all of this his thoughts kept returning to one individual, whom Myron had never felt such hatred before; the mysterious man of Johannesburg.

He had no idea how he was going to find this madman, let alone do the impossible and kill him.

Myron knew he did not have it in to plan somebody else's murder, which was a trait he was simply glad he had. He respected Ishyan almost more than any other man he had ever met, but where his friend could take a life Myron knew he could not.

He knew that blood was indeed on his hands for the Fortuna affair, but it had all been in self-defence, or to rescue Isobel. To plan another's death was something different entirely, although Myron sensed that one day their paths would inevitably cross where he would have to make the simple yet highly emotive decision in a split second. It was also likely it would be this lunatic or Myron.

For now, this enigma would remain at large, and Myron would try and keep under the radar. In the meantime, he would not dare risk contacting Isobel, as he knew only too well that his movements and actions would ultimately find their way back to her eventually. That would do, for now.

The taxi crossed the bridge from Gorskaya to the island and Myron knew they were only minutes away. He just hoped he could help. He thought back to his own condition. Meredith had seemed positive about the effects of the gem, to the point that they could even be controlled. Myron had preferred they could be eradicated completely, but the control of such a release of chemicals into his body could prove as illustrious as Templar's exo-skeleton armour. Maybe it was the best decision he had made this week to pass the suitcase over to DT, as Andrews might well need it before her journey was done.

As the hospital crept into view Myron wondered about all the people he had crossed paths with in the last year, and how disastrous this had proved for many. Hopefully tonight it would be a positive outcome.

Myron thanked the driver and headed up the stone steps into the hospital. The bright lights made him involuntarily close his eyes as he ventured indoors and towards the reception area.

Asking for Kirill the receptionist pointed him in the direction of the nearest corridor. Myron half wondered about how deserted the hospital was, and it took him a good dozen steps before the reality dawned on him. By the time he had fully come to a halt, the stranger to this land had noticed others behind him. Daring to turn around he saw the two figures from the airport. So, he hadn't fooled them, but hopefully he might have tricked anybody else who had tried to keep tabs on him.

Myron noticed how they stayed at the reception area, so he turned and continued alone. The room he had been shown to was only a few more down the corridor, although as he approached something else seemed odd. There were no doctors or nurses either, let alone patients.

He approached the room and simply entered, not even trying to look through the blinds first. Whatever was on the other side he would know sooner or later. The two figures behind him would not let him leave until that was settled, that was for sure.

Myron entered the room and was met with two warm, friendly and ultimately recognisable faces.

'Kirill?' he stuttered.

'I'm sorry my friend,' the older bearded man responded. Larissa stood next to him, her features also expressing the regret of their actions.

'What happened?' Myron asked, knowing he was in for a tale. 'You both had me worried sick.'

'Me too,' Larissa noted eagerly. 'For a short while at least.'

'A very short while,' Kirill turned to her. 'It was about five minutes.'

'It was a lot longer than five minutes babe,' Larissa retorted. 'You were lying on the floor in the kitchen!'

'Ten then?' came the reply.

'Guys?' Myron asked. 'I take it that you needed me here, otherwise you would have got your two friends to turn me right around at the airport?'

'You can say that,' Kirill nodded. 'The gem had an effect on me old friend, but not same as you I expect.'

'What do you mean?' the foreigner to this land questioned.

'It awoke something in my husband that I never knew existed,' Larissa offered. 'That's what scared me so much, and what I kept thinking when I spoke to you on the phone. I could never have fooled you otherwise. We needed you and only you here. Sorry there was only this way.'

'That is true,' Kirill added. 'Although I must quickly add here, it took me as a surprise as well.'

'What do you mean?'

'Pyramidian,' Kirill whispered. 'It is a place from your deepest nightmares and a place someone burned from my memory, until Tuesday evening.'

'It's an old abandoned mining town in the southern half of Svalbard, just east of the global Seed Vault,' Roc explained.

'Yes,' Draven mused. 'I think I remember reading about it in an old journal, although they only mentioned the reason for the abandonment to be the severe weather and the lack of profitable mining.'

'Fairly plausible story,' Roc noted. 'Happens all around the world. The problem here was that once the mine closed down it became a hotbed for Soviet activity. The location was fairly handy, plus the general environment wasn't pleasant.

Details are a bit patchy to say the least,' Roc admitted. 'But if you search deep enough, and when I say deep, I mean into Russian FSB agency territory, then you'll come up with a few answers that will point you in the right direction.'

'If you know what you're looking for,' Anthony guessed. 'Yes, seen that elsewhere too. I almost had to prise the information out of both Soviet and German hands regarding the Kienbaum National Training Centre and the Forbidden "Forest" City of Wünsdorf in East Germany as it was at the time.

The details in the end were hardly worth my effort, guess what some men think as top secret others will dismiss in the blink of an eye.'

'Especially when you're dealing with delicate political issues,' Roc noted. 'I can see why you might have had a few eyebrows raised there. From what I've learnt Kienbaum had an Olympic Games steroid rollout programme working, or at least partially working.'

'Not all the subjects were tested upon,' Draven noted. 'Guess there must have been some controls. However, it did note the potential of atmospheric conditioning, even if the regimental nature on it nearly killed some of the test subjects.'

'And Wunsdorf?' Roc asked. 'What was the thinking there?'

'Long shot,' Draven winked. 'Sometimes you just have to follow every lead.'

'I take it that something successful must have come out of it?'

'I'm here and I'm in the footsteps of Doctor Harding,' Draven announced. 'Something has gone right.'

'Yes,' Roc replied, a bit too quickly and without the enthusiasm that Draven would have expected. However, this was not the first time Roc had shown his disapproval of the doctor and Draven was keen to find out why.

'Tell me,' Anthony began as he stood, picked up the elegant crystal glass decanter and offered his host another drink. 'You've seen my files, haven't you?'

'Yes,' Roc nodded. 'You know that.'

'Humour me,' Draven replied as he sat back before the fire. 'Patrick is here, yet this is neither the time…nor the place to continue my research. As for the twins, well that was a bizarre if profitable encounter. And as for Jake Connelly…'

'The suicide case?' Roc smiled, cradling his drink in his warm hands. 'It did show ingenuity on a whole new level I grant you that.'

'But?' Anthony probed.

'You're going to end up bitterly disappointed,' Roc warned him. 'Harding isn't interested in anything unless it has a guaranteed profit margin attached to it. He's been spending way too much time with mercenaries to justify spending on "what ifs".'

'Really?' Draven replied, but without letting his colleague's words dishearten him. 'How about you?'

'Whoa there,' Roc sat up straight instantly, until he noticed the mischief in Draven's eyes. 'Look, by all means chase up these files with him but my money is on them going nowhere.'

'That's ok,' Anthony ushered him back into his chair. The fire still roared, and the storm still raged outside, but Anthony's mind was calm. Strangely calm given the notion that this Doctor Harding could not even help him achieve his greatest ambitions. 'I have the impression that Harding rates these at the very lowest of his agenda already,' he continued. 'Guess you win.'

'No,' Roc smiled sadly. 'Just because I'm right doesn't mean I win. Far from it actually. However,' he noted. 'There is something on this very American horizon that might benefit us going forward, but for now I have to keep quiet and simply give you the promise of a...chance to exercise your work.'

'Sounds ominous,' Anthony replied.

'Let's just say that what Doctor Harding thinks irrelevant, others find fascinating. For now, I just need the Connelly file, if that's okay? I think with what I know about Pyramidian and what you know about the human mind then we might be able to remedy a very old problem.'

'I'll drink to that,' Draven said. 'But what about Pyramidian? I still have much to learn.'

'You do,' Roc noted as he stood. 'But I must leave you now and sleep, the clients tend not to lie in once the sun rises. Leave Pyramidian for tonight and rest well, for when you know what it is hiding there, you'll understand that the next chapter of your life is starting, and you might not thank me for it.'

'And just maybe I will,' Anthony raised the remnants of his glass before finishing the drink. 'Sleep it is then, if the storm allows.'

'Exactly,' Roc muttered.

Myron accepted the refreshments wholeheartedly and finally let himself relax in the company of his friends. The location was not entirely to his liking, but as ever with Kirill there was a tale to be told.

'So,' Kirill began. 'The background story that I owe to you both.'

Myron looked across at Larissa, but she only smiled back and shrugged.

'The red gem as it turns out is nothing more than evolution of a substance developed by group of military scientists in the Cold War. We knew it as the "Red Juice" back then, but obviously what was first thought as ground-breaking has now gone on and been redeveloped in a much different and, it seems, more potent and crystallised form.

Originally the red juice was nothing more than a drug to allow soldiers to ignore pain and basically keep fighting, even if some went a bit delusional. What we see now is that the actions of a person are still within your control, you just have heightened strengths.

The fascinating part about antidote was that it's on record elsewhere around the world, so this gem isn't something that will fool any scientists for more than a year or two at the max. They'll be able to create something to counter any soldier taking this substance. Therefore, it begs question, why use it and link it to the sarcophagus affair? It doesn't add up. If I were police it simply points arrow back to the developer of the gem, which was Bessek I believe?'

'There's a few names buzzing around right now,' Myron nodded. 'But you might as well plant it with him. One dodgy mercenary is just as good as the other.'

'Anyway,' Kirill noted. 'That web of vipers we can get to later. What has piqued my interest here is what has resurfaced after all these years, and why. I was at Pyramidian for such a short period of time in my military career that those lost days of memory were never noted.

So, whoever ran Pyramidian all those years ago did so very well, and to the point that their influence infiltrated the military,' Kirill pointed out. 'I was not missed, and I was integrated back into my regiment as if nothing ever happened. Which brings me to Wünsdorf.'

'I've heard of that place,' Larissa noted unpleasantly.

'That's my thought,' her husband agreed with her. 'How much links work shared between east Germany and the Kremlin at that time I'm not sure, but whatever it was must have had a similar rival the other side of the Iron Curtain.'

'So, this wasn't a standalone case?' Myron enquired.

'I would guess so,' Krill nodded. 'There were so many defections, double and triple agents at that time that keeping secrets was almost impossible, unless...'

'They found a way to hide it from you,' Larissa noted. 'And I guess at some later point they would have resampled the red juice back into your blood stream where you would have reacted with it?'

'More or less,' the Russian agreed. 'Here the gem did its magic and I recollect a moment in time that I was to forget, maybe intentionally forever. The gem must be as powerful as the juice, probably even more.'

'Unless the gem caused an involuntarily hallucination?' Myron asked. 'It's possible?'

'Yes,' Kirill smiled. 'That's why I want us to visit the abandoned mining town.'

'Really?' Myron sighed. 'Is that why you invited me here?'

'Well,' Larissa gave him her best smile. 'I don't want him going alone.'

'Besides,' Kirill offered optimistically. 'We have help, from special tech department. You'll like.'

'I'll make my own mind up on that one, thank you,' Myron muttered and took one last sip of his coffee. Even that was cold. 'I hate this place.'

Larissa said her goodbyes before she drove off back home by taxi, leaving the two men to stand in the light snow.

'Now what?' the Britain asked. 'I'm not standing here all night.'

'We get next taxi, then grab overnight train to Izhma.'

'I'm not even going to ask if the train has beds,' the younger man replied. 'It better have beds.'

'No,' Kirill shook his head. 'We not need beds.'

'I hate you,' Myron smiled and waved at the next taxi he saw approaching.

'We haven't even got to Pyramidian yet my friend,' Kirill whispered. 'You might want to save some bitterness for that place.'

The overnight train journey was fortunately uneventful, and Kirill had completely tricked Myron into believing there were no sleeping compartments. The train might have only been slightly younger than the Orient Express he had slept on only months ago, but it was clean, comfortable and once Myron had managed to arrange the linen as he had liked it, then slept soundly and warmly.

Myron awoke to the belly laugh of Kirill as he came down the aisle with a full plate of food.

'Happy Friday. Look, breakfast in bed,' the Russian smiled. 'Never say I don't look after you.'

'This just about makes up for last night,' the younger man replied. 'I haven't even started yet about this other place you're taking me to.'

'You worry too much,' Kirill smiled. 'Hurry, we have two stops then we need to get off. Short walk to the hanger where I have a surprise for you.'

'No more surprises Kirill,' Myron noted. 'Just let me know what the score is now.'

'You no fun,' Kirill grimaced. 'No fun at all. Anyway, can't discuss here, if you know what I mean.'

'Yes,' Myron nodded. 'Unfortunately, I do.'

Both men exited the train and stepped carefully over the snowy platform and through the tiny station. Myron understood only too well what was happening here, Kirill had once again taken him to a place that was not on the map.

'There's the hanger,' Kirill pointed over the grassy field and toward a few buildings in the near distance. 'Come on, I'm very excited.'

Myron let his thoughts wander as they crossed the field to get to the hanger. There seemed absolutely no security here whatsoever, and therefore presumed this was simply a civilian operation. That at least calmed his fears a little. However, there was something in Volkov's swagger that allowed the young man's caution to remain just a little bit longer.

He wondered about Isobel but kept his thoughts as positive as possible. Myron did not like the feeling of hatred that washed over him every time he remembered the mystery man's promise, but it was something he had to deal with, and maybe for some time to come.

Kirill walked silently next to him, no doubt enjoying the moment of expectation that comes before revealing a huge surprise to a friend. The Britain had found both the Volkov's friendship easy to come by, almost magical. However, considering what had happened on the Orient Express, in Venice and then Assos, Myron did not hang on this thought for too long. He was simply blessed with good friends.

And Isobel, a blessing that came wrapped as a wonderful, if nerve wracking, disguise. The woman he had known as Miss Fortuna, the then head of *FortunaCS*, had been an excellent figurehead for the company, but once her inner self was revealed Myron had instantly fallen for her. That should have been his biggest mistake of his life, and for a while it almost turned out to be.

Now though, even with both their lives under threat, Myron found he loved her more than ever before. It was not just the absence of her, nor the mundane *FortunaCS* duties that were no longer in his way but knowing that his condition was treatable had removed probably the final barrier from falling for her completely.

Just knowing he had a condition had strangely lifted a huge wait off his mind. There were times where he had laid awake at night, holding Isobel in his arms, when all he had thought about was if he was becoming mentally unstable. The moment he knew, there was again a goal to reach and it seemed to make them both happier together.

Unfortunately, that had only been whilst on the *Angel of the Seas*, but Myron did ponder on what if their meeting with Harrison had gone in another direction. More cold shoulders, Myron refusing to engage with Templar and then they would have gone their separate ways and maybe never talking again.

Myron shuddered. One mistake diverted. However, in doing so he had then placed Isobel in mortal danger, or at least at the promise of a madman. That was easily rectified for now, but it could not go on forever. The longer they were apart the more Myron knew that he would have to hunt down and destroy this man.

The obvious problem was that Myron had never killed another person. And he also had no plans on doing so either. So, Myron needed a plan. He didn't want Kirill involved, but knew that he might need his help along the way. He also needed to get back in contact with Lieutenant Andrews or her soldier DT. It might be a long shot, but any help was better than his current progress with hunting down this man.

Kirill awoke Myron from his thoughts with a simple laugh. They exchanged glances and the younger man let his worries subside momentarily. Myron let Kirill enjoy his moment, the hanger approaching fast.

'You ready?' Volkov asked humorously.

'Come on Kirill,' Myron replied. Whatever it is I'm never going to be ready for it. I can see just by your excitement that if I'm not apoplectic with astonishment then you'll probably only try and surprise me even more in the very near future.'

'Yes,' Kirill muttered; his moment of glory thoroughly diminished by Myron's view of Pyramidian. However, the remission passed, and the smile returned. 'Well, let's see if I've outdone myself anyway. When we get to the hanger, I want you to close your eyes.'

'Okay Kirill,' Myron replied. 'You do realise that as we're heading into a hanger the surprise is going to be relatively limited. I'm guessing a propeller plane or maybe a helicopter, with either needing to be quite fast and able to cover long distances regarding where we're heading to.'

'Good try my young friend,' Volkov hushed him. 'Close your eyes and we'll see if you've won one of my *Hammer and Sickle* cigars.'

Myron shut his eyelids and listed to Kirill unlock the padlock on the side entrance. The door swung open and Myron felt Volkov's hand grasp his arm and lead him forward. The smell hit him first, of aviation fuel and anti-freeze. The door was then shut behind them.

'Open.'

Myron opened his eyes to absolute darkness.

'Brilliant Kirill,' Myron noted. 'I am surprised. You haven't paid the electric bill.'

Next to him Volkov laughed then threw the switch. The lights blazed down and bounced off the immaculately clean huge metal contraption sitting in the middle of the hanger.

'You are joking,' Myron exclaimed.

'I never joke,' Kirill smiled. 'She's a beauty, isn't she?'

'What the hell is it?'

'A Eurocopter X-3,' Kirill sighed with pride.

'Couldn't fit any more blades on it could you?'

'Funny,' Volkov humoured him, before leading him toward the helicopter. 'It's has a traditional helicopter rotor on top, but with two side propellers to aid in forward motion. I modified it a bit so we should get some good speed out of this baby.'

'Well,' Myron began. 'Theoretically I mentioned propellers as well as helicopter, so I don't think you've won this time.'

'Ha ha,' Kirill smiled. 'That not surprise Myron. Look inside.'

Myron followed to where the other man was pointing and noted a pilot, although it seemed far from human.

His heart dropped. Myron did not like the look of this. Kirill opened the helicopter passenger door.

'FEDOR,' he began. 'Say hi to Myron. The robot's head turned.

'Welcome Myrion,' the metallic voice offered. 'I am FEDOR, your pilot for today.'

'Um, it's My-ron,' the young man replied, more flustered at the thought of a robot flying this metallic behemoth rather than pronouncing his name wrong however.

'I'll open up the hanger doors,' Kirill noted. 'Myron, you sit next to our pilot and assist him in manoeuvring the X3 outside.'

'Shouldn't we use a tractor to pull the X3 out safely?' Myron asked, although he quickly noted there was not one around the hanger.

'Nah,' Kirill remarked. 'It has propellers, we use them.'

'Kirill,' Myron suggested quickly. 'I'm no aviation genius, but this doesn't seem to be the best of ideas, even for you.'

'Okay my friend,' Kirill replied. 'You help me open hanger, then we'll move FEDOR to the backseat. Happy?'

'Yes,' Myron relaxed a little. Kirill smiled. 'Oh great. You had that planned, didn't you?'

'You looked better for a second there,' Volkov noted. 'Almost happy.'

'Right,' Myron grimaced. 'That was the robot your government sent into space wasn't it? The one who could not do anything? So, was this the surprise then?'

'No,' Kirill replied coldly. 'I'm not playing anymore, you no fun. And yes, FEDOR is an astro-bot and quite a useless one as it turns out. You were supposed to be more "apoplectic", as you say.'

'Sorry to disappoint,' Myron sighed. 'Glad there's no more surprises. However, don't tell me about Pyramidian until we're safely in the air. You're right, I was almost past my fears for a second there.'

'I'm a psychology guru,' Kirill told him as they first unlocked then pulled apart the hanger doors. 'We can leave them open; I have friend who keeps an eye out on this hanger. He can tidy up after we've gone.'

'Okay,' Myron nodded before they both turned back to the X-3. The two men opened up the pilot door, then pulled out the robot before reseating him into the back of the machine. Kirill strapped FEDOR in as Myron wandered around the front passenger seat and climbed onboard.

The cockpit was full to the brim with instruments but at least they were not sitting within a military helicopter. All of a sudden Myron sensed maybe they instead were going into unknown territory a little too light handed.

'Kirill,' Myron began. 'I know you're going to shout at me, but any chance of a pistol of something when we get to Pyramidian?'

'For what?' Kirill replied deadpan as he climbed into the pilot seat.

'Just in case?'

'Of what?'

'I don't know,' Myron replied. 'But your memory recall wasn't of a mining colony that was normal.'

'First no weapons, now weapons,' Volkov replied despondently. 'Make your mind up Myron.'

'Weapon please.'

'Okay,' Kirill answered. 'Then we make one stop on way, but just for hand weapons only. We go in light and quick.'

'And hopefully out just as swiftly,' Myron nodded.

Kirill flicked two switches and both propellers began to turn slowly.

'The X-3 is a revo...' FEDOR began before Myron turned around to quieten him up.

'Not now,' the young man interrupted him. 'Maybe later.'

'Myron,' Kirill spoke softly. 'You take the dual rudder until we're out in the open, I'll keep my eye on the throttle.'

'Okay,' the young man noted, his concentration shifting to the moment instead. Next to him Kirill smiled, Myron was too predictable. He just needed something to occupy his mind.

'That's it,' Volkov noted. 'Nice and slow, I'm not sure if they've taken her out for a while, although by her polish I'm not so sure.'

'It looks brand new,' McGivney commented as he checked both hanger doors. Due to the propeller on each "wing" the helicopter was quite wide, but there seemed to be plenty of room, and there was a nicely painted central line running out onto the outside runway.

'That's what concerns me,' Kirill noted. 'They never usually keep it in such good condition. They must have done something and felt guilty about it.'

'As long as they fixed her,' Myron replied. 'They do like you, don't they?'

'Ha bloody ha,' Volkov bit back before the outside natural light burst through the cockpit screen. 'Nearly there, you handle her well my friend. Maybe we make a pilot out of you yet?'

'I prefer it on the ground,' the younger man replied. 'Although this is probably the safest looking flying contraption I've been in for quite a while.'

'Capable of 350mph,' Kirill remarked.

'Sorry?' Myron replied instantly. 'You mean kilometres?'

'No,' Volkov answered. 'She is modified but I definitely mean miles.'

'The dashboard says kilometres.'

'Okay.'

'Okay?' Myron replied. 'What does okay mean?'

'It means okay,' Kirill replied as the X-3 turned onto one of the minor concrete roads that interlinked the runways. 'Have you ever travelled at 350mph in the air?'

'Um.'

'Exactly,' Kirill noted. 'So why fuss? Most passenger jets travel faster so no need to worry.'

'And statistically...' FEDOR began before quietening again very quickly.

'Let's just get this over with then,' Myron double checked his seatbelt before Volkov opened up the communications unit to speak to the local air traffic control.

'башня,' Volkov commenced. 'это гений. запрашивающий взлет.'

Kirill held one side of his headset as he motioned with his other hand to Myron which runway they were being designated. He gave the thumbs up as the Britain put the helicopter onto the correct course. Myron took hold of the throttle with his right hand and kept his left on the rudder as he left Kirill to the tower's instructions.

McGivney felt the strange sensation of the red gem's influence as he pushed away all fear of what could occur when flying such a metal monstrosity. Myron almost welcomed it. When it flooded his veins in such a manner Myron had to admit he was half inclined not to want to find a cure, if only he could harness the good parts of the drug from the bad. However, when he thought about the consequences, it was still a drug.

It was still an outside influence. The morality issue was clear for even Templar to see. Myron knew however that he was in a much better position to have the right moral compass to choose when it was right and wrong.

Kirill listened to the tower's instructions, almost completely side-tracked as to what Myron was now achieving on his own. The helicopter was so smooth as it moved across the concrete that Kirill's subconscious simply assumed a competent pilot was at the helm. By the time the tower had confirmed which runway, and that they were cleared for take-off, Volkov was no longer in charge of the X-3. The reality hit him like a sledgehammer.

'I thought you said no surprises?' Kirill remarked as they turned onto the runway.

'Consider this a test,' Myron replied. 'You know the effects don't last indefinitely, so start your watch and report back on how I do.'

'Stopwatch started,' the robot began from the back.

'Actually FEDOR,' Myron said coolly. 'You record everything from now on, and make sure you can send the full transcript to Larissa if required.

'Myron,' Kirill questioned quietly.

'It's fine,' he said. 'And I trust her more than anybody else.'

'Understood,' Volkov nodded. 'Yes, Larissa it is then. FEDOR, just update her regularly, it's the best way for me not to be in bad book when I return.'

'Well,' Myron glanced across at his friend. 'I was actually thinking that she'd be monitoring your movements and would send in the cavalry before you do anything stupid,' he winked.

'Funny,' Volkov muttered. 'When did you learn to fly anyway? Now I worried.'

'Good,' Myron noted. 'Call that payback.'

Kirill gave him a sly look as the helicopter settled to a standstill at the end of the runway.

'You know that it's a helicopter don't you,' Volkov motioned. 'We don't need a runway at all, just go straight up?'

'Usually, yes,' Myron smiled over at him as he pulled his own headset over his ears and clamped the small microphone in front of his mouth. 'However, when in Russia, act like Volkov.'

'Myron,' Kirill warned as the Britain first flicked the overheard rotor in motion and then clicked the two side propellers into rapid mode.

'You worry too much,' Myron smiled at him before forcing forward the throttle. Next to him Volkov pulled his own seat harness tighter as the X-3 accelerated down the runway and almost seamlessly into the morning sky. Myron then banked a hard right and waited until the compass reset itself north-west before stabilising the rudder. 'Let's see if we can set a record here.'

Launch site

Durban: South Africa: Friday; 08:27

Isobel Fortuna looked out of the private jet's window and out toward the vast ocean to her right. The flight from Port Elizabeth to Durban was relatively short and it was a necessary journey due to the recent development for the Templar and Fortuna business relationship.

The Durban International Airport had been decommissioned around ten years ago and the site had yet to have its future decided. Templar once again seemed to have played his usual political games and had managed to acquire the airport and the local labour required to ensure that it could be brought online for the initial unveiling of their joint venture.

Isobel knew Harrison's style and understood only too well that if it made economic sense that the terminal would remain as the initial headquarters, at least until they could profitably relocate it elsewhere. Durban was just as good as any other city and considering the interest in South Africa then Isobel could only agree that it made strategic sense at present.

Also, as far as Isobel was aware, the South African Air Force was still based at this airport, which also offered Templar a handy if not entirely legitimate armed guard. He was good, very good. But she, Isobel smiled, was better.

The flight was near to its end and until now she had managed to keep the one person who meant more to her than the whole world out of her mind, but as ever she could not keep him silent.

Myron, she thought. *Wherever you are be careful my love. And in the meantime, I'll see if I can get us the date in space I always joked about.*

Opposite her Alessendro Fortuna closed the newspaper he was reading and finished off his cup of tea. Isobel looked over at her father as he smiled back, relaxed before the big day.

Yes, there was an unveiling of monumental proportions to look forward to, but it was only a symbolic gesture after all. The aircraft could not even take off yet let alone reach the altitude required to create zero gravity or breach the Earth's atmosphere, but the gimmick was there and needed to be waved in the face of *FoSE*. This *was* business after all.

Harrison Templar stood next to his military escort as they awaited all the various guests from around the world to arrive. Obviously, security was heightened for today's launch, the venue only very recently being announced partially assisting, but hindering also.

Harrison knew that the South African Air Force were formidable in the right environment but providing civilian security for this event was troubling all of them. However, unlike other businesses like the *FortunaCS*, his was one step ahead of any likely terrorist action.

From along the far end of the various aviation buildings Templar caught sight of Ishyan Stölles. He was the *FortunaCS* main bodyguard, who tended to both disappear then reappear at a moment's notice. He was no doubt a worthy asset to the team, but Harrison didn't trust him. Reconsidering this last thought, Templar knew that Stölles didn't trust *him*. Harrison therefore had his eyes and ears firmly on that man, as he had both Isobel and Alessendro firmly eating out of his hands.

Templar thought through the various scenarios that he had planned over the course of the last few years, and the immediate future, but Ishyan was an anomaly that he never seemed to truly understand.

Ishyan's whole life had been one of absolute tragedy, but yet here he was, high up in the *FortunaCS* structure and outliving anybody who ventured too close. The sarcophagus affair only highlighted Harrison's awareness of this individual. Myron and the others had been lucky, but it was this man that such luck had been built. Stölles was the talisman that the *FortunaCS* now drew strength from.

Harrison Templar smiled warmly as Ishyan Stölles arrived at the crowd of military personnel, guests and dignities.

'You've managed to pull off another humongous event Mr Templar,' Ishyan offered politely. 'I was under the impression this airport was a recent acquisition, so it can't have been easy.'

'When you have such fine men and women of the South African Air Force assisting in the operation' Harrison noted loudly to the rest of the crowd, 'then it was always going to succeed. Without them I would have struggled massively.

Now Mr Stölles,' Harrison whispered as he threw his arm around the other man's shoulders and whisked him aside. 'I just want to personally thank you for everything you've done to assist with this merger of businesses. I know it's not easy being a man of your position and having to juggle so many responsibilities.'

'You know Alessandro raised me from young sir,' Ishyan reminded him. 'And he obviously wants this project to run smoothly. Therefore, I'll try to assist where I can but please let me know if I'm starting to interfere.'

'Oh Ishyan,' Templar stopped in his tracks immediately. 'That is not my intention with this chat. Far from it. I wanted to thank you for everything so far and for passing on that little piece of technology to Mr McGivney. I like him but think he has a tendency to get into trouble, yes?'

'Myron is a complicated fellow,' Stölles answered simply. 'However, I'll always put the safety of the family above all else sir. I know how much this project means to you all, but from my perspective I will not let the potential gains ever endanger either Isobel or Myron.'

'Understood,' Templar noted. 'I'll keep an eye on you Mr Stölles.'

'Yes sir,' Ishyan nodded as they began to mingle back with the rest of the group. Right up until the moment I choose to disappear off the map completely and change the rules of the game, thought Ishyan.

Isobel saw the crowd gathering from her viewpoint in the private jet as it touched down in Durban. The whole of the airport, being now in the hands of Templar Industries, was cordoned off and secured by the military. The hanger where the *STaRship* was being stored also visibly guarded. What a pantomime, she considered.

'I know this probably isn't the time nor place' Alessendro pondered as the jet slowly meandered its way to the destination, 'but I can't help notice that Myron has suddenly gone very quiet.'

'Thought you might be happy with that,' Isobel remarked. There was not any venom in her voice, just one of reflection.

'Maybe once,' her father whispered, as if to note that her choice of man was starting to warm on him. 'I did like how he put Templar in his place.'

'And the rescue?' Isobel asked. That after all was his finest hour.

'Which one?' her father simply smiled back at her.

Isobel smiled back before mouthing "thank you".

'I'm giving you your usual space Iz,' her father noted as the plane finally came to a halt. 'But if you, or Myron, need me or my assistance, then just ask.'

'I will,' his daughter said sadly. Isobel did not have the heart to tell him she still hadn't heard back from Myron at all.

'And...' Alessendro began before hesitating. 'Your mother would have approved.'

Isobel wasn't expecting this. Without responding she quickly stepped over to her father and hugged him, not wanting to let go. Alessendro momentarily felt a panic rise up inside of him but forced his arms around her.

Within seconds the father she had thought lost, then returned but at a distance, eventually returned and materialised once more right before her eyes.

'I'm sorry,' he said. 'I only wanted for you to be happy but guess on my terms.'

'It's okay dad,' she whispered from his hold. 'I miss mum so much, she held us all together.'

'She did, didn't she,' Alessendro joked, amazed at how happy this made him feel. 'And kept us out of trouble.'

'Well,' Isobel grinned. 'Most of the time anyway.'

'Come on you,' her father whispered as he heard the cabin doors begin to open. However, for once he didn't take his hands off his daughter. Alessendro kept hold of Isobel's hand as they began exiting the jet and toward the clapping of the crowds and photography from the media.

They walked down the stairs in tandem before reaching the red-carpet area on the concrete. Harrison of course was already there to meet them. Templar also had half of the air force superiors in tow. The sight was indeed something for the media to lap up.

Isobel and her father waved to the crowd as they drew close to Harrison, before greeting him and being introduced to various dignitaries. Isobel felt very relaxed. Ishyan had already sent a code to her watch that everything was running smoothly. The only thing that was missing was Myron, but for now he could wait. Isobel had work to do.

She thanked Harrison for his hospitality and listened to the various officials as they in turned thanked all three of them. Templar then noted that they should make their way toward the hanger and the grand unveiling.

Isobel was used to Templar's swagger as he walked, but today he seemed to have turn the notch right up to maximum. The last time Isobel had seen the aircraft it was crude but effective. She wondered if just within the last few weeks Harrison had managed to achieve the impossible and even make it look like it could fly.

FoSE were ahead of their own schedule, with *FortunaCS* and the *Templar Industries Corporation* seemingly a civilian pipedream. If they could deliver a reasonable punch today, their shares would rocket overnight. Not even overnight considering how early in the day it was here. Templar might be a cutthroat businessman, but Isobel was glad he was on her side. Sort of.

The fanfare from the brass band seemed to reach a crescendo as they approached the hanger. The various types of spaceplanes currently in development had all been listed on social media well before the unveiling today, but design and the technology of their aircraft was supposed to be almost worlds apart.

Well, Isobel thought. We'll soon see how it goes.

Ishyan Stölles stood within the crowd, knowing that the unveiling today would ultimately be a success. He had understood by now that Templar never revealed his cards unless he had already won, or as events had illustrated recently, he thought he had won. The only part of Harrison's personality that Ishyan still hadn't got a handle on was his ability to change sides or perceptions just as victory was taken by another person, or failure was about to land squarely on his lap. Deflection and defection; Templar was without doubt the best in the trade.

From where he was seated Ishyan could view both the hanger, the unveiling of the aircraft and also Isobel and Alessendro. With the sheer amount of security and military around the airport he relaxed his physical guard a little, but his mental abilities were working overtime. Ishyan had researched *FoSE* as well as Boeing and NASA and what they all could bring to the table as regards space travel.

Stölles had no inclination that Templar was hiding something at present. Profit would be minimal for the first few years, even with agreed sponsorship from today. From the outside it did seem as if Templar was simply biding for power but Ishyan knew what Myron was looking for, and it was on a different scale; answers in an infinite universe.

Dark energy was one. Dark matter another. A few months ago, neither had made much impression on Ishyan. Now however, it was different.

Apparently, both made up almost all the universe, yet humans could see neither. It was true that dark energy telescopes had been created in order to discover such secrets, yet Myron had noted to Ishyan that they needed to launch a dark energy satellite in order to make the breakthrough.

Ishyan considered that there was a simpler fact – nobody knew. All he had been shown had yet to deter him from the concept that there was something unknown out there in the universe, and for all they knew, it could quite literally blow up in their face. Highly unlikely maybe, but for Ishyan he now held it as a definitive option.

He also did not like the silence from Myron. Stölles trusted the man to contact him when he was ready but there was always a chance that something was wrong. What if he had been compromised? What if he had been hurt? Ishyan stopped thinking about anything that might be worse than these options.

Stölles allowed the fanfare to break his concentration. The crowd around him had all grown quiet, a sure sign that something was about to occur. Ishyan just hoped it was not an anti-climax as he wasn't sure either *FortunaCS* or *TIC* could come through this unscathed if failure occurred.

Ishyan picked up the cheap binoculars the seated guests had all been given and tried to get a glimpse of Isobel and her father. As ever he was alert to danger. As ever he did not trust everyone here.

The billionaire Harrison Templar took the microphone from the stand and began to wave at the crowd, the seated guests and all the military personnel strung out across the airport.

'Good morning!' Harrison said, his voice carrying easily across the various distances of the aviation centre. 'Today you will witness all the hard work and expertise that the partnerships of *FortunaCS*, *Templar Industrial Corporation,* the South African Air Force and civilian contractors we've been working very closely with.

I must stress that what you see here is simply a prototype, but hopefully it will whet your appetite for what inevitably will follow. The evolution of the spaceplane, of interplanetary travel, of the future.'

There was plenty of applause as Templar held his microphone aloft above his head, which apart from Ishyan and Isobel only brought admiration from the rest of the crowd. Isobel of course smiled and clapped, whereas Ishyan could enjoy the anonymity of the crowd and for once enjoy the little pleasure of rolling his eyes in dismay.

'Now ladies and gentlemen, boys and girls,' Templar offered noting that guests of all ages were here today. 'I now give you...the STaRship.'

This time instead of clapping there was a hushed expectation as the hanger doors slowly drew open. To Isobel it seemed like hours as the huge metal doors slid across the tarmac.

First came the tractor, which pulled the ship behind it. Ishyan noted that whoever had organised this was one for suspense as the metal tow between tractor and aircraft was about twenty metres long. But then came the first sight.

Even Ishyan involuntarily let out a sigh of disbelief as the black tip of the spaceplane was ushered out into the daylight. He had seen shuttles before, but this was not just an evolution but a perspective shift as well. The side windows for the passengers were already there, the ST&R logo on the side, standing proud above the *FortunaCS*, *TIC* and the South African flag illustrated just what Templar needed to do to gain absolute credibility and support from today.

Not the first time Stölles wondered if Templar could achieve the impossible today.

'And now,' Harrison waved his hand around to thank everyone for their cheering and applause. 'We have a change of plan. I understand that *FoSE* have recently listed a list of defects of our ship on social media…'

'Did you know about this?' Isobel asked her father discreetly.

'I knew *FoSE* were raising the heat,' her father noted. 'But you can't take anything they say seriously at the moment.'

'I wonder…' Isobel began before Templar continued his sentence.

'…and you all know I'm not one to shirk a challenge,' he smiled widely. 'Therefore, I have a special surprise for you all.'

Ishyan noted throughout his talk that the tractor was still pulling the spaceplane out toward the runway.

Surely, he wouldn't try to get the bird in the air? His question was about to be answered. He put the binoculars back up to his eyes and studied the STaRship itself. There, he thought. He could just make out a shadow in the cockpit. Ishyan cursed, what he would do for his own binoculars here instead of these cheap imitations.

As Stölles looked again he glided his eyes over the rest of the ship. He thought he caught sight of more silhouettes in the rear, along the passenger compartment but could not be sure.

Whatever Templar was attempting to do, there had to be an end goal that the Fortuna's did not yet know about. Ishyan picked up his mobile and sent a simple message to Isobel's watch. She would soon know what his intentions were, and why.

'You'll notice that our almighty STaRship is now entering the runway, and why you might ask?' Harrison played the theatrics a bit more. 'Surely not even Harrison Templar could defy the space community and create a working aircraft a good month before *FoSE's* due launch date?'

Isobel looked across at her father again, noting Ishyan's message as it vibrated on the back of her watch onto her wrist. People onboard, she considered. That sounded like insanity. Ishyan had found something that they could not let escape. Isobel wondered whom she could call in order to track the plane, but time was against her. The tractor unlinked its tow wire.

'Now, for you,' Templar quietened. 'Witness the STaRship, the future of space travel.'

With the words barely leaving his mouth there was a deafening roar as the spaceplane ignited its thrusters. Some of the crowd threw hands up to protect their ears, others cheered whilst Ishyan recorded each moment within his own memory.

The sound reminded Ishyan of the retired British Vulcan bomber when it used to extend its flight axis to near vertical. The ground shook, the boom elevated his heart and the spaceplane had yet to even leave the ground.

Just then the brakes were released and the STaRship accelerated like a sprinter out of their starting blocks. The sight was amazing, the speed unbelievable and the heat generated as the plane began to climb exhilarating.

All too soon the spaceplane was almost out of sight, but Templar had one more trick up his sleeve. The STaRship banked 180 degrees left and then thundered back over the crowd at a safe, but still mind-bending, height. Stölles did not take much from the final flyby as only the undercover was visible but was impressed with the early demonstration. His next question was soon answered.

'And for those of *FoSE* who are still easy to quip,' Harrison noted. 'We're now linking up the satellites around the globe to track the flight of SS01 to illustrate that we are clearly ready to achieve orbit. Track it yourselves on the website - the address and QR codes are within your program.'

And there it was. Templar had indeed not only attempted and thought of it all, but he had managed to achieve it as well. Stölles did not even need to witness the rest, if Templar had the audacity to promote this to the world then barring a tragedy it was going to be fulfilled.

Ishyan therefore returned to the matter in hand. Who was on that ship? Its next destination was obviously the key, but Templar was too smart to allow it to be tracked as it returned to Earth. Or was that part of the plan? He sent another message to Isobel; she might be able to wring that information out of the billionaire.

Sebastian Nolan kept his eyes firmly closed as the GeForce almost ripped the consciousness from his body. As the craft began to flatten from its 180-degree tight turn Nolan could just make out the thrusters accelerating yet further.

The hold on his body was excruciating. Nolan struggled to even pull up his arms to hold onto his restraints. Sebastian tried to glimpse the others around him, and the sight only pushed him to the point of utter disbelief.

Each Menazee was sitting upright, expressionless and motionless. Nolan sighed heavily. They were not even fazed. If it were not for the nausea he felt, Sebastian would have smiled, but even that in GeForce was a minor miracle.

Still, Nolan kept pushing the same thought through his head to keep him focused. He only had three missions left to fulfil, and two of them now were already in motion.

The first was the priming of the rigged explosives in the Bethelsdorp open cast mine. The mission had come via Harding, but Nolan knew it could only come from the highest command. He also suspected it would be an assassination, although a very messy one. Industrial espionage. The trigger was also with another, so the detonation would come as a surprise to Nolan when it happened, but that also meant he had a convincing alibi if anybody ever linked the two. Nolan doubted it – his facial prosthetics that night had been rather good, and his voice control could fool anybody unsuspecting.

The second was testing this craft and utilising the Menazee's skillsets to identify the limits they were able to achieve in real flight. They had all been tested within the volcano and had passed with flying colours. Here they were also tested as pilots rather than just passengers. It seemed as if this mission would be another huge success.

The third mission was due to be undertaken on American soil, and in a few hours' time. It was a relatively simple task of tying up a loose end. There was something for the accepted reliability of this craft to get them to their military location, and for everything else to run smoothly once entering American space without all the other added complications of flying in a media frenzied spaceplane.

Nolan regained focus as the STaRship suddenly gained altitude and bolted toward orbit. He reached for his oxygen facemask and quickly strapped it around his face. Sebastian knew the ship was pressurised, but he was taken no chances at all, not in his current state.

Fighting against the GeForce Nolan began to control his breathing to keep consciousness and fought to move his neck muscles and look outside the windows at the darkening skies.

Dead end

The Eurocopter X-3 helicopter sped over the Barents Sea toward Svalbard and Pyramidian, the old and now deserted mining colony. Kirill was once again at the helm with Myron sitting across in the passenger seat. The rest of the space within the chopper was taken up by the firearms they had picked up en-route as well of course FEDOR, the robot. Myron turned around and the machine waved back and gave him a digital wink.

'You okay?' Kirill asked subtly, the silence in the cockpit deafening and unsettling him. 'Recovered now?'

'The last time I was in a similar situation I was about to jump from a low flying seaplane,' Myron acknowledged. 'Just hoping this time we can actually get to land this thing.

And as for my condition,' Myron continued. 'It looks like my stats began to drop once you kicked in the autopilot. So, from my point of view my body or brain, or both, seems now to have a handle on it.'

'Well,' the Russian mused. 'If not then we'll get another go soon.'

'Oh right,' Myron turned. 'Thought you were bluffing about that.'

'Why would I bluff?' Kirill asked straight faced.

'Good point,' Myron nodded. 'Do I need weapons training for all of this stuff in the back?'

'No,' the Russian replied honestly. 'How difficult can it be? Point and shoot. Anyway, my friend, I more worried about other matters.'

'You mean your dark history?'

'There is certain things that Larissa is not meant to know,' Kirill stated. 'Some secrets are best kept in shadows, forgotten. Other secrets are imprisoned, where they should remain without end. I fear one secret is no more.'

'Don't downplay the situation at all will you?' Myron sighed. 'I've held a weapon before but yet to fire at anybody. I'm not entirely loving this situation.'

'Maybe what we find not human,' Kirill almost whispered. 'Not in the way you imagine.

Remember when I told you about Vozrozhdeniya? The whole experience seemed holy, yet all were human. What I experienced in Pyramidian I'm not so sure.'

'What do you mean?'

'It's very difficult to explain,' Kirill noted. 'But I get feeling when something is horrible wrong. What happened here was so bad that somebody wanted me to forget about it completely. Now I get flashbacks but am still piecing things together.'

'Yet we're heading straight to the heart of where you thought this all occurred?'

'Yes.'

'Without knowing what we might find?' Myron reasoned sensibly, or so he thought.

'What do we need to know?' Kirill suggested. 'Whatever is there cannot be good. I do not simply forget things. There must have been one hell of a reason.'

'Great,' Myron replied sarcastically.

'When have I ever let you down?'

'Alright,' Myron conceded. 'This seems rash, that's all.'

'Yes,' Kirill smiled. 'That's what Larissa always says. Too rash Kirill, too rash.' The laughing from the pilot did nothing for Myron's nerves.

'To quote Dante,' FEDOR began from behind them. 'Do not be afraid, our fate cannot be taken from us, it is a gift'.

'Fannnntastic,' Myron sighed. 'Now we're quoting delusional Italian poets. This is really helping me feel relaxed.'

Isobel revved the tomahawk in front of the group of men and winked at Harrison.

'Nothing to it,' she shouted through the helmet visor.

'Just be careful,' her father tried to tell her, the sound of the V12 engine slicing most of his words in half. Ishyan stood back from them both, his own mind racing. Something was not right here but it was not the bike. He had been careful and had a quick look himself. However, as with everything that was not enough.

They had returned from Durban after the successful launch of the STaRship and now Isobel planned to take Templar's prized possession for a jubilant spin. Of course, with Isobel, there was an altera-motive.

The Bethelsdorp mining site manager Stölles had also researched very conscientiously. They had even been invited to the gala last night, which showed how much respect some of the companies around the area had from Templar.

Miss Fortuna revved the bike's insane engine one more time before drifting off around the circular driveway that surrounded the entrance car park and central fountain. As she broke onto the highway Isobel let out an almighty roar that almost made Harrison wince.

'My bike,' he whispered. Alessendro put his massive arm around him and hugged the billionaire tightly.

'Don't worry Harry,' he said smoothly. 'She'll look after it.'

As both men turned to re-enter the hotel Ishyan stood staring at the fountain for a few seconds and listened to the Tomahawk disappear into the distance. Isobel was off to check on the mine, one which they had acquired recently, partially to enable them with building up a rapport with the Port Elizabeth businesses and partly to look for new underground facilities for the space program.

Space program, thought Ishyan. The mine. Templar's gala. Something didn't add up, something that had been puzzling him for a while, yet only now had surfaced to the forefront of his mind.

He followed the two men back inside but instead of following them further into the conference area took a right toward the bar. He picked an isolation booth near the rear of the bar and took out his phone.

Bringing up the gala invitation list Ishyan ran through the hundreds of guests, eagerly looking out for the mining name amongst the company list. It didn't take long to find the entry – simply one line listed noting the site manager and all his guests. Probably listed this way to keep the guest list short and sweet, but there must have been another on the door to ensure only those working at the mine could enter. Maybe.

Ishyan wanted to contact Isobel to check about the Bethelsdorp open cast mine but thought better of it than to ring her whilst she was riding a 200mph motorbike. It could wait. For now.

He instead made his way to the conference and events part of the hotel and chatted to the gala co-ordinator for a few minutes. Ishyan feigned complete incompetence to the point where he was basically given everything Stölles required in the form of photocopies, which he took back to the bar to check over.

Ordering a chilled sparkling water and espresso Ishyan waded through the various documents until he found something, but not what he was originally looking for. Templar had indeed invited the mine's workers, but as far as he would see not by the request of Isobel. A simple oversight maybe, but one which probed deep into his mind. A stinging thought which lingered.

Ishyan went through the various documents again then checked against the other records he had for the mine. Something didn't add up. He decided to pick up the phone and put his mind at rest.

It was only a few minutes later that Ishyan sat in the same isolation booth, none the wiser. Koarni, the site manager, was on site but currently in one of the newly excavated tunnels. Therefore, unreachable at present. Ishyan hadn't pressed the matter any further but asked to be contacted as soon as Koarni broke back into daylight.

Ishyan sat and waited. Two things he hated more than anything else in the world.

<u>Appalachian Mountain range: Eastern USA: Friday; 08:27</u>

Lieutenant Gemma Andrews drove her military jeep up the winding dusty track up from the main road which seemed to dissect most of the lush wilderness. She needed answers and the recent disappearance of her commander had driven her to near desperation. This was her last throw of the dice.

The large wood cabin could be seen halfway up the ascent, and Gemma slowed as she approached, half wondering if this was even a good idea. There might have been a number of reasons why Goldhawk had come back here, most of them would have meant she was now breaking their code and violating the sanctity of command. However, there was still something urging her on, something that she knew to be right. At least if not right, then there was a complete absence of being utterly wrong.

The cabin looked deserted, but that didn't mean anything either. There was a small jetty down by the lake which meant the retreat could have been travelled to by foot, vehicle or boat. The commander had also outlived his late wife's illness, so he would be here alone.

Gemma parked the car just shy of the driveway and climbed out of the vehicle. The Appalachian Mountains rose steeply to the west of them, but within this valley there were many vantage points overlooking the cabin. So much for Goldhawk picking a spot where he held the high ground, or maybe this was the point.

The lieutenant walked down the shingled path to the house but decided to venture around the perimeter first. If the old man was anywhere, then probably he was fishing after all.

Andrews wandered around the outskirts of the house before finally she entered the back garden, which had to be a full ten acres including the unkempt forest near the lake. She tried but could not see anything obvious, so instead turned and walked over to the rear of the property.

Maybe she had been completely wrong in this, as there were no visible signs of any life here. Had her instinct completely failed her since she had been rescued onboard the *Angel of the Seas*?

Andrews sighed and stepped onto the decking, passing an old barbeque and stood outside the huge rear lounge window. Nothing, not a soul. Not even a sign of recent activity either.

She turned one last time to view the lake, just in case the lieutenant could view a passing fishing boat. Anything might be a clue, not this complete silence.

The sound of the crash erupting from behind her gave her little chance to react before the heavy mass rushed on her and threw her clear of the decking and onto the grass beyond.

A second impact followed, but this time it was clearly a boot to her side. There came no third blow. Andrews took her time to recover, knowing that whatever had floored her was simply biding their time to gain her full attention.

Slowly finding her feet and turning back toward the house she saw both her attacker as well as another figure.

One held a gun. Lieutenant Gemma Andrews had finally come face to face with the killers from the volcano.

Isobel slowed the Tomahawk as she approached the mine security gates. Obviously at no point had she even attempted full speed of the machine but had enjoyed the looks of fellow travellers along the various highways around Port Elizabeth.

She had even pulled alongside one of the school buses en-route to various schooldays activities, the students onboard cheering and waving excitedly as she throttled the Tomahawk and sped off into the distance.

Engaging the joint footrests, the Tomahawk stood in the settling dust like a torpedo would if it was fitted with a hover mode. Isobel was glad for the loan of extra thick cycling gear, even in the rising morning heat, as the V12 was ridiculously warm between her thighs.

The security guard was obviously expecting her as he did not even let her enter the security cabin, instead walking out to her and admiring the bike where it stood.

'Boy,' he began. 'I was jealous of Templar when I saw him on this yesterday on the news, but it certainly belongs to you Miss Fortuna, if you excuse me saying so.'

'That's okay,' Isobel replied. 'Harrison does things for effect, I do it for fun.'

'Koarni is already down in the tunnels,' the security guard noted. 'I'd tell you not to ride that thing down there, but you'd only sack me, so carry on as you please.'

'My reputation isn't that bad,' Miss Fortuna replied to the guard.

'Maybe not,' the guard replied, slightly embarrassed. 'But around here you're basically a legend. Koarni I know is a big fan, he wouldn't have signed us up with *FortunaCS* if he didn't speak for us all.'

'Thank you,' she replied, slightly astonished at the reception she was getting.

'Ride carefully and stay away from the edges,' the guard said as he returned to his booth and opened up the gate. 'Catch you soon.'

With this Isobel restarted the Tomahawk and crept the bike down the gentle incline and into the central pit area, where the track circled the open cast area, the decline lowering her slowly into the hole.

As Kirill landed the helicopter lightly on a flat level of the outer perimeter of the Pyramidian mining colony, only a few hundred metres from the ice-covered sea, Myron finally let out a sigh of relief.

He was not much of a traveller he knew, but at least he enjoyed being back on dry land. Even if it was stone cold and covered in snow. The site was also one devoid of joy, the abandoned colony a series of nineteen mining buildings set in right angles from each other.

'Great place for a holiday,' Myron offered as the blades stopped rotating. 'We taking FEDOR?'

'What you think?' Kirill responded dryly.

'Right,' the British man replied solemnly before clambering out of the chopper. Kirill had passed him a pistol already, although obviously the Russian had prepared himself a bit better. He had previous after all.

'The map is quite old,' Kirill noted as they stood in the inch-thick snow and looked around the area. It was sunny at least. The area we're looking for should start at the old mining entrance. Come.'

Myron followed the Russian, although his eyes kept reverting back to the colony buildings, abandoned but yet still alive, somehow.

'When did this place shut down?' he asked towards Kirill, his breath causing smoke dragons in the chilly air.

'Lieutenant Andrews,' Nolan began. Next to him the Menazee stood awaiting the next command. 'I must admit you're a very slippery customer.'

'Should I know you?' Andrews replied as cocky as she could muster. Gemma was in a situation that had no control over, so she needed time to work out a way to survive.

'So, you haven't managed to piece this together yet then?' Sebastian taunted her. 'That really makes killing you all a bit pointless but seeing as you're here we might as well implicate you at the same time.'

'You might find that difficult,' Andrews noted, although she was sure this character would give it a go. Just try to keep him talking, she thought.

'Not really,' Nolan noted. 'Goldie's usefulness has run its course. Seems he could not keep his mouth shut after all. Although some might never believe your part in his this, there are plenty that wanted him dead and so will happily turn a blind eye and overlook this unlikely scenario. So, the truth is, in this case, quite irrelevant.'

'You'll have to pardon me by disagreeing with that last statement,' Gemma rallied. 'Someone will put this together.'

'Hardly,' Sebastian replied, venomously.

'Your mate's quiet,' Andrews switched her attention to the Menazee. 'His eyes seemed to have glazed over, can't blame him I suppose.'

'Shut...up,' Nolan whispered, raising his finger as if that alone would silence her. However, Gemma realised her mistake only just in time as the Menazee launched itself at her.

Gemma half ducked and half rolled out of the way of the initial attack, but only managed to aim a glancing blow at the soldier before he jumped past her. The Menazee turned instantly and came at her again, but this time more purposefully.

As the soldier began raining in blow after blow at Andrews, Nolan watched in amazement as the Lieutenant blocked one after the other, until she then created an opportunity to strike back. Gemma fired a quick succession of punches which drove the Menazee back towards the floor.

'Nice,' Nolan admitted as Andrews stepped back, her fists in bloodied agony at the relentless fight. 'Sorry, looks like he's up for more.'

As the Menazee rose to full height Andrews knew she had to finish this fight now and do so using whatever means possible. Gemma coaxed the soldier toward her, allowing the Menazee to rush her once more. This time she brought her knee up into its ribcage, before slipping her arm around its neck and latching on with her other arm, creating a vice.

As the Menazee reeled from the onslaught, Gemma then pulled herself up onto him and wrapped her legs around his waist, interlocking legs and arms around the Menazee to subdue it.

Nolan looked on as the Menazee roared in rage and tried to grab the lieutenant off. Sebastian's first instinct was to pull out his gun, but this was not something he would see each day. An elite against the Menazee. A perfect test. Nolan kept his side arm in the holster, at least for now.

The Menazee stumbled under the pressure of Gemma's grip and fell to one knee, before its weakness became Andrew's winning blow. As the creature began to gasp for air Gemma wrapped both her arms and legs even tighter around the tiring Menazee and flushed the rest of the air out from its body. It fell limply onto its front, followed by Andrews who simply lay panting on top of the creature, her limbs still in a vicelike embrace around it.

Nolan clapped. 'Bravo my dear, bravo. I shouldn't have underestimated you obviously. What's that under your uniform? Some kind of exo-tech?'

'Borrowed it from a friend,' she managed to sigh, rolling off the Menazee and onto the lush green grass. Gemma puffed and tried to regain her feet. As she did so she saw the pistol pointed right at her.

'Not so fast,' Sebastian noted. 'He's got a few friends that want to make amends for his weakness. Just stand there and wait for the inevitable.'

Gemma looked at the man and half-chanced the risk of rushing him herself, but the pistol was already aimed at her head. Andrews forced herself to relax and slumped back down to the ground.

'How many of them do I need to beat?' she asked.

'Another four,' Nolan said, putting away the pistol as Andrews sat back down. Not sure your tech will last that long.'

'I think it's already done,' she mused as parts of it came loose as she untangled her ripped clothing. 'I'll have a word to Templar about this.'

'Oh, it's his kit is it?' Nolan mused. 'Well, you've shown me something unexpected today I grant you that Lieutenant, but now it has to end.'

'Really?' Andrews replied, winking at him. 'Bit slow to respond, aren't they?'

Nolan's hand started to lower again to his holster.

'I wouldn't do that,' Andrews smiled knowingly. Somebody had come to her rescue.

'So, what's your next play?' Nolan asked solemnly.

'Bring you in,' Gemma offered as she slowly stood up. At least on her feet if Nolan had time to draw his gun, he would have to raise it further to strike her a fatal shot. Also, Sebastian was now flustered.

'I don't think so,' Nolan smirked. 'I'm not sure how you've managed to defeat my Menazee but there'll only be one winner here.'

'I can't disagree,' Andrews replied. Here it comes, she thought.

As Nolan whipped his hand to his side the pistol rose almost to Andrew's knee trajectory before it crashed to the floor, the body of Nolan almost instantly doing the same. There had been no sound.

Lieutenant Gemma Andrews walked up toward the house, her eyes drifting around the valley and wondered where DT had managed to place herself to take out the four Menazee and then Nolan. It could only be her. Nobody else was that good a shot. So much for following orders and remaining away from the fight.

Andrews was tired, bruised but thankful to both DT and of course Myron, who had passed the exoskeleton armour over to them. She owed a lot to her friends, and vowed she'd never forget their actions. Gemma approached the terraced decking and the broken patio glass door which the Menazee had first sprung the trap.

Andrews hesitated before entering, knowing only too well what she would find. Gemma wanted it over before DT arrived. Seeing her superior's lifeless body was painful enough without unleashing this horror on her soldier.

Up amongst the trees, DT looked on as her lieutenant entered the building. The area now seemed secure, but there was always a threat, always a risk. So instead she simply waited for the backup to arrive, as planned, a few minutes later.

Isobel brought the Tomahawk to a standstill outside one of the lower tunnels. There was hardly any excavation work on this side of the mine now. Soon the whole operation would shift to another site, very near to here, and the tunnels that had now been built would be left for another purpose. Hers.

As she entered the perfect square cut of rock Isobel caught sight of Koarni with a flashlight at the far end. He waved.

'Sorry Miss Fortuna,' he offered in his strong South African accent. 'We have cut the holes for the cables, but slightly behind on enabling power. Few days delay this end, but ahead of schedule for the install, that I can promise.'

'It's okay,' Miss Fortuna smiled confidently. 'My visit was off the cuff anyway; I was so intrigued when you mentioned that the cutting was already finished.'

'My staff are professionals Miss Fortuna,' Koarni offered. 'Come, look at the main hall. No need for a map here, I personally took control of this part of the project to guarantee the structural integrity of the rock surrounding your project.'

'Thank you,' Isobel replied, awestruck at the how accurate the layout was. It could have been a newly laid concrete structure for all she knew, not cut out of sheer rock.

'Here,' Koarni said as he passed her a face protector. 'Minor dust, don't want you coughing for the next few days now do we?'

Isobel thanked him and placed the kit over her mouth, eyes and nose. It didn't negate her ability to communicate fortunately.

'It's beautiful,' Isobel muttered unintentionally.

'Karoo sandstone,' Koarni replied. 'Finest rock in the land,' he laughed. 'Tough but durable. Brilliant for what you require. As old as Pangaea itself.'

Isobel followed her guide as they meandered through the labyrinth of tunnels, finally making their way into a single cavern, with a dome like ceiling rising above the middle of the circular room.

'This is where you will put the centrifuge,' Koarni said. 'The other rooms are off from the main corridor back the way we came in. Wanted you to see this first. It was the most difficult bit to do, which will probably keep it a secret for a very long time.'

'Yes,' she replied. 'Nobody will suspect a thing.'

'I never ask questions Miss Fortuna, unless my staff wellbeing requires it,' Koarni said. 'You are soon to be my boss so I will only say this. Space training is gruesome, with GeForce at the top of my personal health list. I worry for you, but you are a professional who knows what you're doing.'

'I hope so,' Isobel sighed.

'But,' Koarni said. 'If the race has to be won, then get in the right support. You only have to ask. We are a proud if complicated nation after all. We will help you win.'

'Thank you Koarni,' she smiled honestly. 'Before the end I'm going to need all the help I can get.'

Myron followed Kirill into the old mining shaft, wondering what Isobel was doing right now. Not wandering around darkened tunnels, he mused realistically.

'We'll need to take the lift once we hit the end of this walkway,' Kirill noted sourly. 'There's no other quick way down into the belly of the mine.'

'Understood,' Myron rallied as they approached the lift area. 'Is this it?'

'What you expect?' Kirill asked. 'Old mine, old lift.'

'It's a death cage,' he sighed and allowed Kirill to open up the metal door and usher him inside.

'You worry far too much,' the Russian told him. 'It's no shark cage after all, just cage to stop rocks hitting you. At least you can see where you're going,' he muttered and shone his torch through the grating underneath their feet.

Myron groaned loudly as the torch beam disappeared into the depths. He closed his eyes and hoped, if nothing else, that the lift was safe.

'Hang on,' Kirill spoke as he turned the mechanism on. The lift wheel sprang to life and the cage began it's slow progress down into the darkness below. 'I have kept something from you Myron,' the Russian added as they descended. Somehow Kirill already knew how his comment would be reacted to, so continued quickly. 'I couldn't say at the time, not when Larissa was around.'

'How about the chopper?'

'FEDOR was in there, he might talk.'

'So, you wait until I'm in a locked cage plummeting to hell before telling me one more shocking truth?'

'We're not plummeting Myron,' Kirill whispered. 'Don't exaggerate.'

'I'm really hoping what you've told me about this place was simply an exaggeration intended to scare me.'

'No Myron,' the Russian grimaced. 'I'm not sure what we're going to find down there. I'm scared.'

Kirill waited for a few moments whilst Myron tried to gather his thoughts.

'You're scared?' came the reply, eventually. It was seeped in disbelief.

'Your comment of going to hell is not such a bad one,' was all the Russian said, but it left Myron with a thousand unpleasant images in his mind. He lifted his pistol and took off the safety.

'Maybe I should have been allowed a bigger gun?' he sighed.

Admiral Leffer stood in the lounge area of the log cabin as the military doctor finally finished his post-mortem on Commander Goldhawk.

'I'm sorry Andrews,' he offered his condolences as her figure silhouetted the lowering sun out over the lake.

'Who's Nolan?' she asked, simply.

'From what I can gather he was the one in charge of the ReUnion massacre,' Leffer noted. He half-expected the soldier to react, but there was nothing. The Admiral watched her intensely.

'Who does he work for?' she asked, eventually.

'That we're still working on,' Leffer replied. With that however there was a reaction.

'Don't lie to me,' Andrews whispered as she turned and drew close to him. 'Somebody ordered that hit on us, and it was linked to Goldhawk. What he knew.'

'I don't know what the commander knew,' the Admiral noted. 'But I can tell you this. When we have a lead, I'll give it straight to you. But we have to bring them in alive. There'll be no answers if this trend continues.'

'And what of those creatures?' Gemma asked. 'We had some half-decent tech today, but somebody will only grow them stronger.'

'Yes,' Leffer answered truthfully. 'They no doubt will. Quicker, stronger, more intelligent. You can see why I want...'

'...them alive,' Andrews realised. She almost laughed at the futility of the whole situation. 'You get blood on your hands as well?'

The Admiral looked Andrews square in the eye, knowing nobody else around them had heard her comment. That was just as well. He therefore left it a few moments until her emotions had calmed.

'I want to be the one who brings them in,' Andrews said. 'After that you can do with me as you wish.'

'Quite an offer,' Leffer noted. 'But you undervalue yourself Lieutenant. You *will* be the one to bring in whoever sanctioned this, but currently I have another job for you.'

'Which is?' she replied.

'I have set up a new team,' Leffer began. 'I have the makings of a great squad, and I want you to lead them for a number of undercover operations. Nothing too dangerous, just enough to whet your appetite. Interested?'

'Always,' Andrews replied. 'I want my own sniper though.'

'Already in,' Leffer noted. 'I didn't get here in record time by my own intel. But you can lose the Templar tech for now. Strictly weapons and expertise.'

'Who are you stitching up with us?' she smiled.

'Lieutenant Farr,' the Admiral offered. 'You've worked with him before I believe?'

'Well, yes,' Gemma noted. They had fought side by side but in different teams before now. 'But for that to happen...'

'Yes,' Leffer nodded. 'We can't have two lieutenants in a squad, now can we? Congratulations Commander.'

'Commander?'

'Your position comes due to what you now know,' the Admiral whispered. 'So, it'll stay that way, and from your team. Until the right time.'

'Understood sir,' she replied, her stomach twisting at the thought of keeping secrets from any of her team again. Last time it had cost her most of her squad. The Admiral left her side and began consulting with the medical staff again, leaving her to her own thoughts.

Commander Gemma Andrews looked out at the lake, ignoring the body of the creature she had killed and the corpse of Sebastian Nolan which was now being bagged up.

She looked over the water, over the horizon to what lay ahead. Yes, she would have to keep secrets, but hadn't they all? A slow thought crept into her head. Maybe there was something that Leffer did not know.
A man who had helped her twice already this week, the second time without even knowing, only hoping. Andrews began to let her aches and pains creep over her to avoid having to feign too much injury. It seemed to be her favourite trick at present.
Allowing a small gasp of pain to be shown as she walked into the kitchen, Andrews noticed the Admiral's gaze follow her. Seconds later he'd no doubt send her to be examined before rendezvousing with her new team.
Andrews only wanted to speed up the journey, or even create enough time for a diversionary stop-off. She also needed DT's help.
They had to find Myron, for at present he might be the only one who could hunt down these individuals. Andrews just hoped that she could find him.

Ishyan Stölles finished his double check of the mining staff lists before the obvious struck him firmly between the eyes. All the staff had been invited without question, which meant that either the mine had been shut down for at least twelve hours, or that someone else had come in to babysit the mine.

Considering Koarni's professionalism he doubted either that they had shut down or that he'd let anybody else, locally at least, take the steering wheel of his baby. Something had to give here, Ishyan knew it was going to be big. Stölles knew that neither of the Fortuna's had authorised this, so that left only one other who might have had access to this mine. Templar.

It was a stretch, but any coincidence at this juncture still required more evidence than Koarni simply forgetting his duties of a company he had raised from the dirt up, or down in this case. You do not take nine years away from someone, not likely at all.

Therefore, no matter how unlikely, Harrison was behind this. The big question was why? What would he gain to have access to the mine for half a day? At night also. It did not make sense. Even if he thought Isobel was up to something simply stealing the plans would prove what the Fortuna's wanted with this mine, and to be honest Ishyan knew it was not worth the effort. Stölles knew only too well that Isobel's fascination with the space program would end up with her either achieving it or injuring herself, neither which would hurt Templar particularly.

So, what then? Ishyan stared at his fizzy water as it effervesced to the surface of the glass. So many bubbles. It sent a chill down his spine as he thought back to both Lake Nyos and Lake Kivu, and the gases that had spilled up to the surface daily. Bessek had meant for the methane in Lake Kivu to ignite at the bottom of the lake, creating the ultimate "killing cloud" that would disperse for hundreds of miles around the lake, simply to ensure their new rare find became invaluable.

What was the link with Templar? Was there even one? Ishyan gave up and started to walk out of the bar, just as the noise of ice falling made him turn. It could have been a machine, but there was something about the sound. He looked at the far end of the bar and two barmen were huddled over a huge ice bucket. Ishyan smiled, he knew this game. He approached them quietly.

As one of them turned Ishyan saw him nudge the other worker and they stopped.

'Don't mind me,' Ishyan smiled. 'Who won?'

'Dan here got a five-centimetre radius last night,' one of them spoke quickly, eager to resolve the question and pretend they were working after all.

'Really?' Ishyan asked and looked over the bar and into the ice pit. 'Pretty impressive. Ice right up to the rim?'

'Yes,' the man who was Dan replied. 'It was a long shift, so maybe some of the ice had already melted then refroze, we've got no chance of beating it today.'

Ishyan laughed and looked into the pit just as the sides began to crumble and crashed back into the middle. His laugh started to fade. Something clicked in his mind.

'Shit,' Ishyan swore as he turned and bolted from the bar.

'Ah man,' Dan said to his colleague. 'You think he's going to tell the boss?'

As Stölles hit the curb outside he searched for anything he could use, but without any luck quickly ran toward the nearest taxi rank. He noted one near the rear whom he had chatted to the other day and jumped in.

On any normal day the rest of the taxi drivers would have raised their hands in complaint, but by the way the rear taxi took off out of the car park they all soon realised this was no ordinary ride.

Ishyan had intentionally sat in the front but gave up navigating almost instantly, his instincts had been correct. This driver was indeed the best. Stölles instead lifted his phone and tried to ring Isobel once again.

The image of the falling ice kept repeating over and over again in his mind. Isobel had just walked into the worst of traps.

As they crept along the lower mine walkways, the only sound Myron could hear was that of his own heartbeat. It seemed to want to jump right out of his chest. Kirill had insisted on dead silence, but it did little to make him feel any more welcome down here.

The cold he could cope with, as at least that was a natural phenomenon. The silence should also have also been easily dealt with, but it seemed completely unnatural down here, even unholy. It was no surprise that Myron led with his pistol raised high.

Kirill stopped at a junction and looked down at his map. Myron had insisted on head mounted torches, which at moments like these, with shadows appearing with every movement, at least he felt he had control of. Just.

The Russian signalled to continue straight ahead, but Myron could tell simply from his expression alone that they were nearly at their destination. Neither men dared say anything, instead pressing on through the bitterly cold tunnels.

Myron's torch caught a glare of the ironized metal, and both men halted immediately. Kirill checked his map one more time before glancing across. There was a deep puzzlement on his features.

'Guess we're in right place,' the Russian noted. 'Didn't expect the security though.'

'Would I be correct in assuming there's nobody behind that?' McGivney asked.

'I guess so,' Kirill offered. Myron sensed something underlying in his answer.

'It's not keeping something in is it?'

'That my friend,' Kirill replied with a sigh. 'Is the question.'

'What are you doing?'

'Give me a few minutes my friend,' the Russian offered. 'I remember only very little of these tunnels, yet here we have something built after my time. I need to know what was on the other side. What was really on the other side.'

'Go on.'

'The human mind can only comprehend so much before it implodes,' Kirill noted. 'I have suppressed all memories of this place until your gem released some.'

'Don't remind me about that,' Myron whispered, visibly feeling guilty.

'Were those memories real?' Kirill replied. 'Or only a vague recollection of what happened? A filtered or diluted memory?'

'I hope you don't mean that you've created a flowery hippy version of the past,' Myron responded, suddenly eager for them to simply turn away from this huge metal door. 'What you've said so far is bad, if it gets worse...'

'Here,' Kirill said as he withdrew a small box from his rucksack.

'What's that?' Myron asked innocently.

'Basically, your gem, in liquid form.'

'You've gone and simulated that gem into an easy to swallow dosage?'

'Basically, yes,' Kirill nodded. 'Not as hard as you might imagine. The world isn't as innocent as you believe my friend.'

'Are you talking about all those wonderful places you went on holidays to again?'

'They are just what you know about, and because I've told you,' Kirill smiled. 'There are similar cases all around the word, some which will come to light soon no doubt, once whoever has threatened you is finally held to account.'

'That,' Myron said, suddenly regaining his full strength of purpose, 'will be my pleasure.'

'So,' Kirill suggested as he held the liquid up to eye level. 'Do you partake in a bit of gem juice?'

'You're nuts,' Myron replied. 'But as long as it warms my spirits then I'm game.'

'Good,' Kirill smiled back at him. 'For the women in our lives, for them and all whom we love and care for.'

'Couldn't have put it better myself,' Myron smiled warmly and took a swig from the bottle. 'When you're in the bowels of hell's freezer, what's the worst that can happen?'

'I think,' Kirill suggested as he took something else out from the backpack. 'That we're about to find out.'

'Dynamite?' Myron asked in concern. 'I thought you wanted the gem juice to assist with the memory recall?'

'That could have worked, yes,' Kirill nodded. 'But this is quicker.'

'Great,' Myron smiled sarcastically.

'You told me the gem made you stronger, more aggressive, reflexes finely tuned,' Kirill told him. 'Thought it was a good time to test your statement.'

Myron turned to view Kirill and wondered if he'd brought Ashton then these two wouldn't agree that this was a good plan. As the Russian embedded the dynamite into the sides of the metal and ice, Myron decided to head back to the crossroads they had passed earlier. At least that offered some safety from the explosion.

He turned to the right-hand side of the crossroads and simply walked another few metres before stopping. The walls were almost bare of anything except machinery markings, so if the explosion did send fire his way there was absolutely nothing to stop it. This was a bad idea.

A few seconds later Kirill rounded the right-angled corner and headed over to Myron.

'You might want to put your fin…' the Russian began before the darkness behind him turned to bright light, and a wall of noise catapulted them both from their feet and further along the icy corridor.

The explosion reverberated around the tunnels, with both humans laying on the floor holding their heads in agony. Myron was the first to find his feet, but his whole body ached, and his ears felt as if they had been pummelled by a baseball bat.

Kirill rose from next to him and began to walk back to where the explosion had originated, stumbling a few times in the process. As he rounded the tight bend in the crossroads, he turned back to Myron with a smile on his face.

'We're in,' he mouthed.

Ishyan gave up on Isobel's mobile and instead rang the front gate of the mine. He told them what he presumed might occur and the security team immediately rushed out to find both Miss Fortuna and Koarni the site manager.

Stölles wished he was wrong but knew in his stomach that they were all in mortal danger.

'Good job,' Myron said loudly as his eardrums finally began to return to normal, although the ringing he could hear might have been the noise bouncing back along the tunnels.

'Thank you,' Kirill replied as he stepped onto and over the fallen metal door. Placing the dynamite had the exact effect he had been looking for. He had simply blown the ice right out of the side which was holding the metal secure. Looking up the Russian noted thankfully that the ceiling was still holding.

'What are we looking for?' Myron asked inquisitively.

'Not sure,' Kirill replied. 'What we find, we find.'

'Brilliant,' Myron replied. 'I could have brought your bloody robot to tell me that.'

'I not remember any of this Myron,' the Russian said impatiently. 'We go further, take photos of what we find, then get out. Once we report on our findings then we might come back another day.'

'I do like your attitude of making sure we get out alive,' the Britain replied.

'Look,' Kirill pointed. 'Up there, another doorway?'

'Could be,' Myron replied as he focused his headtorch far up the icy tunnel. 'Seems to be circular though and made of stone, not metal this time.'

'Odd.'

'Come on Kirill,' Myron urged him forward. 'The quicker we take some photos, the quicker we can get back out into fresh air.'

Isobel stood looking around the great hall area for a few minutes until Koarni returned from the other tunnelways.

'Come,' he noted. 'That's enough time down here for now. Still a lot of dust.'

'Okay,' Miss Fortuna responded. 'Thank you.'

'No problem,' Koarni gave her the thumbs up. 'Another week, maybe two and we can get light and air extraction fully working. Then you can come here whenever you wish and start to plan where to put the kit.'

'I will,' Isobel replied as they began the walk back to the open air. She regretted not being able to curb her enthusiasm for the visit and bringing the Tomahawk down to the tunnel entrance, as she'd probably have to push it back up the hill. It was far too powerful to risk motoring back up the dusty tracks, whereas on the way down she had simply glided and pumped the brakes every few metres. Hopefully Koarni could load it onto the back of one of his trucks.

'Ah daylight,' Koarni noted as they rounded the final corner which lead back out into the open cast mine. Something caught the mining manager's eye and his happy demeanour soon vanished in an instant.

'Boss!' a voice shouted from the tunnel entrance as the figure ran down to them. 'You need to get out!'

Harrison Templar sat with Alessandro Fortuna and other guests at the casually laid out afternoon tea in the VIP room. Unlike other Templar gatherings this time the guests simply wandered in, chatted and dispersed as they pleased. Fortuna too was relaxed for once, his mind a nice haze of champagne and hors d'oeuvre.

Harrison, unlike Isobel and others he knew, had decided quite early on not to wear a device that was easily noticeable by others. Currently his ankle tag was relaying in Morse code exactly the location and status of his Tomahawk. Harrison almost found it impossible to contain his smile, the vehicle was actually parked within the heart of the mine. What fortuitous luck.

The Tomahawk motorbike he had leant Isobel. Isobel, the once heir to *FortunaCS* who was currently situated at the bottom of an open cast mine. The mine that Templar had researched as matter of course to his usual business requirements and found an anomaly. An anomaly that now left her exposed.

Harrison smiled across the table to Alessendro, whom Templar had tried to assassinate six months ago and thought he had succeeded, only for the man to rise again from the dead. This time the Fortuna's would not be so lucky.

Although the death of Sergio had been opportunistic, both his and now Isobel's would ultimately both be linked to mercenary groups seeking either wealth or revenge. Templar had utilised Doctor Harding's contacts to ensure the open cast mine could be booby trapped, which had eventually led to Nolan and his prototype troops to carry out an impromptu mission here near Port Elizabeth. It had all fallen together as if planned, but Templar knew better than that. The accident awaiting to occur would be labelled as either terrorism or revenge, but underneath it all was something rather simple in nature. The Fortuna's had simply grown too rich and too relaxed in their kingdoms and were now easy targets those with the strength needed to plot their downfall.

And after their deaths, both companies had so much invested within the space program that templar would simply head up both. The investors would have no other choice. Eventually *FortunaCS* would become just another division of the Templar Innovation Community. This was exactly the reason Harrison had chosen this company name in the first place. The acronym was basically a 'tick' and the name itself invited collaboration, although Templar knew how different this was in real life. He controlled it all.

Harrison picked up his champagne flute and waited for his ankle tag to confirm the Tomahawk was being restarted. Once that happened, he would send the message for the detonation. Nolan and his team were already far from here, and the bombs would never reveal that it was remotely detonated rather than on timers.

There were no strings attached. It would then be a small step to ensure Alessandro suffered a fate of despair, once both his children were laid to rest.
Harrison Templar felt the ankle tag nudge his leg and lifted his phone steadily. Checking his text messages, he simply sent a new one, before returning it back to his jacket pocket.

He smiled and his heart began to race. It was done.

The taxi that drove Ishyan to the mine skidded on the dirt track just outside the security gate. As soon as it stopped the security guard ushered Ishyan over to the edge of the open cast mine, pointing down to where some of the staff had run to ensure Koarni and Miss Fortuna were warned about the incoming danger.

As Stölles made his way to the ridge he caught sight of one of the mine staff starting Templar's bike in order to get it out of the way to get Isobel and Koarni into an awaiting truck.

Then all hell broke loose.

Pyramidian

Myron spent little time hesitating taking photos on the smartphone he was given as beside him Kirill searched for more clues.

The ornate circular stone doorway in front of them stood majestically, encased in ice and seemingly alien to this environment. It obviously didn't belong here, which only posed even more horrible questions for both men.

'There,' Myron noted, pointing at another part of the floor. Something deep within his subconscious was trying to wriggle free. 'You can tell from the light blue shading that those were footprints from ages ago, now preserved in the snow and ice.'

'I'm not disagreeing my friend,' Kirill replied. 'It's just the fact that they do not continue past our blown our metal gateway, nor that they look human, is my point.'

'So, where did they go?' Myron asked the obvious question, before looking back at the monument. 'Surely not?'

'We leave this place,' Kirill said. 'And I think we use remaining dynamite to bury it under the mountain.'

'I agree,' Myron noted, although the Russian had not asked a direct question. 'Pass me some, the quicker the better.'

'Copy my intervals,' Kirill offered as he started to use his ice pick to create holes to place the dynamite sticks. 'They're on remote so one press and all go up.'

'Okay,' Myron replied, his ice pick cutting deep holes in the walls. His strength was undoubtedly growing, but as yet his mind seemed to be his own. Kirill also seemed to be largely unaffected. Maybe this gem juice was not as bad as first thought.

'That's enough,' Kirill noted once they had completed about thirty metres of tunnel. 'With any luck the roof collapse will stop anything that comes this way…' he noted, looking back at the monument one last time along with his friend.

Myron then followed the other man; not entirely sure the reasoning was soundproof, but happy that they were soon to bury it under hundreds of tonnes of snow. They both retreated past the blown metal gate and toward the crossroads where they hid last time.

The Britain was a bit more prepared this time of asking.

'Blow it,' he winked.

The explosion tore apart the tunnel that they had vacated, but the noise did not seem to cease as quickly as before.

'What happened?' Myron asked as he ran back toward the crossroads. He was met with the sight of snow and ice blocking his path, but beyond that either further cave ins were occurring or something far worse, as there seemed to be a constant thunder from behind the white barrier.

'We get out of here,' Kirill muttered from behind him. Myron nodded in agreement and began to jog along the slippery surface behind the Russian. Neither wanted to slip now and hurt themselves, but something primeval told them that time was of the essence. 'Head back to surface and then to chopper.'

The noises behind them failed to slow, something was happening. To Myron's horror it no longer sounded natural either, but strangely mechanical. Next to him Kirill let out a sigh of despair.

He had begun to remember.

Isobel was the first to reach the tunnel opening, just as the first explosion tore apart one of the lower levels below her. The miner holding her bike, with engine running, simply did not know what to do.

'Get Koarni into that jeep and get out of here!' she yelled, just as the site manager exited the tunnel, breathing very loudly. A second explosion. Koarni did not stop but shouted to both to join him and jump onto the back of the jeep.

Any other day Isobel would have joined him, but today her fear forced her to choose a different path. A third explosion, all below them. She vaulted the Tomahawk, revved the engine and took off up the dirt track away from the pit. Each new explosion she could feel vibrate beneath her and although nothing seemed to be happening to the mine, she knew it was only time. Without wanting to look down she assumed at intervals around the hard rock were placed multiple bombs, each explosion weakening the mine until it simply sank into itself.

The Tomahawk skidded sideways as the mine now began to give way. It was almost as if the whole rockface was slowly becoming a landslide. As she threw the bike around the next corner, she chanced a look back to Koarni and could see the jeep, but it was already far behind. Isobel forced her head forwards and concentrated on her own safety.

Up on one ridge of the mine she caught sight of a figure who was unmistakable. Ishyan. He was near a huge crane, but Isobel was unfortunately far from reaching him. The bike might have been powerful, but she did not need power right now, Isobel required the ability to drive right up the near vertical walls. She needed some luck.

As Myron half-pulled Kirill out into the open air he could not believe his eyes. There, out where the helicopter had landed, was a chaotic tribe of humanoid creatures. Some were tearing apart the helicopter, some searching the surrounding area whilst others simply seemed to be attacking each other.

'Kirill,' Myron whispered, hoping that their presence would not be noticed. The younger man half comprehended turning back into the tunnel, an action which the Russian noticed.

'No,' he warned. 'Not back in there my friend. Worse.'

'Really?'

'Here we have a fighting chance,' Kirill told him. 'Come, we must bide time.'

'For what?' Myron asked as the Russian quickly hurried toward the abandoned buildings, both men were easy prey out in the open.

'There,' Kirill pointed as they ran. 'On the horizon. Back up.'

'What are they?' Myron asked. He could barely make out the shapes, but hoped they were coming quickly to their aide.

'My babies,' Kirill replied, his voice strangely edged with concern. 'You wanted automation; I'll show you AI at its finest.'

'Okay,' Myron agreed with him, only wanting to get under cover. 'You can convince me once we hide ourselves.'

'No,' Kirill said. 'No hiding, we must remain on the move. Only way to survive.'

Myron nodded and was relieved when they found shelter. However, just at that moment something else appeared at the tunnel entrance, and it was huge, hungry and very angry.

Instantly it all clicked together. The big cat from Ashton's story was anything but. It could only have been genetically modified.

Isobel stood as the Tomahawk rounded the next corner, her body acting as a lever to swing the bike around the ninety-degree bend. The whole world now seemed to be shaking but she refused to give up.

She knew that Ishyan was over the far side of the mine, but the tracks were concentric around the pit with nothing to assist her. Rounding another corner, she dared to look back but could no longer see Koarni's jeep. Isobel knew she was almost out of time.

Myron pulled Kirill up the stone staircase as they sought higher ground away from the nightmare that was behind them.

'What the hell is that?' the Britain questioned.

'No idea,' Volkov replied. 'But whatever it is it seems to have had a bad day. I say run and hope the backup can do the job for us.'

Myron chanced a glance over his shoulder as they reached a turn in the concrete stairwell and watched through the broken window as first the creature attacked a few of the smaller humanoid figures and then looked up again at the two men.

'It seems to like us,' Myron sighed. 'Although it's clearly an enemy to whatever else is down there.'

'They won't stop it,' Volkov muttered. 'They're only the first order Menazee. Insane creatures. Whatever it is we need some firepower.' He looked at the approaching group of attack helicopters and contemplated their greatest chance of survival. 'We need to keep on the move.

Keep climbing, hopefully we can then find a way to give that thing the run-around.'

'Not sure going higher is the best option,' Myron replied. 'But we don't have much choice.'

Ishyan could see the inevitable occurring right before his eyes so wasted no time as he climbed back into the huge earth moving machine. He swung the crane hook out across the open cast mine's edge and soon found the ground beneath him give way.

The huge crane first leaned slowly forward, Stölles waiting for the exact moment to jump clear and ensure he was safe. Killing himself at this moment in time was not going to help Isobel in the slightest.

Feeling the inertia of the leaning crane take over Ishyan jumped clear and kept rolling and scrambling free from the falling metal behemoth. The dust exploded up around him, smothering him from head to toe with fine dust. The ground beneath him was still stable enough to walk on but there were now huge cracks appearing in different places, most notably around the weight of the crane.

Stölles had no idea how many explosions were still reverberating from around the mine but didn't hesitate to wonder if the worst was over. Instead he jumped back up into the cockpit, which was now on its side, and switched the lever that unravelled the hook at the end of an almighty length of steel cable.

He jumped back out of the fallen crane and saw that the descending landslide had taken the hook down several layers of the pit, and toward where Isobel was heading. She wasn't quite there, but it was now her only chance. Ishyan waved to get her attention before the final explosives all detonated at the bottom of the pit.

'Isobel,' was all Ishyan could whisper.

Myron McGivney reached the top of the derelict building to be met by a sight that brought despair to his soul.

In their haste that they climbed to the part of the building that was not linked to the other areas of the compound. It was a square flat roof the size of a tennis court and the next levels down on either side were steep sloping tiled roofs, no doubt designed to keep snow and ice off.

Myron ran to each edge, easily noticing the lack of the creature down below. As if to answer his question came unwelcome noises from within the building.

'It's coming,' Volkov muttered. He checked the rounds in his shotgun before stepping back away from the doorway.

'There must be something,' Myron noted before running around to the back of the stairwell. There it was. 'Kirill, come on.'

'What is it?'

'Telephone wire, industrial type,' Myron smiled. 'We'll rope slide.'

'Rope slide?' Volkov spluttered.

'It's either that or face that thing before your mates arrive,' Myron noted.

'We have plenty of time,' Kirill noted before the floor below them almost caved in. Myron jumped back as a lethal paw shot up through the roof and almost took his leg with it as it disappeared again. 'Okay, I go first,' the Russian noted and took off his rucksack, swung it around the wire then held on with both hands and jumped.

Both men could see that the wire gradually dipped across to the next building, but Myron had wondered if it would hold their weight. Halfway across Kirill looked as if he was a seasoned veteran doing a training jump as he glided with ease.

'Thanks for making it look easy,' the Britain gave Volkov the thumbs up as Kirill made it to the other side. McGivney tried the same trick, and wrapped the rucksack handles around the wire. He didn't even wait to see what was behind him.

Isobel looked down and saw the dust rise from the centre of the concentric ringed road and knew that whatever had just happened in the bowels of the mine, the sands of time had finally run dry.

She revved the Tomahawk and instead of aiming along the tracks, which were starting to evaporate right before her eyes anyway, she drove headfirst toward the collapsing side of the mine.

As the whole pit fell in on itself the walls began to become landslides, but as they did the angle of the moving slope became less severe. It was this that Isobel now sought as refuge from the despairing thought of being buried alive.

The Tomahawk hit the first part of the oncoming landslide and Isobel thought it was going to catapult her clear of the bike. However, as she rode the moving rubble, something came into view just ahead.

She could not believe her eyes.

Kirill Volkov dropped his shotgun and brought his rifle up to cover Myron as he jumped clear of the building opposite. Almost instantly the creature erupted up through the roof and spent a few seconds looking for both the humans. Once it caught sight of Myron, Kirill fired two shots, although intending to give Myron more time rather than slay the beast.

His plan partially worked. It also made the creature infinitely angrier. It turned and slashed its claws through the telephone wire, sending Myron sprawling to the floor as he landed heavily on the rooftop next to Kirill.

'We should go,' Volkov muttered as the creature started to scale down the outside of the building opposite. Kirill slung the rifle back over his shoulder and picked up the shotgun.

'Yeah,' Myron noted, getting back to his feet. 'Back inside though, it might slow him down. Maybe.'

As the two men bolted inside the building and along the corridors heading away from the creature the sound of the incoming helicopters grew to a crescendo.

'Now we see how good my baby really is!' Volkov shouted. Myron heard his words but decided against correcting his grammar. Unless...

The metal glinted in the sunlight as Isobel fought to keep the Tomahawk upright. By now the pace of the bike was diminishing against the flood of the landslide, but if she kept upright, she could just about outride the flurry of smaller rolling rocks. It would only be a matter of time before the mine literally fell apart.

The silver object grew and was heading straight for her, but instead of trying to manoeuvre out of the way she simply guided the bike toward it. As it levelled with her, she slammed the bike into first gear, slowed to almost a stop, then jumped clear of the bike and grabbed hold of the huge metal hook.

Up above her she heard the whine of a motor kick into action and she knew Ishyan was attempting to pull her up. However, the rocks and stones were lethally close to her hands as first she jumped onto the hook, then held on for dear life. Within seconds she had taken off her jacket and had wrapped it around where the hook and wires were connected.

She stood and leant back, letting her jacket take the strain, and then straightened her legs. Isobel felt like she was surfing the huge metal hook back up the lethal landslide. It seemed to be working.

The barrage of machine gun fire blew apart the northern end of the abandoned building as Myron and Volkov ran ever southwards along the fourth floor. The fact that the helicopters were firing on the building at all was not a good sign, but they were here and were helping.

Myron chanced a look over his shoulder and the sight did little to ease his immediate concerns. It was gaining, either that or they were slowing.

'You ok?' he called across to Kirill.

'No,' Volkov shook his head. 'I never run this far before.'

Myron nodded but nothing seemed to assist them as they ran from room to room. He pulled up his rucksack and pulled anything out that was useful. Volkov took one of the grenades and simply took out the pin and dropped it. A couple of moments later he did the same with a second. It at least made them both keep running.

The first explosion ripped apart the building around twenty metres behind them, the second even closer. Then they came to a bend. Volkov took the rucksack off Myron, took out another pin from a grenade but this time simply dropped the rucksack onto the floor. They then ran westwards as fast as possible before the explosion ripped apart the corner of the building with a huge bone cracking vibration and soundwave.

Both men were flown to the floor, their bodies battered and bruised. Yet still they heard it come after them.

'Come on,' Myron said through the dust. 'What's in your rucksack?'

'Nothing nice,' Volkov muttered. 'If I set it, we don't stop. Ok?'

'That bad hey?'

'Firecracker.'

'Right,' Myron's eyes almost popped out of his head. 'Let's go.'

Volkov tripped the switch on the timer then hurried after his comrade, knowing he might have either given them a fighting chance, or was about to incinerate them in an instant.

Ishyan clicked the switch into the locked position before jumping free from the crane cockpit and looking down into the pit below. The plan was working, although he had not contemplated that Isobel would try to ride the giant metal hook as the huge steel wires brought it back toward the crane.

'She's unbelievable,' Stölles heard himself say. Around him the landscape was still moving like quicksand, and he knew that even if this idea worked, then they were not out of trouble yet. Ishyan also saw the huge dust cloud erupting from the centre of the open cast mine, and although it wasn't probably going to harm them, he didn't fancy trying to survive the landslide without any visibility.

Returning his gaze to Isobel he noticed they were almost there. Just another twenty metres and she'd be safe, unless disaster struck and the whole piece of rock underneath Ishyan gave way,

He turned and looked at the huge crane on its side. That was quite likely given the weight of the metal monstrosity. Ishyan turned side on and looked between Isobel then the crane, time and time again, checking the options they had. Stölles watched and listened, the whine of the crane's winch growing with every second. Ishyan looked at the machine again and moments later realised why. As the crane was on its side the winch was not reeling in the wire in a uniform fashion, the metal wire was being concentrated at one end, simply due to gravity. It would soon jam, and the winch would break.

Ishyan jumped back on the crane's cockpit and turned off the winch. He had literally only turned they key when he felt the crane fall a small distance beneath him. Then it began to slide over the side of the ridge a bit more.

Ishyan jumped clear, only pausing to yell in Isobel's direction to warn her. As he hit the turf the huge dust cloud rushed up the side of the open cast mine and hit him square in the face. Stölles refused to hit the ground or protect himself until he was clear of the crane.

The horrendous nose of twisted metal rang in his ears as he ran from the crane, his feet slipping sliding over the uneven rocks. Eventually he fell, and hugged the ground tightly, trying to breathe as he folded arms around his head to create a barrier.

The noise continued as the crane was pulled over the edge of the ridge and then it skidded down into the void beyond.

Ishyan thought of Isobel but knew she had to have made it. She had to.

Myron felt the intense heat of the incendiary device rush upon them from behind, relentlessly forging along the corridor whence they now ran. At the far end of the floor level he could see a wide window and took his pistol from its holster to weaken the glass as this was now their only means of escape.

Kirill noticed Myron's actions and swung his shotgun out in front of him. Neither man fancied running headfirst into a potentially industrially strengthened windowpane.

From behind, the roar of a beast pushed to the point of agony overtook the fire. The sound strangely prompted more reaction from the men than the approaching fire. Myron fired a few shots towards the glass and Volkov simply held his shotgun at shoulder height, wanting not to waste any of his bullets. If his comrades' shots didn't do the trick, then his would.

As Myron's pistol ran dry of bullets, he turned quickly and saw the creature tear through the fires, itself ablaze, its eyes full of hatred for them both.

'Go,' was all Myron could shout. It was now or never. Volkov pulled the trigger.

Isobel saw the crane tilt toward her and jumped clear of the hook being winched back up. Moments later the hook stopped, and everything seemed to be heading downhill. She kept jumping across sideways to evade the crane, before being engulfed completely by the dust cloud that ascended from below.

Isobel had no option but to try and bury her head within her hands and arms to protect her nose, mouth and lungs and hope that her actions would not be the end of her. Almost like an avalanche she knew to keep on top of the descending rubble, but it would only take one larger piece to hit her. Isobel hoped and prayed.

The sounds around her were so different she almost felt as if she were in a warzone. For the first time she heard shouting, mixed in with the twisting of metal and the constant movement of rock over rock. As the fear began to take her, she instead thought of Myron. She would happily trade places with him right now, whether he was.

Myron hit the shattered glass first, followed by his Russian friend Kirill Volkov. There was no plan, just the impulse of escape. Both men fell, the fall from the fourth floor interrupted as a sloping roof jutted out from two stories up.

Myron hit the tiles first, the impact driving an involuntary groan from his lungs, with Kirill landing moments behind him. The roof was so steep it did little to slow either man, but at least Myron began to spread his body and decrease the inertia of gravity.

All too soon the roof ended and again they fell, this time for another two stories and into a snowdrift. Volkov had the happier landing, a nice padding of British flesh beneath him. Myron moaned. Kirill looked up.

Just then the creature jumped after them, its eyes embedded on Kirill as it plummeted towards them. Volkov had no time to raise his weapon.

Myron turned his head just as the machine guns commenced once again, but this time from the other direction. One of the helicopters had circled the complex and approached from behind.

The creature burst into a thousand fragments as the rounds penetrated the body, the blood and flesh falling onto the two men and the snow around them.

As Kirill moved to protect himself, he caught Myron square in the jaw, the pain muffled by the insane laughter that followed.

'I hope that was the surprise,' Myron sighed. Kirill tried to get to his feet but failed miserably.

'It might well have been,' Volkov admitted. 'I did not tell you but four of those craft were manned, the fifth was automated. FEDOR might be a Russian embarrassment, but my baby isn't.'

'Yes,' Myron acknowledged. 'I guessed you weren't expecting five helicopters. Was it her that saved us?' McGivney asked.

'I think so,' Volkov noted. 'It looks like only one helicopter came this way, that is probably her.'

'And the rest?'

'My old comrade in arms,' Kirill shrugged. 'We might be in a little bit of a bureaucracy nightmare my friend. But it was worth it.'

'Not sure about the "worth it bit",' Myron smiled as he helped the older man to his feet.

Global Seed Vault

Harrison Templar flicked through his smartphone, one of the green lights on an app suddenly turning off. He smiled. So, it was done. There was still the eventuality of identifying the body and proving Miss Fortuna's death, or injury. Whichever it was did not bother Templar. Just knowing that the tag he had had fitted to his Tomahawk had stopped sending a transmission meant that it was irreparably damaged. If everything had gone according to plan, then both it and Isobel were now underneath several thousand tonnes of rock. He flicked through to his email box and sent a draft message he'd saved earlier that day.

Alessendro looked across at him from the table. He was next, Harrison thought, smiling as he did so.

'So?' Alessendro asked. 'Are you going to let me know where that thing landed yet?'

'Of course,' Templar noted. It could not hurt now. Soon the world would come crashing around Alessendro. 'It's in an American military base until we're ready to move it again. I trust the South African's implicitly, but I had to take into account every possible eventuality.'

'That's understandable,' Fortuna replied before something grabbed his attention on the television screen behind the bar. 'Oh no...'

Commander Gemma Andrews sat in the rear of the attack helicopter as it took off from the USS Nimitz which was based in the North Atlantic Ocean. Twin Lockheed F-35 jump jets had transferred both her and DT from the eastern coast of America to the warship, and now she was heading to the *Global Seed Vault* in

Svalbard, where she had the order to apprehend both Doctor Harding and Anthony Draven using all means necessary.

Admiral Leffer had managed to link Sebastian Nolan to first Ulrich Bessek and now Doctor Harding. Anthony Draven seemed to be the unexplained link between them all, but for now that did not matter. It was time to bring an end to this.

Next to her on the helicopter sat Lieutenant Farr, her newest second in command. She had already worked alongside him so knew only too well about his exploits and was, as ever, thoroughly impressed. Andrews hoped this time that she could keep this group together under her command, instead of being split up. Hopefully Leffer could make that happen.

Gemma looked over at DT, who was as ever in "Deep Thought", a skill Andrews had always joked about but one which made her sniper invaluable. DT had once told her how she spent such downtime simply taking her mind to the field, imagining every known variable that could possibly occur once the red mists fell.

Think away, the commander thought. We might need your intuition more than ever under Leffer's command. He might be an Admiral, but Gemma did not trust him. Looking across at Farr he smiled back, giving her the thumbs up before turning to the co-pilot who singled back with five fingers. Farr turned to the rear section's troops and gave them the five-minute warning before all lights went out.

Action time.

Myron McGivney and Kirill Volkov stood in front of the five helicopters as the soldiers exited four of them.

'See,' Kirill noted. 'My baby did save us.'

'Great,' Myron nodded as the soldiers walked their way. 'But your friends don't look very happy.'

'Ah,' Volkov replied. 'There's a reason for that. That's General Fyodor Chugunkin.'

'Kirill Volkov,' the man at the front of the soldiers said loudly as his troopers raised their rifles. 'Once again you tell me one thing but yet we find another.'

'This was a surprise to me as well,' Volkov protested. 'I had intel on a wanted man called Doctor Harding, so we went in pursuit.'

'I read the intelligence report,' the general spoke softly as he stopped right in front of the two men. 'It clearly states that he is based in the *Global Seed Vault*, which is about 50 miles that way.'

'We wanted to sneak up on him,' Myron offered.

'And you,' the general noted quickly. 'You not Russian. Volkov, what is meaning of this?'

'Um,' Kirill stuttered. 'You must know Mr McGivney from the Fortuna incident?'

'Really?' the general looked on impressed.

'Yes,' Myron answered, somewhat embarrassed.

'You kill Bessek?'

'No,' Myron replied, unsure what was the safe answer, so opted for the truth.

'Pity,' the general replied. 'I would have given you key to my city.'

'But you read the news report though?' Kirill asked.

'I read the classified documents,' the general pointed out. 'So, is this linked to Bessek as well?'

'We think Bessek worked for Doctor Harding,' Volkov noted. 'There are others, all in the report.'

'So, you stop Harding, and this terrorism goes away?' the general asked.

'Quite possibly, yes,' Myron nodded.

'Okay,' the general nodded, his thoughts drifting momentarily away. 'How is this?' he contemplated eventually. 'I found my automated helicopter stolen, but without signs of break into the base. We followed in pursuit, which first took us to Svalbard, and the Pyramidian abandoned mining complex.

What we found there horrified us. We therefore had no option but to clean up the complex,' he noted using his hands to describe his intention to use multiple explosive devices. 'Then, as we were cleaning up, we triggered another device in that mountain,' he pointed where the creature had come from. 'To our horror the mountain disintegrates before our eyes, burying everything within.'

'Everything,' Kirill noted.

'Beyond trace,' Myron nodded.

'Then,' the general offered. 'Later we find the helicopter back at our base. It's a mystery but it had returned whilst we were away. No reason, no possible way of finding out who did it.'

'Understood,' Volkov smiled. 'How long do we have?'

'Maximum of three hours,' the general whispered. 'But before you go...'

'Yes?' Kirill asked.

'Was it shut?' the general asked them both. This question threw Myron but not his companion.

'Yes sir,' Kirill nodded. 'From what we saw it had never been opened.'

'Oh, it has been opened,' the general corrected him. 'A very long time ago my friend. That thing was imprisoned for quite a while. But it remembered you I see.'

'Oh great,' Myron sighed. 'This is the bloody surprise. You unlocked that gate and let that thing through in the first place. No wonder you didn't want to remember.'

'Myron, I promise!' Volkov protested, although even he did not truly believe his own words.

'It was both of us Mr McGivney,' the general noted. 'I, for my sins, had no choice but to remember, to protect this place from ever being known to the wider world. My friend here, I could not let him suffer that same fate.'

'You?' Kirill uttered, half angry and half relieved. He was not going mad after all.

'We will need to debrief you,' the general noted. 'But for now, you have a mission. Go and reprimand that Harding, and make sure Russia is covered with this glory.'

'We will,' Kirill noted as he bid farewell to the general and made his way over to the AI helicopter along with Myron.

'Do we fly this thing?' the Britain asked cautiously.

'No,' Kirill replied. 'Let her do her thing. And mind what you say.'

'You are kidding me,' Myron chuckled before stopping as he caught Kirill's expression. 'You're not joking…'

Isobel felt the rubble move near her and dared to lift her head from the ground. It had only been moments since the landslide had stopped, and she was simply so relieved to be alive. Isobel dared not move, just in case she was actually more injured that she first thought.

'You okay?' a croaky but recognisable voice asked from the settling dust.

'Ishyan,' she peered up and smiled. 'You look a mess.'

'You're not looking so hot yourself Miss Fortuna,' Stölles grinned back. He helped her back to her feet, before he took out his phone. Isobel looked over and then asked for it.

'I'll call this one in,' she said softly, and rang the emergency number, her mind racing. 'Hi,' she began as the call was answered. 'I'm up at the Bethelsdorp mine, there's been a huge explosion. My colleagues are buried under the rubble. Please send everyone you can.'

Ishyan watched on, unsure how he could help at present. They also needed military intervention, but Isobel was already way ahead of him. As soon as the call to the emergency services was dealt with, she commenced another call, this time to her contacts at the South African Air Force in Durban. The call was brief, but to the point.

'What now?' Stölles asked as Isobel closed the call.

'Just one last thing,' she sighed, flicking a few onscreen buttons. 'Film me,' she whispered, the reality of what had just happened bringing her almost to tears. 'We can't help them Ishyan, but others can. We need the world to see this as soon as possible.'

'Yes Isobel,' Stölles nodded and started to film Miss Fortuna, standing on the ridge of the open cast mine, tears flooding down her face, as she began to recall the horror that had just happened. Almost within moments she had already pleaded with everyone in the local area for assistance. Ishyan prayed that the miners could be helped, but silently only wanted to leave here and make sure Alessendro was safe.

Somehow, he knew this would be true, as with the live recording Isobel had let the world know that something horrific had happened here today, and it would be investigated. That left her family safe for now, and with any luck would also deal a warning to Harrison Templar. A huge warning.

We know the truth.

The large automated Mil Mi-24 attack gunship helicopter flew low and with great speed across the Svalbard snowy landscape, the two men inside quiet but ready. They had already picked new weapons for apprehending Harding, although Volkov still argued with Myron regarding his choice.

'Tranquiliser?' Kirill asked, stunned.

'I'm not a man of war,' Myron reasoned. 'If I carry a pistol I'll hesitate.'

'Maybe,' Volkov nodded. 'Maybe.'

'I will,' Myron told him. 'I'll think too much and that could be disastrous. This way I can accidently shoot the Head Librarian, and nobody will any worse for wear, after a few days or so…' he trailed off.

'So, your plan is just to shoot everyone?' Volkov smirked. 'You'll need a bigger gun then. Maybe a Kalashnikov rifle fitted with mini tranquilliser pellets?'

'Funny,' Myron returned as the helicopter swerved tight to the right. Strangely McGivney didn't seem worried in a helicopter being piloted by artificial intelligence.

'We're nearly there,' Kirill pointed as the concrete nose of the *Global Seed Vault* crept into view. 'Fortunately for us there's a back entrance.'

'Really?'

'For deliveries,' Kirill winked.

Commander Gemma Andrews and her team of soldiers exited the chopper as soon as it hit the snowy terrain. They stormed the front of the *Global Seed Vault*.

The security guards were quickly moved out of the way as Lieutenant Farr showed them the International Arrest Warrant for Doctor Harding. Scientists stopped their work and also swiftly scattered as the squad moved through the entrance hall with purpose and vigour. The team began to break up, as planned, as the entirety of the installation was searched.

Andrews and Farr took the golden route, the passage to the area of the GSV that probably had the most chance of housing Draven. The other soldiers peeled off in pairs or threes and investigated the rest.

'I never did say thank you for the Cairo affair,' Farr smiled as they hurried down the corridor, halting only to search the single offices off the main route.

'Think we came up even on that one,' Andrews replied. 'Glad you kept your squad together, they always impressed me.'

'What's the story with DT?' Farr asked. 'She always sleep on trips?'

'It's not sleeping,' Gemma whispered as a single office lay up ahead. End of the line.

Farr didn't respond but simply gave his Commander the thumbs up then rose his weapon. He signalled that she would lead, but that he would be the first with a weapon drawn.

As Isobel entered the final room of the search, she saw two figures, one motionless on the floor, the other hunched against a wall. Their eyes met.

'You?' Gemma said in disbelief.

Anthony Draven knew time was of the essence. He had travelled so far to be here today, and still had so much to do. Roc had helped him, although just how the island doctor had managed to orchestrate Draven to this destination, in such a short timeframe still impressed him immensely. Anthony thought he had pulled the strings over the last six months, but now found that a simple conversation with a like minded individual like Roc had helped him transcend to a level he had never before experienced.

The pistol was buried within his coat, the people around him carrying on their duties without a clue to who he was or why he was here. Draven kept walking, liking the anonymity for once. It was odd, now that he had achieved such a goal in his life, he now relished not having to tell everyone who he was. He knew he now had power, so decided to use it wisely.

He had left Roc on Ragged Island, although they both knew other projects awaited. Anthony had found a likeminded soul and almost unbelievably between them it had unlocked a key. Roc had the experience and contacts, but it was Draven who had the knowledge and the thirst to try everything, and it was almost this desperation that pushed him forward now.

Anthony came to the door of his dreams, but unlike his hesitation only days before all that had changed now. He was now the master of his destiny. Draven entered.

Doctor Harding looked up from a microscope, first at Draven, then at the raised gun.

The silencer offered little sound as the bullet was fired and the body fell. Draven closed the door behind him before looking over at the fallen body. It was still moving.

'Never' Draven began coldly, 'hold the answers to eternity in your hand and fail to use them.'

'Wha…,' Harding tried to ask.

'The Gatu Dojan, the manuscripts,' Anthony stated. 'I know all of this now. You had the audacity to play king, yet not once have you pushed forward. Never once tested the impossible.'

Draven leant over the body of Doctor Harding, grabbing at his jacket to search for the key to his safe. It took only seconds, and in the matter of a heartbeat Anthony Draven opened the locked door and pulled forth the ancient bioweapon, as well as several documents.

'This isn't fantasy,' Draven whispered. 'This isn't a game that you can choose whether to play or not. This is destiny, and without forcing yourself on the future you will only become part of the past.

But,' Anthony smiled as he looked down at the bloodied man. 'I have to thank you for finding me. This however is now goodbye.'

A second shot fired from the silenced gun, this time killing Doctor Harding. Draven took a few moments to pocket the Gatu Dojan and read through the documents before he left quickly, leaving only one sheet of paper behind.

It might still have a part to play.

It was not the first time this year that Myron had trudged through sewers, and although he saw the necessity of it on both occasions, it still didn't work wonders with his nausea.

'We nearly there yet?' he joked to his companion.

'You sometimes like child with your moaning,' Kirill smiled. 'Yes, I think we nearly there. We should pop up...'

'...in the toilets,' Myron humoured his friend.

'Almost,' Volkov replied. 'Processing station. It might smell a bit down here, but it could be worse.'

'I think we've already established today what "worse" was,' the Britain thought back to Pyramidian. 'Please tell me you didn't bring any more of those incendiary devices?'

'No,' Kirill answered absentmindedly. 'Here Myron, shine your torch this way.'

Off to the right of them a small tunnel broke off at around waist height. It wasn't very wide, but from the blueprints it should just be enough to allow them access to the plant about ten metres onward.

'Don't think this way was designed as an access route,' Myron noted. 'However, if it works, I'll buy you a Slammer and Fickle cigar once we get back to St. Petersburg.'

'It's Hammer and Sickle you uneducated buffoon. Also, Larissa, she likes champagne,' Volkov smiled. 'I not so much. You just get me a vodka.'

'Really?' Myron exclaimed as he pulled himself up toward the tunnel entrance. He failed miserably the first time. 'You've seen most of the world yet still want Vodka to celebrate?'

'I didn't say which Vodka,' Kirill grinned. 'To celebrate this, and by this, I mean we both get out of it alive and not end up arrested, there is special vodka, in special hotel. You like very much.'

'We'll see,' Myron hesitated before trying a second time to enter the tunnel. This time his upper body made it halfway, then he felt Kirill push him forward. Myron pulled himself onward, a sudden intense sense of claustrophobia creeping over him.

'You keep going,' he heard Volkov from behind him. 'I wait here.'

'Brilliant,' Myron sighed, his quiet comment reverberating through the tunnel. He decided to keep quiet, but still his breathing alone unnerved him.

After what seemed like tens of minutes, he reached the far end of the tunnel and pulled forth his toolbox and moved his head so that the headtorch easily showed him the set of screws he had to loosen.

The requirement was simple enough, five screws. The only issue was that the screws were on the other side of the metal bulkhead. Myron felt for the device in his small toolbox.

'Now or never,' he mused lifting the strange contraption before him. Myron had no idea how it would work, but it basically used an anti-magnet to drive the screws out from the metal casing on the other side. 'Doctor Who would love this.'

He could also hardly move in the tunnel. Myron found himself bending his neck so that he could switch on the screwdriver using his left hand and lips alone. His right arm was slightly forward, which would be great when the operation began in earnest, but right now it only seemed to be cramping up.

Finally, with device powered up, Myron's lips manoeuvred the screwdriver from his left hand to where the right was waiting. From behind him he heard Kirill begin to sing an old Russian folksong, which no doubt was designed to keep hm calm. Strangely, it did start to soothe him.

He held the device up to the metal bulkhead and manoeuvred the small magnetic tip until a little green light appeared on the side. Bingo. It was now lined up with the screw on the other side.

Myron concentrated intensely and kept it still as he pressed the button. He could hear the slight whirl of the contraption but could not tell if the screw on the other side of the wall was actually moving.

Seconds late, the device's light jumped back to red again. Well, it had either worked or the device was faulty. He would be able to tell after four more screws.

The first screw had "apparently" come out easily but was the nearest to his right hand. The others, one by one, were further away and meant he had to suffer excruciating cramp as he held the screwdriver in more and more unnatural positions. Myron knew he wasn't super flexible, but this was stating to push him to his limits.

Three screws down, Myron twisted his body to get better purchase on the position of the remaining two screws. It didn't take long, but by the time the fifth screw had fallen out, Myron was not only sweating but exhausted. He was sure he was becoming faint as well. He must have blocked off the oxygen from the rest of the tunnel where Kirill was standing. Genius.

With that in mind Myron spent no time patting himself on the back, not that he could have done, and simply pushed the unscrewed tunnel lid forward. It was tight but budged a little with his first attempt. The device had worked. Volkov was full of surprises today. Myron's second pounding on the metal lid nudged it further, and with his third it almost fell to the floor on the other side.

Myron pushed at the bottom of the lid, and as it came free from the housing, he slid his right-hand underneath it to stop it falling. Myron had no idea what was on the other side, but he was supposed to be in stealth mode, so decided to at least try and play the part effectively.

Holding the heavy metal lid in his right hand, it made it easier to pull himself forward and out from the tunnel. The fresh air wasn't as sweet as it could possibly have been, an essence of oil was a better description, but it was better than the smell of himself and a serious degradation of his remaining oxygen supply.

Myron turned his head and sent the headtorch beam back down the confinements of the tunnel toward his Russian friend. Volkov gave him the thumbs up.

The Britain withdrew his tranquiliser gun, which now seemed the most ridiculous choice of weapons of all time. However, Kirill must have known that the Russian wouldn't be coming this far, so maybe it wasn't such a mistake after all. Only one way to tell. Onwards.

Isobel and Ishyan stood on the edge of the crater as the emergency crews began to arrive from everywhere. The media also followed, but they were kept back by the police.

'Shall we?' Isobel asked her companion.

'You can do more to help Koarni and his workers by being in front of that camera alone,' he nodded. 'Go for it.'

'What's your plan?'

'I'm going to head back to the hotel,' Ishyan smiled. 'I want to make sure Templar knows who he's dealing with.'

'I think he knows,' Miss Fortuna smiled ruefully. 'But you might as well make absolutely sure.'

'Take care Isobel,' Stölles noted before turning to leave.

Miss Fortuna watched her friend leave before starting her way toward the media. Her thoughts were with Koarni, but this time she couldn't allow the tears to descend again. She had relied on her emotions to draw in the emergency and media the first time. Now she had to play the media for every possible scenario that Templar might have concocted to disable her, her father and their company.

She also had to keep the partnership together, just long enough to find out the truth and to expose Harrison Templar for the murderer that he was. It wasn't going to be easy, but then what was?

Not for the first time she wished Myron were here by her side, and again she was thankful that she had met him. Wherever he was, for however long it would be until she saw him next, she'd carry on and simply wait for him.

Myron exited the processing room and followed his paper map toward the office that was supposed to be that of Doctor Harding. It did not take long to find, and unsettlingly the door was already ajar.

He entered, flicked the light switch and instantly saw the bloodied body on the floor. Myron felt the energy leave his body and stumbled across to where the open safe lay and looked inside. Nothing.

Myron sighed regretfully that he was too late. It had to be the mysterious figure that he was chasing had done this, and maybe he'd never be able to catch him now. Harding was supposed to be the orchestrator, so now who was running this horrific show? Myron looked around the desk for more signs of evidence but only saw a single piece of paper on the side. It was a printed email.

After reading a few words Myron's world crumbled, his legs folded, and he slumped to the floor in dismay. He held his head in his hands as the truth unravelled around him.

Isobel was dead.

Harrison Templar escorted Alessendro to the hotel lobby just as a dusty and bedraggled Ishyan Stölles wandered back into the fray.

'What happened?' Fortuna asked straight away. 'Is Isobel safe? We saw the news report she gave.'

'She's fine sir,' Stölles replied. 'There are a lot of miners trapped though, so the emergency services are all there. Isobel is handling it, but I'm sure she'd like some support from you both,' Ishyan looked at them both in turn.

'Of course,' Templar was the first to respond. 'Alessendro, we'll go straight away. Thank you Ishyan.'

'Just doing my duty sir.'

'You?' Commander Andrews questioned with surprise as she stepped into the office.

'I was too late,' was all Myron could whisper, the pain clear over his features. 'I couldn't save her.'

'What is it?' Gemma asked as she saw his tears, unsure of what had happened. Myron passed her the scrunched-up piece of paper.

'Isobel,' was all he could say before dropping his head back into his hands.

Andrews read the email quickly before heading back out into the corridor. 'Farr,' she began. 'Can you get me an update on the Fortuna's in South Africa. There's been an accident. I need to know what happened.'

Gemma let her lieutenant scurry off and returned to Myron, waiting for the answer on her headset. Between them the bloodied body of Harding lay still. Indeed, Myron had been late, but what chance did any of them have against this evil?

With Doctor Harding and Sebastian Nolan gone, who now ran this freakshow? Andrews had no idea. Maybe Leffer could assist, but she wondered if he had already been hiding secrets from her.

Andrews held her earpiece as the lieutenant's reply came through. Gemma approached Myron, before grabbing his shoulder.

'She fine Myron,' Gemma whispered. 'I promise.'

Myron looked up through blood red eyes in disbelief at the woman he helped rescue only a few days ago. Her eyes were genuine as she gazed down at him. Her expression one full of happiness and hope. 'My lieutenant has confirmed. This email is a fake.'

'But it makes no sense,' he reasoned. 'Why send it if she was alive? Nobody knew I was here?'

'I don't think it was for you,' Andrews thought aloud. 'It was for Harding. The Doctor must have wanted to know. Why though, that's for another day.'

'So, he was betrayed, and we're back to square one?' Myron asked.

'Yes,' Gemma responded. 'Nolan is dead as well. DT killed him in Pennsylvania. It was either him or me.'

'DT is definitely a good judge of character,' Myron tried to laugh.

'And thanks for the armour,' Andrews said as she slumped down next to him in the office. Her trail had now run dry, for now at least. 'How did you know?'

'I didn't,' Myron noted. 'However, I thought you'd run into some trouble, your crash wasn't an accident after all. Just not sure how much anyone onboard the *Angel of the Seas* knew.'

'Someone knew I survived,' Andrews observed. 'However, I'm not entirely sure where I fit in with all this elaborate puzzle, or where the truth now lies since Harding and Nolan are out of the equation.

'There's at least one more,' Myron told her, thinking back to the mysterious man from Johannesburg and now the death of a scientist in this very room. 'I can't tell you much about them though, other than they've warned me to stay clear of Isobel. If I even contact her I've been told they'll kill her. Why, I have no idea.'

'Here,' Gemma offered and passed him her phone, opening the folder of photographs that DT had saved from the airport security room. 'That's the man that spoke to you in Johannesburg. DT tailed him to the airport. You have at least a face now. And you're being targeted because of what you know,' Andrews continued. 'And of who you are, what you believe. You just have a worth otherwise they wouldn't keep an eye on you.'

Myron thought of the red gem and the secrets that he and Kirill now knew. Did other people also know of this? If so then he was indeed a keeper of secrets so dark that Myron knew why he was now a prize asset.

'Maybe,' he reasoned. 'However, we won't be free until I find out who he is and...'

'Kill him?' Andrews asked sternly. She already knew the answer.

'No,' Myron sighed. 'But there are other ways. He picked up the tranquiliser gun and smiled. 'I'll watch from the shadows and will wait patiently,' Myron offered eventually. 'But when the times comes, I'll be there to take him down, you can count on that.'

'I won't stop you Myron,' Gemma nodded. 'I think we both have a common enemy here. Look, I've got to clear up this mess now. How did you get in?'

'Um,' Myron started.

'Use the same way out,' she noted. 'I'll come with you to make sure the route is secure.'

'Thank you.'

'We'll no doubt meet again,' Commander Gemma Andrews noted as they walked along the corridor to the processing plant. 'Until then, just stay out of trouble.'

'I can promise you I'll try,' Myron smiled back at her as he prepared himself for the re-entry to the tunnel. 'You've got an ally. You may never see me coming, but I'll be there when you need me. Even if at first you don't realise it.'

'After what happened on Tuesday,' Gemma told him as Myron passed her the screwdriver. 'I wouldn't be surprised at all if you turned up out of the blue when I'm least expecting it. Good luck with Isobel,' she said finally, waving at him with the tool to get inside the tunnel.

'She'll be surprised when I turn up as well,' Myron whispered to himself. 'Take care Gemma.'

'You too Myron.'

Seconds later Andrews lifted the metal casing and secured it behind him. It was now time to clear up this mess.

By the time Myron had retraced his steps back out of the tunnel, Kirill was already warming up the helicopter. The image of the mystery man was still clear in his mind. The Russian gesticulated to hurry up as the Britain stepped back into the daylight.

'Everything ok?' Volkov asked as Myron opened the door.

'Well, I smell,' came the reply.

'No time to change, just get in,' Kirill noted. 'We need to get out of here.'

Myron understood and strapped himself in as Kirill ran the final checks then lifted the chopper off the ground.

'We're going to be flying low to avoid radar,' Volkov told him. 'I'll need some help.'

'On it,' Myron smiled as he put his headset on. 'Where are we heading?'

'First, we need to find somewhere safe to drop you off,' Volkov reasoned. 'Then, if I'm correct, I'll rendezvous back at Chugunkin's base without any incident. From there we give it a few days until the general decides to contact me again.'

'You think he will?' Myron asked.

'After what we saw today, I have no doubt of that.'

'Guess so,' Myron agreed. 'Why do you need to drop me off first?'

'Precautionary,' Kirill judged. 'Plus, if I'm right you might now be working outside the law. You can't return to Isobel, so you're stuck with me for a bit. If Fyodor knows that then he'll have some jobs lined up for you.'

'I'm no secret agent,' Myron told him. 'And especially no double agent.'

'Double, triple, it doesn't matter to the general,' Kirill said slowly. 'I think he's more interested in what lay under that mountain. It could be that he knows of more locations like it.'

'Really?'

'Probably,' Volkov nodded. 'You're about to enter into a completely different world my friend.'

Calm before the storm

Port Elizabeth; One week later

Isobel waited in the hospital reception area until Koarni's family were ready to welcome her. The mine manager had regained consciousness earlier that morning, and since then he had been inundated with first medical staff now family. Isobel had received the call just after lunchtime that he had asked specifically to see her, so here she was, flowers in hand, waiting to see the man that for a whole week now she had prayed for.

One of the nurses opened the private room door and beckoned her in. Isobel stood, took a deep breath and made her way slowly forward. Koarni and his fellow men had all suffered horrific injuries, but they were receiving the best medical attention possible. Her father was heavily sponsoring everything surrounding the rehabilitation of these men, who somehow had all been saved from the open cast mine explosion.

Koarni had been the hero. He had simply driven the truck into one of the tunnels built into the side of the pit before the landslide buried them alive. They had just enough oxygen to survive the ordeal, although nothing was being left to chance. They were all being monitored and constantly checked even as they left hospital to return home.

Koarni had suffered the worst of the injuries, being the driver of the truck. His ribs and right forearm had been crushed in the crash, but apparently he was making a good recovery. Isobel had already offered whatever counselling and physiotherapy that was required to get him back on his feet as soon as possible.

As she entered the medical bay Koarni's family walked across to greet her. Isobel was hugged and kissed, almost mobbed, by his family before she could hear the rasping voice telling them all to sit down.

'Isobel,' he coughed, calling her over. 'Are you ok?'

'I'm fine,' she almost cried. 'You're the one we're worrying about.'

'That's not what I meant,' Koarni whispered to her. 'You take care, that was no accident.'

'I know,' she whispered back to him. 'I'll find out who did this.'

'In time,' Koarni smiled. 'Be patient. Family, please, allow Isobel to sit for a bit and listen to your stories of how you're going to get me back on my feet.'

'Football daddy,' one of the youngsters shouted happily.

'Hop scotch,' another one chipped in.

'No, no,' an older lady commented from the end of Koarni's bed. 'I'll be round each day to...'

'Actually, I'm feeling better already,' Koarni joked. 'Time to go back to work.'

Isobel couldn't help but laugh as evidently it was either Koarni's mother or mother-in-law that he had just upset.

'Well, you know the rules,' Miss Fortuna said to them all. 'Plenty of rest, physiotherapy and love, and he'll be back on his feet in no time at all. You might as well be the first to know, but your father's actions have helped secure further investment in Port Elizabeth.

The old mine was supposed to be a secret training centre for me to hide away in whilst I dreamt of flying to the stars,' she smiled at them all. 'Now, we want to recommission it to be an open centre for excellence, so potentially we might train the first STaRship pilots from this very city.

And that means,' she turned back to Koarni. 'That your father will start work on the new mine as soon as he's recovered. Until then we'll simply move the machinery around.'

The family all cheered and hugged Isobel, whilst Koarni simply smiled and mouthed a thank you back to her.

Whitby (Turks & Caucas Islands): Southwest of Bahamas

Myron wiped the sweat from his brow as he untangled the mooring line from the side of the yacht.

'You sure this is the location?' he asked his two companions from across the deck. 'I thought we were supposed to be just north of Scarborough? It's changed a bit since I was last there.'

'It's definitely the spot,' Meredith laughed, clearly satisfied that the GPS was working properly. 'Don't you like the sun Myron? Anyway, Whitby was where the mythical Dracula landed so thought this might be more to your liking. As for whether EagleEyes has been programmed prop...'

'She's fine,' Mehrtens rose his head from the laptop. 'We are covering quite a large spot of water here you know.'

'Would there be any point running a seismic anomaly test?' Myron asked, thinking back to something Ashton had mentioned last time they had met.

'As in using the radar, but knocking it down to the seafloor?' Meredith asked quizzically.

'I'm thinking what if we look for every eventuality,' Myron suggested.

'You mean someone has hidden the sinkhole?' Ashton looked across puzzled.

'In Svalbard half of the mine was basically hidden from us until it was too late,' Myron noted. 'What if nobody wanted the sinkhole to be found but didn't bury it. A seismic check might find it.'

'That'll be an impressive cover just to hide a sinkhole,' Ashton nodded.

'It's not the sinkhole that's the problem here,' Myron noted. 'What we found in the mountain was always there, someone simply uncovered it.

Kirill and I did a lot of research last week and this was the best shot at seeing if what I saw in Svalbard is even real.'

'A door, you say?' Meredith asked.

'I know,' Myron reasoned. 'It still feels like a dream, but it was there, until the general buried the whole mountain around it. Which in itself sounds like an Area 52 hoax, let me see 1% of something and my imagination will fill in the other 99%.'

'I was thinking that,' Meredith smiled across at him.

'Okay,' Ashton agreed. 'I've just recalibrated both EagleEyes and TurtleDrone, let's see if they can pick up anything.'

'How's the vaccine working out?' Meredith asked across to Myron as they waited for the data to back in.

'Good, thank you,' he thanked her. 'Kirill took a sample to their labs and between the two he's managed to control his condition as well. No more dreams, not at the moment anyway.'

'Still sounds like the red gem had its uses though, 'Ashton noted. 'But I must admit it must have been a tad terrifying to have something like that going through your body.'

'It was more disconcerting before I realised what it was,' Myron nodded. 'I can only think that the red gem was meant for either Bessek or Sergio to give them an extra edge over matters. When I intercepted it the advantage then began to sit with me, although I had no knowledge of how to harness it.

There's also the potential that Harding created it as a test, maybe not telling anyone?'

'Sounds the most plausible,' Meredith nodded. 'Nothing better than an unsuspecting guinea pig to test the latest technology.'

'So, are you completely cured?' Ashton asked as his head bobbed over his laptop.

'All tests signify that,' Myron replied. 'Looks like any heroics I need to rely from now on will be from my own persuasion. That's the only downer.

Why?' he asked slowly, noticing Ashton's smile widened almost hysterically.

'Because,' Mehrtens began. 'Guess what my little beauties have just found?'

'What is it?' Meredith asked as she got up and rushed to her fiancé's side.

'There,' he pointed at his laptop. 'And that's the minimum depth.'

Myron's heart sank. He knew too well Ashton's loves on this planet, and anything regarding depth accompanied by a smile could only mean one thing, that the sinkhole was deep. Very deep.

'That's insane,' Meredith offered. 'To hide that someone must have built an underwater roof over the hole?'

'EagleEyes and TurtleDrone don't lie babe,' Ashton whistled coolly. 'And those little tentacles off the side must be tunnels of some description. We'll need a proper search to get the 3D image of the sinkhole.

And that's before we even think of looking for a "door",' Ashton muttered.

'Great,' was all Myron could reply with. 'Don't suppose you two want to do the dive and I'll stay here watching over the yacht?'

Their expressions said everything. Another day, another dive. Just then a sound from across the waters made the three look up in apprehension. A seaplane was coming in low, and by its trajectory was heading right towards them.

'Bingo,' Myron muttered. 'This'll soon tell you whether that sinkhole has been hidden.'

'Stick with the plan,' Meredith reminded them. 'We're just scientists checking the waters.'

'With you,' Myron nodded.

'I don't even have to pretend,' Ashton chuckled and waved over at the plane as it touched down a few hundred metres from there.

'Any idea why you're waving?' Meredith asked her fiancé.

'Being friendly,' Ashton remarked. 'I'm going to ask if they have any fresh fruit. Nice ice-breaker.'

'So's a bullet,' Myron noted. 'Just calm down will you, last thing we need is anybody getting itchy trigger fingers.'

'You've been watching too many films Myron,' Ashton rolled his eyes. 'Nobody who flies seaplanes ever shoots anyone. Well, most of the time anyway.'

The seaplane motored its way slowly toward them. Myron could easily see that there was only a pilot onboard, but that did not lessen his concern. Finally, the engines shutdown and the seaplane bobbed up and down in its own wake. The door to the cockpit opened and a man appeared, neatly trimmed beard, and a smile that seemed too friendly.

'Hi,' he shouted. 'Any chance of a dingy ride over to the yacht?'

Ashton was already on the case and gave him the thumbs up. This left Myron and Meredith to wait for them both to return.

'What do you think?' she asked.

'I have my tranquilizer gun with me if required.'

'Do you sleep with that thing? You take it everywhere,' she sighed.

'It keeps me calm.'

'I'd hate to see you panicky,' she joked as the dinghy crept back to them. Myron caught the rope Ashton threw, and soon the two men were on the yacht.

'Afternoon,' the pilot greeted them all. 'Just mentioned to Ashton here that your little expedition hasn't gone unnoticed by the locals. They gave me a quick call.'

'Locals?' Myron asked.

'The Mangrove tribe that live on East Caucas,' he continued. 'You must have seen them fishing and diving for oysters from the seafloor.'

'Yes,' Meredith replied, her curiosity piqued. 'What exactly did they notice?' she tested the stranger.

'Forgive me,' he replied politely. 'I'll introduce myself. My name is Lars Ovaldson. I, like the Mangrove tribe, are protectors of certain secrets and in this instance mysteries of the deep.'

'Deep?' Meredith tried to sound surprised.

'I wouldn't have mentioned it unless I wasn't already sure you knew,' Lars continued. 'There are other ways of dispersing people who get too close. However,' he looked first at Myron, 'when you get a famous adventurer, a rogue scientist and a specialist in biology and find them together on the same yacht, near a hidden sinkhole, then I give up on coincidences.

Svalbard was a burial site, but I understand the need to keep it hidden,' Lars noted to them. 'Here though, we still have time. But I have to warn you, there are dangers everywhere. Some are searching for answers that they cannot possibly comprehend.'

Myron thought instantly to the mysterious man who haunted is movements but kept quiet. Now was not the time.

'So,' Ashton shrugged. 'We going diving or not?'

'Yes, my friend,' Lars replied. 'We all go, as you all need to see. Then once we resurface, we'll stay the night with the Mangrove tribe. They need to know that you're pure, they have a little test, but nothing you should worry about.'

'Truth serum?' Meredith asked, hearing something about it in these parts as a way to separate the good strangers from the bad.

'Along those lines, yes,' Lars smiled. 'You are indeed knowledgeable.'

'Truth serum?' Myron remarked. 'I'm not one hundred percent convinced that this is a good idea.'

'What's the worst that can happen?' Ashton asked him.

'Okay,' Myron answered him, trying not to worry. The image of the beast of Svalbard reappeared in his head, if only for a split second. It was as if it could defy the natural laws of physics and simply burst forth from his subconscious. 'Just want both sides of the argument put forward.'

'Myron has a condition,' Meredith explained clearly to Lars. 'He might react to the serum in a way the tribe might not like...'

'Oh,' Ovaldson replied with interest. 'I see,' he continued as he looked Myron deep in the eyes. 'Well, my boy, maybe we should up the dose and let the demons of hell ride loose?'

'If I didn't think that possible, I wouldn't be standing here having this conversation,' Myron replied, his words chilling both Ashton and Meredith. 'I have already seen too much for one soul to bare.'

'No Myron,' Lars whispered to them all. 'You have hardily seen anything at all. And hopefully, it will remain that way. That is why I am here.

I do not seek power; I do not seek glory nor fame. I am here merely to protect. The Earth is alone in its universe, pray it remains that way.

Now,' Lars continued immediately. 'The Mangrove chief can talk more about that tonight; he is quite good with stories. For now, we need to dive before the light goes, what we find down there you can make your own minds up upon.

I only ask one thing, that these secrets stay with you, always.'

'They will,' Ashton and Meredith replied, holding each other's hands tightly.

'I'm more worried about who else is seeking out these secrets,' Myron answered honestly.

'Then my friend,' Ovaldson said strongly. 'Once we finish here, I have a proposal for you, I need an apprentice to assist me in ensuring these sites are kept hidden.

Up to the task?'

Myron thought of Isobel and the threat that overshadowed them both.

'More than you know,' he replied. This might be the only way to eradicate the mysterious figure.

'Yeah,' Lars smiled. 'Kirill said you'd say yes. He hasn't told you everything about himself yet mind you,' and winked at the astonished man.

'I just want to go diving,' Ashton reminded them all. 'Chop chop, otherwise it'll get dark and the sharkies will come back out.'

'Really?' Myron asked. 'Let's get going then. Make the tour quick please.'

'The dive will be relatively quick,' Lars told them. 'The experience, however, will last a lifetime.'

And with that Myron had begun treading a pathway that he had never dreamed existed only three months ago.

Anthony Draven put down his phone and stirred the spoon once around the rim of his diner coffee. Outside the highway was almost deserted in the constant drizzle. Draven was currently between two tasks, the former a simple necessity that one day might prove very prosperous, the latter a simple pipe dream.

Behind him on his journey lay the Clearwater military installation in Montana, where Roc was currently posted. His elevation to such a senior role in the military had occurred almost too quickly, but neither men had asked too many questions. It was, after all, their goal to have access to such machinery and technology that they had only dared dream of before.

Anthony was convinced that Harding had been involved, and for a split second cursed himself for his own impatience by killing him so quickly only two weeks ago. So be it, Draven considered. Whatever seeds that the Doctor had planted it was now up to both Roc and him to fulfil.

Anthony looked up as the waitress assisted another client. Behind her lay the south, and a very different prospect and challenge. Although Roc fully intended to move Patrick Symions to the installation so they could continue their work, something else had now fallen into their plate.

Harding's insight had noted that the perfect human was one that could fall from a great height, and to do so would need to be saved and then nourished from the jaws of agony to almost divinity.

The Doctor had not failed him. Draven now had an entire page of names at his disposal, but one stood clear of all the rest; Daniel Bruest.

It would take time, a lot of patience and nurturing, but this person held everything Harding had promised. He had been through hell and horribly injured in a war on another shore. Daniel had also baffled medical science by walking again, and above everything else had found love with a woman.

The recovery Draven reasoned was partly down to her, it had to be. There was little else that could ever have allowed Daniel to dream of more. Anthony saw his opportunity only too well.

He would utilise Roc's knowledge of rehabilitation and continue Bruest's recovery, and then, just when time was right, he would strike.

Draven had left the Gatu Dojan with Roc, both wanted it tested on further before allowing Harding's early research to bear any truth. However, if it was what Draven hoped, then it would answer Anthony's most insatiable questions.

And all he had to do was sacrifice one man's life. Templar was right, it was up to Roc and himself now. Their leash had come off.

Anthony smiled as he thought back to Harding's words. The greater they climb, the further they fall...

First Bessek, Nolan and now Harding. He would not make the same mistake.

Draven's journey to find the answers to the afterlife had begun.

The End
of
Ice Ghosts

<u>Epilogue: World of Shadows</u>

<u>*FortunaCS* headquarters: London; Three weeks later</u>

Isobel Fortuna almost had to fight her way through the media frenzy that was awaiting her return to the London HQ of her father's company. Isobel was tired, but knew she had to put on a show in front of the cameras.

Her security team ushered her inside and soon she found herself alone in the lift heading up to her penthouse suite office. Isobel had also requested that it be left unmanned in her absence, so when she returned, she could rest in peace, for at least a few hours anyway.

As the elevator doors opened and Isobel could clearly identify that she was alone she let her heavy heart consume her consciousness once more.

It had been over a month now since she had last seen Myron or heard from him. Isobel felt as if she could not continue, the pain of not knowing was beginning to consume her every minute. Even the usual *FortunaCS* daily grind had become just that, as if all the love Isobel had ever had for her father's company had simply been torn from her soul.

Stepping over to the huge window overlooking London, Isobel stared through the afternoon rain toward the distant horizon. Miss Fortuna had looked out over the city hundreds of times before, but in each instance always had something "important" on her mind, thus ultimately ignoring the sights and sounds of the cosmopolitan city.

Today however, she felt alone, even within this bustling capital. 'I miss you so much,' she sighed aloud.

'Nice to hear it,' came the reply from behind her.

Without looking behind her Isobel simply let out a small laugh. 'I've missed you.'

'I know,' Myron replied. 'But I've been busy, as have you.'

'Well,' Isobel noted. 'We do have a schedule to keep.'

'Yes,' Myron responded. 'And we both have to keep believing.'

'That's easy for you to say,' Isobel offered. 'I haven't heard from you at all since the Angel of the Seas. How am I supposed to simply keep going?'

'You always have?' Myron questioned. 'Surely I can't have made that much of an impression on you?'

'You know you have.'

'Anyway,' Myron said, as Isobel heard his voice travel nearer to her. So much she longed for his touch. 'I've been with you since the Angel of the Seas, haven't I?'

'But that wasn't really you?'

'Wasn't it?' Myron whispered in her ear. Isobel closed her eyes and wanted to be with him, wherever he was.

'Maybe,' she said simply, before thinking this over again. 'Okay,' she conceded. 'You were always with me. So, what does that prove? That black magic exists?'

'No,' Myron smiled. 'Only that something I once thought as cancerous is in fact a stimulant, in the right dosage.'

'The red gem,' Isobel replied. 'That's what Ishyan was hinting at.'

'I guess the experiments were not as confined as first thought,' Myron noted. 'Which actually makes sense if they wanted Bessek, Sergio and...

'That bitch.'

'Yes,' Myron smiled. 'Michelle Glade, to succeed.'

'But why am I thinking of you so intensely again now?' Isobel asked simply. 'Is it returning here, to where it all began? I don't understand it?'

'You already know,' Myron told her. 'Just work it out. For now, though I have to go. I'm being watched, and by eyes of a predator. I need to keep in the shadows...'

And with that he was gone.

Isobel let him go, but felt the weight in her heart disappear, instead replaced with a burning desire to unleash hell upon the worlds of Templar and all of his followers.

'I'll find you my love,' she whispered, talking to herself as she began to turn away from the window. Nobody could hear her ramble here anyway, it was her one haven, a sanctuary Isobel desperately required in order to survive. 'However, although you may believe I have some of the red gem inside me I'm not so sure. What I can muster though is an espresso.'

Isobel fired up her coffee machine to prepare a simple espresso. Well, as simple as you could make the world's best caffeine shot.

Miss Fortuna first opened the cabinet underneath the espresso machine and checked the bags. There were five different bags here, all fresh, four of them Arabica and one Robusta. One caught her eye straight away, which almost made the hairs stand up on the back of her neck.

'He was here...'

Yes, of course he was. Isobel cursed her tiredness. That's why her memories of him had returned so swiftly. She had missed something so obvious, yet her subconscious had caught it yet again. Isobel hated playing these games but had to admit before meeting Myron these events had never once occurred. Maybe it was the red gem. Maybe being near him had affected her, and at the end of the day it had only made her stronger anyway.

So where was it? The sign that he was here?

It obviously was not the espresso bag, as that could be merely coincidence. No, this was only a sign. A finger pointing in the right direction.

Isobel ground the beans, the aroma instantly heightening her senses. Nothing could beat this. She then prepped the machine and the heated water filtered through the ground bean puck to produce the rich, concentrated espresso.

It only took one small sip for the realisation to his her, the smile broadening on her lips as it did.

'Angelo custade,' she smiled and looked back across the room to her desk. Of course, she had seen it before, on the *Angel of the Seas*, yet the ring was sitting quite clearly on her desk.

Isobel walked over, lifted up the ring, gave it a quick kiss before putting it on her finger and walked again over to the window.

'I guess you're out there somewhere,' she smiled. 'Hurry up and come home.'

'You ready?' the voice of Lars Ovaldson asked over the laptop link as Myron lent against the apartment window, looking northwards over the London skyline.
'Yes,' Myron replied. 'Guess this is as close to her as I'm going to get for a while.'

'Maybe,' Ovaldson offered. 'Come on lover boy. We've just got a lead. Pack up your bags, you're off to Venezuela.'

'Okay,' Myron replied. 'But my mum says I have to be home for tea.'

'Funny,' Lars noted as he continued to scroll through documents his end. 'Give Mehrtens a call as well, we might need his help.'

'Why?' Myron asked quizzically.

'You ever heard of tepui?'

'No,' McGivney answered simply.

'Then that's why we need Ashton,' Lars offered. 'Plus, Meredith if she's free, just for medicinal purposes.'

'Medicinal?'

'You know,' Ovaldson began. 'Snake, spider and insect bites, that kind of thing.'

'Of course,' Myron moaned. 'Why didn't I guess? Anything else?'

'Might want to check with Kirill if he knows of any big cats around this area as well? Tell him we're searching the house of the gods,' Lars nodded.

'In English?' Myron queried.

Lars gave the younger man a devilish smile.

'The tepui are ancient plateaus, table-top mountains, some untouched by human hands. We're going to be the first on some of them. Special decompensation. Ever read the "Lost World" by Arthur Conan Doyle? It's based on these unique structures.'

‘No,’ Myron replied as he sat back at the laptop. ‘Watched the film though. Hope we don’t run into any Velociraptors.’

‘Ignoramus,’ was all Lars replied with.

‘Not sure of that dinosaur,’ Myron gave him a half-smile. ‘Okay, I’ll contact Ashton. Anything beats sinkholes.’

‘Glad to hear it,’ Lars said. ‘Catch up with you soon.’

Myron hung up the call and sent Ashton a video link request. Mehrtens’ pet coconut crab answered the call instantly.

‘Hi Ashes,’ Myron said, unphased by the sight. ‘Looking fresh this morning.’

‘Ah man,’ Ashton replied. ‘Thought I’d scare you then. Wassup?’

‘Apparently, I’m off to a Venezuelan tepui, ever heard of them?’

‘Ah man. I’m well jel, My,’ was all Mehrtens could respond. ‘A thousand metre vertical cliff surrounding each mesa, overhangs the size of a Volkswagon Beetle, you get all the fun jobs. It’s a rock climbers dream. Great way to spend an afternoon.’

‘   ,’ Myron tried to reply.

‘What was that buddy?’ Ashton asked. ‘The sound cut out there for a second. Let me check my Wi-Fi.’

‘I said great,’ Myron eventually found his voice again. ‘You fancy a holiday?’

‘I’m invited?’ the other man screamed in excitement. He was physically over the moon, Myron could see. ‘Can Merry come?’

‘If you mean your fiancé then yes. The crab is a no-no. Apparently, Lars thinks we’ll need Meredith’s expertise, something about the wildlife potentially hating me.'

'Sounds a bit OTT My,' Ashton mused. 'Which plateau are we going to?'

'Hold on,' Myron noted. 'He's just sent me a list. One of the mountains is called Matawi Tepui, although he's got that circled as a warm-up climb.'

'You're Brad Pitting me?' Mehrtens almost fell off his seat. 'That's known as the "place of the dead" and is a restricted site. How the hell did you get an invite?'

'I didn't ask for one!' Myron exclaimed. 'At least there'll be no caves this time, I guess. Something to look forward to. Guess I win this time.'

'Oh Myron, your geography stinks dude,' Ashton leaned forward into the laptop camera so his whole beaming face was almost busting into Myron's apartment. 'Some of those mesas have sinkholes deeper than my love for both my Meredith's put together. The canopy cover masks most of the evidence but they're there. Imagine if we find water at the bottom of the sinkholes? A cave system untouched by humans for thousands of years...'

'Hold on,' Myron replied. 'Thought these mountains were restricted?'

'They are now,' Ashton noted. 'There are documents of the ancient Mayans exploring all these tepui in the search of religious wonders thousands of years ago. Basically, we could be diving into the belly of a massive underwater ancient graveyard, with...'

'Yes, thank you,' Myron replied and shut down the laptop instantly. He stood and turned back to the window, and toward the FortunaCS HQ. 'I'm doing this for you, you know,' he smiled. 'All for you. It ain't fun.'

No, the life Lars had offered him was dangerous indeed, but he had no other choice. Ovaldson had contacts, and Myron just had to bide his time. Eventually it would lead him to his adversary, and once that happened, he would have to make a choice. On one hand he'd be able to see Isobel again, on the other...

For now, the sands of time had truly run dry for his stay in London. Time to go. Myron collected all his belongings and turned his back on Isobel, praying one day he'd have the chance to see her again.

Myron, Ishyan & Isobel will return in:

Dark Skies

Bonus stories: Draven's case studies

The following three case studies were reported upon by Suzannah Fray under the watchful guidance of Anthony Draven. Although they are referenced briefly within *Ice Ghosts*, due to the journey Draven was undergoing, the whole stories have remained hidden, until now.

They capture instances of psychological horror and the paranormal, and in doing so will take you the next step towards *Shadow World*...

Transmission #63452
To: Doctor Harding
Please excuse the encrypted message but I too now seem to have prying eyes lingering over both my work and movements.
I have sent three digital files that will arrive separately in your secure drop-box within the next twenty-four hours.
I hope these will not disappoint.
Regards
From: Anthony Draven

Contents

Asylum

Morning After

Patrick Symions felt the early morning sunlight shine on his face, and immediately sat bolt upright in panic. His eyes felt heavy and his vision impaired slightly, lending a hazy blur to the room that he now occupied. The white walls did little to help him in his confusion, the bright sunlight dancing off them with a surreal happiness that seemed to be completely out of place with his current mood.

As his head span with dreariness, Patrick slumped down back onto the bed and sighed a tired groan before closing his eyes once again. He could not remember anything. His head spun wildly as he began to concentrate but nothing came back, no memories stirred, where each second of pursuit only brought him more minutes of panic. His mind seemed to have been completely and utterly wiped clean.

As the day progressed, Patrick quietly began to form a reasonable understanding of his whereabouts and condition. Just after noon a nurse had visited him, but she seemed intent on telling him nothing. She did not fear him though and was optimistic regarding his recovery.

The windows were thick, the glass interwoven with wire and the outside walls displayed a few tightfitting iron bars. He wondered if they were to protect or hold him. Apart from the locked door, there were no other restraints. Maybe with time he would understand why exactly he was here. There were few guards, but the building had a disturbing feel to the air. It was almost as if it radiated an energy, an electric current which held the history of everything that had ever been seen by these walls. Patrick wandered over to the window and noticed the lavish gardens within the perimeter of the buildings. He smiled. Paradise, he thought.

Soon before dinner, Patrick was visited by a male doctor and told that he was to be moved to another cell. According to the detailed notes he was now on the upward curve to recovery. This obviously pleased Patrick immensely even though nobody would tell him what his condition was, and how he had ended up here. Time would tell, he hoped.

Patrick Symions had no belongings and he soon found himself alone again, but this time in his new cell soon after dinner. He felt that he had not eaten properly for months but knew that this could not possibly be true. Still, his mind seemed far more rational after the meal, so he asked for paper and a pencil to begin a journal. He called it 'The Recovery'.

A week passed and Patrick slowly began to grow accustomed to the monotonous daily routine, and fell neatly into the pattern, as it seemed to please all the staff concerned. Each day seemed just like any other, so Patrick began to ensure that he never copied events from day to day. He would differ them slightly so not to lose himself within the void of time. He had already learned that some of the patients in the hospital were less than happy, although Patrick clearly comprehended the fact that this was due to their state of mind. He still needed answers though. They soon came.

On the night of the tenth day of his recovery, Patrick received a visitor in his room. The man had knocked politely and had then asked if he could talk to him. He was not a doctor nor a nurse. He seemed very different. Of course, Patrick had not turned down the offer. Visitors were few and far between and ultimately it might have held the chance to find answers.

His name was Adam and he had been a patient too a long time ago at the hospital. Fortunately, he had recovered but had stayed on to assist others with their illnesses. Patrick at first was wary of this stranger, just in case he was an informer for the doctors. He had seen other patients' being dragged, kicking and screaming off to far away cells, on other levels. With no memory except for this place, Patrick felt a limited trust for the doctors. He had not made any advancement to combat his amnesia, either with or without their help. He felt very alone. He needed a friend.

Patrick had soon realised that Adam was indeed a *bona fide* character and gradually crawled out from his shell. They became close friends very quickly.

'So, what kind of hospital is this exactly?' Patrick found himself asking Adam one windy day, when the front lawn had been covered with the dying leaves from the autumn fall.

'It's a kind of rehab centre,' his friend had corrected him. 'The cases here are quite unique and each very different, hence why you rarely meet some of the more concerning patients.'

'I thought that maybe it was me they were segregating,' Patrick found himself replying honestly.

'No, no, my friend,' Adam smiled. 'Your case might well have baffled a lot of the medics here but believe me, it's nothing compared to some of them.'

An awkward silence descended over the room. Patrick's gaze turned toward the window.

'What is my case?' he asked, breaking the silence but without taking his companion by surprise.

'I can't discuss that,' Adam replied regretfully. 'I do not have the full knowledge, so I'd rather not guess.'

'But would you if you knew?' Patrick asked again. He was desperate to know why. Only then could he come to terms with the problem, to face it and win.

'I could try and find out,' Adam said quietly but he seemed unsure. 'It's very risky. I owe a lot to the staff here. Some people criticise the way they run this centre and treat all the patients in their own way, with their own methods. However, it worked on me so am forever in their debt.'

'Just try,' Patrick urged him as Adam stood to leave. 'I can't remember anything. I need some guidance.'

'Ok. I'll try, but no promises,' Adam answered. With that, he left.

Recovery

The days passed but still Patrick received little encouraging news from his new friend. Adam had repeatedly tried but had not managed to uncover anything about Patrick's history. Both men would not give up hope though. It was late on a Wednesday afternoon, under a heavy sky, when Adam finally consulted his companion. He mentioned that hypnotic regression could be used to delve into Patrick's subconscious and to identify the problem.

'You're sure that you want to try this?' Adam asked as he fidgeted with his fingers nervously, scanning the door occasionally, to see if any porters were checking up on them.

'Sure,' Patrick answered, although he did not know how his companion would assist him at all. Patrick could not recall anything from his past. The doctors had told him nothing, kept him in the dark. 'How will you find out?' Patrick asked eventually. 'If I can't remember anything, how can you make my subconscious recall the past?'

'There are a number of methods,' Adam replied truthfully. 'I just need you to relax totally, to let yourself wander without walls. I need to tear down those barriers that for some reason have kept you from remembering. I heard one of the doctors saying that your case was so rare because you have no recollection, let alone little snippets. It's like your memory has been totally erased, but I have more optimism in your recovery than they do.'

'I'm glad,' Patrick smiled gratefully. 'Guess it's time to start.'

'We already have,' Adam smiled. 'You want me to help. That's the first step. It will take time, but we will succeed.'

Suzannah Fray had seen many special cases in her time but the report on Patrick Symions had prompted her into putting this unfortunate soul toward the top of her screening list. She had travelled far to visit him and hoped that it would not be a wasted journey. Suzannah had so much to offer him. She had the skills to put all that haunted the man far behind him. Suzannah just hoped that she still had a chance.

Patrick lay relaxed and comfortable on the bed, letting Adam's soothing words wash over him and pull him into another time and another world. Patrick left the wards behind and found himself lost where only his dreams had taken him before. His eyelids remain closed as his subconscious released itself of the hidden memories. This time it was different. Patrick had forged no barriers, had sensed no threat. He let himself answer.

'I see it,' he replied to his friend. Adam smiled with a sense of hope, but he did not stop. He continued to urge his friend onwards.

'What do you feel here, what *do* you see?'

'I see walls,' Patrick replied slowly, as if in doubt. 'The walls are not complete though, but…they are building themselves slowly, as if…'

'What do you sense Patrick? Look closely at the walls, what do you feel?' Adam questioned him again.

'I feel something alive,' Patrick answered after a pause. 'Not alive exactly, but a kind of energy, a kind of power.'

'Touch it Patrick,' Adam urged again. 'What does it feel like?'

Patrick reached out and felt the stonework that was building itself right in front of his eyes. There was a chair and a table beside him now. The table was beautiful and ornate, built from ancient oak wood. He smiled with appreciation. He ran his hand over the chair's covers and felt the same respect for its workmanship. Patrick looked back at his other hand and realised that the wall had grown another layer. He touched it again and felt a flicker; something that had just run like a storm through his memory and had jolted something incredible in his past. It felt like...

Love?

Yes, it was a feeling of being alive, feeling young and having something to live for. His heart thumped wildly as he tried to rekindle the image, but it had already left him. He did not panic though. For what seemed like the first time in many years, his soul had been touched.

Patrick moved away from the walls and crept across the ceiling-less room toward the far wall. Here he tried to gaze at what stood outside these walls. The clouds obscured his vision, but he could sense that he was high up here. He understood that he had to try and make it down to the ground. He turned quickly toward the stairs and stepped down from the top step with a sense of hope in his heart. He stopped.

What is it?

Patrick hesitated. He had felt that feeling again. There was also something else mixed in there, something new. I'm going down a new road, he thought.

Yes, you are.

My past? Patrick asked quietly. He now felt a sense of claustrophobia start to surround him. Did he really want to know?

Don't let your fears consume you.

Yes, he wanted to know. He felt for the second step and was relieved when the solid platform did not falter beneath his feet. He placed his weight fully onto it, then sighed heavily. He reached for the next, and the next. Patrick's hand slipped without fear onto the banister as his eyes turned from the steps to that of the walls around him.

The decorative wall design seemed formal to Patrick, and he realised that the stair-carpet on which he stood was laid centrally over the spiralling cold marble slabs – like a red carpet at a gala or ceremony. The lower floor came into view around the sweeping staircase. Everything seemed to become more focused to his eyes, reality shifting from the surreal to reality right before him.

Now what do you see?

I am on another floor.

Your past?

It seemed more of a statement than a question. Patrick quickly understood why. Only he himself could ever break down these barriers. Patrick could be led forever, but it was only within his own mind that the answers that he prayed for could be found.

I have come down one floor and stepped into my past, Patrick considered. Somehow though, he did not yet want to continue down again, not yet. There was a part of his life here which he needed to know first. He searched for any evidence that could help him in his quest. Patrick's heart seemed to be bursting with emotion now, and his arms ached with adrenaline. He no longer cared for caution. He had to find out.

Don't just look.

No, Patrick considered. Search my past for feelings, for the ones I loved. The ones I was taken away from.

The Ones?

Yes, Patrick answered instantly, as he understood. He had loved once. He had also had them stolen from him by another, another who neither cared for him then nor now. Somehow it had destroyed him, left him a mere body without a soul. Something again stirred within him; a battle cry. His dreams. Patrick's eyes glistened with a burning hatred as he fought to collect his thoughts.

Who was it? He asked without thought. He received no answer. He had a guiding hand, that was all. He had to find the answers himself. Suddenly, the whole room seemed all too familiar to him, as if he had lived here all his life. There was bitterness here, and pain, a sense of betrayal that seemed to blame all life, including his own. He could not stay here anymore...

No, you must move on. You decide.

Patrick stepped toward the staircase again and moved to the lower floor for the first time. Again, he was treading on new ground.

What do you see?

Nothing.

Nothing?

No, Patrick answered honestly. The floor was barren of carpet, the walls without paint or paper. The windows were...

What Patrick? What about the windows?

They are barred, he answered. He stepped into the room and instantly felt a deep claustrophobia and loss that haunted him. A loss of something close, something very sacred. He also felt a presence, of which he had never felt before. It threatened him. He pulled his arms close around him. The walls seemed to vibrate right in front of him. He forced his legs to move from the staircase and to cross the harsh wooden floor, to find whatever life these bricks held. He reached out his hand and instantly pulled it back again.

The brickwork was freezing, but there did seem a kind of life trapped within its concrete. He reached again and felt a thousand screams instantly burn into his soul.

Patrick! Pull away Patrick!

'Good afternoon Miss Fray,' the governor addressed his new arrival as she sat down in his neat office. She smiled and accepted his greeting.

'I'm glad to have the opportunity of visiting,' she replied. 'I hope that events have not changed since our last conversation.'

'No,' the governor sighed. He knew that Suzannah had witnessed many cases like Patrick's. He also feared that it so easily could end the same this time.

Patrick opened his eyes and slowly pulled himself up from the wooden floor and to his feet. The daylight now seemed threatened by a darkness other than night. His body ached and he wondered what had happened. Had he fainted?

Patrick searched the room intently, eager to identify his fear, and his breath left him when he realised. From the staircase a mist had gathered, it seemed impenetrable to his eyes. His chance of escape was threatened. He had to do something.

As he stumbled on his tired legs, Patrick realised that maybe he had been unconscious for several hours. His body was freezing, and a severe bout of cramp in his hamstring pinned him in agony for a couple of seconds until he managed to straighten himself out. Steadily he crept toward the staircase and the terrible mist that now engulfed it. He breathed in and gasped, coughing out instantly at the taste in his lungs.

Smoke, he thought. I'm trapped in a fire. Suddenly the truth dawned on him that he might only have a short period of time before the fire breached this floor as well. He looked over the banisters and saw the flames beneath him. All he had to do was to climb the stairs back to safety. That was all. He would however no longer have the chance to continue his journey downwards and into his past.

In the split second of his hesitation, Patrick caught a glimpse of a familiar face in the flames beneath him. The next second brought a frightening rumble as something exploded within the lower floors. Then he heard the sounds for the first time; the voices, the screaming of his name. He remembered her.

Patrick ran down the staircase with alarming urgency as her image flooded through his memory. He did not want to lose her again. This time he would keep her with him. Patrick threw his arms in front of his face as a plume of fire shot up from the wall of the staircase, pushing him away from the voices that called him.

Fighting both for oxygen and against his panic Patrick dived toward the floor. The screams now became more intensified, and more numerous. His memory became flooded with recollected images of them all and Patrick became hell-bent on saving them. The smoke burned his eyes and filled his lungs, but he rose once again to struggle on.

Suddenly the fire lapsed for a second, a pathway creating itself across the wreckage of a room. Charred furniture lay strewn in front of him, smoke billowing like ghosts of misfortune without a decided path. Patrick sought for his inner voice but found nothing. He felt truly alone again. Where was Adam? He had left him here without a hope. Was this the way to his sanctuary? Is this how he had to find his peace?

'Come,' the governor said as he escorted Suzannah down the brightly lit corridors of the hospital. The walkways were crowded with doctors, nurses and porters, all going about their daily routines without a fuss. Suzannah knew that that all had stories to tell, if they hadn't already tried to forget. It was often the only way to survive. Hadn't everyone done the same?

Patrick looked down at himself, burnt and bruised through the ordeal but without any reward to show for his sacrifice. The voices had become silent, all of them. The fires had also died. Seemingly they had died along with his aspirations. She had left him again. They had gone. Patrick was now alone, but with the panful memories of his lost loved ones. He knew this whole tragedy was because of one man's evil. Whatever had fuelled this stranger's hatred had now become Patrick's pain. Why had this murderer taken them from him? Was there no justice?

Suzannah hesitated outside the locked room. She had read the report, formulated her own conclusions and in theory was prepared for any outcome. Now though, this close, Suzannah at last realised just what she proposed to do. She could turn this man against what he had become, and let him live the rest of his life with something to die for, instead of...

Then came a sound. Patrick's heart exploded with pain as he recognised the scream. He had heard that cry once before, on that fateful night. It was full of remorse, betrayal but worse than anything else, a hatred for something that should never have been. Patrick instantly rushed toward the sounds of his forever love, crossing the carnage of the floor in mere seconds before he reached the far doorway. Without a hesitation in his movements, Patrick burst through the door.

Darkness covered him instantly, seconds later followed by a series of vicious blows to his face and ribcage. Patrick fell battered and bruised to the floor. He tried to make out the image of his attacker in the near black. His consciousness shifted again but did not fail him this time. He slowly raised himself to his feet. A voice met him in the dark.

'Patrick, what have you done?'

Patrick felt fear entering his body, his arms trembled and the more he tried to force his mouth to shape an answer, the further away his words seemed.

'Patrick, what has become of you?' the voice mimicked. Patrick felt the words becoming tangible in his mind, forming illusions of his past with terrible regret. A light surfaced slowly from the doorway. It was another fire. This time it seemed controlled as it slowly crept inside the doorframe, illuminating all that was inside with a mystical glow.

Patrick looked around him, searching for answers in a distant land that he had once called home. She lay before him, as did the others. Patrick bent down and touched her face as only a soul that had lost his one love could. A tear surfaced on his otherwise emotionless face. His love had been torn from his life. It had happened once before and now again. Rage burnt in his veins, but any thoughts of revenge could not pull him from her side just yet.

To his left lay the remains of his son, and to the right, his daughter. She had been only three years old. John had only just celebrated his eighth birthday. What had done this to the ones that he loved so much? Why hadn't he been there then and why couldn't he have saved them this time?

'Patrick,' the voice came again. It was a warning. It was not a voice that wanted a compromise, only one that bore commands. Patrick looked around but his tear-ridden eyes seemed to betray him this time.

'You?' he questioned, the comprehension of what he saw too much for his soul to bear at present. His mind raced but no answers could be found.

'Yes,' Adam answered, as he looked right through his companion. 'There can really be nobody else.' Patrick slumped to the ground in confusion. Adam quickly knelt next to him, smiling a continuous and frightening grin as he did so. *'You knew it would be me...'*

The governor waited patiently on the other side of the hallway as Suzannah calmed herself before turning the key in the lock. She felt the cold piece of metal in her palm before she checked one last time that she should enter. She looked through the wire glass.
'Oh my...'

'What do you mean?' Patrick stammered as he felt his world closing in on him again. What did he mean that there could be nobody else? 'Why you?' he stuttered.

‘I had no choice,’ Adam smiled again, sending shivers through Patrick’s heart. ‘I’m you.’

The porters rushed past Suzannah and into the tiny room, quickly securing the patient who had just begun his terrible convulsions again. The governor pulled her from the room and took her to a couch across the hallway.

‘I’m sorry,’ he exclaimed, calming her as Suzannah tried to comprehend what she had just seen. ‘It’s always the same. He recovers a little before isolating himself back in his room, muttering to himself. Then, regular as clockwork, the fits start up again. It’s the same every three months. I’m afraid you’ll have to leave now. He’ll be strapped up for about four weeks. It’s for his own safety.’

‘I had hoped,’ Suzannah started but stopped as she realised the futility of her statement.

‘So had we all,’ the governor answered. Only he knew the real facts of the case. Patrick was in his own personal hell, created and crafted by the demons that had led him astray to kill his loved ones in the first place. There would be no sanctuary for Patrick. His suffering would last an eternity.

Entwined

Bank Raid

'Matt, we have to get out of here!'

'Get back out there, Greeneye,' Matt told him. Behind him, Christine hesitated momentarily from filling full her black combat bag with stolen bank notes.

'It's Dirk, man,' Greeneye pleaded. 'He's gone freaking crazy. Pushing people around, there's a cop out there, he's...'

A gunshot rang out that made the three robbers' hearts thunder. Greeneye was the first back into the huge chamber of the bank.

To his horror, Dirk was now standing over the body of the policeman. The madman fired again at point blank range. The policeman died instantly.

Steven Rakes looked down at the broken china at his feet, his mind only just focusing on what had happened. His companion came close to him.

'Steve,' Lisa asked quietly. 'What is it?'

'I don't know,' Steven replied, unable to trace his sudden loss of thought.

'You seemed to be on another planet just then,' Lisa said, walking over to hug him. 'Don't worry about that,' she continued as Steven began to pick up the broken china. 'You better get to work. Don't want Ray complaining again-' she said before kissing him softly '-and keeping you there longer.'

'No chance,' Steven smiled. 'Not tonight. Everybody on the ward knows that today's our anniversary. Even Ray said that he'll cover me if the needs be.'

'Thanks,' Lisa smiled back at him. 'Don't be late.'

'I won't.'

'Damn it!' Greeneye shouted as he tossed the bag into the rear of the van. 'They're already on to us!'

'No surprise there,' Mouers muttered under his breath before he accelerated the vehicle out into the busy traffic. In his rear-view mirror, he could already see the blue lights flashing. They did not stop at the bank either.

'Hold on!' Mouers shouted, flooring the pedal and weaving throughout the other cars. Occasionally he nudged vehicles around him, sending them swirling amongst the traffic. Chaos was strewn behind them. Mouers smiled.

'We're out of here,' he warned his passengers, as he suddenly directed the van down a deserted backstreet. The road seemed only to head right into a deserted multi-storey car lot. They were cornered. Except...

Steven Rakes rose himself out from his parked car, his attention focused on the activity before him. Three ambulances had just arrived, and the front entrance was bedlam. Quickly, just grabbing his essentials, Steven headed on into the hospital.

The leading pursuing police car skidded to a halt by the alleyway. Without an instance lost, the law enforcement vehicle turned and sped along the perpendicular dirty back road. Either side of the alleyway stood high rising apartment blocks, although there were few windows here for the occupants to witness the escapees' route.

To their right, behind a gate secured with numerous ancient locks, two men were loading a chest of drawers into a large removal lorry. Its rear doors were open, but the inside was apparently bare. The policeman lifted his transmitter only moments before noticing that the road ahead was not a dead end but instead dipped and ran down into an abandoned car park. The pursuers accelerated immediately; their attention drawn toward the tiny back entrance of the disused car park.

'This has all been planned,' one of the policemen offered as their car traced the imaginary steps of the villains. Minutes later, the police car re-emerged back into the sunlight, this time on the far side of the old car-lot complex.

Only a mere hundred metres behind the police car, the driver of the removal's lorry finally closed the rear doors. The police had seen the lorry and had not suspected it for a second. The artwork of the drop-hatch had been good, from metres away at least to cover the small van.

The ancient pad locks and fastenings on the gate had also fooled the police. Only weeks before Matt had fitted hinges to the top of the gate so that it would act like a cat flap. After their van had passed through, the gate had clicked back into place.

As the lorry moved smoothly through to the main street again, the five villains smiled smugly that their carefully organised plan had quite easily baffled their pursuers.

'This has been done before, right?' Greeneye asked Dirk as they headed over the bridge, toward the downtown part of the town.

'The camouflage?' Christine asked him. 'Yeah, got it off a film. Can't remember which one.'

'And the cat flap was my idea,' Matt told them all. 'Class "A" design work. Don't worry mate. Three hours and we'll be out in the country, and this time next week we'll all be over the border, living it up.'

'Internal bleeding,' Steven said instinctively before injecting his patient with another bout of chemical fluids. The nurse on the far side of the bed held the wounded woman still. All around them the other blocked off sections held patients of equally serious conditions. 'Looks like someone's kicked her repeatedly, who the hell would do this?'

'She's been a victim of a bank raid,' Dortman told him as he reached Steven's side. 'I've got this one Steve; you're needed over there. Man's had his head half blown apart. They need you to verify his life signs.'

'Thanks,' Steve offered automatically, although he did not feel thankful for this burden of responsibility. Still, it was his job as the head doctor here.

As Steven Rakes walked over to the far roller-bed, he again felt the strange emotion that had plagued him just earlier that day. Suddenly he became very nervous. Immediately it became very clear why.

As Steven stepped closer, he noticed that there remained little of the officer's face. The whole bed was covered with blood. Yet, through the blood and twisted flesh, Steve saw the ghostly face that he knew only too well. In front of him lay a dead policeman, whose badge and uniform had been torn to erase all identity. Unfortunately, Steven Rakes needed no signs of identification.

Trying to turn away from the sight, Steven Rakes felt his world become unfocused. Seconds later, his body hit the ground hard. He felt hands reach for him, but his mind was now concentrating on someone far from him. Reeling over to one side, Steven vomited over the ward floor before closing his eyes again. The acid from his vomit stung his nose and eyes. However, he did not care for this now. Steven Rakes no longer cared for anything. He no longer wanted to remember.

For above him, lying motionless and without life on the roller-bed, lay lieutenant Daniel Rakes. His brother. His identical twin brother.

Buried memories

Steven Rakes felt his wife Lisa hug him tightly as the wind blew around them. The words hung in the air, but they no longer meant anything to Steven. His world had been torn apart. His eyes lifted slowly to his mother and father, but he no longer wanted to be here. Steven knew that they could feel his pain. He had often heard that twins were more closely linked than other brothers and sisters. Today, out within the field of the dead, he wished that this could never be true.

As the coffin was lowered into the hallowed turf, Steven walked away, leaving his family behind him. Steven knew that his brother was not here. He couldn't feel Daniel at all anymore.

'Are you serious?' Greeneye asked as he looked out of the cabin window. 'Six days here without contact to the outer world? No offence Dirk, but Matt will drive me crazy with his snoring.'

'Then sleep outside,' Dirk countered, knowing full well that the mountain's bitter nights would be fatal for any of them. 'Nobody's risking what we have. Understood.'

'Yeah, boss,' Greeneye replied. 'Can't say that this is my ideal road trip though.'

'Just don't go insane on us, alright,' Christine smiled. 'No wait,' she added, a cruel laugh emitting itself from her mouth.

'Funny,' Greeneye replied. 'Saying that. Six days out here and we're all going to need therapy.'

'What is it?' Lisa asked, waking as her lover rose from the bed.

'I'm going to sleep downstairs tonight,' Steven told her. 'Sorry, I just need to be alone.'

Lisa nodded but ignored her instinct to try and understand him. She did not want to push him away. 'Take Harry,' Lisa smiled, wishing instantly that she had been more sensible.

Steven smiled through his tears back at Lisa. 'Thanks,' he said softly, taking the teddy bear from her. Before reaching the door he turned again, returning to her side to kiss her warmly on her cheek. 'I'm so sorry. Goodnight,' he finished. Lisa let him go.

Greeneye stood outside the cabin door, taking one last drag from his cigarette. Looking out across the partially snowy landscape, the robber let his fears subside. Finally, Greeneye realised that the police would never catch them out here. Dirk had been monitoring the television and radio stations, but the law had no leads.

Greeneye knew that Dirk also had links with the press, who in turn had links with the police. They had got away with it. They would never be captured.

Far across the landscape, Greeneye heard a wolf cry. It unnerved him. The wolf made the ghostly noise again. Greeneye had lived on a farm as a child. He knew that sound. It was not the howl of an animal. It was a cry of warning, a cry for the dead.

As Greeneye left the night and re-entered the cabin, a hundred eyes turned toward the hut and the five souls within. The wolf pack's leader cried again to warn his brothers and sisters from venturing near. The cabin was unholy; the wolves could smell it. There was a shadow of death hanging above it. It had been marked.

Steven Rakes found sleep hard to find but, when he did, he did not wake again until dawn. Nothing had occupied his mind that night; nothing at all. Everything that he had ever known had virtually disappeared over night. However, his despair, hurt, pain and fear all returned when he woke. Everything returned, except the memories of his brother. Daniel Rakes was no more.

Steven stood in the lounge, unable to even think about his day ahead. His world had crumbled around him, leaving only himself, as one.

Later that day Lisa sat with Steven, her hand grasping his tightly. Opposite them sat one of Steven's closest of friends. However, in the circumstances, it was a position that neither of them cherished.

Paul Flint had been a psychiatrist in the hospital where Steven had practised for five years now and had also been friends of Lisa and Steven since college. It hurt him deeply to see Steven so weak, so shallow in his life force.

Lisa realised that Steven's desperately needed therapy, and so left her lover and friend alone. Both needed as much time together as possible, if only to reduce the pain. However, Paul Flint had never dare feared what he might find in Steven's mind. The psychiatrist had never come across this kind of problem before.

After an hour of counselling, Paul heard Lisa leave the house. It was only then that the psychiatrist made his breakthrough. Searching Steven's mind, he would find something that would leave the psychiatrist bewildered, and afraid. Steven Rakes was dying, and there was only one soul that could save him.

Night Calling

As Steven pushed himself from the snow, he caught sight of the moon high above him through the forest cover. His body felt so numb, and his head stung from the intense cold.

As he tried to clamber through the thicket and branches, Steven Rakes heard a sound that was only too easy to identify. It made his heart ice over. He stopped instantly in his tracks, unwilling to risk any movement. He heard the sound again. They were coming closer.

From out of the dense woodland ahead of him, two wolves crept into view. They already knew that Steven was here. Their eyes did not betray their curiosity.

As Steven turned his body away from their advancement, he caught sight of three more to his left. Then he noticed other movements, shifting in the undergrowth. Steven closed his eyes, but the end never came.

When Steven Rakes finally opened his eyes, there remained only one wolf, but the human could still feel *so* many other eyes still watching him.

As Steven looked toward the lone wolf, he noticed that the animal seemed confident in his company, even content. Steven felt his eyes glaze over, his fears finally turning to relief. Then his heart jumped, as four wolves appeared from the forest cover to his right. Steven felt his heart quicken. There was something smaller with them.

Before the wolves reached him, they came to a halt. The cub however did not. It continued to plod forward in the snow; its tiny limbs fighting for every step. He looked back at the lone wolf and stared deep into its eyes. Steven Rakes suddenly understood.

Lisa heard the scream and rushed to Steven's side. She saw his tears and hugged him tight, so tight that she became scared of bruising him. He seemed not to notice her intense grip, however. Lisa would never understand, but Steven Rakes was walking out of his life in the pursuit of another. He had not only forgotten his brother Daniel; he had started to forget himself. As she clung to him, his touch no longer seemed the same.

'You alright?' Christine asked to her companion, as the sun began to set across the red sky in front of them.

'Yeah,' Greeneye answered her. 'It's gone,' he said plainly.

'What's gone?' she asked him quizzically.

'The demons,' he smiled. Christine noticed that his fear had indeed dissipated. She misjudged his last comment to mean instead of his own demons. However, Greeneye meant something different entirely. The wolves had stopped crying at night now. They howled instead. Only Greeneye had noticed this simple difference, but it was only Greeneye who had listened in the first place.

'Let's go inside,' Christine smiled before heading on in. Something still troubled Greeneye but he no longer could reason what it was. He watched the sun disappear and the moon take hold of the night. Letting her drift inside alone, he stayed outside for a while.

Steven Rakes stepped through the huge archway to the bank, eager not to attract any unnecessary attention. Since the death of his brother, the media had been trying to contact him. Constantly.

If someone recognised him here or, more realistically, thought that he was Daniel, then his friend Paul the psychiatrist would freak when he found out. Steven was supposed to be resting the whole of today. Yet here he was. In the bank where his brother had been killed.

There was the cashier whom Dirk first intimida...

Dirk?

'Dirk man,' a voice flittered in his head. 'What are you doing?'

'Get up,' another voice cut in.

'Can I help you sir?' Steven heard, his world suddenly returning to the present.

'Sorry?' he muttered.

'You looked lost-' the office worker continued, '-and a little pale. Just thought I'd see if I could help.'

'I'm fine thanks,' Steven ventured as he nodded his gratitude. The worker smiled and walked away. Steven looked to his left, knowing that the vaults were there. He turned to his right and saw the stairs to the upper floors. In front of him were the main cashier desks, and th...

Without warning, a shotgun bullet erupted into the wall behind the cashier's desk. He turned around only to catch the back end of a shotgun in the side of his head.

As darkness threatened, Steven could hear voices. Scared voices. He heard breathing as well, close to him. The cool tiles of the floor pressed against his cheek, keeping him from unconsciousness.

Too late he realised exactly where he was, and how defenceless he had been left. He closed his eyes and prayed.

'Get up,' a voice said from above him. Steven heard another voice, sounding panic stricken by something. The first voice repeated his words. Steven looked up and saw the figure.

'Dirk man?' a second voice boomed across the bank chamber. 'What are you doing?'

'Get up,' the voice said again. Then his world darkened.

'And what the hell was that supposed to have achieved?' Paul cried out aloud across the living room of Steven's house. Lisa looked on, afraid of what was happening.

'I don't know,' Steven said slowly. 'I didn't plan this. I've never visited that bank before,' he continued, fired up. 'I knew faces, the layout of the room. I don't understand what's going on,' he said before turning to Lisa. Steven noticed her expression. It was one that he did not recognise. The thought chilled his heart.

'We need to work tonight,' Paul told him. It was not a question, but a warning. Steven nodded his agreement. Lisa had her fears, as did Steven, but both were unparalleled compared to Paul's. Little did the psychiatrist know, but he held the answers to Steven Rakes' life in his hand.

'You hear about this?' Rogers told his companion, the hour now becoming late in the office.

'Frigging pipe it down, A-hole,' his colleague advised him. 'Don't want old Parky knowing what we've done.'

'Sorry Klea,' Rogers apologised. 'Still, what do we do?'

'Let them know,' Klea told him. 'Can't hurt can it?'

'So, who is he?' Rogers continued. 'Dead look-alike.'

'Do you come free with this planet, or do I pay tax?' she said, slapping him. 'This is his brother, Rogers. You idiot. His twin in fact.'

'Whoa,' Rogers laughed. 'This is bizarre. What was he doing in the bank?'

'Who cares, just let them know.'

Greeneye looked through the valley ravines, nervous at what he had just been told. Behind him, Matt was making up ground. Greeneye knew exactly what he would say. He would bluff him. Greeneye knew his boundaries, and his superstitions. His companions did not. He had been here three days now. It had been long enough. By dawn he would be out of here; far away from here. Alone if needs be.

The Face

Steven tried to close his eyes, but it was no use. He was still wide-awake. Lisa lay next to him; she at least had found sleep in this godforsaken hour.

Steven pushed away the duvet from his body. His mind was burning, and with every few seconds another painful memory would be released, although none of them seemed to be his.

Paul had reasoned with Steven that his apparent loss of memory, and his new thoughts, could have resulted due to the tremendous tragic loss of his brother. Paul had reasoned that the mind could not survive such a barrage of intense pain, fear and depression. The psychiatrist had told him that in a case where two family members had been so very close, that one's death would often lead the other to a denial of what had just happened. The shock was often too much, Paul had offered.

Steven however understood exactly how he was suffering. He had also researched such phenomena in his days, hoping to assist his own patients. Unlike them, Steven had already cried for his lost brother and, in certain aspects, had come to terms with the situation. Steven knew that his case was different, for he felt nothing. He could not even picture his brother in his mind.

Steven made his way toward the bathroom and looked intensely at the mirror.

'Daniel,' he muttered. 'Come back to me'.

Steven turned off the bathroom light and crept back into his bed. The image of his own face remained in his mind, although it still did not rekindle any memories of Daniel. As Steven stared out into the darkness, suddenly a movement caught his eye.

Focusing his concentration quickly, he realised that it was just the darkness playing tricks on him. As his nerves settled again, Steven watched the banisters of the staircase through the night. As his eyes grew tired, more images seemed to create themselves, until he focused his eyes again. Then they disappeared. He let his eyelids relax again.

The darkness seemed to swirl in motion, unlike anything he had ever seen before. It was as if the night had a will of its own. In his concentrated effort to focus his pupils, different shapes grew and crept away, searching a way to invade his vision.

When Steven Rakes finally found sleep, through exhaustion alone, his brain continued to play over the day's problems in his head. His subconscious thought provoked his right eyelid to flutter involuntarily due to 'rapid eye movement'. In his light and troubled sleep, the vivid dreams began to trouble him even more.

The darkness continued to swirl around the banisters, but in Steven's mind they took on new forms, forms that were re-played by images of his memory.

As the visions continued unabated, Steven suddenly found himself awake. He tried to move but found to his horror that he could not. Out before him stood the landing and the staircase, but it no longer seemed innocent to him. He felt someone's presence in his bedroom, someone else apart from Lisa and himself. He tried to make a noise, but his voice remained silent. Steven tried to move, but not even one muscle seemed to aid his call. He felt completely paralysed. Steven wanted to ask who was there, or to shout out a warning, but only felt the fear of helplessness rise inside of him.

Who are you? Steven's mind asked, searching for an answer.

Steven received no answer but suddenly saw the face approach out of the blackness of night. His prayers were suddenly answered...

'Steven Rakes, I presume,' a voice said discreetly from behind the reception of the police station.

'Uh, yeah,' came the answer, as Steven turned toward the speaker. 'I just wanted to pick up my brother's belongings.'

'Certainly,' Sergeant Pemperton said before showing Steven through to the interior of the office. 'I've cleared it with the commissioner. You can also take Daniel's gun and badge. He was a dedicated policeman and a dear friend. I'm sorry that we've lost him.'

'Yeah,' Steven answered absent-minded.

'Take care of yourself, Steven,' Pemperton offered.

'Thanks Pep,' Steven said before leaving the building.

Sergeant Pemperton smiled and turned away, but moments later felt a trace of confusion dwell up inside of him. Turning around quickly, the sergeant tried to follow Steven Rakes out into the reception. However, the doctor had already left. From the sergeant's side, a colleague stepped toward him.

'What's the matter sarge?' the officer asked. 'Looks like you've seen a ghost.'

'Pep,' Pemperton muttered underneath his breath.

'What sarge?' his colleague asked bemused.

'He called me Pep,' the sergeant continued. 'How would he know?'

'Know what sir?'

'Get me the phone, Reid. Quickly.'

'How far would he have got?' Matt asked the others.

'Probably most of the way,' Dirk told him. 'Klea says that she'll keep a lookout. Do you really think that Greeneye will risk everything just because of some superstition?'

'The solitude's got to him,' Christine offered. 'We have to find him otherwise we'll all in for it.'

'So, where do we head for now?' Matt asked again. 'Steven Rakes?'

'Who else?' Dirk asked them. 'I just hope that we find him before Greeneye.'

'What about the cash boss?' Mouers questioned, a sense of concern holding in his voice.

'Bury it out here, under the floorboards somewhere,' Dirk offered. 'Only we know where it is. It'll remain that way and none of us will return here, not until it's all over.'

The money's the least of our problems now,' Christine noted as she slipped her pistol under her belt. 'Let's go and catch us a rat.'

Greeneye saw Steven Rakes enter the house alone and so headed around to the rear of the building. With precious seconds to waste, Greeneye pushed himself through the already broken lock of the back door and headed into the kitchen.

He raised his pistol and hoped for good fortune. Greeneye could still hear the wolves crying in his head. They were warning him. There was still a shadow of death looming over them all.

Greeneye headed up the stairs, the silence threatening his own sanity. There was no sign of Steven Rakes, nothing at all. What if somehow Rakes was still downstairs. Had Greeneye missed him?

Just then, high above him on the landing, something moved. There was a distant thud, like the sound of footsteps on the floor a couple of rooms away. Greeneye's heart sprang into his throat, but his grasp on the pistol calmed his nerves.

With the utmost care, Greeneye raised his head to the level of the first floor. Out from the last room along the corridor, steam was creeping. Greeneye could tell from the way the hot vapour was acting that the bathroom door was still open, if only slightly ajar. Rakes had to be here somewhere, but where?

Slowly, step by carefully taken step, Greeneye made his way along the lonely corridor. There was a complete absence of movement or sound. The robber felt his trigger finger twitch. Greeneye wished that the others were here but knew that he had chosen a road that had led him here alone.

Greeneye had felt the watching eyes of the wolves at the cabin lodge in the highlands. At the time it had haunted him, but now he only wished that he could return there. At that time, he had been surrounded by nature, and some of it deadly, but at least he had felt that the world out there was alive. Here, here was different.

Greeneye's pupils shifted intently around the manmade terrain before him, jumping quickly from doorway to doorway with every passing step. Ahead of him the steam still leaked out from the half-closed bathroom door. Greeneye raised his gun and stepped forward again.

There were three rooms that led off from the corridor: two on one side - the bathroom and spare room, and one master bedroom on the other. Greeneye slowly pulled open the spare room's door, before gliding his body quickly through. The room before him was small, but well lit. From out of the window, Greeneye could just catch the sun reclining over the horizon. Dusk was coming. But would Steven Rakes see dawn? Would Greeneye?

Without hesitation, Greeneye crept back into the corridor, eager to find his prey. Greeneye switched his vision from the bedroom to bathroom and back again. Which next? The robber clutched tightly at his pistol but did not feel the calm return to him this time. He wanted to bolt, to leave. Greeneye did not want to end this. He knew something was horribly wrong.

Suddenly, just as Greeneye was prepared to turn and run, a noise emanated from the bathroom. It was a strangely domestic sound, but a sound nevertheless, like the clanging of a toothbrush in the sink. Greeneye turned back once again, raising his gun, a new flow of adrenaline firing through his body. He would make the others proud of him. He would kill the link. The robber's hand gripped the bathroom door tightly. It was now or never.

Pushing the door back hard, and nearly slamming it right off its hinges, Greeneye burst into the bathroom. The steam instantly swept past him, the cold air creating whirlwinds around the doorway. Greeneye's pistol targeted every inch of the room but to no avail. His heart sank. Steven Rakes was not here.

Greeneye turned instinctively back around, his search now becoming a more terrifying hunt. The terms had been changed, and they seemed no longer in his favour. Greeneye stepped back out into the corridor, his finger itching under the strain of suspense. He had to be in the master bedroom, there was nowher...

'*Wolves,*' something whispered from behind him.

Greeneye span around instantly, and in that split-second caught sight of Daniel Rakes in the mirror, except that it was not the man that they had killed.
'What?' Greeneye found himself saying underneath his breath. 'You're not...' the robber continued as he stared into the mirror, and into those eyes. 'It's not you,' Greeneye muttered toward the mirror again.

Those eyes were different. Those features were the same but those eyes; they seemed to reflect another life, another time. Greeneye found the strength return to his body, and his fear diminished. He lifted the pistol and fired, again and again.

The mirror shattered into a thousand pieces, but the figure remained in front of him. Out from the sides of the room, a black void began to plummet inwards. The broken glass hit Greeneye on his outstretched arm, and the fragments bounced off him, before drifting slowly to the floor. His head swayed from one side to another, before finally the void closed in around him and he crashed unconscious to the floor.

The last thing that he remembered was a voice. 'The wolves-' it had said, '-will always be here.'

'What do you think?' Matt asked the others.

'Well,' Mouers pondered. 'No sign of anything but probable forced entry.'

'How can you tell?' Christine asked as she looked down the hill and towards the Rakes' residence.

'I served remember?' Mouers told her. 'Look, no medical crew, no chief inspector and especially no media.'

'Low key then,' Matt agreed. 'So, what now?'

'Well, whatever happened here, there's no sign of either Greeneye or Rakes,' Dirk noted. He was unsure to whether this held good or bad fortunes.

'What do you reckon? Go after Rakes' girl?' Christine queried.

'Yeah,' Dirk shrugged. 'We have no other choice.'

'What do we need Rakes for anyway?' Mouers asked.

'Look, we've been through this. Rakes knows nothing, but Greeneye has got it into his shit-for-brains head that this twin has some kind of link with the dead. If Greeneye does anything stupid, then we're in deep trouble. Right?' Dirk offered, losing his patience slightly.

'Yeah,' Mouers responded instantly.

'Come on,' Dirk gave him a smile. 'We can still turn this to our advanta...'

'What is it?' Christine asked as the mobile phone rang suddenly.

'If you let me answer the damn phone then I'll tell you,' Dirk sighed underneath his breath before picking up the receiver and listening carefully to the message.

'So?' Matt asked concerned as his colleague put down the phone.

'It's Greeneye,' Dirk said quietly. 'He's taken Steven Rakes hostage.'

'Where?' Matt continued.

'The old oil refinery,' Dirk told him before collecting his thoughts. 'Right, remember all of you. Greeneye has crossed us all. He has risked everything that we have worked for, and all for an insane venture. He is no longer one of us.'

'I have already chosen a bullet for him,' Christine said.

'Strange,' Mouers added. 'So have I.'

Next to them, Matt said nothing but answered the other three with a simple nod. He had no intention of killing Greeneye. Somehow, there had to be a way to save him. Somehow.

'Good,' Steven said as he tossed the mobile phone aside. 'Now when they come for you, let them know that you're back here behind the crates. Remember, no tricks. I have no quarry with you. Only the one who killed my brother. Just shut it and wait for my signal.'

Mouers drove the car slowly through the grounds of the oil refinery. Dirk sat next to him, neatly slotting a couple of shotgun pellets into his gun to aid his concentration. Matt and Christine sat behind him and were quite content not to disturb the silence either. They all knew only too well that the calm would not last much longer.

'Park it over there,' Dirk told Mouers as the main storage warehouse came into view. 'We'll start with the warehouse then move out toward the coolant towers. Greeneye's brought Rakes here for a reason and I bet it's to re-negotiate his side of the bargain. Rakes I want alive. Greeneye has crossed us once. It won't happen again.'

'Right boss,' Matt said from behind him as he banged his fist against Christine's shoulder in a fake sign of camaraderie. She smiled back before opening her door.

Rakes saw the foursome walk steadily across the dusty forecourt of the warehouse entrance, untroubled that he was cruelly outnumbered. He had something that they did not.

'Up you get,' Steven told Greeneye as he pressed the pistol up against the head of the robber. 'Play this right and you'll live.'

Matt led the group into the warehouse, his shotgun raised in a menacing poise. Behind him Christine and Mouers targeted the upper walkways whilst Dirk let his eyes do the tracking. His patience was limited.

'Greeneye, are you there?' Dirk asked strongly.

Say yes, a voice told Greeneye.

'Yes, boss,' the robber answered.

'Is Rakes with you?' Dirk continued as he tried to pinpoint the exact location of his accomplice's voice.

Say yes, the voice reasoned again.

'He's with me,' Greeneye replied. 'I had to do this boss. I had to come back.'

'I understand,' Dirk said with a smile. 'Kill Rakes and then come out. They'll be nobody to stop us then.' He'll kill you, the voice told him. Take the first shot. Be ready for them. The wolves are out tonight, and they will take no prisoners.

Greeneye nodded before stepping away from Rakes. Bending down to the floor, Greeneye picked up the spare pistol that Steven had kicked out before him. He checked the clip and found it to be full. For a split second he found himself turning back towards Rakes, with murder in his thoughts. But then he saw those eyes again. They were cold, dark as the night. Then he heard those cries again. The wolves.

He fired one shot into the floor to signify Steven Rakes' death.

Greeneye subtly moved his head from around an empty oil drum and caught sight of Matt. Matt, who had been with him when they had completed Route 99 down in Mexico. Matt, who had pulled him from the car wreck at Forecast Bridge and had hidden him from the police within the mountains until they had finally managed to escape. Matt, who had always been there for him.

Slowly the cries of the wolves lessened, and the noise of the outside wind began to rattle around his mind instead. Greeneye stepped out into the open. His eyes met Matt's.

'Hi,' Matt smiled. It was not a smile of vengeance, hatred or of betrayal. It was an honest smile. However, Greeneye could also make out something sinister in his expression.

'Welcome back Greeneye,' Mouers stated from across the floor to his left. Dirk was standing behind Mouers but made no effort to come closer. Christine was now to his right, and her gun was still raised.

'I'm sorry,' Greeneye said slowly. 'Rakes is gone, and I want to go. I'm sorry. There was something wronged that I needed to right.'

'Yes, there was,' Mouers said as he raised his pistol.

Greeneye caught Matt's eyes close, as if in prayer. Greeneye's life ended.

Christine dived to the ground as a wild shot from Mouer's gun rebounded on a canister behind her. Instantly she tried to raise herself and her weapon toward Greeneye but there was no longer any need. Greeneye was lying motionless on the floor. Out beside him two other figures lay, and both were still.

'Get up Christine,' Dirk told her.

'What happened?' she asked her companion, as the woman finally found her feet.

'Mouers took it into his hands to sort out our little problem. Unfortunately, Greeneye's reactions were still as fast as they've always been. Mouers also managed to dispose of Matt, although both knew little about it,' Dirk sighed as he raised Matt's bloodied head off the ground. A large gaping hole was now situated where the left eye should have been.

'Greeneye got off three shots before Mouer's finally leaded him with the shotgun. Unfortunately, Mouer's dropped his shotgun as he fell, and it fired off a single shell into Matt. Can't believe he just stood there. Damn fool didn't even raise his gun against Greeneye.'

'Did you expect him too?' Christine asked him.

'I had hoped,' Dirk said quietly. For both, a moment of silence was all that was needed. It never came.

'The wolves are calling for you too,' a voice boomed. 'Do you care to run with the night?'

'What?' Dirk shouted over the sound of the wind outside.

'The wolves...' the voice said again, this time fading out into the distance.

'Dirk,' Christine said quietly. 'Who the hell is that?'

'It's the reason why Greeneye returned here,' Dirk replied as he reloaded his pistol. 'It's Rakes. He's still alive, for now. Guess he wants to join his brother.'

Steven heard the two figures move slowly through the dark labyrinth of empty petrol canisters. His head still felt light on his shoulders, but the rest of his body seemed calm. His eyes ached, and his mind hurt even more, but the visions before him were becoming steadier by the second. Soon they settled. From out of nowhere, he was now standing between the two villains.

'Greeneye found me,' Steven told them. 'He could not tame me though. Neither of us.'

'Rakes,' Dirk smiled through the near darkness as he turned toward the man who stood alone within the aisle of canisters. 'Want to see your brother so soon?'

'My brother hasn't gone yet,' Steven smiled. From behind him, Christine moved closer, raising her pistol up to shoulder level. He was now surrounded – front and back.

'Hasn't he?' Dirk suggested. 'I think I remember wasting him in the bank. Kind of a hard thing to forget, don't you think?'

'My brother's still here,' Steven smiled again. Christine felt her finger tighten on the trigger. Something scared her, but it wasn't the eerie darkness of the warehouse. Suddenly she understood. As her eyes grew accustomed to the light, she saw the first feint trace of a figure standing between her and Dirk. However, she could not push the fear of death from her mind. She could not even emit one warning scream.

'They said that twins have a special link,' Dirk said. 'They call it death,' Dirk laughed as he fired a single bullet toward the body of Steven Rakes.

Something hit the ground hard and remained there. Slowly, the weeping wound let loose its crimson life force, and slowly the soul found its own way home. Dirk looked over at the motionless body with a startled look on his face. He looked down at the pistol and then back to the dead figure. His expression faltered.
Dirk noticed the light waver slightly around the man still standing before him but could not understand this premonition to be true. Slowly Dirk could make out the motionless outline of Christine through the ghostly figure of Steven.

'They call it life,' Steven corrected him. Moments later Dirk heard movement from behind him but dared not look around. He already knew who it was.

'They call *this* death,' Daniel Rakes offered with a whisper before firing the pistol.

Dirk fell to the ground, his soul already fighting with the devil. His body lay motionless before the twins, but neither had the opportunity to view the blood of their revenge killing. Their time had come. The pistol fell to the floor, clattering an almighty thunder throughout the silent warehouse. Seconds later there stood only one man.

Steven Rakes walked out into the last remaining rays of the evening sun, with a new fire in his heart. Instead of feeling a loss, he now felt the emotion of immense binding, a binding for someone who he would never truly be apart from ever again.

Out in the distance, Steven heard the oncoming sounds of police sirens. Back in the warehouse behind him, the fingerprints of Daniel Rakes were over the pistol that had shot Dirk. Although that would no doubt baffle the police, it would be an easier interpretation when they noticed that Dirk's fingerprints were over the gun that had killed Christine. The others had killed each other, through both mistake and intention.

Steven knew that he could walk away from the crimes here, but that would never be enough for him. He wanted more, a lot more from life. For he had touched death and had let it consume his own body. Now, Daniel Rakes had fulfilled his destiny and had begun the next step of his unique journey.

Steven finally felt the grip of his brother loosen from his soul and drift away. He might now be physically alone, but the memories would always remain. He knew that. The memories would always remain...

The Bridge

Two years ago

The rain continued, unabated in its quest to soak the town of Muhoi, whilst the citizens hurried themselves through the monotony of their daily lives. The autumn fall was now well and truly upon them, with the start of summer half a year away at least. For the region of Kings' Mount, this was just another day of just another week.

The Police Marshall's four-wheel drive drove slowly through the muddy tracks of the town's outer rim, in search of her call. Maxine caught sight of a male up ahead of her and recognised him instantly. Bringing the vehicle to a halt, she stepped out and greeted the figure.

'Thanks for coming, Max,' the young man smiled. 'It's just Winston again, locked himself in. I wouldn't have called but I heard what I presumed was a shotgun. Don't really think he's capable of anything stupid though.'

'Don't worry Jake,' Maxine nodded. 'The factory laid him off last week. He's just angry,' she began.

'And very drunk,' the young man interrupted.

'Give the deputy a call, I'll handle this from here,' the Marshall replied as she headed toward the residence of Winston Laine, her hand unclipping her pistol holder just in case.

The young man reached into the jeep and clicked open the transistor channel. 'Cope, this is Jake Connelly. I'm with Maxine, we need assistance up at Winston Laine's place. Possible sounds of gunfire have been reported.'

Jake listened to the confirmation before stepping back from the vehicle. Then, suddenly, the world seemed to explode.

The sound erupted from Winston's front door, and before Jake could even move, Maxine had already fallen back down the porch steps and onto the muddy pathway below. The young man felt his heart tighten as he saw Winston step out onto the porchway. Without thought, Jake stepped forward slowly from the police vehicle. Winston looked up at him.

As Jake viewed right into the old man's eyes his fear subsided. The young man ran to Maxine's side, and quickly threw his jacket over her. Her face was covered with blood and dirt, but Jake could quickly identify her wounds. The Marshall's left shoulder had suffered the intensity of the blast, but she seemed more shocked than hurt. Jake turned back toward Winston.

High up the porch, the front door had been blown apart by the blast. Jake knew that Maxine had been lucky and that her wounds were mostly superficial. Fortunately, this was mainly due to Winston firing the shotgun through the door. The question was, why?

'I just wanted to be left alone,' Jake heard the old man's voice cry out. 'I just needed to be alone, Jake. Alone.'

Jake turned to face him and saw the old man's tears flow freely down his cheeks. 'I didn't mean to hurt her. It was an accident. I didn't even know who it was.'

Jake tried to speak but could not find his words. He could not offer anything at all to Winston Laine. Then, as Jake heard the sirens creep up from the main road, the old man lifted the shotgun once again. Jake felt Maxine's grip tighten on his arm, but his thoughts were already far from here.

As the sound of the shotgun filled the air, Jake could only focus on Winston's last words. *I just needed to be left alone, Jake. Alone.*

Present day

Jake stood out on the balcony, as the winds blew unsteadily around him. Above him, the moon lay partially hidden by the dark cloudy skies.

After three months of intense training Jake finally had the chance to return home for a few days at least. However, what once had almost been a dream for him was now turning into a nightmare.

He hoped that somehow, he could prove them all wrong. He would find a way.

As Ephraim's Bridge crept into view, Jake wound down the cold windowpane and turned down the stereo. At this time of year, you could often hear the rapids, even above the jeep's engines.

Jake looked far below him as the vehicle crossed the ancient bridge and indeed the water was high. Another season of rain. Another Fall. Yet another year.

Jake quickly stowed his luggage into his old room at his parent's place before heading straight over to Ceri's house. Communications with her had been growing fraught and more distant for several weeks now, and his mind was now becoming clouded with desperate thoughts.

Jake had been away from Muhoi now for well over three months, and nothing between himself and Ceri should have changed. He pushed his fears away again before they threatened to destroy him. He needed her. His aspirations had become so shallow with the institution and his finances had brought him near to despair, but through all that, he had somewhere to retreat, to build again.

As the jeep ploughed its way through the muddy puddles that seemed to riddle the street, Jake noticed Ceri's residence creep into view. He slowed the vehicle, but as the jeep drew close to Ceri's house, his heart began to tighten. Then, without warning, Ceri stepped out onto the patio with a man embracing her.

Without hesitation, Jake turned the vehicle away and down a nearby alleyway. He did not care nor notice whether Ceri had seen him. It no longer mattered.

Ceri stepped away from the porch as Jake drove off up the lane, unaware of the events that she had just set in motion. She pushed away the loving touch of her companion, uneasy in his warmth. She still had thoughts of another, and now it seemed to haunt her now more than ever.

Ceri let her concentration wander and felt vaguely guilty that her emotions were not focused on the male with her. Ceri suddenly felt a loss for Jake like none she had suffered before. For the first time, she felt as if she had lost him.

Their conversation still rung in her head from all those weeks ago, and she still had a thousand unsaid words in her thoughts. Ceri had never wanted to end their relationship this way, and in the last few weeks she had no choice but to come to terms with their separation. Then she had met someone else. He was not like Jake, and that had helped. She knew now that it had been for the wrong reasons. She let a tear flow down her cheek.

'It's over,' Ceri pleaded. 'I'm sorry.'

For Ceri it had ended. For others, this was only the beginning.

Jake looked out over Ephraim's Bridge, the rapids beneath him filling his mind with a deafening roar. The rain had become sparse now, although Jake's thoughts were only on the torrent below.

Jake felt most of his fears diminish as the time crept by. Slowly, one by one, his thoughts drifted away under the moonlight. His heart ached more than ever though. Ceri had been his whole world for the last year. She had been the reason to keep plugging away at a dream that was clearly only a delusion of grandeur. For the first time in his life, Jake no longer believed that he mattered.

The young man knew that he should just walk away, but to Jake, this was not an option. There were boundaries to emotions and thoughts, but his world was built and fuelled by the people around him. He did not really care for himself. He had never wanted to be left alone.

Jake turned his eyes to the stars and wondered if, in any other life, he would have stepped from this bridge. No doubt, in another life, he might. He felt his eyes swell, but quickly bit back the tears.

'It's a cold night to be out here alone.'

The voice startled Jake, and his reactions obviously showed this.

'There is no need to be afraid,' the figure continued. 'My name is Ryan. I am a traveller, of sorts,' the stranger offered.

'What brings you to Kings' Mount?' Jake asked suspiciously. 'Muhoi is a few miles from here. Apart from that, there's not much else.'

'Not much here?' Ryan laughed. 'My boy, you've been standing here watching the rapids for ages. You dare call them nothing?'

'No,' Jake answered back. He let the silence threaten. He did not feel happy in this person's presence. However, the stranger had no intention of simply walking away.

'Your thoughts trouble you,' Ryan said quietly. 'Do you see any light at the end of the tunnel?'

'Not anymore,' Jake replied honestly, mesmerised somehow by the figure's questions.

'You'd be surprised,' the man continued. 'There are, other ways,' he smiled across to the young man.

'I wouldn't jump,' Jake offered coldly.

'A part of you already has,' Ryan returned, his voice equally emotionless. 'You have to find a way of reclaiming all that you once had.'

'Leave me,' Jake started, his pain again trying to claim him.

'There is a way, son. There is always a way.'

'And that is?' Jake asked, his pain turning to anger.

'That is to step away from yourself,' Ryan replied. 'But not literary,' the stranger smiled as he took grip of the bridge rails to illustrate his point. 'You'll find that to win anything in life, you must first care more about yourself than anyone or anything else. That is the only way to succeed. Become cold in your ambitions, whatever they are. Never let your strengths become threatened by your weaknesses,' Ryan said as he looked over at Jake.

'You are a soul who has none of these traits. You are too innocent,' Ryan told the man. 'You are too naïve. That can be changed. Just step back and reclaim what is rightfully yours.'

'How do I do that?' Jake asked, unsure where this conversation was going.

'I said that a part of you has already jumped from this bridge,' Ryan told him. 'Only you and I know that. Your jeep is parked over there. It will be found by midday tomorrow at the latest.'

'What are you saying?' Jake asked, fearful of what Ryan was thinking.

'Walk away from your life for a week,' the stranger said coldly. 'You will soon learn never to think so carelessly about life again. You will soon appreciate just what you have to offer,' Ryan explained as he turned his own eyes to the heavens. 'And believe me, so will everybody else.'

Jake's eyes followed the figure as Ryan headed back from where he had come. The young man looked down at the rapids one last time before his decision was made.

Maxine Johnston left the Connelly residence at just after ten the next morning, after a report had been issued that Jakes' van had been found. Her initial thoughts had been uneasy, even chilling. She knew that this would not be pleasant for her or the town. Not Jake, she thought.

Ceri pulled the duvet high over her head. She had awoken in the last few minutes, but already some part of her had sensed that something terrible had happened. She heard the voices of her parents and could easily tell from their tone.

She heard the stairs creek and knew that one of them was coming to wake her. Ceri suddenly felt very cold.

Maxine looked down at the river beneath her, and then to the skies. The autumn very frequently abated in its rainfall. She knew that Ephraim's Bridge was "popular" for suicides, but this was the first apparent jump of someone whom she had known.

Although Ceri was not here, nor Jakes' parents, everyone else of the volunteers would without doubt be very familiar with both his family and friends.

The Marshall made her way over to them to begin the search.

Jake looked through the binoculars down upon the road and bridge before turning back to his companion.

'Do you think that this is wise?' he asked.

'You promised me that you would go through with this,' Ryan told Jake. 'You will only hurt those that you love if you go back to them now. I promise you that everyone will benefit if you trust in me. I will deliver Jake. You can trust me.'

'I can't watch this,' Jake said as he climbed back into the rear of the van.

'Ye of little faith,' Ryan smiled. Out below, the search for Jake Connelly's body had already begun. Ryan turned toward the vehicle. They were about to take a trip right into the heart of Muhoi. Ryan wanted to see what reaction Jake's disappearance had created.

'You've been ages,' Jake told his companion after Ryan had returned. Ryan turned around from the driver's seat and looked back into the rear compartment of the van. There were no windows back here, and Jake felt safe from any prying eyes.

'Well?' Jake asked, although he did not feel too much pride in his enquiry.

'Visited the garage, chapel and the local drinking house,' Ryan told his companion. 'This whole place is like a ghost town, son.'

'Welcome to Muhoi,' Jake smiled.

'No,' his companion warned him. 'I mean that the garage was shut, and I found the chaplain assisting the co-ordination of your search in the bar. These are sad times for your town.'

'This was your idea!' Jake whispered with venom. 'This is serious. I've trusted you so far, but this has to end.'

'No,' Ryan said as he looked out over the street. 'You cannot win without becoming cold, Jake. Just let a few more days pass, at the most. You want everything back don't you?'

'Yes.'

'And I can give you it all,' Ryan said. 'Just trust in me. All your problems will disappear, because all your family and friends will take you under their wing and put you back on your feet. And Ceri...' Ryan began.

'What about Ceri?' Jake asked sternly.

'She was due to leave Muhoi for New York today, yes?' Ryan stated. 'She is also in the bar, with your mother. From what I could assume, your father is out there looking for you now,' Ryan hesitated. 'Jake, you can't go back yet. You must believe in something that you cannot control, and that must be difficult. You will find out a lot about yourself before you return. So will your friends.'

That night Jake slept uneasily, and not for the first time reconsidered whether he was doing something heartless and insane. Jake had become so concerned about his family and friends that the young man had even begun to dream up his own excuse for disappearing.

However, by next morning, his wish had already become reality.

'This is the day,' Ryan told his companion as he turned to view the rear compartment of the van. 'Today, you will return to Muhoi and your new life.'

'How?' Jake asked him seriously. 'I spent the whole of last night trying to think of an excuse for my disappearance. This isn't going to work.'

'Yes, it is,' Ryan told him. 'You look like hell already. I'm glad that you didn't sleep.'

'Ryan,' Jake pleaded from the darkness. 'How are we going to do this?'

'With this,' Ryan smiled as he withdrew a large knife from his satchel. 'Come here,' he said, his eyes widening with excitement.

'No,' Jake heard himself utter before he pushed himself to the rear of the van.

'The back doors are locked,' Ryan told him, his voice icy cold. 'Nobody will hear you out here in the woods. Did you actually think that I would let you return to them?'

'No,' Jake said again, this time more of a cry than of words. The young man forced himself to look into Ryan's eyes, to maybe guess at the other man's thoughts. Seconds later, Ryan's whole expression changed.

'You can do it, son,' Ryan nodded as he put the knife back away. 'You just needed a story.'

'What?' Jake asked, still rigid with fear.

'I have given you your life back,' Ryan told him. 'You won't even have to lie. Just twist this tale a bit, and everything will be yours. You didn't even need to get hurt. You'll have to imagine how you escaped from this van though, but I'm sure that you'll come up with something.'

Ryan stepped from the vehicle and unlocked the rear doors before wandering away toward the edge of the ridge. Out before him lay most of King's Mount. Behind him, he could just make out the muffled banging of Jake Connelly. Ryan could only guess to what injuries the young man was inflicting on himself, but it would be worth it, in the end.

About ten minutes later, Jake was standing at Ryan's side. Jake's right hand was covered with a torn rag of his own clothing, and he seemed to be covered in blood from head to foot. His jeans were littered with both dirt and blood, and his head had a nasty gash just above his right eye.

Ryan was impressed with the lad but kept his emotions within. The young man's work was not finished yet.

'Are you ready?' Ryan asked him.

'Yes,' Jake smiled. Ryan could easily read the pure happiness in the young man's voice. Jake looked at him. 'Thanks,' he said. There was nothing else that neither of them needed to offer.

Ryan watched him walk away.

'Ryan! Ryan!' Jake shouted as he ran back to the part of the wood where the stranger had parked. Ten minutes had passed, and Jake was relieved when he found him easily, although Ryan was clearly ready to depart.

'What is it, my friend?' Ryan asked him.

'Come, to the ridge,' Jake pleaded. 'There's something down by the riverbank, I'm sure. I think it might be human. It looks as if it's trapped in the bank's branches.'

'Hold on,' Ryan told him as he reached into the van for his binoculars. 'Right, show me the way.'

Jake stepped over to the bank's edge, his eyes focused on the mangled and bloated body of the drowned human. The young man hesitated slightly; unsure as to whether he should call the town first.

'Ryan?' he asked but received no answer. Jake turned around.

The mysterious man looked up from the ground and met his eyes but remained quiet. Jake misunderstood the other man's silence to be a fear of death, and that the corpse had rattled him. Jake could not have been further from the truth.

'I haven't told anyone this,' Jake said suddenly as he viewed the motionless body. 'Two years ago, someone I knew killed himself with a shotgun in front of me. I'll never forget the words that he used. "I just needed to be left alone, Jake. Alone"' Jake uttered quietly, his memories now flooding back. 'I can't believe that even the thought of suicide could enter my mind, and certainly not after all that I've seen.'

Ryan looked up at the midday sun and then back to the young man in front of him. 'Pull in the corpse,' he said.

The mysterious figure stepped closer. Jake was like every soul in this world. They were just trying to find a way. Just trying to win. Sometimes they had the will to fight, sometimes they were lucky if they did not cave in and cry.

By the time that Ryan was by Jake's side, the boy had already pulled the corpse nearer to him in the water and had turned it over to face the sky. Ryan heard the man's cries but didn't have any emotion to comfort him. This one soul was no different to all the rest.

Jake turned to him, the tears flooding down his face. He could not manage to speak with comprehension. Jake had recognised the corpse and this humble truth would destroy him.

'I'm sorry,' Ryan said quietly without remorse. 'This is what will guide you now, through the greatest fight of your life,' Ryan told the young man. 'What I have shown you over the last few days will haunt you, but ultimately might save your soul. I will not stand by and let your flame be extinguished. I will not watch you die for nothing,' Ryan said before turning away.

'I am not a cruel man. I am not a monster,' the mysterious man offered before turning to leave the corpse of Jake Connelly behind him. 'I just want to find the answers. Now, you must fight your demons and maybe we both might find what we're looking for.'

Jake looked up from his own corpse and understood where he was. He was about to lose everything. Jake had managed to solve every one of his problems, but it was now too late. The young man now understood that his life would have been perfect, but he had also thrown that away. He had let himself be consumed by his own fears and now he had lost it all.

'Why?' Jake asked quietly. His thoughts could only cling to Ceri, for she meant more to him than anything else in the world.

He looked toward the sun above him and heard distant voices in the wind. Jake could just identify the sound of Maxine's voice above the rest.

As the voices came close, the soul of a suicide stood above his own corpse, unable to move. He realised that his pain would never end, because this memory would not die. Not yet.

As he searched behind him, there was no longer any sign of Ryan. There was no evidence that the mysterious stranger had ever been here at all. Jake closed his eyes. Now he was truly alone.

Jake struggled to keep his eyes open, concentrating hard again at the rapids before him. He sat beneath the bridge, and the sun was now dipping slowly behind the mountain peaks. His body ached from fatigue, and his mind battled constantly to avoid the threat of unconsciousness.

Every time Jake closed his eyes, he heard *their* silence and it threatened his very existence. But he was so very tired.

As the young man's eyes closed involuntarily once again, Jake's head slipped from his palm and instantly his body startled itself awake. Jake Connelly felt his panic return. As the young man looked around himself, he realised that it had happened again. His world was slowly becoming a forgotten memory.

Out on the far hillside, the trees had now become sparse, with only a dull void replacing the background. Jake knew that he had to stay awake, and only then could he fight his demons. Soon his whole world would loosen itself from his memory and he would become nothing. All he had to do was to stay awake. But he was so tired.

If only he could keep consciousness until dusk, then maybe someone would pass back across Ephraim's Bridge. Then he could shout up to them. Then he could fight his demons, with his friends' help. But he was so tired.

So very tired.

Maxine Johnston looked down at the corpse, tears flooding from her eyes. She noticed Jake's pupils dilate once again and held him tighter. The Marshall hoped that he still wasn't suffering, not after all this. Maxine had been holding the body now for over five minutes but knew that there was little else that anybody could do for the boy.

As Jake Connelly's asphyxiated brain finally collapsed under the accumulated pressure of osmosis, Maxine noticed the boy's pupils lose their intensity and finally become motionless. Gliding her fingertips gently over his face, she closed his eyelids and said a prayer for Jake's soul.

The Marshall looked down at his battered and bruised body and hoped that Jake Connelly had not suffered too much. She could only guess of what journey, if any, now awaited this reckless soul.

Maxine would never know but there would be no journey. The boy would have no chance to fight for his soul. For Jake Connelly had committed suicide, and that one act had extinguished his soul's flame. He was now no more. Nothing.

Draven will return in:

Shadow World

Story order:

Smoke Dragon

Ice Ghosts

Dark Skies & Shadow World (both stories run simultaneously)

Border World

Fallen World

Also by *Midn13ht*:

Turtle & Co. Private Detective Agency (inc. Misfits)

Rock-ish music: Out of time/Nothing to lose/Firecracker/Out on the track

Acknowledgements:

For the stories, huge amounts of appreciation & gratitude to...

Rupert for editorial and publishing advice
Owen for slightly dubious military weapons knowledge
Keith & Ben for kind words of encouragement
Simon for the artwork nod
Jon & Ian – for inspiring characters
And, of course, to my parents and brother who at some point have all been force-read at least one story...

For the music, I am forever indebted to...

Ben for editing, sound levels, encouragement, and general all-round knowledge of music
Simon for listening to countless demos and for giving artwork nods (and advice)
Julian/Mike/Matt, Stu, Woz/Mike, CB/Richie/Fitzie/Stevo/Laurie – for all those I've played alongside over the years and kept me passionate with playing and writing music

And finally to my kids for enjoying made up ad-hoc stories and music – and to my wife for putting up with my ridiculously loud typing at unearthly times of the night & for understanding that on horrible wet and stormy nights I'll be in the shed practicing vocals...

Printed in Great Britain
by Amazon

74997153R00248